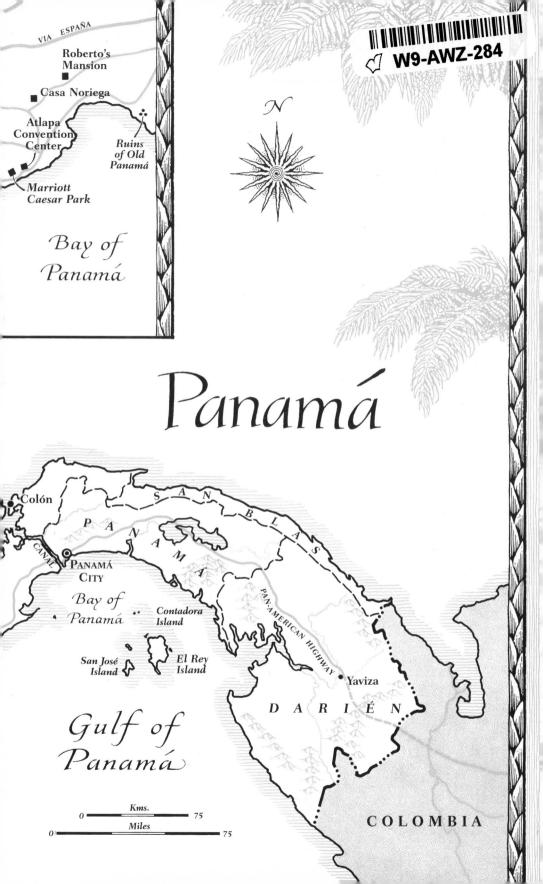

LAWRENCE WRIGHT

GOD'S FAVORITE

A NOVEL

SIMON & SCHUSTER
New York London Sydney Singapore

SIMON & SCHUSTER
Rockefeller Center
1230 Avenue of the Americas
New York, NY 10020

Simon & Schuster and colophon are registered trademarks of
Simon & Schuster, Inc.

Designed by Leslie Phillips
Manufactured in the United States of America

1   3   5   7   9   10   8   6   4   2

LIBRARY OF CONGRESS CATALOGING-IN-PUBLICATION DATA
Wright, Lawrence, date.
God's favorite : a novel / Lawrence Wright.
p.   cm.
1. Panama—History—1981—Fiction.   I. Title.
PS3573.R53685 G63 2000
813'.54—dc21
99-048508
ISBN 0-684-86810-5

TO WENDY WEIL

CHAPTER 1

For twenty minutes the policeman sat with the villagers watching the golden frog. As long as the frog did not move, the Indians from the village did not move, and therefore the policeman waited, knowing that there was no need to hurry. If he broke the frog's spell it might be seen as a bad omen, and so he rested on his haunches, as he remembered doing in his own village many years before.

The frog seemed to be growing ever more powerful as it defended the little patch of sunlight that squeezed through the guayacan trees in the ravine. Its ancient wedge-shaped face pointed directly at the policeman, as if he knew that the matter now rested between them. But the frog was in no hurry, either. He was in a paradise of flies. He was sleepy from eating, and the lids bobbed on his gold-slitted black eyes, but he gripped the sides of the large canvas mailbag like a miser clutching his purse. Two human feet protruded from the mailbag.

"And who discovered this?" the policeman said in a low voice.

After a pause the oldest of the men responded, "The boy. He came to fish in the river."

The policeman saw a child half-hidden behind his mother's dress.

"At what time of day?"

"It was evening."

The policeman absorbed the fact that a night and part of the morning had passed before anyone had come to El Roblito to notify him. Perhaps they wanted to own this mystery for a while, before giving it to him. Certainly the frog had not been sitting here all that time.

The policeman glanced at his camera and thought about taking photographs of the scene, but then he saw the villagers shift like grass stirring in the slightest breeze, and so he relaxed again into mindlessness. He was scarcely aware of how much time passed before a cloud shadowed the mailbag and the frog leapt into the ferns, but when the villagers abruptly rose to their feet, he understood that he could now go about his work.

The policeman unrolled a yellow tape that he tied to bushes and trees in a rough square around the crime scene. This was what the villagers expected, and they nodded approvingly, having seen such actions on television. The policeman took his time. He was alone in this outpost, and he did not feel that he had the authority to order the villagers to leave. Also, he enjoyed making a show of professionalism. He put on rubber gloves and took out a plastic bag from his kit, along with a pair of tweezers. There was a gum wrapper on the ground that he picked up and examined.

"Has anyone been down here?" he asked in general.

The Indians looked at one another, and the same old man responded, "No."

The policeman took photographs of the footprints on the edge of the ravine, then walked down to the riverbank to get water for the plaster casts. He knew what the villagers were waiting for, but he also knew that their anticipation was worth savoring. They would not hurry him.

He could tell from the tire tracks that the body had been dumped out of a truck with double tires on the back, and already that worried him, because the only such trucks he knew of in the area belonged to the Panama Defense Forces. He did not want to find one of their victims. It was also obvious that the body was meant to be found. There were hundreds of square miles of jungle around them, places few humans had ever passed through, but this village was just across the border of Costa Rica, along a road everyone used. It appeared that the body had been driven across the river and dumped in the nearest ravine. Done quickly but carelessly. With arrogance. This also worried him.

Finally the policeman moved through the electric curtain of flies. He looked closely at the weave of the mailbag. There was some printing on the underside that he could just see, so now he touched the bag and felt the sodden heaviness. It took real force to turn the bag to one side, so that the twisted, naked knees of the corpse inside were now pointing upward, and the bare, exposed feet were hanging in the air. U.S. MAIL, it said on the bag. The policeman lowered the bag into its original position and sat back on the ferns.

Presently, he stood and began to tug roughly at the bag, but the body was stiff and ungainly and did not come loose willingly. He had to grasp one of the legs to work the knees through the opening. He did not like to touch the dead, and he could sense the villagers withdrawing a bit into their own reluctance. It was not like anything else. The hardness of the limbs felt wrong and alien. The hair on the dead man's legs was repulsive to him, but he could not stop until he had gotten the body out of the bag. His audience was quietly insistent on this.

Now that the bloody legs were out, the policeman pulled again on the corners of the mailbag, and he felt the canvas surrender its cargo. He heard the villagers gasp, and one of the women screamed, but his own thoughts had not yet focused on what he was actually seeing. The wrongness was blinding his senses. And then he understood that the corpse's head was gone.

He did not mean to vomit, it just came out of him, perfectly naturally and spontaneously. He stood gaping in surprise at the sight and at his own violent reaction. Then he came to himself and began to do the things he knew he was expected to do. He took pictures. It helped to see the corpse through the lens; it was as if he were viewing something in another element, underwater, as it were.

The body was covered with purple contusions and deep wounds that were not meant to kill. The genitals were swollen to the size of mangoes. The policeman did not want to think about what the man had endured before death spared him. He knew that he was going to become very drunk tonight.

When he had taken enough photos of the front, he took a breath, then heaved the body over. Now he saw something else that he didn't want to see: *F-8* was crudely carved into the dead man's back.

The policeman stood. He reached into his evidence bag and took out the gum wrapper, which he dropped back onto the ground. There would be no further investigation.

THE LIBRARY of the papal nunciature was a pleasantly formal room, and although the building lacked the most basic tropical appliances—central air-conditioning and a dehumidifier—the library itself remained remarkably cool and free of mildew, a sanctuary from the steam-bath climate and the unnerving, noisy vitality of Panama City. The library floors were made of Italian marble, and the walls of thick limestone bricks in the classic colonial style. Here is where Monseñor Henri-Auguste Morette, the official representative of the Vatican, spent most of his working days. Morette was seventy-one years old, and although he was still hearty and erect, lately he had begun to bend and shrink with age, so that his hatchet nose and great Gallic ears appeared to have been borrowed from a much larger man. His skin—so unsuited to the tropics—was starkly pale and marbled with blue veins, and his thin, white hair lay close to his skull. All this pallor was in shocking contrast to his shining dark eyes and his riotous, exclamatory black eyebrows, which gave him a look of predatory ferocity.

Many vanquished opponents had underestimated Morette's cunning and resourcefulness. His native talent for intrigue had been sharpened to a fine edge by twelve years of Vatican politics. Within this intimate arena, Archbishop Morette had been a figure of speculation and controversy. His excoriating intelligence and snapping wit set him apart from the bureaucratic herd, and his linguistic skills—he was fluent in five languages—made him indispensable within the Vatican Secretariat of State. Even his most jealous colleagues had marked him as a future member of the College of Cardinals, while conspiring to limit his influence.

In the end, however, it was Morette who brought himself down, through a turn of events that would otherwise have seemed like a great advance. He gained an appointment to the powerful—and much feared—Congregation for the Doctrine of the Faith, which at that time was conducting a purge of free-thinking theologians, particularly Latin American liberationists. It was a job he attacked with characteristic vigor. At his hand, many of the finest priests in the church were expelled or humiliated into submission. Morette personally took no position on the great doctrinal battle in which he played one of the leading roles. It was not his task to debate theology, only to implement policy. Gradually, however, he began to notice the change in the expressions of his colleagues when he entered a room or sat at the table with them for dinner. They were afraid of him. Some hated him. He could see them struggling to be civil.

There was a penalty to be paid for serving his office so efficiently. Morette recognized the forces that were being arrayed against him, and recognized that his own position was becoming increasingly hopeless. He would be sacrificed. Like a marauding knight on a chessboard, he had accomplished his mission. Now he would be taken. In the larger game it was a tactical necessity.

The attack came in the form of a whispering campaign. His faith was called into question. This did not surprise him. He had never been pious. He quickly made a confession of his loss of faith and was sent to a kind of spiritual rehabilitation center on the southern coast of Sicily. When he returned to Rome six months later, his standing was so reduced that he was transferred back to the Secretariat of State, which banished him from the center of power to this remote, rather disgraceful posting.

Much like a prisoner facing a lengthy sentence, the Nuncio had arrived in Panama with a crate of books and crossword puzzles in various languages, which he hoped would occupy his years of exile. Included in the crate were thirty-seven volumes of Aquinas. He had told himself that Aquinas was going to be his great pursuit; he had remembered the *Summa Theologica* as his passion in seminary; but after forcing himself through four hundred pages of commentaries, he put the books back on the shelves. In a subversive frame of mind, he then thought of writing his long-postponed, definitive treatise on the history of appearances by the Virgin, but he discovered that he somehow had lost interest in the Marian cult as well. The artifacts of belief seemed only curiosities now; there was nothing vital there to grip his interest. For long stretches of time, the Nuncio confined himself to his study, watching Mexican soap operas and playing bridge by correspondence.

By nature, however, the Nuncio was not a hermit. He was a man of the world. He enjoyed good wine and lively talk. To his surprise and immense pleasure he soon awakened to the fact that both were readily available in this amusing little country to which he had been pocketed. Panamanians rarely took themselves seriously—a delightful quality. They were dedicated to pleasure and business and the multilayered intimacy of society. The entire country was Rome all over again, the Nuncio thought, soft and shallow but also beautiful and dear.

In his brief time here, the Nuncio had come to realize that there were really two Panamas, one of appearances and the other an underworld of secrets. There was, for instance, the nominal Catholicism that most of the country adhered to, and yet behind that mask of orthodoxy there was a primitive and highly inventive spiritualism, which was everywhere—the country was steeped in it. The Nuncio could stand on his balcony and see the hand-painted buses rushing past with their vivid depictions of Indian legends and tribal gods. Nearly everyone he met in the country consulted a spiritual guide of some sort—an astrologer, a fortune-teller, a voodoo priest. He even knew some nuns who wore amulets around their necks, a practice he tried in vain to stamp out. The Nuncio had the feeling that modernity was a transitory condition in Panama, and that the country's magical past, like the jungle, was chewing at the margins, always threatening to break through and reclaim the vulnerable campsite of civilization.

From his balcony the Nuncio could also see the heavy freighters chesting through the Bay of Panama toward the canal. One could follow their wakes as they wobbled shoreward, until the waves crashed against the seawall at the foot of the towering financial district. This was one economy, built on shipping, import-export, duty-free shops, tourism, bananas, and the mighty American military presence. Behind the façade of legitimacy was another, much larger economy, one of numbered bank accounts and laundered drug profits. Smugglers and arms dealers swaggered through the hotel lobbies. Pilots for the drug cartels paraded through the jewelry stores on Via España buying gaudy trinkets with great green rolls of Yanqui dollars. Guerrillas who were engaged in one revolution or another sat at the same gaming tables with Middle Eastern weapons merchants and CIA officers and Colombian cocaine dealers. Like peacock tails, extraordinary fortunes opened themselves for display in the form of fantastic seaside palaces and country retreats. One took care not to inquire too closely about the sources of wealth or to comment on a sudden improvement in a person's financial status. In such an intimate nation, people tended to be complexly related by blood or marriage or both, so it was easy to give offense even to the most decent citizens.

13

Real political life had been smothered by two decades of military dictatorship, which hid behind a counterfeit democracy. There was a congress and a president who came to power through graft and fraud. Indeed, that was the whole point of political office. Most Panamanians accepted this with a shrug or a wink, as if the concept of government was a kind of genial farce, not to be taken seriously. The Nuncio supposed that this fatalism must be a predictable consequence of the artificiality of Panama's creation. The country had never had the opportunity to fight for its independence; it had simply been snatched away from Colombia by the Americans and fashioned into a surprised and awkward and wholly unprepared republic.

It was no accident that General Noriega had been chief of military intelligence before he made his grab for power. Intelligence was the one commodity everyone traded in this two-faced commonwealth. The Americans had listening posts burrowed into the green volcanic hills above the city, from which they could overhear conversations all over Latin America. Satellites and high-flying aircraft with high-speed lenses patrolled the skies. Antennae studded the mountains like the spines of a hedgehog. But the Americans were by no means the only spies in Panama. The Japanese and the Taiwanese depended on the canal as a lifeline to Europe, so they monitored every political development, spending millions each year to keep their interests alive and their paid lackeys in office. No one could even guess how many Cuban agents and informers there were in the country, not to mention the Mexicans and Colombians and Israelis and Russians and even South Africans. The entire country was like an espionage trade fair.

And the Nuncio loved it. He adored the secrecy, the scheming and plotting, the intricate connivings, the hidden meanings that made life in Panama a study in human duplicity. In this, his Vatican training served him well. After ten years in Panama, he had become the most recognized and trusted diplomat in the city, gaining a reputation for his craftiness and his access to juicy intelligence—qualities deeply prized in a country that dines on gossip. Many of the Nuncio's sources were reporters, dissidents, or fallen political figures who had, at various times, come knocking at the back door of the old stone mansion at the corner of Avenida Balboa and Via Italia, where they might wait out the latest government purge. At this very moment the Nuncio was harboring at Vatican expense a columnist for *La Prensa* as well as two former members of the cabinet who had been there for nearly seven months, draining the wine cellar of many of its finest labels.

Aside from his network of political refugees and the deeply guarded but sometimes surprisingly useful information garnered from the confession box, the Nuncio had trained his staff to cultivate sources. Even the nuns brought in useful bits from time to time, rumors picked up from the schoolchildren—it was surprising what you could learn about a country by listening to its children—or complaints in the marketplace. But the Nuncio's prize student in the art of espionage was Father Jorge Ugarte, a handsome young Salvadoran whose talents reminded the Nuncio of himself nearly fifty years ago—cool, intelligent, and dispassionate. With training and encouragement, Father Jorge might attain the offices that the Nuncio himself had once aspired to. In fact, it was Father Jorge's step that the Nuncio recognized echoing in the marble hallway, and presently the handsome priest entered the room and shut the pocket doors behind him.

"It's raining," Father Jorge announced superfluously. He was drenched. "Just the walk from the bus stop." Without asking, he took a seat in the silver brocatelle wing-back chair opposite the desk.

The Nuncio started to protest, but thought better of it. He knew he had a reputation for being finicky; and besides, his affection for the young man inclined him to forgiveness. He thought Father Jorge one of the most interesting, attractive, and original young men he had ever met. Father Jorge had been orphaned in El Salvador during the cruelest civil war in Central

America and had taken refuge in a Catholic orphanage. The nuns, seeing his extraordinary promise and his natural piety, had arranged to send him to Madrid for schooling, where he was Europeanized and fashioned into an intellectual. A mestizo with dark Indian skin and liquid black eyes, which he hid behind round tortoiseshell glasses, Father Jorge still bore a slight trace of Castilian accent, which somehow added to his charm without making him appear at all pretentious.

"You've heard the news, of course."

The Nuncio nodded. That very morning the city had been electrified by the report that Panama's most famous revolutionary, Dr. Hugo Spadafora, had been murdered.

"He was on his way to the capital to make charges against Noriega," said Father Jorge. "Everybody knew that he had been promising to reveal the connections between the General and the narcotraffickers."

"Yes, I heard him on the radio last week. He said he had a briefcase full of evidence. What do you know about it?"

"These remarks come to me privately, but they are not under seal," Father Jorge said, betraying no emotion behind the shiny, round lenses. "Let us say they are observations of one who was intimate with a certain lieutenant."

The Nuncio had given his secretary permission to spend part of each week ministering to the poor in El Chorrillo, a vast slum in the center of town that surrounded the Panamanian military headquarters. He thought it might add to his protégé's portfolio when the Holy See began looking for prospects. Happily, there was an unexpected dividend in this part-time assignment: many soldiers came to the Chorrillo parish to pray, as did their women—the wives and girlfriends and mistresses who were such invaluable sources of intelligence, especially for Father Jorge, whose dark good looks and scrupulous chastity made him a sought-after curiosity in female society.

"As we know, Hugo left Costa Rica on Friday, the thirteenth," Father Jorge continued. "He took a taxi across the border and had a serving of rabbit stew in a small cantina. Then he boarded a minibus for the capital. It appears that he got as far as Concepción. He was taken off the bus by a PDF officer and escorted to military headquarters. That is the last sighting of the living Hugo Spadafora. Three days later his headless corpse was discovered in a U.S. mailbag on the Costa Rican border."

"Unburied?"

"Exactly, dumped on a riverbank, obviously meant to be found. By the way, I have secured the coroner's report," said Father Jorge, trying to suppress the note of triumph in his voice as he passed the photocopied document to the Nuncio, who eagerly snatched it up. "As you can see, he was quite extensively tortured."

"And raped, I see," the Nuncio said as he examined the report, which was slightly damp from Father Jorge's clothing.

"Yes, apparently they severed his hamstrings so he couldn't resist. And when they finished they drove a stake up his ass."

The Nuncio cast an uncritical but surprised look at his secretary, who never, in the Nuncio's memory, had ventured anything like a vulgarity. The impassiveness of the young priest's expression assured the Nuncio that he was merely speaking clinically, with his usual harrowing exactitude.

"At the end, a PDF cook cut off his head," Father Jorge added.

"Are we to make anything of that?" asked the Nuncio.

"What do you mean?"

"The entire country is in love with witchcraft. No doubt they believe that there is some juju to be gotten from such practices."

"I think it's just a show to terrify the masses."

"Perhaps," said the Nuncio, "but before the drug money came to Panama, Noriega would never have stooped to this. This is not his style." He reached for one of Sister Sarita's sugar wafers and held it in front of him, as if it contained some vital mystery.

"But as long as he is out of the country, he can maintain that he knew nothing about the assassination."

"I doubt that will help him." The Nuncio placed the coroner's report in a slender drawer in the center of his desk, which he locked with a key he kept in the pocket of his cassock. "The great Hugo Spadafora," he said meditatively. "You know, this time I think the Little General has gone too far."

THREE FRIGHTENED men entered the driveway of a handsome villa in Fort Amador, a former American military base that had been turned over to the Panama Defense Forces. A high stone wall topped with shards of colored glass surrounded the grounds. As the car approached, the iron gate opened to receive it, then abruptly shut behind it with a clang of doom.

The door chime played "Lara's Song" from *Doctor Zhivago*. Presently a shirtless butler in Bermuda shorts opened the door. "Mr. Escobar is expecting you," he said with pity in his voice.

The three men—César Rodríguez, Floyd Carlton, and Kiki Pretelt—exchanged desperate glances, then followed the butler through the living room to the private office of Pablo Escobar, the chief of security for the Medellín cartel.

The office was tasteful but surprisingly modest for a man of Escobar's wealth and resources. House-decorating magazines covered the coffee table. The shelves were bookless, lined instead with eight-track tapes and exotic Oriental vases. The centerpiece of the room, Escobar's desk, was an elegant sheet of black slate. A paused Pac-Man game blinked on the computer screen. Behind the desk was a picture window opening on a resplendent garden. Hummingbirds dodged frantically through the blossoms.

Escobar was sitting on his Exercycle with a towel around his neck, watching CNN. He did not seem to notice the men when they came in. They stood nervously aside and listened to the reporter describing Panama as a drug haven and a sanctuary for internationally known mobsters, such as the Ochoa brothers and Pablo Escobar. "Unlike many people here, Dr. Spadafora had the courage to speak out against the criminal element of Panamanian society," the reporter continued. "His death could mean the end of popular resistance to the Noriega regime, but judging from the reaction to his death, it is only the beginning."

Escobar stopped pedaling.

"What do you want to drink?" he asked. "Strychnine or cyanide?"

Kiki collapsed, banging his head on the slate desk as he fell.

"Get him off my rug," Escobar ordered. "He's bleeding on my fucking Karistan."

Floyd and César pulled Kiki to his feet. His eyes rolled slowly back into focus.

"It was a joke," said Escobar. "Ha, you should see your faces. You must have a very bad conscience to react in this manner."

Kiki tried to speak, but his lips seemed to be glued together.

"Low blood sugar, Mr. Escobar," said Floyd. "I think he missed breakfast."

Escobar gave them all a look of such disdain that Kiki began to wobble again. Floyd and César held him up.

"The Bible says a man cannot serve two masters," said Escobar, "but you work for me and you work for Noriega. The time has come to choose."

"Mr. Escobar, there is no choice. You know our first loyalty is to you," said César as the others nodded.

" 'Loyalty'—this is an interesting word," Escobar said as he toweled off. He was a pudgy man with a frowning mustache. "Perhaps it means something different in Panama. In Colombia, when we pay a man for his cooperation, we get his cooperation. If he doesn't wish to work with us—okay! He doesn't take our money. But this! I give Noriega five million dollars. I entrust it to you. You tell me he appreciates it."

"He was very grateful. I am sure of this," César said.

"Yes, he even sends me this vase," said Escobar, indicating a delicate blue ceramic, which resonated in a pleasing low hum as he traced his finger around its rim. "It's Ming, you know, one of the finest pieces in my collection. Very rare, a genuine treasure."

"It's exquisite," Kiki said in a hoarse whisper.

"This is true. He also rents me this villa, but he charges me so much I wonder if I can afford his generosity. Now I learn that he has closed down our new processing lab—a world-class facility, the finest I have ever seen, a work of great genius. Twenty-three of my workers captured—highly skilled men, men with families—taken off to jail. As if they had no protection. As if they had no assurance from me of their safety."

"This is wrong," said César indignantly. "Most definitely a very wrong thing."

"Yes, it is. And now I want that you deliver a message to the General," said Escobar, his face turning black with fury. "You tell that little wart he's going to die! Right here! I'll rip out his balls! I'll feed his liver to the house cat! Do you think he can understand that? This is *business!*" With that, Pablo Escobar hurled his prized Ming vase through the picture window, sending shards of glass into the hibiscus and scattering hummingbirds into the sky.

D R. JÜRGEN SPRACHT, the world-famous Swiss dermatologist, carefully unwrapped the gauze from the face of one of his most difficult cases—M.N., as he was known in the medical literature, a middle-aged Latin man badly scarred by multiple lesions of acne vulgaris that continued to erupt long after adolescence. It was a challenging case, one that Spracht had been working on for nearly a dozen years with admittedly modest success.

"*Ja,*" he said as the gauze lifted to reveal a raw red scab covering the patient's entire face. "It's clearing, it's definitely clearing."

The patient started to smile, but the scab cracked like a boiled egg. M.N.'s eyes registered a bolt of pain.

"Not moving ist best," advised Dr. Spracht. "No expression. Even talking *ist nicht so gut.*"

The patient grunted in response.

"Now the nuss will apply special ointment, and we will bandage all over again. Agweed? No movement."

As a blond nurse in a gratifyingly tight lab coat leaned over and began to swab a stinging green unguent on the throbbing wound, ignoring the muzzled cries of pain, the door opened, and a very alarmed receptionist stuck her head in. "There's an emergency call for General Noriega!" she announced.

"I am busy," the patient said through clenched teeth.

"It's the *president* of Panama," the receptionist exclaimed in an awed voice.

"Nicky, what the fuck do you want?" the patient asked as Dr. Spracht held the phone to his ear.

On the other end of the line there was a brief transatlantic pause, then President Nicolás Ardito Barletta responded, "Tony, I have serious news. Something very important has come up. Incidentally, Roberto is also on the line."

"Hi, Tony!" said Roberto Díaz Herrera, the colonel who was second in command of the Panama Defense Forces.

"What is the problem?" Tony demanded.

"Hugo Spadafora has been murdered," Barletta said in a strangely neutral tone of voice.

"Good," said Tony. "This is good."

"Uh, yes, of course we agree, but the people are not taking it so well," Barletta continued. "I don't know if you can hear the honking outside. I'm holding the phone out the window for you."

Tony listened to the cacophonous traffic outside the presidential palace and the distant chanting of his name.

"There is great agitation," Roberto added unhelpfully. "The people hold you responsible."

"Listen, Nicky, I can't talk about this now," said Tony. "You should call me in New York next week."

"Next week!" said Barletta.

"Tony, what we're saying is that the situation in Panama is very unstable," said Roberto. "Maybe it is more important for you to be here than in Paris, or Switzerland, or New York, or whatever."

"We think either you should come home right away, or else . . ." Barletta's voice trailed away significantly.

O R ELSE?" The threat implicit in that phrase echoed in Tony's mind as his limo crawled through the Geneva traffic. What did they think of him—that he would abdicate? Live the rest of his life in Switzerland? Who did they think they were dealing with? Did Nicky and Roberto imagine that they could run Panama without him? The thought would have made Tony laugh if the consequences weren't so painful.

His thoughts flew about in confusion. Hugo dead. Tony's nemesis gone. Out of his life. Out of life itself. It should be an occasion to rejoice. It was certainly an opportunity to reflect on the nature of divine justice. Hugo had been everything Tony was not: tall, handsome, rich, loved. And now dead, a nothing, his fame turned to vaporous memory. Delicious victory, especially after the noise that Hugo had made about Tony and the narcos, the threats he had made on the radio, the "proof" he had boasted about having in that little book of his.

But panic was banging on the door demanding to be admitted. Hugo—dead! Everyone would blame Tony for it. They already were! Something enormous had shifted in Tony's universe, and only God knew how it would throw the planets out of alignment. A little change was containable. Too much change made everything crazy.

But in any case, he had a more pressing concern impatiently awaiting for him at the Bank of Credit and Commerce International. Tony glanced at his watch and shuddered.

Twenty minutes later, the limo came to a halt in front of BCCI's imposing Geneva headquarters, and Tony darted out, carrying a weighty valise.

"Four o'clock!"

Tony periscoped his head toward the sound of that stony-hearted voice. There she was, sitting on a divan, surrounded by shopping bags and stroking the head of the dead fox attached to the fur around her shoulders: Felicidad, his formidable wife, staring at him with the eyes of an assassin.

"You said to meet you here at four o'clock and you show up at ten to five!" Her voice echoed in the oddly rapt lobby.

"Sweetness, the traffic—"

Felicidad made a clucking, dismissive sound that caused Tony's knees to go weak. "But I have arranged a surprise for you," he pleaded. "This is something I am sure you will appreciate."

"I've got a massage at six."

"Please, dearest, this is most important to our future, I swear it."

"This had better be worth it."

A few minutes later Tony and Felicidad were seated in a small but luxurious conference room in the high-security subbasement, decorated with investment-quality folk art and hand-painted Haitian furniture.

"Very tasteful," Felicidad decreed as she surveyed the room. "We should do this, Tony. We should do this in the den." She seemed to be mollified by the prospect of extensive redecoration.

Tony nodded agreeably, although the thought of turning his den into a replica of a Swiss bank office filled him with—well, mixed feelings. On the one hand, how pathetic, how derivative, how frankly weird to come upon Caribbean handicrafts in this chilled subterranean Swiss vault; on the other hand, he had to admit, it looked better here, it looked like real art. A ghoulish frieze of skeletons tangoed on the painted tabletop. Life in death: it was so primitive, so unreconstructed, so strangely powerful now that Tony saw it out of context. Perhaps something in the cold Swiss soul longed for chaotic tropical vitality. Tony considered himself an expert on the Swiss, since he had been coming here annually for a decade now, both to do his banking and for the spa where Felicidad got massages and Tony received Dr.

Spracht's savage facial treatments—and also fetal-tissue injections that gave Tony a more or less continual erection. Of course, the Swiss claim they don't deal in voodoo, but Tony recognized magic when he saw it. He would have to get the recipe for those injections.

It occurred to him that there was a correspondence between his own radical Latin soul and the mountain-bound conservatism of these magical, cheese-eating blonds. Perhaps he should stay here after all, he reflected; life would not be so bad. Here, in frumpy Geneva, Tony could experience his own Swissness. He, too, had a longing for neutrality. He, too, yearned to step out of the arena of conflict, to achieve the spiritual contentment that seemed so native to the curtained horizons of Europe's dairyland. He supposed it was mere cultural difference that allowed this bank, which had been established for the sole purpose of hiding drug profits from Colombia and stashing away large portions of the Third World GNP in numbered accounts, to appear so respectable, so within the bounds, so spiritually untroubled. *"Pecunia non olet,"* the bankers liked to say: money doesn't smell.

Presently the door opened and a nervous young teller appeared. Behind her was a bulky man in shirtsleeves and an apron who was pushing a heavy metal cart. The man in the apron took a quick glance at the General, then cast his eyes into middle space as he pushed the cart into the conference room. Tony waited until the bankers were gone, then he opened the valise and dumped $13 million on the table.

Felicidad looked at him with scorn. "Tony, did you think you could buy me off?"

That, of course, was exactly what he had thought. He took a key from his pocket and opened the vault on top of the cart. There were stacks of currency inside, mounds of it—dollars, francs, yen, marks—and a dozen shining gold ingots. Tony lifted one of the gold bars and pressed it over his head like a dumbbell. "Heavy," he said, noticing that the underside of the bar was stamped with a swastika.

Felicidad drew the fox close around her shoulders despite the thin bead of perspiration that had formed on her upper lip.

"Tony, what is this?"

"Money. Lots and lots of money." Tony casually began to stack the new currency into the vault.

"But where did it come from?" Felicidad asked hesitantly. Her breath was shallow and faint.

"Hard work. Investments. A few gifts. It's retirement benefits, mainly."

"They could hang you for this."

"I didn't *steal* it! People give me things—it's part of my job to do favors, and in return, they give me little donations."

"Tony, this is a lot of favors."

"Many favors, many donations."

"I don't want to know the details," Felicidad said as she cautiously fanned through a bundle of thousand-yen notes. "And what do you expect from me, with all this?"

"Understanding. Patience. Perhaps a little forgiveness. A man like me, I am not so perfect, but you must admit there are compensations. Take that into account, that is what I am saying."

"Even so, Tony, the power, all this money—it's not infinite, you know."

"Not infinite, but isn't it enough?"

"Tony, you ask for the forgiveness of a saint. I am not a saint. How many times you have wronged me! Did you expect to buy me, like one of your whores?"

"Fela, I ask you please to respect the fact that I have made you one of the richest women in the world. It is not so small a thing."

Felicidad looked at Tony and then at the mountain of cash and bullion. "You have been a good provider, this I agree. So I can tell you this much: what's in the past is past."

"That is all I ask," Tony said gratefully.

"But do not expect that this pardons even one more sin against me or your family!"

25

"No, of course . . ."

"You can ask this only once, Tony. The slate is clean. From now on, you must behave yourself. Do not try to find the end of my patience—it is very near!"

Tony put his hand over his heart. "Fela, I swear to you, from this day forward, I am a new man."

CHAPTER 2

THE FUNERAL procession for Dr. Spadafora began at the airport, where the plane carrying his body from Costa Rica arrived at noon. Thousands waited for him, including many of his comrades from the Victoriano Lorenzo Brigade who had fought with Hugo in Nicaragua against the Somoza dictatorship and then with the Miskito Indians against the corrupt Sandinistas. The spies in the crowd worked furiously, snapping up anecdotes like sharks feeding in a fertile lagoon. "He came to my house with a briefcase," said one of Hugo's many beautiful lovers. "He said he could prove Tony was in bed with the narcotraffickers. And he patted the briefcase like a pet."

"Someone said he implicated the CIA as well."

"Is it surprising? Tony and the CIA are together in everything else."

"Certainly this could not have happened without the Americans agreeing to it. They must have wanted Tony to put a stop to the threats." Heads nodded. Nothing transpired in Panama without the Americans being involved.

The motorcade brought the city to a standstill. The Nuncio

watched with great concern as the procession stretched along Avenida Balboa like a lizard's tail. He knew that Father Jorge was in the lead vehicle with the Spadafora family. His young secretary had been chosen to preach the funeral oration.

It seemed as if everyone in the country were either in the march or standing on the seawall, making the sign of the cross as the garlanded hearse carrying Hugo's headless corpse passed by. No one had ever seen such a public outpouring—not even upon the death of Omar Torrijos. And as the crowd mourned Hugo, they also mourned that former time, which now seemed so innocent. Under Torrijos, political dissidents might have been jailed or exiled, but they were rarely murdered. Until now, the country had avoided the savage civil wars that had ravaged Salvador, Honduras, Guatemala, and Nicaragua. The people had not known, when Torrijos died, what would follow. Now they knew.

Of course, they remembered that Torrijos himself had thrown Hugo in La Modelo prison, but even that action now appeared harmless, almost playful. When Hugo had come back from Africa, where he was fighting with the guerrillas in Portuguese Guinea, he had come to stir up revolt against Torrijos's military coup. But Torrijos being Torrijos—that is to say, cocksure and crazy—and recognizing these same qualities in the adventurous young medical man, he had often come to visit Hugo at La Modelo, preaching to him about his own vision for Panama, seducing him with his sympathy for the poor. Eventually he made Hugo the vice minister of health. If only Hugo had stayed in government service, people said, the destiny of Panama would have been different. But Hugo was by nature a fighter, not a civil servant. When the Nicaraguan rebellion began, Hugo formed his own freelance brigade and led his men into the jungle. Torrijos sent his own fifteen-year-old son, Martín, to join him. There Hugo learned about the secret network of pilots and jungle airstrips that the guerrillas had established to run guns to the Sandinistas. Noriega was using this network to operate a private drug-trafficking ring. Hugo informed Torrijos and also warned him that Noriega was plotting against him. Perhaps if Torrijos had acted quickly, he might have saved himself and Hugo as well. But a few days later Torrijos's Dehavilland Twin Otter aircraft crashed into a hillside. The cause of the crash was never explained. Of course, everyone in Panama suspected the CIA's man in Panama and Omar's eventual successor, Manuel Antonio Noriega.

With Hugo's death, people sensed that some final barrier of civility had been crossed and that they were rapidly hurtling toward barbarity. Rumors about the aborted investigation of Hugo's death flew around the city. The bus driver and several passengers who had ridden with Hugo the morning of his capture had spoken to the press. They had talked about the soldiers who had taken Hugo away. But they recanted their stories after being interrogated at PDF headquarters. An elderly woman who refused to change her story disappeared. Later, her body was found. She, too, had been decapitated.

Occasionally someone in the crowd would start a chant, which would go on for some minutes, soaking up the anger and frustration, but then it would lose conviction and the people would shift about nervously, casting glances at unfamiliar faces. Everyone knew that names were being taken. Had Hugo been there, the living Hugo, he would have given them the courage to express their defiance, but the image of their mutilated hero settled into their minds, dousing their ardor and shaming them with the knowledge of their faint hearts.

The priest that the Spadafora family originally had sought for the occasion pleaded illness, and perhaps he really was ill, people joked: he had the Noriega virus. The diocese subsequently offered several alternative priests, most of whom were on the take from the PDF and one who was so elderly and addled that he drooled and stared into space for long periods between sentences. Finally the family settled on Father Jorge, who was practically unknown outside the Chorrillo slum. His association with the Nuncio compensated for the fact that he was an Indian. Besides, there was something about the young priest's looks and demeanor that reminded Hugo's father of his own martyred son.

And so Father Jorge found himself in the position of celebrating the funeral mass for a famous man he had never met. He rode to the city of Chitré in the third row of seats of a ponderous Chevrolet Suburban. Hugo's younger brother, Winston, an attorney in Panama City, sat up front with the driver, and the priest sat with Hugo's father. Don Melo was the former mayor of Chitré and governor of Herrera Province. He was a popular figure in the country, well thought of, with a reputation for honesty that was quite remarkable in this congenitally corrupt society. There were six more cars immediately behind them filled with Spadaforas— Don Melo had twelve children by various wives—and behind them came the cousins and in-laws and then the thousands of friends. The Spadaforas were one of the most prominent families in Panama, and the farther the caravan proceeded into the heart of the country, the larger it grew and the more absurd Hugo's murder appeared to be. Father Jorge did not consider himself a political sophisticate, but it was obvious even to him that the Spadaforas were not easily intimidated. They had friends and resources that could not be discounted.

The procession picked up friends and relatives at every turn in the road. Sometimes the entire funeral cortege came to a halt because of the crowds that surrounded the cars in the little villages they passed along the way. Crying faces were pressed into the windows. Women stood on the corners screaming oaths at the government. A group of schoolchildren took up the chant "Death to Noriega!"

Father Jorge sat quietly, feeling a bit carsick from the undulations of the road through the jungle. He was also suffering misgivings about the mass. Without really dictating what he should say, the Nuncio had begged him to be restrained, to minister to the spirit but to avoid addressing the political explosion that had followed the atrocity. Whatever he said, the Nuncio reminded him, would be heard by the entire country, and certainly by Noriega and his PDF thugs. No purpose would be served in making some brave statement that resulted in Father Jorge's body being found with *F*-8—the signature of Noriega's death squad—carved into it.

The sermon Father Jorge intended to deliver was much as the Nuncio advised, a plea to God for compassion and mercy and understanding. Of course, the occasion also demanded a call for justice. He and the Nuncio had discussed terms that would not be too offensive to the government but that would serve to appease the crowd. Father Jorge realized that if he followed the Nuncio's advice to the letter, he would be politely despised by Hugo's admirers; moreover, he would think himself a coward. Hugo's sacrifice was too great to be discreetly acknowledged. Father Jorge could sense Hugo's spirit hovering over him, urging him to take up his cry for vengeance and revolution.

He suddenly shivered and blocked the memory of his parents lying dead in the sawdust on the floor of his father's workshop. The scene was like a snapshot that never changed—the strange arrangement of their limbs, the curlicues of planed wood caught in his mother's bloody hair. They had not been brave and reckless rebels like Hugo. Their death meant nothing. There were no fawning crowds to grieve their passing. Father Jorge was not even sure who had killed them. Some said the military, but there were also rebels who assassinated anyone thought to be against them. Revolution gave license to murder on all sides.

Father Jorge was a man of faith, not of action—at least that is how he thought of himself—and therefore he regarded Hugo with mixed feelings of admiration, envy, suspicion, and disdain. All his life he had avoided such men with their contagious passions. Politics held no interest for him. When he entered the priesthood, he had hoped to close the door on the world as it is. And yet he had been pushed back into it, apprenticed to a semidisgraced Vatican bureaucrat in a country that was just beginning to heave itself into a political cataclysm.

"Of course Nicky made assurances, but what of it?" Winston was saying. He was speaking of President Barletta, who had called for a complete investigation of the murder.

"Talk," Don Melo said hopelessly. "They talk, they offer sympathy . . ." He trailed off into the silence that had consumed him from the moment his son's body was discovered.

These people don't just want me to make sense of their grief, Father Jorge thought. They want me to bring their son back to life. He stared out the tinted window at the Indians who stood silently on the roadside watching the funeral procession go by. The priest saw his own sober reflection passing over their faces. He belonged out there with them, he thought, not inside the car with these upper-class whites.

"What do you think, Father?" Don Melo was asking him, interrupting his thoughts. It took a second for the priest to mentally retrieve the bits of conversation that he had been overhearing without really listening to it. Don Melo had been complaining about the propriety of burying Hugo's body without the head. This was an obsession with him.

"From the Church's point of view, it makes no difference," said Father Jorge. "His soul does not reside in one portion of his body or another. Our Hugo is no longer on this earth at all. He is safely with his Lord and Savior in heaven."

It was clear from Don Melo's mournful eyes that he did not accept this line of thinking. "If it offends me so much, it must offend God as well," he said.

"I am sure God shares your suffering, but be assured that he understands the sacrifice that Hugo has made. He will surely judge those who committed this horrible deed."

Don Melo nodded doubtfully.

When they reached Chitré, the crowd was spilling out of the Cathedral of Saint John the Baptist and standing in the light drizzle in the plaza. They had been waiting restlessly for hours.

Finally the casket entered the cathedral on the shoulders of Hugo's comrades, and at last the mass began. Father Jorge would not remember all the words he said that afternoon, but he would never forget the faces of the mourners and how they had sought him out, how they had turned to him for solace and meaning. And for some reason, his words did console. They were his words; they did not belong to the Nuncio or to Hugo. He had spoken of the majesty of God's gift of life and the nobility of Hugo's sacrifice. He reflected on Jesus' entry into Jerusalem in his last week of life, placing himself willingly in the hands of the Roman despot. Like Jesus, Hugo had accepted death as an inevitable consequence of a radical life, and the torture and humiliation that he had endured did not diminish him; rather, it raised him up in the eyes of God. "Hugo's head is missing," said Father Jorge, "but his soul is not—it is here with us. It is inside everyone who yearns for justice and freedom. We must honor Hugo by remembering his sacrifice; but we must also honor Jesus by remembering his example of nonviolence. For earthly justice is transitory and imperfect, but divine justice is eternal."

Afterward, the mourners remarked on the mysterious power of the occasion and the healing words of the young priest that no one knew. "He came when others refused," Don Melo said later. "He is one of us, even if he doesn't know it yet."

O N TOP OF New York, Tony reclined in the four-poster, king-sized bed, wearing a white terry-cloth robe embossed with the regal seal of the Helmsley Palace Hotel, listening to President Nicolás Ardito Barletta on the speakerphone. Half a dozen chairs were pulled up to the foot of the bed to accommodate the retinue of CIA officers and State Department officials.

As it happened, the Panamanian president was only fifteen blocks away, at the U.N. Plaza Hotel. The fact that he had not been invited to be present in person at this meeting was a fillip of humiliation evident to everyone in the room, and of course to the president himself. "What are you saying?" Barletta asked in an aggrieved tone of voice. "That the U.S. position has changed?"

"We can only speak for the agency," said Rollins, the chief of the Panama station. He was a small, wiry man with bad teeth and nicotine-stained fingers and weak blue eyes that floated like balloons behind thick, dirty glasses. "The agency is behind you, Mr. President. Isn't that right, Ginny?" He turned to the crisp brunette in a chintz armchair.

"From Casey on down," she agreed.

"But from a public-relations point of view, it's a disaster." This came from Mark Ortega, the executive on the Panamanian account at Nocera, Lemann & Fallows, a top-dollar Washington public-relations firm.

"Agreed," said Ginny.

"Is that your view, Rollins?" asked Tony.

"That's why we brought Mark with us, General," said Rollins. "I think you ought to listen to him."

Tony sized up the bulky suit with the pushed-up sleeves and the round black glasses. "The whole Spadafora thing is undermining the image of Panama," said Mark. "We've got to make a dramatic gesture that will reassure the American people that the Panamanian government is not involved in political assassination. And by the way, I hope that's true."

"I assure you that our hands are clean," said Barletta.

"What do you suggest, Mr. Mark?" asked Tony.

"Elections. Press loves 'em."

"But we *had* an election," Barletta said plaintively over the speakerphone. "I won."

Tony thoughtfully scratched his balls while the others stared at their shoes.

"Free and fair elections," Mark said gently. "Supervised by international monitors, like the U.N. or—"

"Jimmy Carter," suggested Gabriel Vargas, the white-haired Panamanian ambassador to Washington.

"Great idea, Mr. Ambassador!" said Mark. "Brokered the canal treaties. Both the Americans and the Panamanians trust him, even though the Americans don't like him very much. Actually, that could be an advantage."

Tony shot a glance at Vargas. The old man had never been reliable. He was one of those white-assed aristocrats who had made a fortune off the backs of fruit pickers.

"We've got another problem in Washington," said Ginny. "Senator Jesse Helms is asking for an investigation into the Spadafora business."

"We *welcome* an investigation!" Barletta said defiantly. In the silence that followed, Tony signaled to his doctor, who was quietly reading a comic book in the corner. Tony rubbed the center of his forehead, and the doctor reached into his bag for a bottle of Excedrin.

"Helms—he's loco, right?" asked Tony.

"Completely berserk," said Mark. "That's what makes him so dangerous. But it's not just Helms. You got Kerry on the Left saying the same stuff. Lot of people on both sides of the aisle are worried that Panama is turning into some kind of refuge for drug lords. They don't want to see the canal fall under the control of narcotraffickers."

"Drugs! Drugs!" Tony shouted. "Don't they read the newspapers? Don't they see the television? We just raided the biggest cocaine plant in Central America—in Darién! Twenty-three narcos arrested!"

"You're right, General, and kudos to you," said Mark.

"Noriega is a leader in the war on drugs. A rock!" said Tony.

"We know that, General."

"A fucking rock!"

"We know that you're a good guy, an anticommunist democrat," Mark continued, "but you've got to realize–the American people perceive you as something other than that. And, frankly, the Spadafora business hasn't helped."

"How do they see me, Mr. Mark?"

"They see you as a little tin-pot fascist, which, Lord knows how they got that impression, but—" Mark threw up his hands. "Bad PR management in the past, I suspect. But we're here to change that, General."

"We've got to make a gesture, Tony." This from Vargas, who seemed immune to Tony's icy stare.

"You know, I have already anticipated this myself," said Barletta. He had a slightly giddy note of triumph in his voice. "Even before you called, I have taken action."

The people in Tony's suite exchanged worried glances.

"Yesterday, I appointed a commission to investigate this crime," Barletta chirped from the speakerphone. "A blue-ribbon commission, composed of the most respectable men in the country." He named half a dozen people, all of them, like Vargas and Barletta, members of the white upper class. "Anyone would have to say that these men are incorruptible. Moreover, I have invested this panel with subpoena power. I think you will see us getting to the bottom of this terrible business quickly. Senator Helms should be congratulating us! He will see who is in charge in Panama—the narcotraffickers or the true democrats!"

Tony's headache was ringing like a church bell.

"Well, I'm sure you've done the right thing, Mr. President," said Rollins. "The problem with an investigation is you never know what they might turn up, if you don't have control. If you know what I mean."

"Imagewise, it's tricky," Mark agreed.

"We'll get to the truth, believe me," Barletta assured them, failing to follow the drift of their conversation. "I can make a pledge to you, a pledge to all the American people, that—"

"Nicky, hold on, I've got another call," said Tony. He punched the button of the second phone line.

"General, is that you?" said the surprisingly girlish voice of the hotel proprietress, Leona Helmsley.

"Oh, Leona!" Tony made smooching sounds into the receiver.

"Did you get the flowers?" she asked.

"The room is full of their sweet aroma. And the champagne! You are so thoughtful. Now all I need is someone named Leona to share it with me."

A trill of nervous laughter came through the speaker. Tony's audience sat blankly as he murmured several indiscreet proposals. "You know, I love you very much," he finally said, grasping his balls emphatically.

When he got back on the line with the president, Tony's mood was much improved. "Don't worry, Nicky," he said cheerfully. "Look on the bright side. Hugo was a pest and now he's dead. Maybe people are upset now, but they'll forget about him soon. Why don't you forget about this commission and just leave it to me? I know just what to do."

CHAPTER 3

A HOLE OPENED in the sky and *Panama One* fell five hundred feet. Felicidad screamed and Tony grabbed the vomit bag.

"It's the tail of the hurricane, General," the pilot apologized over the intercom. "We're going to try to fly above it."

The sleek Learjet had never felt so fragile as it climbed through the bank of thunderclouds that were scurrying before Hurricane Gloria. The atmosphere was at war with itself. The little jet jerked and hawed and bounced and stumbled, its engines straining, as lightning exploded just beyond the wingtips.

Prayers and promises came rushing into Tony's terrified mind. Thousands of feet below him the great Atlantic Ocean stretched out like bottomless death forever and forever.

There had been a sense of foreboding all along, even though the trip had been a triumph from the very start. After Geneva, he had spent a delicious lost weekend at his country house near Verdun with a former Miss Panama, whom he rewarded by appointing her cultural attaché to France and Spain. In Paris, Mitterrand had given him a medal and kissed his cheeks—in itself a surprisingly sensual experience. Then off to Washington, where Tony picked up another award from the Drug Enforcement Agency for the Darién bust. Afterward, he had drinks with his old friend Bill Casey, the head of the CIA, to talk about the Contras, Casey's obsession. As long as the Sandinistas were running Nicaragua, Tony was the king of Central America. It was the greatest little war.

Another plunge. Tony vomited violently into the bag.

The oxygen masks dropped without warning. Felicidad cried out. Even her steel nerves were shattered. She made a cross before pulling the mask to her face. The wings of the Learjet were bending; they almost seemed to be flapping in their effort to climb over the storm. The shuddering aircraft pitched abruptly upward, popping open one of the storage bins and spilling shopping bags from Givenchy and Yves Saint Laurent.

"Oh, my God, I am heartily sorry for having offended thee," Tony prayed urgently. "I regret the loss of heaven and the pains of hell, but most of all I regret that I have offended you, O Lord, who art all good and deserving of my trust." He realized this was a pre–Vatican II act of contrition, but he was so out of touch with the Church that he wasn't sure what the latest formulation was. He hadn't gone to confession in nearly ten years, since he turned to Zen. But Buddhism was no consolation in a hurricane.

And then suddenly, miraculously, they burst into sunshine, a blue zone of safety. Tony and Felicidad looked at each other in mutual astonishment and relief.

"God, Tony, look at the mess you made."

Apparently he had mostly missed the bag.

"Really, you're going to have to do something. Clean yourself up," she said as she picked up her novel and dismissed him.

Tony came out of the rest room wearing a crisp new uniform. He was suddenly horny—probably it was his brush with death—and he wondered if Felicidad felt the same way. He watched her drinking her Campari and soda and reading *The Thorn Birds*. She could stand to lose a few pounds, but the pretty young teacher he had married was still evident—preserved with all the science and magic a woman could bring to bear on the matter. Her hair was still glistening black, her teeth gleaming white, her skin lustrous pearl, her eyes—well, her eyes were weapons, one couldn't talk about them in the same way. The adolescent, moony love-lust that Tony had once felt for her had long since been replaced by an amalgamation of other, equally intense passions—primarily awe and fear. Everybody in Panama believed that she had already killed one of his lovers—an ambassador's daughter, a terrifically sensual girl who always smelled of jasmine—who had either jumped or been pushed off a downtown hotel balcony. Tony had never had the nerve to question Felicidad about it. He had already paid a fortune to Dr. Spracht to repair the scratch marks Felicidad had left in the face of another beauty.

Despite all that, Tony could still imagine being with Felicidad sexually, tearing into each other, biting and clawing . . .

Felicidad looked up from her novel and gave him a look of such scorn that he felt his balls slip into his body cavity, like mice fleeing the cat. He'd never known such a woman.

"I think I'll go up front," he said fumblingly. "I need to talk to César."

He walked through the cabin and tapped on the cockpit door. The copilot, a grim-faced lieutenant in a PDF uniform, bumped his head on the overhead controls and made his salute.

"César and I have business to discuss," said Tony.

The copilot quickly removed his headset and left the cockpit.

César Rodríguez looked up and grinned. His curly chest hair burst through his half-open tropical shirt. He had rough, muscular features and a face that always looked two days unshaved. A heavy gold chronometer coiled around his wrist. "What happened?" he asked as Tony sat in the copilot's seat. "Did you shit in your pants?"

"César, why do you talk to me like this?"

César merely laughed. "I tell you what you *need* to hear, not what you *want* to hear. That's why you can't live without me. Because no one else has the balls to tell you when you're fucking up."

Tony frowned. "And how am I fucking up?"

"Too many ways to count. You take too much for yourself, man. People get upset if you don't leave more money on the table."

"I give money to everybody in Panama already," Tony said irritably.

"Plus you made a huge mistake with Spadafora. What were you thinking, Tony? Everything was going fine till all this shit happened. You look like Al Capone in the news, man. Even the Colombians are upset. Bad publicity for them."

"I'm not afraid of the Colombians," said Tony.

"Well, I am," César said fervently. "That Escobar, man, he's crazy enough to do anything. They kill people every day, and they're not even nice about it."

"They need me too much."

"I'm just saying you got to watch your ass, you know what I mean? We're not talking about rational human beings. Lay some serious money at their feet. A peace offering. Maybe they'll forget about all the trouble you caused them."

"You abuse me and you know too much," Tony grumbled.

César took the warning and began to do a navigation check; the storm had thrown them several hundred miles off course. Tony looked out the window at the bright sky. He could still see the storm below them and the lightning in the clouds exploding like radiant bombs. His mood improved. He reached over and put his hand on César's thigh, feeling the alarmed muscular response to his touch.

"I love to fly," Tony said happily.

"General . . . !"

"Put it on auto, César," said Tony. It was an order.

* * *

41

Rain had suddenly soaked the marching band, which remained standing at attention on the tarmac through the downpour. Just as the low clouds broke apart and the rain moved on to the green mountains behind the city, *Panama One* appeared on a ray of sunlight, and the band struck up the "Washington Post March." Tuba players spat out rainwater. The dignitaries rushed out of the hangar where they had taken shelter and lined up beside the sodden red carpet. The jet bounced heavily as it touched down, being so overladen with purchases that it had barely been able to take off from La Guardia earlier that afternoon.

Resplendent in his dress whites, Tony stepped onto the stairs and observed the upturned faces of the cabinet members, the judiciary, military officers, and various ambassadors, all waiting expectantly in the drenched sunset for the uncrowned head of state to descend to his native soil. Tony lingered a moment in the doorway of the aircraft and waved a white handkerchief triumphantly overhead. He always did that when he left or when he returned—a trademark gesture.

Suddenly he noticed that hundreds of citizens—well-wishers? —were surging against a line of police officers beside the terminal. Many of them were waving white handkerchiefs in response. Were they welcoming him home?

"Hey, Tony, where's the head?" a voice cried out.

To his horror, Tony realized that people were mocking him. They were waving posters with Hugo's picture on them, which asked the same question—where's the head? Where's the head?

Tony stomped down the steps. Roberto was the first to greet him. He stood with a sickly fixed smile on his face like a rictus. "I won't forget this, Roberto," Tony said over the jeers of the crowd. "Also, I know all about your little barracks uprising. You think because I am out of the country that I don't know what is happening?"

Roberto wobbled and his face went pale. "What are you talking about, General?" he said anxiously. "I only moved the troops because of these demonstrators. As you can see, we need even more. I've been waiting for additional instructions from you!"

"It's a good thing your balls are so small. You may be eating them for breakfast," said Tony as he moved on to the next in line, Eric Arturo Delvalle, the first vice president. "Tuturo" was a glamorous playboy, far more at home at the racetrack than in government offices. Freshly barbered and shaved, his nails even and gleaming, the vice president grasped Tony's limp, damp hand. "Welcome home, General. I hope you enjoyed your well-deserved trip to Europe and America."

"You make it sound like a vacation," Tony snapped.

"Why, no—I mean, I certainly did not think of it in such a way, only that in matters of state, it is good that Panama can be represented abroad, and who, of course, can do that better than . . ." Delvalle sputtered to a stop as Tony moved on.

Tony continued down the receiving line, greeting cabinet members and supreme court justices, each of whom trembled in his embrace.

"So, General, you came home," the Nuncio said in as polite a tone as he could muster, when Tony finally approached the diplomatic corps.

Tony laughed. "Did you think I would become an exile? It's not my style, Father." The Nuncio had always amused him despite his known sympathies for Tony's opponents. "A few malcontents—well, it's the price of freedom, eh?"

"And it is a very small price," the Nuncio replied over the screams of the demonstrators as the police bludgeoned their way through the mob.

The Nuncio had met Noriega many times before on official occasions such as this one. Initially, he had been impressed, as everyone is, by the General's moonlike face, which was cratered by acne scars, and by his short stature, which made him look like a stocky child in a man's uniform. These were the physical qualities everyone made fun of. They called him Pineapple Face because of his complexion and made jokes about his manliness, but at the same time they were terrified of him. His cold hands, and his oily skin and hooded eyes, gave him a reptilian quality. But as the Nuncio came to know him better, he had also been struck and a bit alarmed by the sheer sensuousness of the General's presence. He exuded sexuality and power.

"In any case, I forgive all Frenchmen today," Tony said. "You see what your countrymen have given me."

There were so many colorful medals on Noriega's chest, most of which he had awarded himself, that the Nuncio had not really noticed the *Légion d'honneur* among them. He was so astounded that for a moment he couldn't speak. He reflected quickly on the probable cause of such a gift—France's highest honor—and he decided that it must be a very public payment for the secret dirty work that Noriega had recently performed. The French secret service had captured six Basque terrorists and then didn't know how to dispose of them. Panama was the only country willing to offer them asylum. Now the terrorists were living like pashas in a beach condo a block away from the nunciature. One of them, a chef, had opened a restaurant on Via Argentina with valet parking and a dress code.

Tony had started to move on to the next ambassador—a Rastafarian from the Bahamas who was about to present him with a tortoiseshell inscribed with the image of Harry Belafonte—when he turned back to the Nuncio. "One other thing," he said.

"Yes?"

"I want to ask your opinion about something that has been troubling me. I'm asking you as a scholar and a theologian."

"You flatter me. But if it's of any value, I'll be happy to offer it."

"Do you recall when Saint Augustine made his break with the Manichaeans? They asked him how the Christian God could favor men who killed, men who had many wives, men who sacrificed living creatures. I myself have often wondered about this paradox."

"It's an interesting question," said the Nuncio, "but to be honest, I haven't read the *Confessions* for many years."

"Don't you suppose they were thinking of King David?"

"The Manichaeans?"

"He murdered women and children, he took hundreds of wives and concubines, he even cursed God, but God still loved him above all others."

"Yes, I suppose that's what the Bible tells us."

"Surely there is some catechism they taught you in seminary that covers this matter."

"I suppose your question is covered under the heading of 'unmerited grace,' " said the Nuncio, a little miffed by the General's familiarity. "I don't know if I can adequately explain the Church's stance on this matter here on the tarmac, but if you'd like to call me sometime . . ."

"Yes, very much," said Tony. "I am quite sure you can enlighten me."

As Noriega moved on to the Rastafarian, the Nuncio felt strangely let down, as if he had just failed an examination. He also realized that although he had been in Panama for years, he had just seen a human being behind the mask of power. He was intrigued and charmed—but then he remembered who he was dealing with and quickly turned away.

NOTHING IN Panama should be constructed of wood, Father Jorge thought as he walked through the streets of Chorrillo. One might as well have built this slum out of cardboard. The rotten buildings slumped against one another like a bunch of packing boxes that had been left out in the rain. They were nearly all one-room apartments built at the turn of the century to house the West Indian laborers who dug the canal and were never intended to last more than a few years. Their foundations had long since buckled under the insatiable appetite of tropical termites. Balconies and windows melted into hallucinatory angles of repose.

Because the entire neighborhood had been condemned decades ago, it was against the law to charge rent. This, of course, had led to a population explosion, which made Chorrillo even more dangerous than ever before. Extended families crowded into single rooms, cooking with hibachis and sleeping in shifts. The streets were crammed with children and aimless young men. Music rained down from the rooftops, the smell of coffee and simmering beans choked the air, and clotheslines crisscrossed the alleyways. Father Jorge jumped aside as a worn-out tire rolled out of the doorway of a mechanic's shop into the street, where it wobbled into a gaggle of children playing stickball. In a moment, the tire had become a part of the game. No one came to retrieve it—it might sit in the middle of the street for a century.

In the heart of Chorrillo was La Modelo, a prison that once aspired to be, as its name suggested, a model reformatory. Such ambitions had long since slunk away, and now the name had a sinister ring to it. La Modelo was little more than a three-story cage, like a human zoo. Arms and legs dangled through the bars of every window. The prisoners stared vacantly into the street, idly smoking marijuana and calling listlessly to the women who tended the graves at the cemetery next door. Father Jorge had been into the foul prison many times to minister to the men inside. Once he had seen a dead man hanging from a basketball goal. The man had been handcuffed to the hoop and beaten to death by the gang members who ran the place. The guards simply left the body as a bleak reminder of the futility of resistance.

Directly across the street from the prison was the Comandancia, the headquarters of the Panama Defense Forces. Inside a low-slung wall there was a military courtyard and the barracks for several hundred soldiers. Many of them came from the same teetering Chorrillo apartments that loomed over the concrete parapet. Those who had gotten into the army, through merit or connections, considered themselves lucky. For the unscrupulous, it was a path to wealth and power. The sentries could stand on the wall and talk to their neighbors and the admiring boys on the rooftops or, for that matter, the prisoners in La Modelo, who had little more to do than sit in their windows and watch the troops march in review. Strategically, as much as Father Jorge understood such things, the fort was absurdly located, but there was an intimacy about life in Panama that pressed all experiences together.

Father Jorge walked toward a large apartment house that rose out of a field of rubble. On the blank side of one wall there was a giant face of a Marlboro Man in a black cowboy hat, staring down upon the heart of Chorrillo—the prison, the fort, the cemetery, the teeming street—with savage indifference. Behind these apartments there was another street of wooden slums, which seemed, in Father Jorge's opinion, even more degraded than the crumbling shanties he had already passed. It was called Mariners Street. The balconies on Mariners Street were like a long frozen wave, a bit nauseating to focus on. The thought of people actually living in these perilous apartments filled him with outrage. Much of the wood was so rotten that he could push his fingers straight through the walls. Many times he had presided over funerals of people who had died when a floor suddenly gave way, or a balcony collapsed, or a cooking stove caught fire and the entire structure had burned like a scrap of newspaper. If he chose to, Father Jorge could spend every day of his life campaigning for sanitation and medical attention for his parishioners. Chorrillo was a pesthole, everyone knew it. Too many children had died of diseases that were easily curable. And yet all this was a natural result of the corruption and indifference of military rule. The people themselves lived like rats, moving into abandoned quarters and staying until they simply overran the space, or until they were run off by other, more unscrupulous and dangerous competitors, or until disease or accident destroyed them, leaving their squalid living space for new squatters to occupy.

A small girl sat on a stoop painting her toenails lime green.

Father Jorge recognized her from catechism class. She looked up and greeted him happily.

"Is your mother home, Renata?" Father Jorge asked.

"She's upstairs."

There was no front door. Father Jorge walked into the stair-well, which was crammed with trash. A child came bolting down the stairs, heedless of the missing steps, and skipped past the priest, who picked his way through the dark corridors, his eyes not yet adjusted to the gloom. He could hear music from a transistor radio coming from one of the rooms. He waved at the dark spaces in front of him and made his way toward the noise.

A young woman who Father Jorge took to be Renata's older sister answered the door. She was wearing the same lime green polish on her very long fingernails.

"I'm looking for Señora Sánchez," he told her.

"I'm Gloria Sánchez, the mother of Renata and Teófilo," the young woman responded, avoiding the implications of Father Jorge's clumsy statement. Very few women here were actually married. He admired her tact.

"I've brought you some supplies for Renata's studies," he said, setting a package on the small table beside the stove.

"Do you want some coffee, Father?"

The priest sat at the table and watched the young woman put the pot on the burner. She was some mixture of black and Indian and Chinese—a typical Panamanian racial gumbo. Her bare arms were strong and shapely, and her skin was the color of polished mahogany. She wore her hair in a ponytail, which was one reason Father Jorge had mistaken her for a teenager, but he could see now that she was a grown woman, in her early thirties, he supposed. There was something especially delicate about the line of her jaw and her fine, thin neck. The intersection of these two appealing vectors was highlighted by a pair of tiny gold crucifixes in the lobes of her small ears.

By Chorrillo standards, the Sánchez household was spacious and well appointed. They even had electricity, although how they managed to get wiring into the apartment was a mystery. A single bulb illuminated the small room. On the floor were three mattresses, which had been carefully rolled up in a noble attempt at housekeeping. A calendar picture of the Virgin of Guadalupe occupied one wall, and a poster of Sylvester Stallone occupied another. A framed certificate from the Mirabella School of Beauty testified that Gloria Sánchez was a recent graduate. Renata's schoolbooks were in a stack on the floor. The radio rested on the windowsill, with its antenna pointing outside for better reception. Beside the table and chairs, there was a futon and a bureau with several photographs on it. Father Jorge was curious to see them closer; he was looking for hints about Señorita Sánchez's life. But then he looked at her green fingernails and smiled to himself.

"Do you know my son, Father? He is the reason I asked you to come."

The boy was standing silently in the doorway. He looked to be about eleven, although malnutrition often caused the children of Chorrillo to appear many years younger than they actually were. He had his mother's high cheekbones and delicate nose, but he had the eyes of a bitter old man.

"This is Teófilo," said the mother.

"Are you in school, Teófilo?" Father Jorge asked.

The boy stared at him impassively. His mother answered for him. "He went for five years, but now he never goes. He only wanders the street with the gangs, isn't that right, Teo?" When the boy gave no response, she continued wearily, "If he doesn't get away from them, God only knows where this will end. Already he is fifteen years old. He has intelligence. He doesn't need to become a gangster."

"Gangster," the boy repeated, with an embarrassed smirk on his face.

"Don't laugh, it's happening already. The stealing, the lies. You're becoming a criminal."

"So what? Next year I'll join the army."

"Even the army requires you to read and do your sums," said

49

Gloria. "Do you want to be ignorant all your life? You need a trade. You need to study. On the streets you only become a no-body. Look at those other boys, they're all going to wind up in prison. Just because they have made stupid choices doesn't mean you have to follow them."

"They're not stupid," Teo said angrily. "At least they got money to buy nice things."

Gloria turned to Father Jorge. "That's all he thinks about, money. He doesn't think about the consequences. It doesn't oc-cur to him that maybe someday he might die out there. I have prayed about this, Father. You must take him. I can't control his life. He needs a man to control him."

Teo cast a quick look at the priest, then contemptuously rolled his eyes and looked away.

"I certainly can't control him, or any of the other children we raise in the parish," said Father Jorge. "Every child we take in has to agree to certain rules. They have to study and they must at-tend mass every day. They cannot commit any crimes or they will be expelled immediately. I don't know if Teo is ready to accept our way of life."

The boy studied the cracks in the ceiling for a moment. "I heard you got a basketball team," he said casually.

"We've got several sports teams," Father Jorge said. "We also have a band, if you like music."

"He sings like an angel," said Gloria. "But his voice is still changing."

"We have a choir, of course," said Father Jorge, "and work-shops where you can learn a trade. There are about twenty other boys there now, all ages. If you want to go visit, I can take you there this afternoon. This is a decision you have to make for yourself. Nobody is going to make you do anything."

"Can I visit Renata?" the boy asked.

"Of course. Anytime you are not in class. And she can visit you. It is a church, not a prison."

The boy nodded an almost imperceptible assent.

CHAPTER 4

D<small>ON'T THINK</small> you can intimidate me," said Nicky Barletta as he sat shivering in Tony's overly air-conditioned office in the Comandancia. "We do have laws in this country. We do have a constitution. I realize that you are the head of the military forces, but I am the president, and that fact must be respected."

Tony poured himself an eye-opening dollop of Old Parr. It was nine in the morning, well before his usual rising time.

"You are the president, but you serve at the will of General Noriega," said Roberto, who sat beside Tony's desk, in front of the Panamanian flag.

Nicky started to respond, since he knew very well what the Panamanian constitution said about this, but he chose not to press the point. "In any case, I am here, making every effort to be helpful."

Nicky had just gotten off the flight from New York, and now he wished he had never left. He was a stiff, owlish-looking creature, with slicked-back hair and thick, squarish bifocals that framed his eyes in a perpetual expression of alarm. A former World Bank bureaucrat, Nicky saw himself as a soldier of economic enlightenment, imposing the stern teachings of Milton Friedman on the Third World, much as the conquistadors had imposed bloody Christianity on the savages of the past. Now he shifted uncomfortably in his chair and stared at the warmly inscribed photographs of John Wayne and Mother Teresa on Tony's desk and the brass menorah and the golden Buddha on the shelf behind him. He felt as if he were in a religious museum of some sort—or a crypt. The air conditioner shuddered as the condenser kicked in. Moisture was forming on the windows. Overhead the ceiling fan moaned. Nicky's teeth began to chatter.

"We still have a problem, Nicky," Tony said politely. "We have to take care of this problem."

"As I said, I am here and ready to help. What is the problem?"

"I said when you were elected that you had three hundred and sixty-five days to turn the economy around. Frankly, we expected more of you."

"Does this meeting really have anything to do with the economy?" Nicky asked doubtfully.

"The people are suffering," said Roberto, "but you are deaf to their cries."

"Oh, stop it, Roberto," Nicky said impatiently. "I've only instituted the very measures proposed by the IMF and the World Bank—the same ones any country must adopt in order to have respectable credit."

"Nonetheless, the legislature is in revolt," said Tony. "They are demanding that I make a change."

"Nothing has been mentioned to me," said Nicky. "Besides, the legislature is not even in session."

"They are calling you a traitor," said Roberto.

"Who is saying this?" Nicky cried indignantly. "I love my country! I have served her valiantly! I have sacrificed my own interests!"

Tony yawned deeply.

"I do not intend to sit here and watch this charade any further," Nicky said, gathering his dignity. "I am a loyal patriot, as every Panamanian knows. I refuse to be treated like some junior officer. If you want to discuss economic decisions in a civilized manner, you can call me in the morning in my office. Cecilia has my schedule."

With that, Barletta walked purposefully out of Tony's office. Tony poured another glass of whiskey and leaned back in his oversized executive chair. Felicidad had picked it up at Sotheby's during a shockingly expensive weekend getaway. It had belonged to Admiral Karl Dönitz, the Nazi U-boat commander who had been Führer for three days after Hitler's death. The sentimental value alone was worth whatever she paid for it.

Presently a white-faced President Barletta reappeared in Tony's doorway. "Apparently, I am your prisoner," he said.

"Let's just say that our discussion hasn't concluded," Tony said amicably.

"What do you want? You want me to resign? Is that going to solve your problem?"

"I think it is the only solution," said Tony. "Naturally, we are prepared to make your transition an easy one."

"You're making a big mistake, Tony. People are going to say that the only reason you're doing this is to avoid creating the Spadafora commission. If you really felt this way, you should have told me! Okay, perhaps I should have consulted you before I acted, but you were out of the country, and people were demanding a response. I had to do something! It never occurred to me that this would concern you, since I knew you would never have had anything to do with his murder. I only did what I did to bring his killers to justice. I am sure that you want the same thing."

"Of course," said Tony.

"But don't you see, if you remove me from office, people are going to say you are covering up! It'll create the wrong impression."

Tony shrugged. "People talk, who listens?"

"But everyone will suspect you, Tony. They'll say, 'He must

have something to hide.' They'll say, 'Hugo knew the truth.' It won't stop. Finally, somebody's got to take responsibility for his death—and you know very well that you'll never be able to pin it on me."

"You should be careful, Nicky," Roberto warned. "The way you talk, it is very disrespectful."

"What have I got to lose?" Nicky said defiantly. "If you think you are going to force me into signing a letter of resignation, you're completely off track. I will never do such a thing. You will have to fire me. Think how that would look."

"That would be unfortunate," Tony agreed.

"Very unfortunate," Nicky said. "Essentially, we are talking about a military coup. And do you know how this will be received in Washington? Do you know what my friend George Shultz will say? I would think your future would be very short, Tony. The Americans will step on you, I guarantee it."

Tony wasn't thinking too clearly; the scotch had not had time to lubricate his mental gears. Moreover, there was a larger and more pressing problem that he had to deal with. "Why don't you continue talking this over with Roberto, Nicky?" he said. "I've got an important meeting. Roberto, you explain to Nicky the retirement package we are offering. Make sure he understands."

"Do I have a choice?" Nicky asked coldly.

"You don't have to talk," said Tony. "But you do have to listen."

*H*ey baby hey baby hey baby!" The scarlet macaw on Tony's shoulder was having an anxiety attack as he faced the open elevator doors. His talons knifed into Tony's flesh. Tony could feel the force of the powerful wings backpedaling them into the lobby.

"Shhh, Romeo! Behave!"

"*Fuck your mother! Fuck your mother! Fuuu-aaawwck! Aa-aaawwk!*" Romeo cried desperately, whistling and weeping and batting the air.

"It's an elevator!" Tony said, trying to reason with him.

"Yanqui go home!"

Tony removed his hat and plopped it over the parrot's head. Romeo squirmed for a moment, then relaxed his grip on Tony's shoulder, surrendering to the blindness. I wish women were so easy, Tony thought.

He pushed the number of Carmen's floor.

On the way up, Tony rehearsed his apology. He hated this more than dentistry.

"Say, 'Carmen is a pretty girl,'" Tony told Romeo as he removed the hat in front of Carmen's apartment. Romeo imitated the sound of the door buzzer.

Tony waited. No response. He could hear a slight stirring inside.

"Carmen, my love?"

"I'm not here," her voice replied.

"How can you say that? What does that mean? Please, dearest, open the door. I have a little present for you."

He could almost hear her weighing his offer. In a moment, the door opened. Carmen Morales and Romeo exchanged sideways glances.

"Your money or your life!"

"Do you think this fucking bird will make everything different?" Carmen asked furiously.

"I trained him myself," said Tony. "He is the most intelligent of all my birds. He has something to tell you, don't you, Romeo?"

Romeo's bill clacked shut. He studied Tony's ear and pretended not to hear.

"Anyway, I'm allergic," said Carmen.

"Let me in," Tony pleaded. "I've got trouble."

Carmen grudgingly stepped aside.

Romeo took one look at the apartment and whistled in admiration.

"Just be glad you missed Paris," said Tony. "Rain all week. And Geneva—how do they live in that place? You would freeze there,

I swear it, even in the summer." Tony set Romeo on the back of a plush chintz couch in a bold floral pattern that caused the bird to become slightly euphoric.

"Maybe Europe doesn't make me as miserable as it does you. He better not dirty the fabric."

"You could not have gone on the same trip with Felicidad! Do you want her to kill us both? What were you thinking?"

"That I should go and she should stay, for once! Me, not her!"

Carmen's eyes were on fire. When she got like this, it was a little frightening, like trying to ride a horse that refuses to be tamed.

"I try to make you happy, but you are so crazy," Tony complained. "I know I promised to take you to Paris, but not this time! This was an official trip. Photographers! Press! When we go to Paris, it should be for romance, not for business."

"Is that what you think I want? *Paris?*" Carmen spat out the word. "I don't give a fuck about Paris."

"I thought you loved Paris."

"I do love Paris, but that's not what I *want*, Tony! Not Paris. And not some stupid bird."

Romeo cackled nervously.

"God, you're both so weird!" Carmen rushed out of the room, brushing away tears with her fingers.

Tony waited. He had developed a theory about women that had come from his work with parrots. Like all creatures, they sought rewards and feared punishment. The trick was to take them by surprise, keep them off guard, never let them know what was coming. He made a lot of promises and every once in a while he would deliver. Hope kept them on the hook.

But Carmen was a riddle because she really didn't know what she wanted. It was a constant source of frustration. If only she could say, "I want a million dollars!" or "I want a career in the movies!" There was really very little that was outside Tony's grasp. Oh, she loved fashionable clothes and jewelry, et cetera, but she was so beautiful that she simply accepted such things as a natural right. It was as if she walked on a beach where diamonds and rubies routinely washed ashore at her feet. Now here she was, mistress to a man who only wanted to please her—a man who could give her nearly anything—but she suffered from an inability to name her price. Nothing satisfied her. Since puberty she had been the object of men's desires, but she herself was curiously desireless.

That left open the question of why she stayed with Tony at all. She had always been too much for him. She was fine in ways that kept Tony off guard. He didn't know how to act around her. She had everything. She was well bred, well educated, at ease in society. She enjoyed European movies and Japanese food, tastes that Tony simply could not comprehend. On the wall of her bedroom there was a publicity photo signed by some pasty French movie director with a scarf around his neck who seemed to be a kind of sexual icon for her. Tony couldn't understand such refinement. She was in so many ways the positive print from Tony's negative. The bottomless mystery of their affair was her interest in him. Granted, his ugliness was, to some women, a source of appalling fascination, but that didn't seem to hold much interest for her. In the end, he supposed Carmen was simply drawn to power. There was some elemental joy in harnessing a tyrant with her sexuality. It was beauty's way of ruling the world.

"At least Felicidad can hold her head up in public," Carmen said as she abruptly returned, blowing her nose in a tissue, "without people pointing at her and saying, 'There goes Noriega's whore!' "

"Just give me their names, Lollipop. I assure you they will never make such statements again."

"God, Tony! I don't want them killed—I just want to be accepted in society. I guess it's hopeless now—no one will ever think of me as anything other than . . ." Carmen looked out the window at the cormorants perched on the rocks in the surf, their wings spread like opera capes. "Than what I am," she concluded. "Your little *chica*. I can't believe that this is what my life adds up to."

"Is that what you think I think about you?"

"Tony, this is the truth. Don't try to make our relationship into something it's not. I'm not your wife."

"Believe me, I've talked to many priests about this. Annulment is out of the question, even for a man in my position. Too many children."

"Tony—why? Why do you do this Catholic business with me? You are the worst Christian in Panama. You just use it as an excuse."

"Look, I am not a Christian," said Tony as he absentmindedly poured another two fingers of Old Parr into a crystal tumbler. "But Catholic—it is like a race. If I move to Miami, does my skin turn pale and my hair become blond? No! I am mestizo! You look at me and you know who I am. Inside, I am Catholic. Belief, faith—they mean nothing. But Catholic, it is a condition of life. You want a highball?"

"So this 'condition' means I am supposed to be your mistress forever? I do not accept this, Tony. And it is not even noon. I don't see how you can drink at this hour."

"Sit down, please. I'm asking you to sit. Be calm and listen."

"I can't sit," Carmen said. "I'm too humiliated."

Carmen's blond hair spilled into her face, and her skin was turning patchy from crying. For some reason, it made her even more desirable. But in this mood she was so out of reach she might as well be the Virgin Mary.

"Maybe you're right," said Tony. "I am a hypocrite, I admit it. But what good does it do me? It's my life that suffers because I am afraid to act in my own interest. Why can't I just do what I want with my personal life, no matter what the Church says about it?"

"Exactly. This isn't the Middle Ages."

"Moreover, it is not fair to you," Tony continued. "I should be proud to be seen in public with you. I shouldn't be hiding the most important relationship in my life!"

Carmen's tongue moved appraisingly across her upper lip. "I guess I'm not sure what you mean by that," she said.

"What I mean is that I am ashamed of how I have treated you. You're right to be scolding me. It should have been you with me in Paris sitting at the table with Mitterrand."

"Tony, I wanted to go to Paris, but this is getting a little far-fetched. You don't take your girlfriend to a state dinner."

"Agreed. That's why I will talk to my lawyer on Monday about getting a divorce. I'll do everything I can to make an honest woman of you. Even divorce. Yes, even that."

Carmen looked at him for a moment and then ignited. "God damn you, Tony, you lie so easily it just scares me."

Tony's face darkened with embarrassment. "What are you saying? Are you calling me a liar?" He shouted furiously, acting outraged, but Carmen could see right through him. She had some kind of x-ray vision for emotional truth.

"You say things just to see what might happen," Carmen continued in her ruthless, completely accurate assessment. "Sometimes I don't think you even realize that you're lying. Well, it's sick, you know that? You're not going to divorce Felicidad! Come on, Tony, admit it! You're so full of shit! Do you have any idea how much it hurts when you say things like that? I could just kill you, you lying bastard!"

Tony calmly took his pearl-handled .32 from his holster. "Here, do it," he said, handing her the revolver. "If you think I could ever lie to you, I don't want to live."

Romeo shifted nervously on the coach.

Carmen pushed Tony's hand away. "Get that away from me! What do you think—that I'm going to shoot you in my living room?"

"Do you want me to step out on the balcony?"

"Just put that gun away and leave," she said. "And take the damn bird. It's over, Tony."

IT WAS NEARLY midnight when Tony returned to his office. He was feeling a little stultified from the pasta and the wine at dinner and gloomy from his fight with Carmen. He couldn't get her out of his mind. The world was falling apart all around him, and all he could think about was Carmen! Their relationship was too volatile to last. But the thought of being without her was too awful to consider. "A long day," he said as he sat heavily in his high-backed chair.

"I think Nicky and I have come to an understanding," said Roberto.

"Is that right?"

Nicky made a grunt of assent. A cloud came out of his mouth in the deep chill of the room.

"Rollins called," Roberto said significantly. "He wants to hear from you right away."

"I really need to go for a walk," Tony said by way of apology after a noisy burp. "Jean-Luc's chocolate mousse is a little too rich."

Roberto bowed in agreement. The remains of his own sumptuous dinner were sitting on the desk between them.

President Barletta looked ravaged and half-starved. He was visibly shaking, partly from the cold and partly from indignation. "You have the nerve to threaten me," he said. "You hold me illegally. And then you even threaten members of my family. God damn you, Tony—you can't get away with this!"

Tony shook his head. "Roberto is a little anxious, Nicky. He's worried because he knows I know what he is up to. He is trying to get rid of both of us. He thinks that if I unload you, pressure will be brought against me—by the Americans and everybody else. So maybe he exceeds his authority."

"You see it, too?" Nicky said excitedly. "That's exactly what I realized myself! This whole business has been Roberto's plan! He has been planting rumors, making people upset, scheming with the troops! *He's* the one who has been disloyal! Not me! I'm only trying to do the right thing! I just want to help you, I swear it. Together we can fix everything—it's not too late! We can make this country great, Tony! But first we have to get rid of Roberto. He's the problem—not me!"

"What do you have to say about this, Roberto?" Tony asked.

Roberto was smiling uncertainly. He realized that Tony was in a mischievous frame of mind; in any case, one could never be too confident about his support. "You know very well that Nicky has been using the Spadafora case as a way to incriminate you," Roberto said indignantly. "Surely you cannot tolerate such disloyalty. If I have gone too far in my efforts to protect you, it is simply because of my desire to serve my country."

Tony looked from one man to the other. "It's hard, you know. Every day people bring me their problems and ask me to solve them. Sometimes I think the whole fucking country is waiting for me to make their decisions for them."

"Take this also into account," Nicky said, leaning forward urgently. "If you remove me, you will be left with Tuturo Delvalle. He is the king of the white asses. Is that the kind of man you want running your country? The people won't respect him. Everybody knows he's a donkey's behind."

"Everything you say is true," Tony conceded. "And yet, you do not see the complete picture. This is what leadership requires, my friend. You see, there is some value in knowing that Roberto is a Judas. He cannot afford to be too clever, because we occupy the same milieu. I always know what he is up to. A man like that, he will work very hard to prove himself to me. You, on the other hand, have no such obligation. Every day of your life you will be working to get rid of me. And this is only human. I respect you for it. But I cannot allow you to stay in office."

The phone rang. It was Rollins. Tony put him on the speaker.

"Tony, I hear you're about to make a change in government," Rollins said.

"This is a possibility," Tony admitted. "But to tell you honestly, Nicky says that if we remove him, the Americans will destroy me."

"Nicky, did you say that?" Rollins asked.

"I only say that because the Americans want the same things I want—stability, a democratic government, a commitment to sound fiscal policies. And of course, justice in the Spadafora matter."

"Nicky also says his friend George Shultz will crush me," Tony added. "Tell me, Rollins, do you think that is true?"

"The State Department will be very upset, I can guarantee it," said Rollins. "And he's right about Shultz—he'll want your scalp."

Nicky shook his head meaningfully.

"So what do you think the White House reaction will be if we make this change?"

"The president will have to disapprove in very strong terms," said Rollins. "Just make sure it's constitutional, Tony. As long as it's constitutional, you'll be okay."

"Of course," said Tony. "In fact, the legislature is already assembling to consider the matter of Nicky's impeachment."

"Well, then, it's an internal matter," said Rollins. "None of our business."

Nicky seemed to collapse in on himself, like a ruined soufflé. "Very impressive, Tony," he said. "You've covered every base. Even the Americans have washed their hands of me." He laughed in disbelief—an empty, despairing laugh. "But you still have the problem of Hugo. Getting rid of me won't change anything. People are demanding justice. They won't let you get away with this."

"I think you would really rather resign than be impeached," said Tony. "I tell you this as your friend. Think of your family. Think of your future. Why don't you sign the letter Roberto has prepared? Then perhaps we can all go to Naomi's and spend some time with the girls."

*   *   *

FATHER JORGE sat in the antechamber of the massage parlor, feeling like a spy. He rarely wore a Roman collar, except in the confessional and during Sunday services, and because he was dressed very simply, with no outward indication of his vocation, he supposed the women responded to him as they did toward any other potential customer. He had expected either boredom or else highly exaggerated interest. Although they looked at him, of course, simultaneously sizing him up and selling themselves with their eyes, they were mostly polite and familiar, accepting him as if he were a classmate or a cousin, which left him with the disconcerting sense of being entirely at home in their company. Once they determined that he did not want to make a selection right away, they went back to watching cartoons on the cable. Father Jorge and the whores watched and laughed companionably. He tried not to think about the fact that he could pick one of the women, have sex with her, then return to the next Roadrunner cartoon without causing the least comment. No one would know but God.

A businesslike older woman came out of a small room that Father Jorge guessed must be an office. She introduced herself as Naomi. Unlike the other women, who were dressed in nightgowns or tank tops, Naomi wore a dark suit. "Have you made a selection?" she asked. "Or are you waiting for someone in particular?"

"Actually, I am here on personal business. I'm a priest," he added, feeling an odd sense of embarrassment. But the whores did not even look up from the cartoons.

"We service all kinds, Father," Naomi said.

"I've come to talk to one of your employees. Her name is Gloria Sánchez."

"If this is Church business, you should meet somewhere else."

Father Jorge explained that he had only been given the address on a form. "Believe me, it's a very important matter or I wouldn't be troubling her at work."

Naomi considered for a moment. "She's with a client. You can wait for her. But please conduct your business in private."

Presently, a man buttoning up his bus driver's uniform came out of the dark hallway that led to the other rooms. Behind him was a woman whose hair was fluffed into an airy bouffant, and her almond-shaped eyes were highlighted with purple mascara and gold glitter. Father Jorge would not have recognized her except for the lime green fingernails and crucifix ear studs.

"This gentleman has been waiting to see you," said Naomi when the bus driver had departed.

Gloria looked at Father Jorge and smiled in recognition. The priest silently wished that someone would be shocked by his presence.

"It's about Teo," he said in a low voice.

Her expression immediately changed. She led him down the hallway to a small room lit with a black light. There was a water bed and a massage table and a cabinet full of oils.

"He left the dormitory last night," Father Jorge said in answer to the urgent questions in her eyes. "Frankly, we've been having some trouble with him. He was suspected of taking money from the collection. It happens all the time," he hastened to assure her. "Boys in the mission don't have an income. We try to get them odd jobs, but occasionally they steal. It's never much. But when I tried to talk to Teo about it, he became very agitated and refused to discuss the matter. He didn't admit anything, he simply left. I was hoping he had come to you."

"He wouldn't come to me. He has gone to his friends in the street."

"If he's still in Chorrillo, I am sure I will find him," said Father Jorge. "But unfortunately he cannot return to the church. He has violated our rules."

The glitter above Gloria's eyes shone like neon in the black light. "God must be so angry with me. He makes me suffer by punishing Teo."

"God does not punish the children for the sins of the parent," the priest said.

"Then why does he punish Teo? Why does he give him such a difficult life? This is a good boy, at one time he was a very good boy. But nothing works for him."

"God has given him a life. It is not all bad. Many other children have more difficult situations. It is up to Teo to take advantage of what is offered him."

Gloria began to cry softly and unself-consciously. "If you want, we can say the rosary," the priest suggested.

Gloria got her rosary out of a drawer in the cabinet with the oils. Father Jorge took her hand. As they prayed to Mary, he thought how strange her hand felt in his, as if he were holding a rare and delicate bird.

CHAPTER 5

THERE WERE only six limousines in Panama, so when the long black Cadillac snaked up the hillside of Via Porras, a stream of children playing in Omar Torrijos Park ran after it, waving and loudly demanding that the windows be lowered so they could see inside. But the smoky windows stayed shut, and the limousine left the howling children behind.

Policemen in their coffee-colored uniforms watched respectfully as the limousine slowly passed by. In the manicured yards, oversized purebred dogs stuck their muzzles through the fences, as if they smelled trouble. The limousine turned on Calle Andre into Golf Heights. Here lived the drug barons and the upper ranks of the PDF in tacky stucco mansions set behind tamarind trees and high walls draped with bougainvillea and crowned with shards of colored glass. Immense satellite dishes crowded the rooftops, with their receptive faces raised to the sky. Torrijos had believed that the best way to gain the loyalty of his officers was to make them rich, and it was a policy that Tony grudgingly continued. The more loyalty an officer displayed, the larger the unaccountable, untaxable cash bonus he received in his monthly brown envelope.

The grounds of Casa Noriega were surrounded by a low stone fence behind a bed of petunias. The house itself was large and U-shaped, also built of stone. One entered through a broad foyer that housed Tony's extensive collection of porcelain frogs, which were his talisman and spirit guide. The kitchen and large public rooms were on one side, along with a handsome chapel; on the family side, there was an art gallery, a library, a beauty parlor for Felicidad, a dojo where Tony practiced karate, and bedrooms for the Noriegas and their three daughters. Mangoes and hibiscus filled the courtyard between the two wings. The girls' old playhouse was still there, and a toy windmill, and a reproduction of the Liberty Bell that was given to Tony by some American fundamentalist Christians for promoting democracy in Central America. Crimson-backed tanagers and social flycatchers could usually be glimpsed flitting about in the foliage. More exotic birds occupied the aviary in front of the house, in a grove of orange trees, where Tony kept his prize parrots and macaws. In a cage by himself was his vicious battle-scarred rooster, Fusilero.

A policeman slumped in a wicker rocker at his post in the guard hut at the front gate, his automatic weapon lying at his feet. He was snoring loudly, unmindful of the distant cries of children or the barking of the hysterical Dalmatian across the street. But a light tap on a car horn brought him splashing back into consciousness. He licked the crust off his dry lips and shielded his eyes against the blinding Panama afternoon and the fiery sheen of the limousine.

The guard slung his weapon over his shoulder and regarded the limo with wonder. The window lowered.

"Take this to your boss," said the man inside the cool puddle of gloom. The guard saluted and accepted a package the size of a shoe box wrapped in green foil.

FRANKLY, ROBERTO, you have never struck me as a military man. It is not your special gift, in my opinion."

Roberto Díaz Herrera shifted uncomfortably in the stiff cane-back chair he had been offered in Tony's game room. It was Tony's aerie in the treetops, which could be reached only by way of a spiral staircase from his second-floor library. Through the windows one could see the city and the Gulf of Panama and the verdant hills of the Canal Zone. "Tony, I do not have to defend my military record—it speaks for itself," Roberto said indignantly, ignoring the chuckle of Ari Nachman, an Israeli intelligence agent and arms merchant, who was sorting through Tony's record collection. In the background, the Dallas Cowboys were playing the Pittsburgh Steelers on a fuzzy giant-screen TV.

"Haven't you ever imagined another career for yourself?" Tony asked as he poured a whiskey for himself at the bar beside the faro table. "It would solve a lot of your problems. Something that might take you abroad?"

"Are you telling me to get out of the country?" Roberto said incredulously. "What have I done wrong? Everything you have asked of me I have done! Every day, I am only trying to prove my loyalty to you!"

"My God, Tony, how can you listen to this shit?" Nachman interjected. "Ray Conniff, Vikki Carr—the Osmonds?"

"I only want to help you, Roberto," Tony said.

"What, exactly, is my problem?"

"The Spadafora business," said Tony. "Many people suggest that you are responsible."

"Me! Tony, we agreed that Nicky was responsible! He resigned! Now you say I am also responsible? How can that be?"

"People are saying it was a conspiracy."

"Tony, we are your friends! Even Nicky, I count him as well. Why do you seek to punish the people who have stood by you, who have worked for you—my God! You would turn your back even on me?"

"You know, Roberto, my balls are my friends, too. But when I run, they bump into each other."

From the stereo, the voices of Donny and Marie Osmond

sang "Make the World Go Away." Nachman began dancing slowly around the room with a martini in his hand.

"Obviously, I need to take actions that will signal my intention to resolve this terrible matter," Tony continued. "I am prepared to be merciful, but don't test me, Roberto."

The guard stuck his head through the opening where the spiral staircase arose. Tony looked at him sharply.

"A man brought this for you, General," he said as he set the box on Tony's desk. "A Colombian."

Tony nodded, then looked expectantly at Roberto.

"This won't work, Tony," said Roberto. "I am not Nicky Barletta. I won't just go quietly."

"I understand your needs, Roberto. I am only saying some changes will have to be made—at very high levels. The situation demands it."

"You can make all the changes you want, you can stab your friends in the back—but it is not my name that people in the streets are chanting."

"The people in the streets," said Tony dismissively, "are only having fun. This waving of handkerchiefs—do you think it troubles me? It's amusing, really. They are only teasing me. But even so, they are saying in all seriousness that actions must be taken. And I hear them, Roberto. I am responding to their plea."

Roberto's jaw clenched and bulged. "I want to stay in government service," he declared defiantly.

"Mmm-hmm. In that case, perhaps a consular post."

"Ambassador rank," said Roberto. "If you want to blacken my reputation, I insist on this."

Tony's stomach grumbled, an incipient ulcer, no doubt. "You ask for too much, Roberto. Be practical."

"I am second in command of the Panama Defense Forces! I am your number two! How can you say anything is too grand for me?"

"He has a point, Tony," the dancing Nachman observed. "You need to consider the precedent."

Tony stroked his chin thoughtfully. "Perhaps," he said, "from the goodness of my heart, I can find a place for you. I was thinking of the Dominican Republic, our Caribbean trading partner and loyal ally . . ."

"Japan," Roberto said abruptly.

"Japan!"

"Look, Tony, you ask me to be practical. How can an ambassador make any money in the Dominican?"

"He's right, Tony," said Nachman. "They can't even afford decent automatic weapons."

"But Japan is out of the question," said Tony. "I've promised the post to Carmen's cousin, an expert on the Japanese."

"He's a judo instructor!" Roberto said. "This hardly qualifies him as an expert."

"If I try to satisfy everyone, then no one will get what he wants."

Roberto turned sulky. "I'm not playing games, Tony. Don't think this will come cheap."

"What about the Vatican? You are still a Catholic, I believe. And life in Rome cannot be so bad," Tony added, winking for emphasis.

Roberto's eyebrows knitted in concentration as he figured the Roman cost of living into the probable financial benefits. "Well, it's not Japan," he said slowly, "but it's not out of the question. You could make up the difference in the form of a bonus."

"A bonus!" Tony said furiously. "You've made millions already! Look at the mansion you live in—finer than Casa Noriega by far! Wouldn't you say I've been generous to you? Do you really need more?"

Roberto sat stonily, not responding.

"All right, all right," said Tony, "a million dollars. Take it! Take it, take the Vatican, then you disappear."

"A million dollars?" said Roberto. "You expect me to sell my reputation for a million dollars? A million dollars to take the blame for Hugo's death? Tony, you insult me. Ten times a million and we will talk. But don't ask me to bargain with you. You know what it is worth. Think about it carefully."

When Roberto had gone, Nachman asked, "So what are you going to do with him?"

"I'm going to nail his tongue to the gate of the Comandancia! He should be an example to any whore's son who tries to blackmail me."

"Friends can be a problem," Nachman agreed.

"The son of a bitch made millions selling visas to Cubans, and now he tries to rob me."

"He should be on his knees to you," said Nachman. "But still, you've got to get this Hugo thing behind you. If you can pin it on Roberto and hustle him out of the country, it's worth the cost."

"I suppose I really could let him go to the Vatican."

"That's what I'm saying, Tony. It's an option."

"But then he would try to take advantage. He would feel strong. If I were in his shoes, I would be the same way. He would think he controlled me. Inevitably, he would ask for more favors."

"Still, he would be very far away."

Tony stared moodily at the football game and then abruptly clicked it off. Nachman got the message and found a reason to leave. "Just don't let it fester," he advised on his way out. "You gotta act, Tony. Declare yourself, one way or the other. Maybe send a few guys to a firing squad. Get it over with. Let the healing begin."

Now that he was alone, Tony went to the window and stared at the sea. His whole world lay before him—the city, the Comandancia, the Presidential Palace, the jungle, and the mountains, everything and everyone so familiar to him, every street corner, every nuance of conversation, every turn in the weather. It was *his*, his world, it belonged to him as it belonged to no one else. He had fought for it. He had the balls to take it. He began with nothing and now he had it all.

He was feeling his age, for once in his life. He was fifty-four years old and he had just started dyeing his hair, which was now so black it shone in the dark. A man in his position couldn't afford to display the slightest sign of weakness. Even gray hair was a signal to his enemies that he wouldn't be around forever. But he couldn't fool himself—the pressure was mounting, the fun was gone. He couldn't hold on indefinitely.

Roberto was obviously bluffing. Well, he had some balls of his own; Tony had to give him credit for that. Maybe he was a little crazy as well, which was useful in this line of work. Tony had been cultivating his own craziness for years. People dealt with you more respectfully if they thought you were a bit psycho.

Tony remembered the foil carton sitting on his desk, which cheered him. There was no card, he noticed, and if he hadn't known that the box had already been tested for explosives, he might have been more cautious about opening it. Inside was a highly lacquered box—a humidor, he supposed with a jolt of disgust. He thought the Colombians knew him better than that. He detested smoking, especially cigar smoking. One of the hazards of his job was a considerable amount of exposure to secondhand smoke from drug dealers and fellow dictators. The Colombians were particularly bad.

The box was beautiful handiwork. Tony opened it, expecting to find the customary Havanas. Instead, there was a carved wooden skeleton wearing the uniform of a PDF general.

Tony sat down. He felt a little light-headed. The meaning of the gift was obvious. It was war. They were waging voodoo war on him, the fucking Colombians, with the squadron of Santería priests they kept on staff.

He gingerly lifted the skeleton doll aside and set it on his desk. He wasn't certain how to deal with the ghoulish object. Perhaps he should burn it immediately to keep it from working its malignant influence. On the other hand, it was him, after all, or a version of him, a spiritual representation. Some other voice in his head warned him not to be so hasty.

Under the skeleton there was a videotape. Inscribed on the side of the tape was a single handwritten word: *Hello.*

Tony went to the bathroom. He was sweating profusely and he felt like passing out. He knelt on the floor facing the toilet bowl, but nothing happened. Downstairs he could hear Felicidad bossing the maid around and the girls fighting over their wardrobes. Life was blithely going on without him.

He didn't want to know what was on the tape, but he also had to know. He mentally rehearsed putting the tape in his VCR and watching whatever dreadful information was on it. Curiosity was also tugging at him. That *Hello* had not sounded threatening. It could be a joke or a simple greeting from friends.

Fortified by these thoughts, Tony returned to the room, placed the tape in his machine, and stepped away from the television set. Snow and static. He backed into his BarcaLounger and took a long swallow of Old Parr. An image swam onto the screen—it was Tony, standing in his aviary, stroking one of his parrots, then turning to wave to someone in the house. The camera was dead still—a fixed surveillance post, Tony realized with his professional eye, probably attached to the telephone pole across the street. It was a little galling to think that, with all his security, they could get so close to him.

The next clip on the video showed Felicidad in her bra in a department-store changing room—an overhead shot, the camera buried in the light fixture. She was trying on clothes. Now she took a small pair of scissors out of her purse and began very deliberately to cut the buttons off a blouse. Tony regarded her shoplifting as an amusing twist of character—Fela was, after all, the most powerful woman in Panama—but it was upsetting to see it documented. This was the sort of thing that could be easily reproduced and spread around the country like video samizdat. There were more pictures of Tony in the Comandancia, Fela at a garden party, the children in school, his oldest daughter, Sandra, walking on the seawall with her boyfriend—apparently they had surveillance everywhere. Now there was a picture of a man watching television. Tony realized with appalled fascination that he was watching himself—here! In this very room! A clip of Tony masturbating to a Czechoslovakian porno flick!

That was yesterday.

Tony turned and looked at his bookshelf. The camera must be there. In his sanctuary. Spying on every private thing.

He now heard the tiniest sound, like a long exhalation, but it was not his breath he was hearing. He moved a step closer to the sound and stood on tiptoe. The Panama Lions Club 1981 Man of the Year Award, a bronze lion on a wooden plaque, was humming. Tony looked directly into the lion's open mouth and listened to the microscopic roar.

"You think you can fuck with Tony Noriega?" he screamed into the lion's mouth. "You think you got the balls?" He ripped the award off the wall. Wires and circuitry spilled out of the back as Tony smashed it across his desk. "Fucking mob! So tough— but I got a fucking army! I got my own voodoo! We'll see who has the balls around here!"

But then he collapsed into his recliner and began to tremble. He put his head between his knees to keep from fainting. César was right, he realized when he got his wits back. These people were crazy. They would kill him without even thinking about the repercussions. He had counted on them being rational, but they were psychopaths! Moreover, they knew his every move.

There were only two alternatives with the Colombians, war or peace, and in either case it was going to cost a fortune. He knew in his heart that it wouldn't be over until blood was on the ground. His—or whose?

In the Nuncio's experience, priests were divided into three personality types: ecstatics, penitents, and bureaucrats. He knew himself to be firmly in the third camp. His calling, if one could dignify it by such a term, was to be a modest part of the grand, ancient hierarchy of the oldest bureaucracy in the world. He was a worker bee in the Roman hive, and by nature he nursed a certain distrust of holy men. In his opinion, too much praying, too much love of the hidden mysteries, too much longing for transcendence, were evidence of an unhealthy personality. There had never been a single moment in the Nuncio's life when he had been blinded by the light of faith. There was nothing ecstatic in his nature. Nor had he a strong inclination toward service. He was undistracted by the tricks of belief or by the need to apologize for his life by serving the poor. He was aware that his motives for choosing the priesthood were unusual, but his devotion to office administration, combined with his interest in intelligence, perfectly suited him for the clerical life. Still, when he thought about his peers, he often wondered if he was inadequately guilty for his calling. A little more guilt would make the frustrations of the job easier to swallow.

Most priests he had known were physically bland. Group photos tended to be of roundish, lumpy men wearing cheap eyeglasses and sporting rudimentary haircuts. Some of them were distinguished in manner, but rarely were they the sort that caught one's gaze. That left open, in the Nuncio's mind, the question of exactly what force had drawn Father Jorge out of the normal sexualized world. Presumably, Jorge was the penitent type. The Nuncio had never heard the young man express thoughts of a mystical nature, and although he served perfectly well as a secretary, he had no flair for minutiae. Nor did he have the brutal gaming instincts of a bureaucratic insider. He was still a little naive and politically uninformed, qualities that the Nuncio believed could be remedied with education. This was to take nothing away from Father Jorge's admirable abilities as a spy.

No, whatever psychological chemistry was operating in Father Jorge's brain, it was obvious that guilt was heavily in the mix. The Nuncio did not believe that his secretary had some unconfessed sin in his past that was so great that it had pushed him into the priesthood. Sin, in the Nuncio's opinion, rarely worked like that. Perhaps Jorge was vulnerable to life's disparities in a way that most of us are not. His sensitive nature, combined with the legacy of being orphaned and raised by nuns, explained the whole matter so convincingly that the Nuncio only occasionally wondered about it.

And yet he found himself pondering these questions once again as Manuelito drove him toward Amador, where he was meeting Jorge for dinner. They had planned to ride out together, but the young man had to attend to some pressing business at Our Lady of Fatima and promised to arrive by bus. The necessities of that parish were taking up most of Father Jorge's time, leaving the Nuncio shorthanded and a little jealous, even though he had personally arranged it. The whole scene of the simple parish priest working with the poor made him feel inadequate and nonplussed.

But as soon as he passed through the gates of Fort Clayton and entered the Canal Zone, the Nuncio perceptibly relaxed. Although he hated giving in to the calculated ambience of the place, which reminded him of what he supposed an American theme park must be like, he had to admit that this obsession with order, sanitation, and niceness had a calming effect. Here the door closed on poverty and hopelessness. There was an utter absence of litter, or for that matter, honking. No blaring radios, no smoke-spewing buses. No beggars or prostitutes. Here, with the majestic Panama Canal Administration Building set like a Greek temple on a hilltop, ablaze in the sunset, and a McDonald's on the perfect little nonchaotic American street below, and American high schoolers walking casually on the spotless sidewalks like actors on a movie set, schoolbooks clasped to their chests, the contrast with the city outside the gates seemed pointed and almost mean.

Past the McDonald's was a charming train station where passengers could wait for a train that no longer ran. The railroad was the first part of the zone to be turned over to the Panamanians under the Carter-Torrijos treaties. For more than a century trains had traversed the country several times a day, like clockwork, until Panamanians assumed control. Now weeds grew through the tracks, and the locomotives rusted in place. By the year 2000 the canal itself would be theirs, a prospect that filled most Panamanians with dread. The Nuncio had never met a people so cynical about their capacity for self-government (and this included an intimate acquaintance with the Italians).

Most of the military bases in the zone still belonged to the Americans. The Nuncio could never understand why there had to be so many of them—thirteen altogether. Those he could remember were Fort Clayton, Fort Gulick, Howard Air Force Base, Rodman Naval Station, and until the treaty, Fort Amador. Together they formed the U.S. Southern Command—or SOUTH-COM, one of those conglomerated military terms that the Nuncio abominated. SOUTHCOM sprawled across Quarry Heights, the volcanic rise where the officers lived. The highest point of Quarry Heights was Ancón Hill, an abrupt little peak that loomed over Chorrillo and the old city. An immense Panamanian flag flew from the mast on its crest, the surface of the hill having reverted to national control. The Americans, however, still operated a vast cave inside Ancón known as the Tunnel. Here the world's most sensitive listening devices monitored conversations all over Central America. When the Nuncio first arrived in Panama, he had had no idea of the sophistication of the equipment or the prurient interest the Americans had in hearing what everybody had to say. Now he simply assumed that they heard everything, the way God is supposed to hear prayers.

Parallel to the railroad tracks was the canal itself, which was merely a dredged-out industrial river until it reached the Miraflores Locks at the foot of Fort Clayton. There the ships ascended the first of those gravity-mocking elevators that caused the waterway to rise above the natural riverbed and made the ships appear to hover giddily above the landscape. They entered the canal from the Caribbean port of Colón, floated over the mountains, and dropped into the Pacific beside Panama City.

The Nuncio rode past the port, which was strongly lit by mercury lights and the slanting rays of the setting sun. There was a long line of lorries parked beside the warehouses, and beyond them were the crowded wharves and the huge cranes cutting tangents across the orange horizon. Manuelito drove so slowly that the workers who were finishing their shift walked casually across the road in front of the embassy Toyota, laughing and smoking, some of them casting curious looks at the yellow-and-white Vatican flag and the Nuncio inside.

Just past the port lay the Amador peninsula. The military base there was now home to the Panama Defense Forces. As he rode through the base, the Nuncio mused that the clerical life was a near cousin to the military one. He, too, had spent most of his life in the company of men, living in comparatively spartan quarters not much different from the barracks that these young soldiers occupied. He wondered how his rank would translate into military terms. He supposed that as an archbishop he would be the equivalent of a colonel—at least he hoped he wasn't lower on the chain of command than that.

The peninsula narrowed into a spit of land not much wider than the palm-lined causeway. The canal lay on one side and the Bay of Panama on the other. Absorbing this inspiring view were several of the choicest houses in the entire country. Once they had been the quarters for senior American military personnel. Now that Fort Amador had reverted to the PDF, the houses served as homes for Carlos Lehder, the Ochoa brothers, and Pablo Escobar, the fugitive leaders of the Medellín drug cartel. More than a hundred other Colombian lawyers, accountants, bodyguards, and personal trainers were living in the best hotels in the country. The cartel's business was now run from the lobby of the Caesar Park Marriott. Since Noriega took power, Panama had become a safe haven for the worst people in the world.

There was a little outdoor bistro at the tip of Amador that the Nuncio favored, more for the view than the food. He sat under one of the Cinzano umbrellas, which lent a nostalgic Roman ambience to the spot. An endless wavering line of running lights of the great ships, queued to enter the canal, stretched far out into the Pacific. Closer at hand, the catalpa trees were filling up with chattering parakeets, which were settling in for the night. Across the bay, the wicked city was getting dressed for the evening.

Father Jorge finally appeared, trailing apologies.

"Perhaps we should go ahead and order," the Nuncio said. "I can recommend the grilled corvina, only because there is so little that can go wrong with such a dish. With a taste of garlic and lime, it's quite reliable."

"I'm not at all hungry."

The Nuncio looked at his secretary with open exasperation. He had been looking forward to this dinner all day. Moreover, the young man's asceticism was becoming annoying. "Look at you, your watchband is sliding nearly to your elbow," the Nuncio chided. "You do yourself no merit by starving yourself."

"I'm not starving, I'm just not hungry. But I'll watch you eat."

"At least get a bowl of bouillabaisse," the Nuncio pleaded. "Otherwise, I'll feel like a glutton on display."

When the waiter came, the Nuncio ordered the *pescado alca-parrado*, a striped bass in caper sauce. "I recall that it's prepared with minced carrots and something odd that I can't bring to mind."

"Turnips," said the waiter.

"Ah," the Nuncio said appreciatively. "The turnips are a surprise. So then you must have something a little bitter to balance the flavors."

"It's garnished with almonds."

"Of course," the Nuncio said. He sensed Father Jorge's amusement. Well, it was his loss that he didn't appreciate the soulfulness of food. The Nuncio never felt more in tune with the glory of creation than he did at the dinner table.

Father Jorge obediently ordered the bouillabaisse.

"So, what pressing business at the parish detained you?" the

Nuncio inquired testily. Part of his displeasure was that he missed seeing Father Jorge, who had gotten so involved with the parish, and he simply felt neglected. He was surprised when the priest averted his eyes.

"In fact, I was not at the parish," Father Jorge confessed.

"Really? I thought you said you were tied up in Chorrillo."

"That was a lie," Father Jorge said.

The Nuncio stared at him speechlessly.

"I was told not to let anyone know where I was," Father Jorge said, stammering in embarrassment. "I hope you'll forgive me. I can't allow myself to deceive you."

The waiter poured a sip of wine, and the Nuncio pretended to taste it.

"A few citizens have formed a group," Father Jorge said in a low voice when the waiter had gone. "We are studying nonviolent ways to resist the tyranny. Right now it's important that we meet in secret."

The Nuncio was so alarmed by this news that for a moment he could not manage a response. Father Jorge had never expressed a single political opinion that the Nuncio was aware of, and now he was engaging in an activity of surpassing dangerousness. The Nuncio tugged nervously at his tangled eyebrows. "There is nothing secret in this country," he warned.

"I'm sure you are right, and it is my belief that we should be open about our goals and methods. We are talking about a peaceful transition to democracy—marches and strikes, that sort of thing, not some kind of armed insurrection."

"Still, if such actions are even being discussed, then you are signing your death sentence," said the Nuncio. "Moreover, I should warn you that the Church also condemns involvement in such movements. I'm sure I don't have to remind you of its abhorrence of liberation theology and its determination to remove the clergy from politics. You will not find support from your superiors if you pursue this course of action."

"You are my superior."

"I am your superior, yes, in both age and rank, if not in wisdom. And whatever you think of me, I hope that you do not believe I am an enemy of justice. It is a laudable pursuit, God knows. I am certainly not an apologist for the status quo."

"Silence is also a statement, Monseñor," Father Jorge said evenly.

Never in their relationship had the younger man questioned the Nuncio's judgment or authority. Certainly his secretary knew how perilous his actions might prove to be. Central America was a graveyard for idealists. Even if General Noriega spared him, his promising career in the Church would be ruined. Unwelcome memories of priests whose careers he personally had crushed flooded in on the Nuncio. Like Father Jorge, they had been earnest, pious men, committed but naive. Those who survived the repression they fought against were destroyed by the institution they served. One day a man would come, a man like the Nuncio—canny and hard—and the ideals of the priest would mean nothing to him.

"You must be careful that you don't stir up too much wrath," the Nuncio warned. "I would not presume to lecture you on morality. But on tactics—this is an area of expertise that I hope you would grant me. To navigate these difficult waters, you need to have a clear plan and a knowledge of what lies ahead. You can't go sailing into the storm heedless of the consequences."

"Tactics are important. But more important is public pressure. The people should be marching in the streets, not strategizing in the coffeehouses. Noriega will not be outmaneuvered. He must be overthrown."

"If that is what you are talking about, then I beg you to disband immediately," the Nuncio pleaded. "Be certain that you have already been marked by Noriega's men. We should find you another post out of the country as quickly as possible."

"That may be your choice, Monseñor, but if it is my decision, I prefer to stay."

The Nuncio held his chilled wineglass in both hands. How

much easier it is, he thought bitterly, to be young and defiant than to be old and cautious. The rebel who is fighting for a change is so much more appealing than the old man who only wants to survive. "There was a young priest I met when I first arrived in this country," he said. "Father Gallego—he held a small parish in the countryside. Probably you would not think of him as a radical. I know he did not think of himself that way. He attempted only a few simple, decent things, such as organizing peasants for housing and setting up agricultural cooperatives. But somehow he offended a relative of Torrijos. He was arrested and then disappeared. Of course, you've heard this story hundreds of times in Salvador, but it was unusual in Panama. No one thought that he had committed such a great offense. Later, we heard he was beaten into a coma, then taken into a helicopter over the Pacific. The name of the soldier who pushed him out of the helicopter was Noriega. For many of us, it was the first time we had heard that name."

"I know about his capacity for violence," said Father Jorge. "I promise you I am not that naive."

"I didn't say that. The point about poor Father Gallego is that he did not become the martyr he deserved to be, either to the people of Panama or to the Church. He became a joke. People laughed about why, if he was so holy, he couldn't fly. His reputed killer became the ruler of the country, the confidant of American presidents. Even the pope receives him. So what is the lesson one draws from this?"

"If you are suggesting that the righteous suffer and evil is rewarded—well, this does not come as a surprise to me," said Father Jorge. "Our actions still must be based on what we know is right. One only hopes that God will judge us more fairly."

The Nuncio saw the hopelessness of changing his secretary's mind. "Well, then, allow me to become involved," he said.

"You? But you said you are opposed to everything we are doing!"

"I am opposed to the way that you are doing it—meeting in

secret, whispering against the government. Such actions are bound to draw attention and brutal reprisals. If you are plotting revolution, it has to be done openly and in such a way that it appears to be harmless. And the best way to do that is to let an old man be your leader. It is youth that power fears."

"What about the Church?"

The Nuncio shrugged. "For some time the Vatican has paid no attention to me. I think they expect me to die or retire momentarily. They are not likely to notice the idle talk of an old renegade. We can meet in the nunciature, as if it is perfectly normal. But please, promise me that there will be no more of these underground conspiracies."

When the waiter brought their dinners, the Nuncio stared at his garnished sea bass without appetite. He watched as Father Jorge dumped chili sauce into his soup—a puzzling Latin habit that turned all food into an overheated sameness. There was a new game to be played, and despite what he had said, the Nuncio knew how dangerous it could be. His career—and his life— had nearly run their course; Father Jorge's were just leaving the gate. He must do what he could do to save him.

CHAPTER **6**

O LLIE, YOUR GLASS is empty," Tony observed. He signaled to one of the several topless stewardesses aboard his yacht, *Macho III*. "Chiquita, another carrot juice for Colonel North."

Chiquita curtseyed and disappeared into the cabin.

"These ribs are terrific," said North, wiping his fingers on his bathing suit. "Aren't you having any?"

"Actually, I don't eat meat."

"I'm surprised," said North.

"I think it's a sin to eat the flesh of other animals. Of course, you should enjoy your meal, don't worry about the moral consequences."

North studied the pork rib in his hand and then took another bite. "You know, this really interests me. I mean, all through history, man has eaten meat. In First Timothy, the apostle Paul warns us against vegetarians."

"Yes," said Tony, "and because of such foolishness I have turned to the Buddhist faith."

"Gosh, I don't know much about that," said North, wiping the sauce off his chin.

"I used to tell Bill Casey, 'Buddhism is the only spiritual discipline for a rational man.' But the Jesuits had him hypnotized."

Both men were quiet, thinking of the recently deceased CIA director. For Tony, the loss had been particularly worrisome. Casey had been his sponsor for decades.

"But you have other fish to fry, as you Christians say," Tony continued. "So, how can I help you? This thought is always in the front of my mind—how can I help my American friends?"

"First of all," North said, smiling brilliantly as he accepted the carrot juice from Chiquita, "thanks for all you've done. No, I mean that sincerely. Our two countries have had some misunderstandings. I won't hide the fact that there was some upset over the Barletta ouster. The thing is, that's all in the past. There are more important things to consider. We want to continue our special relationship with you. You've always been on our side when it counts. Especially with the Contras. The president wants you to know that he appreciates it. From the bottom of his heart. You've been at our side in the battle for freedom in Nicaragua."

"I tell you, Ollie, we're going to win that war."

"You don't need to tell me!"

"I've had enough trouble, believe me, with the commies in my own government," said Tony. Occasionally it was wise to wave the red flag in front of the Americans. "They need a firm hand. To be honest, I think they also need to be a little afraid. Otherwise . . . another Cuba."

"I would hate to see that, General. We all would."

"Sometimes a leader in this part of the world has to do things that Americans don't understand."

"Well, there I would agree with you," North said as he watched Chiquita stretch out on the sundeck. He forced himself to look out on the gentle gray swells of Balboa harbor. "Speaking of things that are hard to understand, there's something else we need to talk about. This is a hard thing to tell a friend. You know about the Senate investigation."

Tony remembered hearing about it in the CIA briefing in New York.

"Now it turns out that Helms has proposed an amendment to the Intelligence Authorization Bill."

"Really? Who would let him do that?" asked Tony.

"Well, of course there's nothing unusual about that, General. You know these senators—always trying to get their way! But this particular amendment requires the CIA to report to the Senate about these . . . I guess you'd call 'em 'allegations' about the involvement of the Panamanian military in drug trafficking and money laundering. Also, about the death of this fellow Spadodifera."

"Spadafora."

"Right."

"What does the president think about this proposal?"

"You can count on him to stand firmly against it."

Tony leaned back and exhaled in relief.

"You seem to be taking this pretty well," North observed.

"Part of the training we receive as Buddhists is to detach from worldly events," said Tony. "You give me this information, I ask myself: What can Tony Noriega do about it? The answer is, nothing. Tony Noriega cannot change the course of destiny. He can only observe and realize that all things pass by in the great river of life."

"Wow," said North. "I'd like to get to that place, General. That's the right way of looking at things, that's for sure. But the thing is, the son of a bitch Helms has the votes."

"Tell me what you mean exactly," said Tony. He had never quite understood the nuances of democracy.

"I mean, the Senate is going to have a full-blown investigation. Helms is dead set on it. And it's going to be a stinker, you can be sure. They'll subpoena every little gunrunner and dope dealer who ever passed through Panama."

"I know that my friends at the agency will take care of me."

"Of course, they'll do what they can. But it's a different place over there without the old man. He really loved you. This new guy, the jury's still out on him. Oh, and speaking of juries, there's something else I have to tell you. There's this renegade prosecutor down in Florida."

"A prosecutor? Have I committed some crime?"

"This jerk is just trying to make a name for himself. They say he's got your name on a drug indictment."

Tony laughed genially. "And what are my American friends going to do about it?"

"Gosh, General, there's not much we can do. They went to a grand jury. I don't know how much you know about our country, but—"

"After all the favors you ask of me, this is how you repay me?"

"I just feel awful about it."

"And what about my friend George Herbert Walker Bush?"

"I'm sure he feels awful about it, too."

Tony stared at North in disbelief. "You and I have an arrangement, Colonel," he reminded him. "You came to me. 'General Noriega, we need your help in Nicaragua. We want to stop the spread of communism.' And I said, 'This is also Tony Noriega's goal. Together we will fight to make our part of the world a haven for freedom.' So I gave you what you wanted."

"Yes, sir, you did."

"And when the CIA asks to set up special companies to do espionage in Panama and launder money, I say yes to this as well—even though we know these are illegal activities in Panama. I don't call the prosecutor! I even permit Contras to be trained at SOUTHCOM, which is against the treaties. All these laws I broke—for you! To help my American friends."

"You are a special friend, all right. And we appreciate it. No kidding."

"So this is what you offer in return?" Tony thundered. "Your politicians slander me in Congress, they make up charges against me, they even pursue me in the courts? And they send you to insult me in this fashion—you, a man who has asked me for so many favors? Now you should be doing favors for me instead."

North nodded and looked guiltily at his pile of ribs. "The truth is, General, I've got some legal problems of my own."

The two men were quiet. A school of dolphins rolled past the yacht, drawing the excited attention of the stewardesses, who raced to starboard, pointing and throwing canapés after the indifferent creatures.

"I've got a proposition," Tony finally said in his most reasonable tone of voice, "a goodwill gesture. You take it to my friend George Herbert Walker Bush. We can get rid of these Sandinistas in one—what do you say? One sweep? One swoop?"

"One fell swoop."

"One fell swoop. I have men there, as you know—good men, in Managua and the countryside—waiting for my command. They will do what I say. You know this is true."

"I've seen it," said North, remembering with awe the one-eyed demolition expert that Noriega had provided for a top-secret raid that North had organized out of the White House basement. The little guy was a genius at explosives and a stone-cold killer. He and his gang of mercenaries had managed to blow up a military complex and a hospital in Managua. The hospital, of course, had been a regrettable mistake, and luckily no one had been killed.

"Give me a little money for these men, and they will kill the comandantes," Tony said cheerfully. "A dozen heads will roll. Tomás Borge, the Ortegas—the whole bunch! One fell swoop."

North grinned in admiration. "I gotta hand it to you, General. I mean, it's such a neat idea. But I just—"

"You take care of my problems, I take care of yours."

"Can't. I just can't do it. It's against the law."

"Are you being . . ." Tony groped for the term. *"Amusing?"* He spat the word out of his mouth. "Your whole fucking war is 'against the law.' So why is it the only one who gets indicted is your good friend Tony Noriega?"

"I wish I had a good answer for you."

"You will wish it very much before all this comes to an end," Tony promised darkly.

THE POLICE substation on Avenida Central was a noisy and confusing place. A rowdy procession of small-time criminals passed through the informal booking procedure and then disappeared into the basement holding cells, where they would await trial or else simply await . . . nothing. People spent months and even years here with no resolution or even an official hearing. Without pressure from important families or influential personages, a prisoner in the substation was likely to remain there indefinitely, until the system finally noticed him and either brought him to trial or arbitrarily expelled him.

Finally the steel door in the back of the substation opened and Teo Sánchez appeared, looking rumpled and disdainful and wearing cheap imitations of brand-name American clothes.

"So what are you going to do with me, Father?" he asked, but his tone reflected little interest in the answer.

"What if I take you to lunch?"

Teo looked surprised and a little suspicious. They walked down to the Kentucky Fried Chicken around the corner. It was midafternoon, and the place was nearly empty except for the flies. A radio behind the counter played a salsa tune by Rubén Blades.

In jail, Teo had grown out the wispy hairs of his mustache, which was so thin that Father Jorge had not noticed it until he was seated directly opposite him. He was a good-looking child, like his mother, except for the hardness in his features. He ate the chicken greedily, without looking up; and when Father Jorge didn't object, he helped himself to both rolls.

"You want some dessert?"

Teo didn't argue. He ordered a large cone of chocolate ice cream. "They don't feed you much in jail," he said.

"Your mother doesn't know about this. She's been very worried."

"She worries," Teo said. "She doesn't know what else to do, so she worries. Look where it gets her. She's working in a whorehouse."

"That must be very upsetting."

Teo shrugged.

"Do you ever give any thought to what you want for your own life?" Father Jorge asked.

"Yeah. Every day."

"Would you like to tell me about it?"

"Just, I'm not going to be poor, that much I know. You got to take what you want in this life." He said this with absolute conviction.

"The police said you were selling stolen shoes."

A cross-eyed beggar stood in the window watching Teo eat his ice cream. Teo looked at him indifferently. "It's a good business. I can make some real money."

Father Jorge stopped himself from trying to counsel Teo, although the boy's future was dismally clear to him. His view of the world was already formed, and there was little that anyone could do to change it. Nor was Teo inviting Father Jorge's advice, at least not now. The most he could hope for was to establish a tiny ledge of trust. And yet the priest deeply believed in the flexibility of human nature. He always assumed that God offered life-changing moments of decision, even to the most jaded person. Teo would make a choice between a life on the streets or something better. Father Jorge believed it was the choice between damnation and salvation. He could see how circumstances forced young men to make appalling choices about their lives, and he wanted to be there if Teo needed someone to show him a way out. He felt a sense of urgency that was difficult to explain. He had dealt with other boys as hard and hopeless as Teo, but with indifferent success. Perhaps he had kept a couple of them alive when circumstances might have led them down a more dangerous path.

More often than not, however, his ministrations had had no effect. Chorrillo was a mistress to despair. There were thousands of
Chorrillos and thousands of Teos inside them—and so little hope
for change. Even one priest with one boy was overmatched. In
any case, Father Jorge was conscious that he had nothing to offer
now, and Teo was in no mood to receive it if he had.

"Look at your number, Father," Teo said in a moment.
"Maybe you won."

Father Jorge looked under the bottom of his Pepsi cup as Teo
had done.

"What does it say?"

"It says, 'The Force is with you. You win a free action figure.' "

"How about that, Father? You going to cash it in?" His voice
betrayed a bit of envy.

"I don't need an action figure. Why don't you get it?"

Despite himself, Teo's eyes brightened. He returned in a moment with a small plastic doll. "Which one is it?" Father Jorge
asked.

"Boba Fett."

Teo set the doll on the table and studied it closely. He is still
such a child, Father Jorge thought, feeling a surge of anger at the
world that Teo lived in, which had so little space for innocence.

"I'm afraid you can't come back to the parish," said the priest.
"We have a policy—"

"They told me the rules, Father. I know all about it."

"I'm sure your mother wants you to come back home."

Teo didn't answer. He seemed to be weighing the truth of that
statement. "Will you take something to her?" he finally said. He
took a wadded-up bill from the watch pocket of his Levi's and
carefully smoothed it out. It was twenty dollars. "Tell her this is
for Renata. She's going to need a dress for her First Communion." He seemed to be very proud as he placed the money on
the table.

If Teo had given that money to the policeman, Father Jorge
thought, he might not have gone to jail.

"What shall I tell her about you? She'll want to know where you are."

"I got friends. They'll take care of me."

The priest stopped himself from responding. He knew who Teo's friends were—delinquent boys, like Teo himself, who ran the gangs in the street. He wanted to save the boy, but he knew that Teo had to be willing. That might never happen, but if it did, Father Jorge hoped he would be ready for him. There was something about the child that called to him. He was still capable of love, unlike some of the toughs that Father Jorge had dealt with. But the more the priest tried to close the distance between them, the farther away Teo seemed to be. It was like running after a train. The child was on his way to some awful destination, and Father Jorge was unable to pull him back.

At least he's alive," Gloria Sánchez said, when Father Jorge appeared at her apartment. She wasn't surprised to learn that her son had been arrested. She took the twenty dollars without a word and placed it in a plastic glass in her cupboard. As she did so, Father Jorge allowed himself a glimpse of her legs, which were slender and shapely. Now that he had seen her as a prostitute, he couldn't keep his eyes off her body. She had already been the subject of several memorable dreams.

"Who cuts your hair, Father?" Gloria asked unexpectedly.

"I suppose I do."

"That's what I thought." She laughed lightly.

Father Jorge touched his hair self-consciously. It was long and disorderly—in fact, the Nuncio had recently made some critical remark about the need to maintain a tidy appearance. "I guess you think I should give it a trim."

"Let me do it. I need the practice."

"Are you planning to be a barber?"

"That's my dream. I'm saving to open a shop."

The priest hesitated.

"Look, I've already got the tools," said Gloria. She showed him a kit with an electric trimmer and several pairs of scissors.

"Well, it's one thing they didn't teach us in seminary," Father Jorge admitted.

She made him take off his glasses and bend over the sink while she washed his hair. Her fingers were firm and sure, and his scalp tingled with pleasure. Then she toweled him off and sat him in a kitchen chair with paper napkins tucked into his collar and spread over his shoulders. "How long do you want it, Father?"

"Whatever you think is right."

Gloria stood in front of him and sized him up. "I think shorter is better."

Father Jorge had not had his hair cut professionally in years—not since Spain, in fact. It was such a small service, he thought, but disarmingly intimate. There was no mirror for him to look into, but he could sense Gloria standing behind him and imagine what she was doing and the look of concentration on her face. His damp hair fell like fronds from a tamarind tree. He struggled against the erection that announced itself with a rude lurch.

"Your hair is very thick," Gloria said admiringly. "It's got a lot of body also. I would kill to have hair like this."

"Your hair is okay."

Gloria laughed. "'Okay.'"

"I mean, you have beautiful hair," he said, feeling deeply embarrassed by the erection, which was now quite obvious.

"Well, it's not my best feature, but it doesn't embarrass me." She moved to his right side and began trimming around his ear. He was extremely conscious of her skin and her breasts, which were so close to him and somewhat more exposed because of her bent position. She was wearing shorts and a halter top. She smelled like coffee and cinnamon. His nerves were so acute that he could feel her touch even before her fingers actually reached him. He could feel her hands moving in the air. He could also feel the throbbing in his penis, which was like a gorilla pounding its chest. He closed his eyes and made a quick plea to God to put the beast to sleep.

"Did I hurt you?" Gloria asked.

"No, no," he said faintly. "I was just wondering where you got this talent for barbering. I can tell you have a gift."

"Well, thank you. Hugo used to tell me I was born to make men happy, which I guess is also a talent."

"Hugo?" the priest said in surprise. "Did you cut his hair as well?"

"Yeah, you could say that, Father."

"I'm sorry, I didn't mean to be indiscreet."

"I don't mind. He was a wonderful man. He was always very good to me, and he often sent money for Teo. Don't you think he favors him?"

"Is Hugo his father?"

Gloria set her scissors aside and brushed the hair off the priest's neck. Her manner seemed a little brusque. "Hugo didn't claim him," she said. "I don't blame him, it wasn't possible to know for certain. But I always believed it was Hugo, and I think he didn't mind. I just wish Teo could have known him. Maybe he would have a little pride, you know what I mean? Instead, he's so hurt inside and so angry at the world. He thinks I'm responsible for all the bad things that happen." Her voice broke, and she turned away.

"I'm sure he loves you, he just can't show it," Father Jorge said. "It's obvious to me. He just doesn't want to be a child anymore. He wants to take care of you. Give him a couple of years, you'll see."

Gloria took the electric trimmer and began to buzz the back of his neck. The cool metal made him shiver. "I'm going to tell you a fashion secret, Father," she said. "When you start getting gray hair, you should grow a beard. It'll make you look like a saint."

"Appearances don't always tell the truth."

Gloria put some lotion in his hair and combed it back. Then she stood back and looked at him. "You better be careful, Father," she said. "I may have done too good a job." She said it as a joke, but he noticed that her eyes lingered on him as she put her scissors back in the sheath.

CHAPTER 7

GILBERT BLANCARTE, the famous Argentine psychic, was in a trance. Tony could just see the whites of Gilbert's eyes through the peroxided braids that draped the witch doctor's face. Gilbert wore a red chiffon scarf over his naked shoulders, which glistened with sweat in the small, still room. The scene was a little spooky, even to Tony. Sometimes he thought it was all so ridiculous, but whenever Gilbert entered the spirit world, Tony felt surrounded by ghosts.

In the legends of the Afro-Cuban gods of Santería, Tony found a divine echo of his own life story. His personal orisha, or guardian angel, was Oshún, the yellow goddess of the rivers, who was primarily worshiped by women because she looked after childbirth. But she was also the goddess of beauty and sexual power. Vain and amorous, she gave away her children to her younger sister, Yemayá, just as Tony's dying mother had given him away to his godmother, Mama Luisa. Tony revered Yemayá, but he wore the amber beads of Oshún. In the end, he had to worship beauty.

Few people knew about Tony's secret studio in Chorrillo, but then it was a district where people didn't ask many questions. Tony could be alone here when he needed to conjure. On the walls were bottles of special potions, herbs, exotic medicines. A chicken carcass was being drained of its blood in the corner, plop-plop-plopping into a mayonnaise jar to be used later. Obviously Tony was going to need all the help he could muster to counter the massive Cuban wanga that the Colombians were putting out. A shrine to Shango and to Saint Barbara dominated one corner, and on a low altar before it was a soup tureen filled with polished stones and cowry shells. Facing the tureen were the pin-filled dolls of Tony's enemies, a pudgy Pablo Escobar and bespectacled Jesse Helms, which Tony had personally constructed out of burlap and papier-mâché.

"A fat man from Colombia," Gilbert muttered in his high-pitched trance voice, which sounded as if it were floating on helium.

Tony looked at the Escobar doll. "What does he want?"

"He wants to have you killed."

Tony shuddered. "You've got to protect me, Gilbert."

"Are you wearing your ribbons?"

"Of course!" Tony raised his pant leg to show Gilbert the red ribbon tied above his ankle. But Gilbert's eyes were focused inward, on another plane entirely.

"There is another disturbance."

"What? Who?"

"A rival."

"I have many rivals."

"This man is a slave to women."

"Is his name Roberto?"

"Roberto," the witch doctor repeated. "This could be."

"Roberto is a problem, I agree. But he is useful to me."

"He can cause you much trouble. Beware of him."

Perhaps Japan, after all.

"Who is this?" said Gilbert. "Another powerful figure arises in the spiritual realm. He is wearing robes."

"Robes? Like a priest?"

"He is a very high priest."

"The papal nuncio? He provides refuge to the opposition, but I did not think of him as an enemy."

"He is big," said Gilbert.

"He is very tall," Tony agreed.

"I mean, spiritually, he is big," said Gilbert, sounding a little vexed despite his trance. "Much mojo."

"Really? We're talking about the Nuncio? Old man with bushy eyebrows? I thought he was harmless."

"He can be treacherous, like the tides. Do not go over your head with this man—he will sweep you away!"

With that pronouncement, Gilbert suddenly coughed up a wad of black goo. Then he sprang back into present reality, delicately wiping the foam from his lips. "So, bad reading, huh?" he said in his normal lisping voice. "Sometimes it goes like that."

"You can help me, though?" Tony tried to keep the pleading tone out of his voice. Gilbert was so vain about his powers that it wouldn't do to let him know how much Tony depended on him. There were so few people he could trust.

"I can help you, Tony, but you have to be careful. Lately, you've been up to a lot of tricks. You're going to have to simplify, my friend. These enemies, they gain power as they multiply. Spiritual geometry. It works against you."

"I know," Tony said miserably.

"Look, don't be so worried. We'll put you on a special program, an enemy-reduction plan. We'll keep on casting the usual spells, but in the meantime I want you to try to imagine what you personally can do to make your enemies into your friends."

"But Escobar and Helms, they are crazy people."

"I'm not saying you can reason with them. But perhaps there is some thoughtful gift you can give them. Something personal. Something that says, 'I hear you and I understand.' "

"Money," said Tony. "Money says that."

"If I were in your place, I would get someone to speak for me.

An intermediary who will talk to the fat Colombian. I think this is your main piece of work right now, Tony. Because really, this guy has a lot of juice. And oh, man, he's very fucking angry."

Tony grimaced and rubbed his temples.

"The headache again?" Gilbert asked.

"Make me a potion, Gilbert. It's killing me."

"Tony, you overdo the potions."

"Why does everyone want me to suffer? I'm hurting and I need treatment."

"You should listen to me. It's not a gin and tonic, you know."

"Gilbert . . ." Tony said, the pleading now apparent.

Gilbert reached over victoriously and patted Tony's hand. "I'll make you a special. You'll feel like a king."

Tony sighed and closed his eyes. Total defeat. But he also felt relieved. Gilbert was powerful. Gilbert was wise. His advice was sound: offer a gift. Tomorrow morning, Tony decided, he would release the twenty-six Colombians who had been captured in the DEA raid in Darién. That should appease Escobar. Okay, the Americans would be upset, but some jurisdictional excuse could be offered. They were Colombians, after all. Tony could release them and tell Colombia to extradite them, which would never happen. In the meantime, the men would disappear. In a few weeks, they'd be forgotten about entirely.

"Where do you keep the powdered rooster toenails?" Gilbert asked as he thumbed through the glass vials in Tony's cabinet.

"In the left-hand drawer. All the ingredients are alphabet-ized."

"You are so organized," Gilbert said admiringly. "That's how you got where you are, I guess."

IT WAS A RARE occasion when the Nuncio was invited to dine at the Union Club. For generations the Union Club was where the white elite conspired to run their country over cocktails and caviar. When Torrijos seized power, one of his first actions was to appropriate the original facility and turn it into an officers club. The power that the old members once exercised was considerably reduced, but eventually they built themselves another Union Club, which was even more elegant, with wide verandas and lovely dining rooms with porthole windows overlooking the bay. In this manner they reminded themselves that although they no longer ran the country, they still owned it. And that was something.

The mood among the members, however, had soured even in the several months since the Nuncio had last dined among them. Torrijos had hurt their pride, perhaps, but Noriega was ruining their business. He and his PDF mafia were creating one new enterprise after another. Money was flooding into Panama, but it was dirty money; and even worse—it was filling the pockets of Noriega and his henchmen and no one else. Legitimate businesses had little chance to compete against the smugglers and black marketeers and money launderers whose skyscrapers were rising along the waterfront. Everyone in the club had learned that they had to pay protection money if they hoped to continue to operate. Most ominously, the Americans were turning over the prize properties in the zone to the Panamanians, bit by precious bit, and Tony's gang was getting all of it—not even scraps were left for the deserving members of the Union Club.

The Nuncio was also surprised by the identity of his host for this luncheon—Roberto Díaz Herrera. They hated Roberto here. In the minds of the members, Roberto was a traitor to his class. True, he was a first cousin of Torrijos and therefore he might be forgiven for making a career in the military, where his family connection would do him the most good. But Roberto was also white. He was one of them. They had expected that after Torrijos was buried under his monument to himself in Fort Amador, Roberto would return to the fold and accept his proper place in Panamanian society. Instead, he continued his military career, serving the odious Noriega, the thief of their birthright. So Roberto's uniformed appearance at the club was bound to cause a stir, especially because he was now in disgrace and he brought his troubles with him like a disease. Indeed, the Nuncio wondered if Roberto had invited him to act as a social bodyguard. Who would attack a man who was dining with a priest? He could already anticipate the gossip columns in *La Prensa*.

"They think I'm spying on them, you know," Roberto said as he unfolded his linen napkin—the size of a bath towel—and laid it across his lap. "And you know what? They're right. If you could see the reports I get—hah! It makes me wonder why I would want to be a member of such a club."

"Yes, I was wondering that as well," the Nuncio replied.

"Do you see the man over my right shoulder?" asked Roberto. "Serafín Mitrotti? You know him? He has become the leader of the opposition. They call themselves the Committee for the Redemption of Moral Values. Now they all go around dressed in white, as if they are so pure. But I think it's because they are all so proud of *being* white."

So—Noriega's men knew all about it, just as the Nuncio feared. He discreetly glanced at Mitrotti, whom he knew casually at the Rotary Club. Mitrotti gave him a quizzical look and went back to his lamb chop. If Roberto knows about Mitrotti, the Nuncio realized, he must know about Father Jorge as well. All of us.

The waiter appeared, and the Nuncio ordered a roulade of veal, dressed with an anchovy mayonnaise, an arugula salad, and a glass of Orvieto.

"I'll have the fruit bowl and a bottle of still water," said Roberto.

"That's all?" the Nuncio exclaimed. "I should reorder. I didn't realize you were just snacking."

"No, no—this is all I eat now, fruit, fruit, more fruit. Occasionally, some tofu." Certainly Roberto appeared very thin, almost haggard.

"Is this some special diet, Roberto? Because frankly you look like you should be gaining weight, not losing it. Are you in good health?"

101

"Never better. I'm in top shape—not only physically, but spiritually."

"Are you saying that eating fruit has spiritual consequences?"

"Absolutely! Fruit is full of positive energy." Roberto fixed the Nuncio with a discomfitingly intense stare. "I'm sharing this information with you because I know you interest yourself in all sorts of religious matters."

"I like fruit well enough, but I have never thought of it as having this extra dimension," the Nuncio said. "Besides, at my age, it loosens the bowels."

Roberto continued his intense and quizzical gaze. "Surely you notice something different about me?" he finally demanded.

"Besides the fact that you are so gaunt? I can't say that anything jumps out at me. Have you changed your hair?"

Roberto looked crestfallen. "Many people say they notice immediately," he said. "They say they detect a change in my aura."

"There might be such a change, Roberto, but I assure you it would be invisible to me. I've never really known what people meant when they were using such terms."

The Nuncio had nothing against religious ecstasy. When he was young, he still had hopes that some transforming mystical experience would happen to him. But that had never occurred. Nor had he ever seen a ghost or had an out-of-body experience. He supposed he was not receptive to supernatural events. When he first joined the Congregation for the Doctrine of the Faith, he had been given the task of documenting miracles. He personally investigated 112 alleged sightings of the Virgin Mary and found cause to disbelieve every one of them. Few of his colleagues in the Holy See were miracle mongers, and at first they had enjoyed the intellectual gamesmanship. When he exposed the plumbing leak that had caused a statue of Mary to weep in a little chapel in Lodz, near the pope's home village, he was hailed and pointed at in the corridors. When he diagnosed the schizophrenia of a twelve-year-old girl in Bosnia who was channeling Mary's prophecies, the Vatican issued a statement in *L'Osservatore Romano* repudiating her divinations. Monseñor Morette then turned his attention to the shroud of Turin. His lengthy and daring review of the shroud's history had never been published; although only a few Vatican insiders had actually read the document in its entirety, it was rumored to be so devastating in its conclusions that the pope quietly canceled a planned public exhibition of the venerated icon. Strangely enough, he never stopped 'hoping that one of the miracles would prove to be true so that he could see God's hand with his own eyes; however, he had long since stopped expecting such events to occur—at least in his presence.

The Nuncio looked guiltily out the window as the waiter set the sumptuous plate of veal in front of him and then placed a halved cantaloupe filled with berries before Roberto.

"Shall I tell you why I invited you today, Monseñor?" Roberto asked.

"Yes, by all means," said the Nuncio, "but if what I hear is true, I should begin by congratulating you on your appointment to the Holy See. I suppose you will want to know all about Rome. I am sure you will adore it. Do you know the city at all?"

"Not at all, and unfortunately, I believe I never will," said Roberto. "Yes, Tony made me the offer, but—without going into details—we did not reach a final agreement."

"You are still negotiating?"

"We are negotiating, but one gets the feeling it is a game of charades. The truth is, Tony wants to get rid of me."

"Sending you to Rome would not accomplish that?"

"Not in the ultimate sense that the General intends."

The Nuncio arched his brows. "The nunciature is always open to you," he said. "We've housed many of the General's political opponents, but you'd be the first PDF officer."

"Thank you for your offer, Monseñor, but I have an entirely different course of action in mind."

"And what is that?"

Roberto forked a strawberry and examined it with interest before popping it into his mouth. "It's a radical idea, I confess. I am hoping to enlist your assistance in carrying it out."

"You know I have an official policy of neutrality. I can't afford to take sides in the internal politics of the country. At least," the Nuncio paused, "not obviously so."

"I'm not talking about political action," said Roberto. "I'm talking about good and evil. In that case, I believe you have already declared yourself."

"I'm sorry. I'm at a complete loss as to what you mean."

"Spiritual warfare, Monseñor. That's what I'm saying."

The Nuncio supposed that excessive fruit eating had worked its unsettling effects on Roberto's brain. "Perhaps you should be more explicit, Roberto. How can I help you?"

Roberto's eyes discreetly surveyed the room before returning to the Nuncio. "This is ultraconfidential," he said in a low voice. "I am trusting you with this information with the understanding that it is to remain only between the two of us."

"Should I consider this a privileged conversation?"

Roberto looked miffed. "Certainly not. This is a plot, not a confession." He leaned forward and continued in a theatrical whisper. "What transpires must be limited to those who have been initiated at the highest levels of spiritual authority. Really, there's no one else in Panama who can help us."

The Nuncio nodded in bewilderment.

"Some weeks ago Maigualida and I made a trip to Brazil," said Roberto. "We had arranged a secret meeting with Indra Devi, the famous Indian yogini. You know her?"

"I confess I know nothing at all about yoga."

"You would be astonished. She is eighty-eight years old, but she appears to be a woman of no more than fifty. She's the most transcendent being I've ever encountered. She was the one who introduced me to the works of Sai Baba. I'm sure you've heard of him, at least."

"I fear not."

"Really, Monseñor, I understand that you are Catholic, but I suspected that you had an interest in the larger spiritual world," Roberto said impatiently, the disappointment evident in his voice.

"He's some kind of swami?" the Nuncio asked hopelessly.

"Many believe he is a reincarnation of God himself."

"Ah." The Nuncio caught the waiter's eye and signaled for another glass of wine.

"I myself have not met him, but he is reputed to have extraordinary powers," Roberto continued. "He is a healer and a psychic. They say he can even stop rainbows and transform himself into nonhuman forms. Occasionally he brings the dead back to life."

"Indeed?" said the Nuncio wearily. He had investigated so many similar claims that he had stopped being surprised.

"Through Indra Devi, I have learned of this man's holy power. I can even say that I have come to share in these powers—in a far more modest fashion, of course," Roberto added with a self-deprecating laugh.

"So you can float in the air now?" the Nuncio teased.

"Not yet," Roberto responded in all seriousness. "Nor have I achieved the ability to be in two places at once. But Indra has helped me understand the nature of my destiny. The fate of our country is on my shoulders. She knew this within minutes of meeting me. I can tell you, it gave me a chill."

"But is that, perhaps, the reason you visited her in the first place?"

"You are right to be skeptical. It did confirm an inner sense that I had been born for some great calling, and I suppose that does account for my initial interest in seeing her. Still, her insight into my situation was so immediate and profound that it swept away any doubt that this woman was a true prophet. Right away she told me I was going to enter a great battle and that I would appear to lose, but in the end I would be vindicated. I must have faith, she said, and I must not hate General Noriega. 'Your karma and his are totally independent,' she told me. So I asked, 'What, then, should I do with this man?' And she told me this: that I should send him love and light."

"That sounds like good Christian advice," said the Nuncio.

"That's what I thought as well. Christ is not the only prophet who has told us we must love our enemies. Anyway, Indra Devi put me on the fruit diet and told me that I must refrain from drinking alcohol. This alone, however, would not lead all the way to enlightenment. She then revealed the key to achieving true spiritual mastery."

"Really? May I ask what it is?"

"Chastity, alas."

"In my own case, I believe the effect has been comparatively modest," said the Nuncio.

Roberto looked momentarily confused. "I'm sorry, Monseñor, I'd forgotten that others have had to endure similar disciplines. For me, and of course for poor Maigualida, this has been an enormous sacrifice. But I can tell you, it does bring the mind into focus on the higher things. And if it prepares me for the battle to come, as Indra has prophesied, then it will have been worth it."

"So you are trying to bring some of this spiritual force to bear on General Noriega? I am told that he puts quite a lot of stock in his own various spiritual pursuits."

Roberto nodded his head in grave assent. "I always got the feeling that Tony was invoking power from the black side of life. Once he told me we must get rid of all moralisms. Tell me, Monseñor, as a student of theology, what you would call a spirituality that is without morality?"

"Witchcraft."

"Exactly," said Roberto. "And do you know about Tony's voodoo practices? Once he gave me Santería beads and told me he was a priest and could hex our enemies. He said the true source of his power was that he worshiped the devil."

"I have heard rumors about black masses and such things, but I have also heard the General is a Freemason, a Rosicrucian, and a Buddhist, so I don't know which to believe."

"It's all true. Beliefs are like radio stations to him; whenever he gets bored he changes the frequency. I will tell you something that may surprise even you," Roberto said, adopting his confidential whisper. "There is an actual shrine to Noriega at the foot of Mount Fuji."

"A shrine to Noriega in Japan?"

"I know it sounds bizarre. Some exotic Buddhist cult Tony has become associated with, called the Value Creation Society—they put up a statue to him and they worship him or something like that. I think Tony must have given them a fortune. In return, they awarded him the title 'shogun.' He actually thinks he is a reincarnated spirit of some thirteenth-century warrior monk."

"Well, I am surprised," the Nuncio confessed.

"The things some people believe!" Roberto exclaimed, shaking his head.

"Yes, it's continually amazing," said the Nuncio, watching Roberto scrape the sides of his cantaloupe for some additional bit of nourishment. "I hope your yoga and fruit prove equal to the task."

"I'm still going to need your help, Monseñor. Certainly the Church is opposed to satanic practices. I'm only asking that you act in the interest of your own faith."

"Exactly how do you see my role?" the Nuncio asked reluctantly.

"I think you should perform an exorcism on Tony."

Whatever appetite the Nuncio had enjoyed now vanished. "I'm afraid that such a ceremony is completely outside my field of expertise. I've never even seen it performed. Moreover, these days even in Panama the liability laws are such that you can't just go off exorcising people without their permission. I imagine one would need legal releases with witnesses and notaries and all that—I wouldn't even know where to begin."

"But you are a priest!" Roberto protested. "Aren't you interested in the man's soul?"

"It's true I am a priest, but my primary role in Panama is to serve as ambassador. I represent the official interests of the Church. I'm not here to minister. It wouldn't be very diplomatic for the papal nuncio to exorcise the leader of the country to which he is assigned."

Roberto sank back in his chair. "I think you underestimate the man we are dealing with, Monseñor. Unfortunately, I know him very well. We have been friends and competitors all of our lives. He's a wicked man, and a clever one. You and I should work together on this. Otherwise, each of us will have to face him alone."

"I'm afraid I really must decline," the Nuncio said firmly. But to himself he admitted that Roberto's final words had an ominous ring of truth to them.

I CAN'T BELIEVE you are doing this, Mama," Carmen said to her elegant, slender, and wonderfully well preserved mother, who was installed at the head of the baronial dining table like a queen. Señora Olga Ramona Morales was a middle-class shopkeeper—she operated a women's clothing store in the Bella Vista district—but her royal bearing boosted her social status, and her clientele included most of the female aristocrats in the country. Her customers depended on her for advice not only about fashion but also about food, romance, and even politics, since it was well known that La Olga had her fingerprints everywhere. She was widely feared because of her genius for social etiquette, which kept even her richest clients in a dependent and slightly cowed condition.

"I am simply acknowledging the facts of a relationship you choose to hide," said Señora Morales. She glanced significantly at the other end of the table, where Carmen's erstwhile boyfriend, Tony Noriega, studied the array of silverware at his place setting with a knitted brow.

"For the first time in three years, I'm not hiding anything!"

Carmen cried. "It's over! I'm free! I don't know why you're trying to bring it back to life!"

"I am only acting in your interest."

"My interest is to have an ordinary life—husband, children. To be respected in society," Carmen said. "But as long as I am Tony's woman, forget it! I'm radioactive."

"What we are talking about is more important than social respect," Señora Morales chided.

"Mama! You don't believe that! Why would you say such a thing? What has he paid you?"

The nostrils in Señora Morales's fine nose flared like a wild mare's. "Do you think I would betray my daughter for any price in the world?"

Actually, Tony had promised her a seat on the Canal Commission, an incredibly lucrative partnership for both of them.

A servant with an expression of a beaten dog entered with a soup tureen and ladled a serving into Tony's bowl.

"He's a married man!" Carmen protested. "You've told me this yourself countless times. Do you want me to be a kept woman for the rest of my life?"

"Believe me, chère, love is too rare a thing to be traded away for"—she waved her hand in the air—"social convention. What do you care about the opinion of the people in the cafés? They are only speaking out of envy." Señora Morales looked down at Tony, who had picked up the wrong spoon for the soup. "How do you like the vichyssoise, General?"

"It's cold," he said in a puzzled voice.

"Yes," she agreed. "Perhaps the General would like some chives." Señora Morales nodded to Carmen, who gave her a brief outdone look but then proceeded to pick up a small pot of chives on the silken tablecloth and snip the tops into Tony's soup. Tony smiled at her gratefully.

"Señora Morales," Tony said, his voice heavy with emotion, "I wish sometimes that I had had a mother and she would have been like you."

With that, Carmen burst into tears and ran out of the room.

Tony and Señora Morales watched her go, then returned to their soup. He stole a surreptitious glance at her figure, which was still admirably formed. Señora Morales caught him staring and smiled. There might even be a bonus in this arrangement, Tony realized.

CHAPTER 8

"Welcome to the workers' paradise," Tony muttered to Felicidad as they entered José Martí Airport in Havana, a squalid spot half-lit by yellowed lamps and stinking of overflowing urinals. A chorus of children greeted them, singing "The Third World Debt Must Be Canceled." When they stepped outside the terminal doors, souvenir vendors swarmed toward them bearing pirated Gloria Estefan CDs and mother-of-pearl key chains imprinted with the image of Che Guevara. A mob of illegal cab-drivers stood in front of some of the oldest American cars Tony had ever seen, and a dozen fabulous hookers screamed for attention. One day, these people will be the richest people in Cuba, Tony thought. Perhaps they already are.

A gray-haired soldier came to greet them and escort them to the Protocol House, a former Soviet Army resort on the Bay of Pigs. The place was even grimmer than Tony had expected. Tony and Felicidad sat by themselves in a cavernous room, waited upon by three grinning bartenders. Furious oversized portraits of the heroes of the revolution stared down at them in sullen admonishment. Outside, the surf crashed and crashed against the

111

beach, like Time pounding itself on the forehead, wondering what it had forgotten.

"Tony, you are drinking too much," Felicidad warned quietly as he signaled the waiters for another Cuba Libre. "Do you want Fidel to see you like this?"

"It's the custom," he assured her.

"You've got a duty to your country to behave yourself," she said sternly.

"You know, you shouldn't concern yourself with matters of state, Fela. Fidel will not be here until midnight. He always keeps his visitors waiting, that's his style. I know very well what he's up to. Nothing will be accomplished tonight. He's probably out enjoying himself, expecting that we'll become nervous and impatient. That we'll lose confidence. Then, when we think he's forgotten us, he'll walk in full of apologies about the official duties that detained him. It's an old strategy—I've used the same tricks myself. There will be no actual meeting until tomorrow, believe me." Tony turned to the bartenders. *"Viva Cuba!"* he said.

"Viva!" they cried in unison.

"Viva Fidel!" said Tony.

"Viva!" they said, less enthusiastically.

"You see," Tony said. "It's a very simple country."

Three hours later, just as Tony had predicted, the doors banged open loudly, and Fidel burst in, flanked by a half-dozen revolutionary bureaucrats wearing chinos and Izod shirts—the new Cuba. Tony was snoozing noisily in his chair.

"Comrade!" Fidel said.

Tony startled awake and stood up groggily, his tie askew and his shirttail ballooning over the back of his pants. He made a frantic attempt to straighten up before Fidel crushed him in a bear hug. Tony disappeared into his wiry gray beard.

"Forgive me, my dear friends," Fidel said. His uniform was green and crisp. "I have been speaking to the cane farmers. It seems whenever I open my mouth, it takes several hours to get it closed again."

"We were simply enjoying your hospitalality," Tony said, realizing that hadn't come out quite right.

"Apparently so," said Fidel. "And now, Señora Noriega, will you excuse the men for a while? We have business to discuss."

Fidel put his arm around Tony and escorted him out of the room and down a dismal corridor to a small stale conference room with a poker table and a peeling poster of Mao on one wall.

"Please join me in a cigar," Fidel said as he steered Tony to his seat.

"Actually, I don't smoke."

"Ah, well, this is not the same thing as smoking," Fidel assured him, pressing a Cohiba the size of a catfish into Tony's hand. "And besides, it would be a favor to me to be able to witness your discovery of this great Cuban treasure."

Tony reluctantly accepted the light.

"And so, Manuel Antonio, it is good that you requested to see me." Fidel exhaled a huge toxic cloud of blue smoke. "For some time I've been concerned about what is transpiring in your country. I've wondered why you haven't come to me until now. I have thought about this many times."

Tony coughed and held his cigar as far away as possible. "I hope I didn't offend you, Fidel."

Fidel laughed, and then everyone else began laughing, so Tony laughed as well.

"You know, Manuel Antonio, it's okay to give offense if you offend the right persons. Correct?"

The functionaries in the room nodded.

"You offend me, and it is fine, because I forgive you. I know you. You are a little stupid, and I take this into account. You offend the Americans. In my opinion, it is good policy to offend the Americans. Up to a point. But Tony, you never offend the Colombians. These are serious people. You make a big problem—for Panama, for Colombia, for everybody. And for me. Because the Colombians are very helpful."

"That's why I have come to see you, Fidel. If you will only speak to them for me . . ."

"Haven't I spoken to them already, many times? Unlike you, they consult me, they take my views into account. Unfortunately I must report that they are inclined to take drastic action. They believe that you sold them out to the Americans. They gave you five million dollars for protection, and then you let the Americans confiscate their most modern processing plant—without even the courtesy of telling them in advance."

"Fidel, it was an accident! Some Indian fishermen saw helicopters flying into the jungle and told the police. The Americans found out, they tracked the helicopters by satellite—there was nothing I could do!"

"You made a deal. You took the money."

"I know, I know, it was a mistake. I've made a lot of mistakes. In fact, I've decided to get out of the drug business completely."

Fidel looked at him incredulously. One of the bureaucrats tittered impolitely.

"You are on a one-way street, my friend," said Fidel. "You cannot turn around now."

Tony began to feel sick, from either the smoke or the implications, he wasn't certain which. "What should I do?" he asked helplessly.

"I recommend a change of identity," Fidel replied.

Tony grinned sickly, unsure how to respond. Was Fidel joking?

"Oh, Tony, Tony, Tony!" Fidel said, shaking his head with pitying affection. "Okay, we understand each other. Perhaps I can speak to someone. Make certain assurances."

"Yes, of course—anything! Anything—within reason."

"The return of their investment," said Fidel.

"Five million dollars?" Tony said weakly.

"*That* they gave you for protection, and how little you honored it. It was the premium on their insurance, as the capitalists would say. No, their loss was much greater than that. The plant, the machines, the helicopters, the loss of production time, the inconvenience of the men you imprisoned, the necessity of building a new facility—all this amounts to a billion dollars, in their opinion."

Tony started to speak, but the words wouldn't come—all those zeroes had formed a traffic jam in his mouth.

LATER THAT EVENING Fidel relaxed with his arm around Felicidad at the nearly empty Copacabana. A French tour group divided its attention between Fidel and the bare-breasted showgirls onstage. They were surely the most beautiful girls in the world, but everyone in the club was openly staring at Fidel. After more than thirty years in power, he was still an object of obsession in his own country. Tony thought he himself must have become completely invisible. No one knew who he was, or cared—even his wife had spent the entire meal gazing at Fidel adoringly. Tony was shocked to see her relaxing into the old guerrilla's embrace.

Strobe lights gave the whole scene a hypnotic silent-movie effect. Blinkety blinkety blinkety.

"It's the only way we bring in hard currency," Fidel said as a way of explaining the decadence of the nightclub—and the prices. Another bottle of French wine manifested itself on the table, adding five hundred dollars to the Cuban trade deficit.

"Your husband should bring you to Cuba more often," Fidel said. "Next time, I will take you to the Sierra Maestra. I will show you where the revolution began."

"I love the mountains," Felicidad said breathlessly.

Fidel cast a triumphant look at Tony, who sank further into obscurity. An amazingly beautiful showgirl with her breasts resting on a nest of flamingo feathers passed by their table and put a familiar arm on Fidel's shoulder. Without even looking at her, he brushed it away. Felicidad pressed against him a tiny bit more.

"I'm worried about you, Manuel Antonio," Fidel said in his now familiar, gratingly avuncular tone. "Politically speaking, you're on an anthill. You need some protection for yourself, you know what I mean?"

"The Colombians may have powerful resources, but I have an entire army to protect me."

"I'm not speaking of the Colombians. If they want you to disappear, your army will mean nothing to them. I'm talking about the Americans. Soon they are supposed to turn over the canal to the first Panamanian administrator."

"Of course, the first day of nineteen-ninety."

"And you believe they will do this?"

"Why not? They have already given us authority over most of the zone. Everything is proceeding according to the treaties. To the letter."

"I am telling you as a fact, as long as you are in power, the Americans will never let the canal out of their hands. If I were you, I'd be watching my backside."

Tony knew that Fidel was insane, but he did have a paranoiac's genius for seeing patterns that others might miss. For instance, the little complication with Senator Helms might turn out to be serious. That prosecutor in Florida with the drug indictment—could that be a part of a larger conspiracy against him? And yet Reagan had treated him with respect, consulting with him on appointments and even inviting him to White House dinners. And now Bush was campaigning to succeed Reagan in the Oval Office—George Herbert Walker Bush, who had been Tony's paymaster when he was head of the CIA. Bush knew better than anyone what a friend the United States had in Tony Noriega. All in all, Tony thought his relations with the United States were excellent.

But the canal was too valuable for the Americans to simply give away. Tony realized that he had always secretly believed that the treaties were a ruse, a stalling tactic, and that when the time came the Americans would invent some excuse to dishonor them. Certainly that is what he would do in their place.

"I'm telling you this as a friend, but also as an interested party," Fidel continued. "If the Americans block the transfer of the canal, they can use it against us. Without the canal, Cuba is lost. Our trade with Asia—it's over. The sugar industry dies, then we die as well. For this reason, I'm going to give you some free advice. Who will the Americans turn to if they decide Noriega must go?"

For the sake of argument, Tony considered this. No doubt Roberto had his own contacts with the CIA, and if the agency chose to execute a quick 1950s-style coup, that could be easily done, especially while Tony was out of the country (like now). Nor was assassination out of the question. The kill order had already been given once, early in his career, when Nixon demanded that Tony be "totally and completely immobilized"—a phrase that still resounded in Tony's recurring nightmares. And how many times had they tried to kill Fidel? By poisoning his cigars! Tony knew enough about the "new" CIA to realize that there were plenty of dirty tricks still in their bag. They just covered themselves a lot better these days.

"I suppose they would groom some young colonel," Tony said, trying to think realistically, "some power-hungry egotist they can control."

Fidel shook his head gravely. "You're out of date, my friend. Look at what they did in Nicaragua: they used the middle class to subvert the people's revolution. No, the gringos are not interested in the military anymore. In fact, they are trying to wipe Latin America clean of its armies. They want to turn us all into Puerto Rico—little American subdivisions and unarmed tourist resorts." Fidel snorted. "The first item on their agenda will be to eliminate the Panama Defense Forces. Then, even if they actually turn over the canal, you will be completely unable to defend it. You will have the Americans always. They will still control the canal, but they won't have to pay for it. To achieve this, they will turn the middle class against you. They will prop up the newspapers and the business interests. They will finance candidates to run against your men. All this will be done in the sacred name of

117

democracy. But the real goal is to eliminate the Panamanian army and control the canal forever. And to do that," Fidel said, stabbing Tony in the chest with his brutal forefinger, "they must first get rid of General Manuel Antonio Noriega."

The clarity of this fiendish vision struck Tony with overpowering force. It fit with trends he could already see emerging—little stirrings of complaint in the press (which up till now he had graciously tolerated), a bit too much grand talk in the Union Club among the white asses who wanted to run their own candidates, and most of all, the suspiciously obstacle-free progression of the canal treaties toward the ultimate day of Panamanian control. It all came into focus through Fidel's paranoiac lens.

"He's right, Tony," Felicidad said unhelpfully. "You have placed yourself in a dangerous position. You need to protect yourself—and your family."

The strobe lights were giving Tony a migraine.

"Even if this were the American design, which I doubt," Tony said unconvincingly, "how can I oppose it?"

"Have you ever seen a dog try to eat a toad?" asked Fidel. "He cannot do it. He puts his mouth around it, then he spits it out. You know why this is? Because the toad is poison. One taste and the dog knows he cannot swallow this thing or he will die. You must do the same as the toad, my friend. You must make yourself indigestible."

"Listen to him, Tony," Felicidad advised.

"So how do I become indigestible?"

Fidel tugged on his beard in an impressive display of cogitation. "Well, one thought does occur. It's the same as I suggested to the comandantes in Nicaragua. Organize the poor to be on your side. This is my suggestion. Make yourself their hero. Train them. Give them arms. Let everybody know, if the Americans invade, the people of the streets will rise! *And they will kill the bourgeoisie!* The people—they will be your poison!"

"Beautiful," said Felicidad.

The waiter brought a silver platter containing the bill and set it in front of Tony. Tony stared at the sum in disbelief.

"The *advice* is free," said Fidel.

GENERAL DELMAR HONEYCUTT pinned the last ribbon on his uniform and sized himself up in the full-length mirror. The newly appointed leader of the U.S. Southern Command was an exceedingly large man—at six foot seven, he had had to receive a special waiver to enlist in the military. As a tight end at West Point, he had broken scoring records that had stood for fifty years. He came out of Vietnam with a chestful of ribbons, medals, and oakleaf clusters that might have seemed outlandish on a man whose chest was not so massive. With his sun-bronzed skin, General Honeycutt sometimes looked more like a larger-than-life, Soviet-style statue of himself than a middle-aged divorced man with a bleeding ulcer and credit-card debt who had been shunted off to Central America to guard a big ditch.

"Give me that line again," he said to Lieutenant Cheever, his fussy assistant.

"The 'bridge to two cultures' thing?" Cheever was brushing the lint from the general's expansive shoulders. "You've already been over it four times, General. I'm sure you know it by heart. Anyway, you'll have a TelePrompTer."

"Makes a better show if you look spontaneous, like you're thinking it up as you go along," said the general. "Remember that when you're writing my speeches in the future. Nothing too pretty. Rough it up a little."

"I'll keep it in mind, sir."

"I want everybody to know that we mean business here. We're tough, but we're on their side. Like the cop on the corner. Friendly, but there for a good reason."

"I'm sure they'll understand that, sir."

"What's the president's name again?"

"Delvalle, sir."

"They change them with the seasons here."

"Yes, sir."

"Am I ready?"

"You're ready, sir."

"Then let's do it."

T HE PARADE GROUND AT SOUTHCOM was crammed with Panamanian officials and American military brass watching the U.S.
troops march in review before their new commander. The elite of
Panamanian society had fought for the tickets in the grandstand,
eager to see the panoply of lethal gizmos that rolled out of the
hangars and caverns of Fort Clayton. The crowd was at once
cheery and ironic, like schoolchildren watching a faculty play.
Overhead, a modest squadron of F-16s roared past, trailed by a
wing of Tomcat fighters from the USS *Forrestal*, which happened
to be in port. In truth, there was only a modest representation of
advanced weaponry stationed in Panama, since the real danger
to the canal, in the way of a military threat, was thought to be
very small. Most of the armament was left over from the Vietnam
War. Nonetheless, it impressed the natives, General Honeycutt
believed. He sat next to President and Mrs. Delvalle and patiently explained what they were seeing. "That's the Sheridan
tank, ma'am, more maneuverable than its high-tech cousins.
Still a formidable fighting machine." "They *are* neat little mis-
siles, aren't they, sir? Nuclear-tipped." And so on. He always rel-
ished the splendor of men and arms on display.

General Honeycutt was so absorbed in the spectacle that he
failed to notice the stirring in the crowd that marked the well-
past-fashionable entrance of General Noriega. Tony arrived with
his usual air of ownership, his gold buttons glinting, his ceremonial medals and his *Légion d'honneur* practically on fire in the
tropical sunlight. Around his neck he wore the symbol of the
supreme military commander, a heavy silver medallion inscribed
with the image of the Panamanian eagle, surrounded by the in-

signia of each of the country's military units. His ski-slope hat rose to a peak, with the gold seal of state on the front and gold laurel leaves on the bill. And under the hat: Tony's hooded, viperous eyes and pitted, implacable face.

When the air show had concluded, leaping in an instant from the Atlantic to the Pacific over the inconsiderable spit of land that constituted Panama, General Honeycutt approached the unshaded podium. To his great annoyance, the TelePrompTer screen was blank. He shot a glance to the communications specialist first class who was manning the equipment. The suicidal look on the young man's face amply expressed the situation. The general tapped his breast pocket, realizing that there was no copy of his speech there, either. Goddamn lucky thing that he'd read it before he got into this spot, he reflected, choking down the panic of public speaking that two years of attending Toastmasters Club meetings at Fort Hood had failed to overcome.

The general looked into the grandstand, hoping to recapture the long list of names that he was supposed to officially recognize. President Mountainous? Was that it? The general remembered associating the president's name with a geologic feature. Remember the image and the name would spring to mind: that was the theory. But he'd forgotten which image he was supposed to remember.

The crowd was beginning to look at him curiously. "Welcome," he finally said, "or perhaps I should say, 'Thank you,' for it is you who have made me feel welcome." The general relaxed a bit. He'd done this before. "I particularly want to thank"—he made a stab at it—"President Valley and his lovely wife . . ." General Honeycutt caught a concerned look on Lieutenant Cheever's face and quickly moved on. Next to the president were two vice presidents, one named Manuel Solís Palma and another whose name was completely blank in the general's mind. He couldn't very well acknowledge the first without the second, so he merely thanked "the two sterling gentlemen who stand beside the president in everything he does, vice presidents not only in name but in deed." What did that mean? The general began to realize that his steering was gone and the speech was taking on its own wild momentum. "As I gaze upon the faces in the grandstand, I see—what? You know what I see, ladies and gentlemen? I see the faces of Panama's cabinet, men and women who will lead this country into the next century. Their names—too many to mention—will one day be recorded in the textbooks. Their names will be on the streets and avenues of this great city. Schools will be named after them! I see the judges, the judges, yes—sadly enough, they often labor in anonymity, but surely their names will be in the lawbooks, you can count on that! I see the members of the Canal Commission. Boy, there's an important group of guys! Let's give them a round of applause!" He was really sailing now, completely rudderless, trying to avoid the puzzled expressions of the dignitaries in the crowd, who obediently applauded the flustered commissioners. "Priests!" the general cried. "I see the representatives of the Church here today, and I want to say that part of what makes this country great is religion! So, lots of priests. When the roll is called up yonder, you can bet that there will be a lot of priests on it! I say 'priests,' but I don't mean to exclude representatives of other denominations. Catholicism is still a fine religion. Family values kind of thing. I know President Reagan relates to it, or I mean them, the values that I was referring to. So, summing up: good people, good values, Panama is a bridge between them, and as I think about it, we are all on that bridge of life . . ."

Tony listened to the mysterious speech with growing incredulity. Obviously there were significant signals being sent out—the occasion demanded it—but the most important one dawned on him, as it had on every other Panamanian in the crowd, with the force of a thunderbolt: the Americans are not recognizing Tony Noriega! People were shifting uncomfortably in their chairs. There was a perceptible movement away from Tony, a united leaning away, as if he had leprosy. In a few enigmatic sentences the huge American officer had signaled that Tony was contaminated, expelled, cast into the non-American darkness.

Fidel was right, Tony thought savagely; he would have to make himself indigestible.

CHAPTER 9

OLD PARR. Very Old Parr. Very much very Old Parr. Every other sip, an enlisted man appeared from the shadows with a freshener to keep Tony's drink maximally stiff.

Tony was holding court at his round table in the back of La Playita, the private club owned by César Rodríguez and some of his Colombian pals. Ari Nachman was there, and Dr. Demos, Tony's psychiatrist and political pollster. Several girls from Miami who specialized in consolation rubbed Tony's knees. But with every drink, Tony could feel himself becoming more dangerous.

"Tony, why are you taking this personally?" César asked. "The Americans know they can't do business in Panama without you."

"He even thanked the priests!" Nachman said in disbelief.

"Maybe he needs a little welcome party," said Tony. "A demonstration of the people's righteous anger."

"I know what you're thinking, Tony, but you should be careful," said César. "Don't pull the trigger right away." César was drinking White Russians as a tonic for his new ulcer.

"What the Americans did was very clever," Dr. Demos said. "If you make too big a stink, they can say you are paranoid."

This point really rankled Tony. He had to give the American general credit. Not mentioning Tony's name had been far more damning than if he had singled him out and criticized him. This way, the general made his point while giving Tony nothing to reply to. That was part of his humiliation, that he had been so cleverly handled, with a subtlety rarely associated with American diplomacy.

"I think they are only playing with you," Nachman offered. "If you give them a little something, they'll remember who they are dealing with. Tell them what Fidel had for dinner—they'll jack off to that."

"More arms to the Contras," said César.

"Maybe I'll give them a few names," said Tony. "People in the drug business. It's like catnip to them."

Frozen smiles all around the table.

Tony turned to one of the girls, a sophomore in telephone marketing at Miami-Dade Junior College. "And you, my mercenary little friend, what would you advise me?"

"Fuck 'em, Tony," she said eagerly. "Fuck 'em right and left."

Tony grinned. He looked across the room, where Roberto was sitting alone. The sight of Roberto's sly eyes peeking over his champagne glass made Tony's blood pressure hop.

"Look at him," Tony said. "He's spying on us."

"Roberto's gone loco, haven't you heard?" said Nachman. "They say he found some guru who made him stop having sex. He became completely insane."

"Technically," said Dr. Demos, "I believe he's suffering from delusions of persecution springing from type-two schizophrenia."

"Can you believe it?" said César. "And just when the Miss Universe pageant comes to town."

"The most beautiful women in the world, and Roberto decides to become a virgin again!" Nachman marveled at the mysteriousness of that.

"Hey, Roberto!" Tony called out, silencing the rest of the room. "Do the Americans know you are a communist?"

Roberto looked stricken, but he quickly put up a brave smile. "What communist drinks Dom Pérignon?" he asked lightly.

"Dom Pérignon? It's for cunts!"

Tony's companions laughed, but they were uneasy. Everyone else was dead quiet.

"Waitress—hey, beauty," Tony said, "bring Roberto a man's drink. Johnny Walker—*Red* Label."

Tony laughed as Roberto walked out of the room. For a moment he simply sat staring down the dress of the future telephone marketer. Then he sighed. "Now is the time to teach the Americans a terrible lesson."

"So what are you going to do?" Nachman asked. "You can't make them too mad, you know."

Tony drained off the rest of his scotch. "Tony Noriega is a good friend, but he is also a terrible enemy," he said. "The U.S., it is like a monkey on a chain. All you do is play the music, and the monkey performs."

"Well, the U.S. is also like an elephant," César said cautiously. "It takes time to get him to move, but when he does, it's a heavy move."

THE EXTERIOR OF the Atlapa Convention Center was bathed in floodlights when Tony arrived with his retinue of bodyguards. In the vast hall, waiters carrying trays of lobster wove through the tables and potted palms. The reflections of the many-faceted jewels on the bosoms of Panamanian society shown like a galaxy of infinite value. When the national anthem concluded, a beaming President Delvalle, wearing a tuxedo and the red, white, and blue sash of his office, approached the podium. "Tonight, the eyes of many nations are on Panama," he said, "as we go about the serious business of choosing the most beautiful woman in the world. Welcome, ladies and gentlemen, to the Miss Universe pageant."

Tony noticed Pablo Escobar entertaining a half-dozen bankers at the table closest to the stage. Escobar was disconcertingly at ease, and when he glanced up and caught Tony staring at him, he winked. This gesture was so threatening that, despite himself, Tony gasped. That Escobar has balls, he thought admiringly. They might become friends if one of them didn't kill the other first. He signaled to his bodyguards and walked quickly out of the crowded room, down the escalators, down another flight of stairs, to a labyrinthine complex of subterranean walkways that connected the convention center to the subbasement of the Marriott across the street. His grim-faced bodyguards walked on either side of him, and a pair of PDF lieutenants raced ahead like hounds, opening doors to various rooms.

"What's going on?" asked a busboy when one of the soldiers poked into the kitchen.

"Where's the reception area for the contestants?" the officer demanded.

"We're not supposed to say."

The soldier pulled the boy into the hallway. His eyes widened when he recognized Tony. The boy quickly pointed to a double doorway at the end of the corridor. "But what's going on?" he asked under his breath.

"The General is going to fuck Miss U.S.A.," the soldier informed him.

At the end of the corridor was the Venetian ballroom. A policeman at the entrance was peeking through the crack in the doors when the approaching footsteps captured his attention. He quickly jumped to attention. The bodyguards pushed him aside and burst into the room.

Two hundred of the most beautiful women in the world stood there like wood nymphs. Short and tall, dark and light, intense and silly, husky and shrill: variety, wonderful female variety, offered itself in ball gowns.

Swarming around the nubile contestants was a fawning mass of handlers and cosmeticians and fashion consultants and relatives and reporters and agents and personal trainers and ass-patting pageant officials. Tony wandered through them like a hunter, his eyes seeking a single quarry, shoving out of his mind the appetizing distractions that arose at every point of the compass.

Suddenly there she was, tall, blond, strikingly beautiful if a bit horsy, her sash cutting a hypotenuse between her ample midwestern breasts. Half a dozen photographers were circling and firing at the scene of the highly favored Miss U.S.A. talking to Miss U.S.S.R., a staged event meant to echo recent developments at the summit talks. The Russian contestant was trim and muscular, standing a bit on tiptoe to match the statuesque American. Both of them were talking to a third party—an amusing third party who made them laugh and blush, a third party Tony recognized with an abrupt start: Roberto.

"Oh, General!" Roberto said in alarm as he noticed Tony hissing in his ear.

"General?" said Miss U.S.A.

Tony now took her in completely. She was a type who particularly appealed to him: a green-eyed blonde with luminous, downy skin. A small gold cross lounged in the billows of her breasts.

"Welcome to Panama, Miss U.S.A. and Miss U.S.S.R.," Tony said, offering a little Prussian, heel-snapping bow. "If there is anything you desire, it is yours."

Miss U.S.A. gave him an interested look. "You must be the fella in charge," she concluded.

"Excuse me very much," said Roberto, hastily introducing Tony to the two contestants, who were obviously flattered to be meeting "Panama's beloved leader," as Roberto graciously described him.

"Pleased to meetcha," said Miss U.S.A., pumping Tony's limp hand several times with shocking vigor. "I'm Brandi Thistlewhite."

"Brandi—such an intoxicating name."

"Yeah," she agreed. "Roberto said the same thing."

Tony turned to Roberto and grinned ferociously. Roberto abruptly excused himself.

"See ya later, Mr. Ambassador," Brandi said as Roberto rushed away.

"My name, Tatyana Chernyshevskaya," said Miss U.S.S.R., seizing Tony's hand as if it were a Baltic republic.

Faced with the towering actuality of Brandi Thistlewhite, whose disinfected sexuality presented no obvious approach, Tony nearly lost heart. The entire enterprise suddenly seemed hopeless; she was a fortress of nonchalance—uninterested, unavailable, and blandly incorruptible.

"My God, these American women!" Tony finally exclaimed. "They are so clean!"

"Well, thank you, I guess," said Brandi, "but I don't think I'm any cleaner than the other girls. I mean, everybody washed, I'm pretty sure."

"Still, somehow you seem cleaner. And your teeth, I think you have never had a cavity. Is this true?"

"They got sealed when I lost my baby teeth."

Brandi's lips demurely closed the curtain on her gleamingly perfect incisors, but not before Tatyana cast them a covetous glance.

"I always feel, when I meet a beautiful American woman, that she has just been created, that God has just made her fully adult, like Eve, innocent and fresh, with the dew of creation still upon her," said Tony.

"You make me feel a little self-conscious," Brandi said through her pursed lips.

"May I ask what is your special talent?" said Tony.

"Birdsongs. It's a little strange," she said apologetically.

"Birds?"

"Yeah, you know, like—" Brandi suddenly emitted a loud croaking noise like the sound of a rusty nail being prized out of an old board.

"Toucan," said Tony.

"Right," she said in surprise. "The keel-billed toucan! I'm majoring in ornithology at Ohio State."

"I, too, have an interest in birds. Tell me, what noise does the falcon make during intercourse?"

"Pardon me?"

"To me, this is the noblest bird of all," Tony said, turning slightly to include the vixen-eyed Miss U.S.S.R. "When the falcons make love, it is in the air—*plunging*." He illustrated the point by clapping his hands together and swooping them down in a headlong fluttering dive.

"That may be true of chimney swifts," Brandi said doubtfully.

"And if the male does not climax before the ground arrives—" Tony smashed his fist into his palm.

"Is very beautiful, this story," said Tatyana.

"And what is your special talent?"

"I am contortionist."

Tony had to steady himself.

"Have you met all the judges?" Tony asked Brandi. He was edging toward his central proposition. "The two Panamanians are close friends of mine."

"Oh, wow, thanks. But we're really not supposed to fraternize. People might get the wrong idea."

"Yes, but it is another matter when the supreme leader of a country takes an interest in your welfare."

Brandi's eyes narrowed into tiny emeralds. "We had to sign all these documents. They pretty much frown on girls having anything to do with the judges."

"In my opinion, is okay if it is the custom of the country," said Tatyana.

But Tony had one last trick. "You appear to be interested in my complexion," he said cruelly.

"No!" Brandi cried. "I mean, oh, my God, was I staring? I'm sorry!"

"You are charming when you blush," he said. "Look how red you become."

"Oh, God, I'm so embarrassed. And usually I'm not like this. I mean, I volunteer in the state school, so I've seen it all, if you know what I mean."

"You know the story of Beauty and the Beast?" said Tony. "There is some universal human truth in this childhood fable."

"For sure," Brandi said desperately.

"This beast, he was not such a bad fellow inside," said Tatyana.

"I agree," said Tony. "And it makes me wonder: why do people think that beautiful people are all so good and ugly people are evil? Tell me, Miss U.S.A., do you think I am a wicked man?"

"You've been perfectly nice to me."

"I am glad to hear this, but many in your country say I am almost a devil. I think it is because they don't know me. They only see this face."

"That's so unfair," Brandi said fervently. "And by the way, you shouldn't think that just because a person is beautiful on the outside that she is, like, holy or something. You should see how some of these gals behave! I think there's a few of them that would kill their own mothers to win this thing."

"But still, you are on one side of my face and I am on the other. To make the journey across, from the beautiful to the ugly, it is asking too much. No one can expect that Beauty will sleep with the Beast by her own choice. In real life, the Beast sleeps alone. It is his fate."

"Is that really true?" asked Brandi. "I'd think a guy like you, with his own country and all, could pretty much have his pick."

"It has happened," Tony conceded. "Many women come to me. But after a while, you see what they are up to. They do not come because of who I am. They come because of what they want. They don't see me. They see power. They see money. They see their dreams coming true. Because in Panama I can give them anything they want. It's a paradox, isn't it? I am like the genie in the bottle. Women make wishes on me. But no one gives the genie his own wish."

"And what is this wish?" asked Miss U.S.S.R.

"That just once in my life a woman would come to me because she really wants to be with me, because she sees my soul instead of my face."

Brandi looked a bit distant and troubled. "This conversation sure has gotten personal. I mean, I'm real sorry if I was staring at your complexion. But, you know, we've just met, and you're like the head of a country and I'm a junior in college. So, I don't know where you're going with this, is what I'm saying."

"What he says is he wants love, like anyone else," said Tatyana. "In Russia, we understand this. Does not matter, old and young, beautiful and ugly. Matters only that two souls recognize each other. Even Stalin, he was an ugly man, but a great lover. He fathered many Russian children."

Tony felt his resolve wash away in this tide of Old World wisdom. Besides, there was more than one way to accomplish his goal. He would just have to learn to be more flexible. He had a powerful feeling that Miss U.S.S.R. could teach him something about that.

THE PARTY GUESTS at Roberto's powder blue mansion in Golf Heights were still gossiping wildly about the unexpected triumph of Miss U.S.S.R. in the Miss Universe pageant.

"Rita told me that Tony took the Russian girl on a joyride in *Panama One*."

"How would Rita know?"

"She is the cousin of Tony's pilot's mother."

"Some say he uses the plane to engage in exotic sexual practices."

"In the air itself?"

"Everyone agrees the American girl was far prettier."

"Perhaps this is the reason the Americans have begun to investigate the narcos in Panama."

"Tony should have let her win. He will ruin business for everybody."

"Have you read the *New York Times*? On the front page they say he is responsible for Hugo's death."

The Nuncio paused at this last conversation. He, too, had been surprised by the unanticipated change in American foreign policy toward Noriega, which was reinforced in the article by Seymour Hersh blatantly accusing him of running drugs and laundering money and setting up Spadafora's murder. People here generally assumed that the *Times* was the official organ of the American government. The Nuncio also knew that Hugo's relatives had been making frequent trips to Washington to talk to influential American politicians, but he found it inconceivable that the Americans would turn against their long-standing regional ally and reliable intelligence asset, particularly after the Americans had supported far more appalling and repressive regimes in Guatemala and El Salvador.

These days the Nuncio worried all the time about Father Jorge, whose increasingly provocative sermons placed him in the center of the growing middle-class rebellion. The Nuncio had welcomed the opposition leaders into the nunciature, and so far their meetings had gone unremarked. Age had rendered him harmless, at least in the eyes of others. But Father Jorge was another matter. At every mass he invoked Hugo's name, keeping alive the shock and the anger over the assassination to his growing number of parishioners. One saw Hugo's face everywhere now; posters were pasted all over the city—even in the provinces, the Nuncio had heard. The country was smoldering, volcanic, more unstable than ever.

"Monseñor, can it be true that the Americans have ordered Tony to leave the country?" asked one of the partygoers, an attractive daughter of a shipping executive. "They say he is being investigated in the American Congress."

"If they had really turned against him, he'd be gone, wouldn't he?" said the smart young man who was with her. Like most Panamanians the Nuncio came in contact with, the young man had an exaggerated idea not only of the omnipotence of American power but also of the capacity of American intelligence and its interest in the affairs of other countries. America was an obsession with them, occupying spiritual territory that the Nuncio believed properly belonged to God.

"From what I hear, the Americans investigate scandals all the time," said the Nuncio. "They even put them on television. It seems to be some kind of national sport."

"But who would ever testify against him?" the young man demanded. "Nobody has the nerve."

"Even if someone did, it is unclear what difference it would make," the Nuncio observed. "It is one thing for the Americans to investigate their own politicians, but quite another for them to meddle in things they don't understand in a country where they have no jurisdiction. But then, quite extraordinary things have been happening these past several months. I've stopped trying to predict where they might lead."

The Nuncio detected a strange restlessness among the partygoers, who were mingling around the pool and the garden, drinking daiquiris and wine spritzers and gossiping with an intensity that no longer seemed fun. Many of them were dressed in the white garments that had become a characteristically ironic Panamanian political statement, meant to symbolize Tony's handkerchief—the one they hoped he would wave as he said good-bye to Panama permanently.

"Has anybody seen our host?" one of the guests asked.

People shook their heads no.

"I hope Roberto isn't ill."

"Perhaps the chastity has affected his immune system."

"Do you notice who is here? Everybody in the opposition."

"Shit! You don't think we're being set up?"

"Roberto? No, he's too crazy."

"But he is PDF all the same. And he has invited all the opposition—we are all rounded up in the same place."

As the partygoers chatted and fretted, a silence began at one end of the garden and spread like a shock wave around the poolside and the snack table and the gazebo under the mango trees where the drinks were being served. The Nuncio looked toward the source of the reaction. Roberto stood on the stairwell overlooking the pool house. The Nuncio had never seen him without a crisp military uniform and spit-shined shoes. Now he was barefoot and garbed in a sheer white robe. His wife stood beside him wearing a look of total chagrin.

"My friends, don't let the change in my appearance alarm you," Roberto said. "For some months I have been on a spiritual journey, and the clothes you see me in now are only an outward manifestation of my inner transformation. I know it must seem strange to you, but for the battle to come I am going to need the assistance of a higher power. A few minutes ago, I made a prayer to myself and to my guru, Sai Baba, whereupon I solemnly declared holy war on General Manuel Antonio Noriega."

Several people laughed and then abruptly stopped, unsure how to react. Was it a prank or had Roberto gone completely insane?

"My only weapon will be truth, but against the truth no evil man can stand for long," Roberto continued. "Do not fear for me, my friends. Sai Baba will protect me. His power is greater than any witchcraft. With your help and prayers, we will purify our country and restore civilian rule." Roberto put his hands together and bowed. Then he walked back up the stairs into his house and disappeared.

It was quiet for a moment, then the partygoers turned to each other and began speaking in urgent whispers, saying Roberto's mad, he's berserk, the whole country is a laughingstock. They were shocked and embarrassed but the fact that they were whispering betrayed their fear. The Nuncio wondered what was going to come of this bizarre turn of events. He had always thought that Roberto was vain and superstitious, but he never questioned that the man was also competent and clever. Possibly there was more to this gambit than mere religious mania. In any case, Roberto was right: the truth is a powerful weapon. The Nuncio just hoped it didn't blow up in his face.

BLESS ME, FATHER, for I have sinned."

Through the screen in the confessional, Father Jorge could distinguish the shadowed outline of a middle-aged military man. Lately, it was becoming unusual for soldiers to attend mass at Our Lady of Fatima because of Father Jorge's growing reputation as an antigovernment priest. But still, in this overly militarized society, nearly every mass had a smattering of uniforms among the pews, some representing families that had lived in this impoverished parish for generations.

He asked the officer to recite his sins, expecting the usual response. The rate of infidelity may not be as high in Latin America as popularly believed, but in Father Jorge's experience no Latin man ever missed the opportunity to talk about it. He sometimes thought that was the entire reason they came to confession. He usually dosed them with a novena.

"It's a very grave offense," said the smoke-scraped voice behind the screen.

"God forgives every sin that is truly repented."

After a pause the soldier said, "A murder was committed."

"Did you commit this murder?"

"No, Father. But I knew about it, and I think I could have prevented it."

"Why didn't you?"

"I was ordered to be silent about it."

"Did you take part in it in any way? In the planning or the execution?"

"Not in this one," the soldier said hesitantly.

"Were there others?"

"Yes," the soldier said. He was quiet for some time. "There was another man. Someone they described as an enemy of the state." Once again the soldier became quiet, and when he resumed, his voice was thick. "I wasn't part of the execution team, but I did gather information on this person. He was not a communist, as some have said. He was a brave man, a sincere patriot. I gathered the intelligence they needed to find him and kill him. That is the only way they could have planned this. I didn't know how they were going to use it. But this weighs very heavily on me."

Father Jorge wanted to know more, because he was convinced that the soldier was referring to the death of Hugo Spadafora. But the task of confession was only to assess the nature of the sin and prescribe an appropriate act of contrition. Moreover, it was obvious from the soldier's statements that he was an intelligence officer, so each of them was cautious about how to proceed. "These also were actions you were ordered to undertake?" the priest asked.

"Yes, and if I had refused to carry out my instructions, my career would have been finished—like that! I was afraid and so I obeyed the commands. But now I have the blood of two good men on my conscience."

"We all must take responsibility for our actions," Father Jorge said.

"Yes, I believe that, Father. But I have seen what happens to others who have tried to stand up—nothing is spared to make them regret their actions. I feared the consequences to myself and to my family if I resisted my superiors. Also, I am a soldier. It is part of my nature to obey my officers' command. And yet, as a Christian, I know that I will be judged for my behavior. My commanders will not take my place in hell."

Father Jorge was moved by the officer's moral awareness and his expressive understanding of his dilemma, but he also realized that the man was involved in evil of the highest order. "It's true that we often do things we know to be wrong just to be able to exist safely in the world, but Christ has called us to a higher duty," he finally said. "I ask you to pray on this. Ask Jesus to intercede for you. Open your heart to him and heartily repent of your sins."

"I have been praying, Father."

"And I will pray as well. But you must also refrain from any further sin to protect your immortal soul."

"This is what concerns me, Father. How can I do what you ask? I know that my soul is in peril. But what am I to do? I must follow orders, even if they are illegal or immoral. My children depend on me. I'm too old to start again. And I don't want to face the consequences of resistance."

"God requires us to be his servants every day. You can take encouragement from the fact that he will not ask of us something we cannot deliver. For every problem we face, there is a Christian solution that God provides. You must search your heart to understand what God wants of you. I am sure you will find a way to the right action. Indeed, you have already begun—just by making this confession you are opening your heart to his guidance. Rejoice in this and do not be afraid."

But when the soldier left, Father Jorge wondered about his own advice. What choice was there for such a man? He was caught up in a system of wickedness that was so total that it offered no obvious means of escape. Father Jorge worried and prayed about the situation until well after midnight and then slept poorly all night.

CHAPTER 10

THE MORGUE WAS on a small side street behind the Hospital Santo Tomás, a block away from the American embassy. The Nuncio had been passing it for years without ever realizing what it was, and as he waited in the outer office for the chief pathologist, he devoutly wished that he might have been permitted to continue in his ignorance. There were some tasks that he was simply not suited for. He was too ridiculous, sitting here in his brilliant white cassock and wearing a mask over his nose that the receptionist had provided him. Even in the outer office the odor of decay was frighteningly penetrating. The Nuncio tried to concentrate on the soap opera that was playing on the staticky television. There was a colored engraving of Jesus on the wall and a gallon jug of bleach on top of a file cabinet. An elderly couple were staring at him from the slumping couch across the narrow foyer. They were probably waiting to identify a dead relative. Perhaps he should make an offer to pray with them. He decided not.

Finally the pathologist appeared, a small man with a wavy black toupee. His name, Crespo, was printed on the breast pocket of his blue cotton scrub suit. "You are here to see Mitrotti, I understand," the pathologist said. "Very well, come on, they are bringing him out right now."

The morgue looked nothing like the gleaming and hygienic rooms that the Nuncio had seen on American television shows, where the dead were carefully tagged and filed in orderly spaces, like books on a shelf. Here the dead were in a state of arrested chaos. Instead of the individual drawers that the Nuncio expected, there was a large chilled room like a meat locker filled with undraped corpses dressed in the clothes they died in, many of them frozen in agonized contortions, twisting, resisting, eyes open, paralyzed screams on their mouths. A stiff, dead arm reached eerily into the air. Death seemed frightfully unpeaceful.

As they entered the examining room, an orderly wheeled in a gurney bearing the waxy corpse of Serafín Mitrotti. "We tried to clean him up a little before you came," Dr. Crespo apologized. "He was rather messy. As you see, he's been dead for several days."

The Nuncio tried not to breathe. He felt deeply embarrassed for Mitrotti to be seen in this appalling condition. Only a month before, he had seen him at the Union Club during his lunch with Roberto. The stinking corpse on the gurney was barely recognizable. His face was horribly battered. There were deep cuts on his forehead and arms.

"When did you receive him?" the Nuncio asked.

"He came yesterday from Penonomé. That is where the autopsy was performed."

"And they ruled it a suicide?"

Dr. Crespo grinned wryly. "May I ask what is your interest in this, Monseñor?"

"The family wishes to have a Christian burial, but the Church cannot sanction such a ceremony in the case of a self-murder. So I have been asked to examine the body and give an opinion."

"I am an atheist myself, so these matters are immaterial to

me. And I cannot believe this poor fellow has any further concerns."

"In this case, Doctor, I believe there is a political dimension as well."

Dr. Crespo shrugged. "Politics is another area that I try to avoid. In my business, you so often see the consequences."

The Nuncio did not doubt that statement. "I take it you knew Serafín."

"Everyone knew him. He was very brave, but perhaps a little foolish. One saw his name in the paper too often."

"So it would seem. Could any man have done this to himself?"

"If you are asking me for a professional opinion, then I will tell you that the cause of his death has already been officially established. He bled to death from self-inflicted wounds."

Obviously, Dr. Crespo did not want to be drawn into this affair, and yet the Nuncio felt inadequate to the task of overruling a medical decision. "Let us simply discuss the matter theoretically," he said.

"Theoretically?"

"As you know, we priests often deal with matters that are mysterious or even irrational. I suppose such things happen in your business as well."

"Sometimes," Dr. Crespo said cautiously.

"On those occasions, there may be some details that defy rational explanations. Such as why a man who intends to commit suicide would break his own nose."

"Yes," Dr. Crespo agreed. "It is a mystery."

"Also, these cuts around his head, wouldn't they have bled copiously? Would he then have been able to hurt himself in more profound ways? I would think he would have been in shock."

"Yes, it is especially peculiar given that no blood was actually discovered in the motel room where he was found."

"That is exceedingly strange."

"I would say it is practically a miracle," Dr. Crespo said with a strangely blank expression.

"I've always been interested in miracles, but I've never actually found one," said the Nuncio.

"Well, then, you may be curious about this as well." Dr. Crespo held up one of Mitrotti's mutilated arms. "This man cut his hands nearly off. Look, you can see the bones."

The Nuncio forced himself to examine the deep gashes in Mitrotti's wrists, which had severed the tendons as well as the arteries. "One would think it would be impossible to cut one's wrist so badly, and then have the strength remaining to cut the other one."

"Another miracle," said Dr. Crespo.

WHEN HE FINISHED lunch at the Economic Café, Father Jorge walked down the Avenida de los Poetas, which ran along an inlet of the bay. A dozen empty fishermen's boats bobbed at anchor, their gunwales lined with droopy pelicans. He was thinking about Renata Sánchez's First Communion, which was soon approaching, and the opportunity to see Gloria again. He wondered at the nature of his interest in her. He couldn't get her out of his mind. Her eyes were so vivid and receptive, her voice was so soft and playful, her touch was so electric. Her smell hovered over him like a confusing cloud.

The traffic on Avenida Central came bursting through the signal lights like greyhounds at the racetrack. Father Jorge abruptly snapped into awareness and stepped back on the curb just as a pickup truck with oversized tires roared past. One saw these vehicles everywhere in Panama, these big pickups and four-wheel-drive sport utility trucks. People got tax benefits because they were described as agricultural vehicles, and yet they all seemed to be driven by middle-class teenage boys playing the radio at seismic levels.

Litter from yesterday's antigovernment demonstration still

filled the streets—confetti, torn posters—and some of the office buildings were still draped with signs of support made from computer printouts. This budding revolution had an odd holiday feel about it. In the distance, Father Jorge could hear the sounds of a crowd and the screech of a microphone. He supposed it must be another demonstration.

Out of curiosity, he walked toward the noise, which emanated from Terraplén. The streets were too narrow for two-way traffic, and they were made even more constricted by the many kiosks selling cigarettes and lottery tickets. He could smell the harbor and the fish market and the stale beer that wafted through the doorways of the bars, which were busy even at noon. A man slept in a garbage can. Dark young boys ran toward him begging him to buy pralines or homemade sugar cookies. There was one child trying to sell empty lard buckets. He could tell by their accents that they were Cuban. Thousands of Cuban families lived here. They had purchased falsified Panamanian passports in misplaced hopes of getting to America. Instead, they were stuck in Panama, unable to get legal employment, their children not allowed to go to school. They had become a new underclass in a country already teeming with paupers.

He realized that the amplified voice he was hearing belonged to General Noriega. He couldn't make out the words yet, but that squeaky, awkward sound was too distinctive to belong to anyone else. Soon the priest found himself at the back of a crowd of several thousand people who were watching the General speak. He stood on a makeshift platform on the seawall, directly in front of a statue of Balboa, wearing a turquoise guayabera and a straw hat, his Santería beads clearly visible around his neck. He looked like any ordinary Panamanian man.

"I am home," the General was saying. "I am back in the streets of my youth. People say to me, 'General, why have you avoided returning to Terraplén?' I tell them that I have always been here, I have never left these streets. They are my real mother. Like many children, I ran free and wild here—perhaps too wild for my own good." The General laughed as several of the mothers in the carpet of faces before him shook their heads in agreement. "Hey, Grandma, you remember that, don't you?" he called to an elderly woman standing on a balcony, who giggled and then put her hand over her mouth to hide her missing teeth. "Yes, the people of Terraplén know Tony Noriega," the General continued. "And so when I come to apologize to the people of Panama, it is here in my home that I must begin. That's right, I am here to beg your forgiveness—for letting you down! For allowing the white asses who own this country to continue to control your lives! You see what they have done to our beloved Panama—and to us! We have the highest per capita debt in the world—and for what? Do you see any money for improvements? Terraplén is the same as it was when I was a boy. Many years have passed, many promises have been made, but what has come of it? Nothing! They were lies! One president after another has come forward with a suitcase full of empty promises, and when he leaves office his suitcase is always full of money! You know this to be true. The white asses think that we owe them this!"

Father Jorge surveyed the faces of the crowd. As usual, most of them were civil-service workers who were paid to attend, but there were also people looking out their windows, and on the margins of the crowd stood hundreds of unschooled teenagers and unemployed young men. It was to them that General Noriega was speaking. He repeatedly looked and gestured in their direction. Father Jorge couldn't quite understand what he was witnessing. In his memory, General Noriega had only rarely made political speeches; he much preferred to be a silent presence rather than a public figure. The gist of the speech was very disturbing, but also puzzling, since everyone knew that it was General Noriega who placed the corrupt presidents in office—and removed them at his leisure.

"They own our land, but they don't own our souls!" Noriega cried, and the audience shouted out in affirmation. During the speech, young men in colorful T-shirts that said *Dignity Battal-*

ion roamed through the audience, passing out fliers. Father Jorge accepted one of the crude recruiting brochures. There was a drawing of a muscular teenager carrying an automatic weapon. "I say to the white asses, 'The people are going forward now—get out of our way! We are fed up with your lies! Tony Noriega is standing here in the streets of Terraplén saying it is time to take what we deserve!' " The famished young men on the margins of the crowd began to press closer. The General paused for a moment. "Now when the white asses hear this, they will want to get rid of Tony Noriega. But you won't let this happen, will you? You can tell them, 'If anything happens to General Noriega, the Dignity Battalion will come to your homes! We will drag your wife into the street! We will eat the food in your kitchen! We will shit in your fine commode! Your house will be our house! So don't go fucking with Tony Noriega, because the people of the streets will not let this happen!' Am I right?"

Father Jorge turned and walked hurriedly through the battered neighborhood, leaving the cheering crowd behind. As he passed unclaimed trash in the squalid street, sewer water gushing out of cracks in the ground, abandoned burned-out hulks of cars, idle women on the corners, harelipped children begging for coins, his anger boiled over and he raged to himself about the hypocrisy, the injustice, the waste, the soul-crushing despair of Panama's lost people. What did Noriega offer them? Not hope but revenge.

The soldier's confession was still weighing on his mind. Father Jorge was thinking how good people can be made bad merely by consenting to the evil around them. There is always evil in the world, only sometimes it is so much in control that there seems to be no possibility for good to flourish or even survive. Then he thought about Gloria Sánchez, a good woman, he believed, but with no obvious escape from the driving poverty of her environment. Perhaps prostitution was a kind of moral sacrifice she made to support her children. He would like to think of it that way and to forgive her for it. And yet one can't just give in to the evil of the system. One has to confront it, to resist it. But how? What good was a priest when the only counsel he could offer to such people was to pray to God to make impossible alternatives obvious to them? Perhaps, he thought ruefully, I am no more than a freelance meddler in the affairs of others. I have nothing to give them but prayers and false hopes.

In this state of mind, he looked up and saw that he had already arrived at the nunciature and Sister Sarita was waving to him and telling him to go immediately to the library.

THE NUNCIO WAS drafting his weekly report to the head of the Vatican Secretariat of State. Although it was a routine task, there was much to say, even if, as the Nuncio hoped and expected, such reports went unread. He supposed that Cardinal Falthauser merely glanced at the monthly budget that he was required to append. And yet, out of his compulsive sense of duty and a certain secret vanity concerning his talents as a correspondent, the Nuncio faithfully fulfilled his obligation to keep the Vatican current on Panamanian events:

"Although GENERAL NORIEGA remains very much in charge of this country, the middle class has begun to turn against him. The press has been quite outspoken about the farcical investigation of the SPADAFORA assassination and openly speculates about the likely involvement of government agents. Everyone here believes that the General ordered the killing. The tragedy has been extended by the shocking death of Spadafora's father, CARMELO SPADAFORA, at a rally in Chiriquí last week. He was about to speak when he suddenly fell out of his chair and died onstage, the victim of a heart attack. He had been in fragile health for many years, but the stress of events, and the weight of his grief, overwhelmed him in the end. There seems to be no end to this national calamity.

"Demonstrations against the government, practically unknown in the past few years, have become a common occurrence despite the lack of leadership and the frequent beating of the protesters by PDF troops. The General has responded by threatening the bourgeoisie with class warfare. Cuban arms have been ferried into the country secretly and hidden in caches to be used in the unlikely case of an American invasion or in the event of political insurrection by the middle class.

"NORIEGA's more immediate problem concerns his relationship with PABLO ESCOBAR, the ruthless drug chieftain of the Medellín cocaine cartel. The cartel paid the General a substantial sum of money to avoid extradition and to set up a giant cocaine processing plant in Darién Province, on the Colombian border. The Americans found out about it and shut it down. Since then, Escobar has threatened to have the General murdered. It is believed that FIDEL CASTRO is negotiating between the parties, but the matter remains unresolved and highly unstable. As long as the General is threatened by drug lords, he will be unwilling to negotiate his own departure from power; it would be like signing his death warrant.

"The situation is made even more volatile by an ongoing American investigation into Panamanian corruption. This seems wildly hypocritical, given the several dummy corporations established here by the Central Intelligence Agency to launder drug money from the Contras. One of Noriega's pilots, FLOYD CARLTON, a well-known narcotrafficker, was arrested recently in Costa Rica and flown to the U.S., where it is presumed he will offer evidence to the American Congress about NORIEGA's involvement in the Central American drug trade. Others who might have provided additional testimony have disappeared or been found dead. The brutality of these people is difficult to overstate.

"If you will permit a personal aside, once again I would like to request reassignment to a European country . . ."

The Nuncio always added a petulant note at the end of his missives, just in case anyone happened to read them. He had learned that the best way of keeping his enemies at bay was to allow them to believe in his continued misery. He was just finishing this complaint when he heard Father Jorge's knock.

"Am I in time?" the young man asked as he came into the library. His face was still flushed from his vigorous walk.

"Don't worry. Roberto called not two hours ago. He said the interview will not air until six. We've got a few moments yet."

Everyone in Panama was talking about Roberto's sudden revelations. He had given an interview to *La Prensa* that afternoon, in which he accused Noriega of Spadafora's murder. The whole country was waiting to see what else he had to say on television that evening.

"Did he ask you to come to his house?" Father Jorge asked. Roberto had surrounded himself with prominent people, especially churchmen, in an attempt to protect himself from Noriega's wrath.

"I declined," the Nuncio admitted. "The last thing the Vatican wants is to have its emissary caught up in the middle of a civil war. That is why all our contacts with the opposition must be kept in strict confidence. Something like this, with press and television—" He shrugged and drew down the corners of his mouth, staring heavenward—a Gallic gesture of complete hopelessness.

Promptly at six Roberto came on the screen, looking weirdly exuberant in his white robes as a nervous interviewer asked questions that had never been publicly posed in Panama. "First, let me confess my own sins," Roberto said. He pointed to his palatial living room, with its Louis XV furniture and Rubenesque frescoes on the walls. "Look at my beautiful home. It's at least half-stolen. I say that because much of my own fortune has come from selling Panamanian passports to poor Cubans. And this is just my share! Everybody on the general staff made fortunes. It was expected! It was the nature of things! But I can't take my millions to heaven. I ought to be in jail, I know that. Only I do not wish to go there alone. Noriega should go with me. And many, many others."

The Nuncio and Father Jorge exchanged an amazed look.

"Why are you telling about this now?" the interviewer asked in a shocked whisper.

"Because I am a little crazy, and you know what they say about crazy people—they always tell the truth."

Roberto then began to ramble about "mystical guerrilla warfare." He showed a plaque, which he propped up against his feet, that contained the symbols of all the world's great religions—it was a spiritual shield, he said, to guard him against General Noriega's voodoo. "There are people who are concentrating their mental powers to crush me, but they will fail! My own power is far greater than theirs. See how I extend my hands with the palms facing upward? As I do this, I am receiving the positive energy from the universe. Now you can tell me what you wish to talk about. Anything. Anything at all. For instance, I am quite prepared to discuss the fraud that elected Nicky Barletta. In fact, the final preparations were made by General Noriega and myself right here in this room."

"Here?" said the interviewer. "You planned it all right in this place?"

"It's historic, no? The truth is that the real president of Panama is Arnulfo Arias Madrid, the man people voted for by a great majority."

"This is quite shocking," the interviewer said.

"If you are so easily shocked, I am worried for you," said Roberto. "The murder of Spadafora, do you want to hear of that? Some have said that I am the intellectual author of this assassination, but I can tell you the truth: General Noriega planned this action personally, just as he also conspired with the American air force and the CIA to murder our beloved Omar Torrijos."

"Torrijos!" the interviewer gasped. But then the power was

149

cut to the central part of the city and the nunciature plunged
into darkness.

IMMEDIATELY AFTER the lights went out, thousands of Panamanians took to the streets—a spontaneous, utterly disorganized
outpouring. Many found themselves on the grounds of the Díaz
Herrera mansion in Golf Heights. Some of them came because
they were galvanized by the political moment, the sense that the
destiny of their country hung in the balance, but just as many
wandered through the grounds of the mansion out of curiosity
and to see the way a crazy rich man lived. The following day, and
then day after day for the next several weeks, people milled about
on the lawn and slept on the expansive porch behind the gilded
plaster lions, while Roberto wandered through the traffic with a
Bible in his hand, blessing the protesters and handing out
brochures listing General Noriega's crimes.

In characteristic Panamanian fashion, the protest quickly
turned into a party. Rioters barricaded the downtown streets,
hoisting pineapples onto the traffic lights and banging pots and
pans in a Latin clave. After a few days the riots settled into a
cheerful routine: half an hour of demonstrations at lunchtime
and an hour before cocktails.

"This is the most peculiar revolution," the Nuncio observed
as he escorted Father Jorge to Golf Heights in the embassy Toyota. "More revelry than revolution. I can't decide whether it is
comedy or farce." The traffic was backed up for blocks by ecstatic young people cruising up and down the boulevards in
their BMWs and Land Rovers, leaning out their windows and
waving handkerchiefs. "I certainly don't wish that the situation
in Panama ever be more serious than this," the Nuncio continued. "But still, one wonders what will happen when these happy
warriors meet real resistance on the part of the government.
The dirty secret in this country is that General Noriega has
never needed to apply much force to stay in power. For the most

part, as long as Noriega kept the Americans appeased, the Panamanians were content—especially *these* Panamanians," he said as a carload of teenagers wearing gold chains and bracelets roared past in a blast of salsa music. The young people leaned out of the car windows, laughing and talking on their cell phones. "Manuelito, you must stop honking," the Nuncio told his elderly driver. "What you do on your own time is your business, but in the papal Toyota you must conduct yourself diplomatically. We are carrying the flag of the Church, after all."

THE INVITATIONS, TONY. Get back to the business at hand," Felicidad commanded. "We've got blue embossed, which looks very head of state, or the white on lavender, which is beautiful but I don't know if it sends the right message. They will be pasted onto bottles of Moët et Chandon—isn't that a darling idea? We've already ordered two hundred and fifty cases. What do you think?"

Tony stared at the invitations to his eldest daughter's marriage. Three thousand bottles of forty-dollar champagne and the wedding hadn't even taken place! Along with the champagne, each invitee would receive a Baccarat crystal glass engraved with the young couple's initials. "Which does Sandra like?" he asked.

"She's too excited to be trusted with this decision."

"Fela, I also have things on my mind."

His wife shook her head sadly. "This is the biggest moment in her life, Tony. It should be one of the biggest in yours. But you don't ever stop to think about the important things."

"Okay, the blue one," he said wearily.

"Really, the blue?"

"Perhaps the lavender is better."

"For God's sake, Tony, make up your mind!"

The truth was, Tony hated to declare himself. He felt trapped by the need to make choices. All of his life he had managed to remain in the background, like a puppet master manipulating the creatures on the stage, but now he found himself pressed into the spotlight. He was having to make decisions in full view, which was not his style.

He should never have allowed the least amount of resistance, he thought bitterly. The moment the first protester shouted Hugo's name, Tony should have had him shot. That would have saved many lives. It would have been the most humane and economical approach. Although there would have been an outcry abroad, Panama soon would have gone back to the life it had always known. But that was not what Tony did. Instead, he was tolerant. He had allowed the opposition to build, financed by American liberals, overseen by the burgeoning corps of international press. The American Congress had just passed a resolution demanding that he resign. The CIA had cut off his paycheck after Casey died. More worrisome was the fact that the Panamanian resistance had begun to assume the form of real leadership. An alliance of business leaders, calling themselves the Civic Crusade, was meeting every morning for breakfast at the nunciature. That was no matter, but lately these business leaders had been refusing to pay their taxes and utility bills and were openly organizing among the trade unions and the hospitals and the Rotary and Lions Clubs. Even the American ambassador's daughter was a part of it. The streets were streaming with brazen protesters playing to the cameras of CNN. Roberto's house had become a haven for the opposition, although perhaps he should call it an asylum because Roberto had clearly jumped off the narrow ledge of sanity he had enjoyed until now. Tony blamed himself for letting things get to this point. So far, he had limited his response to arresting some of the most prominent protesters and confining them to the Hilton. But soon he would have to clean out the vipers' nest.

And now the head of G-2, his intelligence division, called with more terrible news. "Tony, there is talk of a general strike, and I am ashamed to tell you that the day they have chosen is the tenth of July."

Tony's eye fell on the lavender invitation in front of him. The tenth of July, his precious daughter's special day.

"They'll pay for this," Tony told his intelligence officer. "They are trying to intimidate us, to make us fear them. But it is we who will create the fear. Summon Giroldi. Tell him it is time for the Dobermans to do their work."

CHAPTER 11

The Nunciature
Panama City, Panama
July 26, 1987

His Eminence Hans Cardinal Falthauser
Secretariat of State
Vatican City

My Dear Cardinal Falthauser:

Matters in this quaint republic have taken another turn for the worse. Early Tuesday afternoon a gang of children—most of them in their teens, but some as young as ten—attacked the Mansion Dante, the largest department store in the country. It is owned by a leading figure in the opposition, ROBERTO EISEN-MANN, who is also the publisher of *La Prensa*. The gang calls itself the Dignity Battalion. They were carrying AK-47s and gasoline bombs. As the store employees watched, the Digbats opened fire on them. Some of the children were knocked to the ground by the powerful recoil of their weapons. As it happened, the store windows had recently been replaced with bulletproof Lexan, so the bullets ricocheted wildly into the street. One of the older boys commandeered a city garbage truck, and he drove it directly into a display window full of the latest fashions. Then the Digbats rushed into the store, grabbing clothes and jewelry and setting fires. We could easily see the flames from the nunciature. A fire engine arrived and sat in the street for several hours, doing nothing.

In the middle of this chaotic scene, PRESIDENT DELVALLE appeared to personally rescue his niece, who sold dresses in the store. He waded through the looters and the mob of armed children. All this happened while the firemen sat on their truck watching the store burn to the ground.

The wedding of General Noriega's eldest daughter, SANDRA, took place several days in advance of her announced date, quietly, in a small, highly secure chapel in Fort Amador, with fewer than a hundred guests. We were not invited to this much-reduced event. I have heard reports that the General was in such a dark frame of mind that even his friends trembled for their future. Some of them came home from the reception and promptly booked airline tickets to Miami.

Two days later, an Israeli-trained brigade called the Dobermans rolled through the streets firing tear gas and birdshot into the crowds and rounding up anyone they could find who was wearing white. Apparently the color itself has been outlawed. Even grandmothers who were waving handkerchiefs on the balconies of their apartments were shot at from helicopters. Fifteen hundred people have been arrested and jailed. Amazingly, no one was killed.

As you can imagine, the nunciature is overrun with new refugees fleeing this latest crackdown. We accommodate as best we can, but our guests have seriously taxed our budget. We are now having to feed an additional fifteen persons as well as our staff. We fervently pray that you can put in a word with the exchequer to increase our allotment on an emergency basis. We have been working with our colleagues at the Costa Rican and

Brazilian embassies to handle our excessive number of guests, but for whatever reason the nunciature remains the sanctuary of first resort. I do worry that we have increased our reputation as a hostel for the opposition.

A foreboding atmosphere of dread and uncertainty hangs over the country. Some days the government declares a state of emergency, other days it rescinds the emergency and tries to carry on as usual. The constant vacillation keeps everyone on edge, waiting for the General to make his next move. One expects that it will come soon.

Until then I remain

Very sincerely yours,
H.-A. Morette

THE WEIRDNESS of the scene was beginning to take a toll on Father Jorge. For the past week he had been sleeping at Roberto's house, along with a handful of other priests and nuns who were offering themselves as a human shield for the dwindling number of sympathizers, reporters, and hangers-on who made up the shrinking resistance movement. There were still perhaps two hundred people in and out of the mansion, however, and some nights they made enough noise that General Noriega was said to be disturbed in his own house, a couple of blocks away.

Nearly everyone here laid claim to some particular spiritual genius. There was an abundance of psychics and astrologers and, for some reason, chiropractors, who were making free spinal adjustments as their contribution to the revolution. Posters of a giggling Sai Baba were taped to the walls. Somewhat to his embarrassment, Father Jorge had been persuaded to give up his shoes and wander about barefoot like everyone else. Roberto had convinced them that only in this way could they keep in tune with the harmony of the earth. Although he recognized the absurdity of the scene, he had to admit that these people were standing up for their beliefs—unlike most of the conventional religious leaders in the country. Perhaps the revolution required a bit of lunacy to keep itself going. But who was he in this affair? He felt dismayingly sane and ineffectual.

One night, about two in the morning, everyone was suddenly summoned to look at the moon. To Father Jorge's eyes, it was a perfectly normal gibbous moon, and yet nearly twenty people claimed to be able to see the number seven inscribed on it. "Look to the right side, Father, among the shadows. It's very clear. Perhaps you need glasses." Roberto then brought out the Bible and began to quote from the Book of Revelation, in which Saint John spoke of the seven stars and seven golden candlesticks, and the Lamb with seven horns and seven eyes, and the book with the seven seals, and so on. By the time the group had finished its discussion of numerology and apocalypse, the sun had come up.

Father Jorge had undertaken to have the weapons removed from the house so that the government would not have the excuse to use military force. He filled a station wagon with pistols and automatic weapons and even a bazooka that a PDF defector had smuggled into the house, and he made sure that the press was there to record it when the weapons were taken away to a neutral spot. He wanted the world to know that the occupants were defenseless and did not intend to resist with force.

Therefore he was dismayed to discover Roberto wandering around the kitchen at five in the morning, wearing his robes and carrying an AK-47.

"I thought we had an understanding," said Father Jorge.

"Yes, we do, of course," Roberto replied, completely unabashed. "But last night I arrested my personal bodyguards and confiscated their arms."

"Why would you do that?"

"They were PDF. They could not be totally trusted. I let them go. We are now completely without protection. Only a few weapons remain, enough perhaps to defend the inner perimeter, if it should come to that."

The kitchen stank of leftover pizza. Father Jorge rummaged through the dirty dishes looking for the coffeepot. "Shall I make you a cup?" he asked Roberto.

"I'm only allowed juice." Roberto was now so thin he looked completely starved.

"You make me grateful that my vows are limited to poverty and chastity," said Father Jorge. "If I had to give up coffee as well, I'd never have made a priest."

Roberto pushed an empty pizza box onto the floor and sat down. "Last night we had a secret council. We assembled some very interesting intelligence on General Noriega."

"Ah."

"As you know, he has always kept the details of his background classified."

"But we do know about his illegitimacy and the godmother who raised him and such things."

"Of course. But the really useful information he has kept to himself. He would hate for it to fall into the hands of people who know what to do with it."

"What sort of information are you speaking of?"

Roberto leaned forward and said in a quiet and meaningful tone, "His birth date, for instance."

"His birth date?"

"A state secret."

"I didn't realize."

"Fortunately, because I have my own contacts in intelligence, we have been able to learn some interesting things. The General is an Aquarius."

"Really?"

"It makes sense, doesn't it? Smart, nervous, a quick but unstable mind, a modernist who thrives on change."

"So you know the date of his birth?"

"Not only the day. This is important, but it is not everything. We have managed to work it out so that we are within several hours of the exact *moment* of his birth. We deduced that Scorpio must be his ascendant star—he being an extremist in all things. Scorpio is also associated with strong psychic powers, which is why he is so interested in espionage. He was born to be either a great mystic or a great criminal."

Father Jorge watched the coffeemaker as it sputtered and spewed.

"I'm sure this is a breakthrough," Roberto said after a moment. "If Tony knew we had this information . . ." Then he laughed gleefully. "Oh, man, if he knew!"

T ONY SOAKED IN the hot, sulfurous vat, mud dripping from his hair. The hut in the jungle was dark, but light broke through the cracks in the palm-thatch walls, and he could see little Indian children peeking through, trying to catch a glimpse of their naked leader.

The old bare-breasted Indian crone who was bathing him roughly slapped yellow branches of a guayacan tree across his shoulders. Tony grunted. "Enough," he said in the language of his mother's people.

"Wait," the woman commanded. "Takes time. The water makes you powerful." Her torso was painted in geometric designs and her breasts drooped down to her navel.

"And for sex, it's good, eh?"

The crone laughed, a weird pagan whinny. Tony imitated her, which caused her to laugh louder, and then the children outside began laughing as well, like donkeys braying.

"Tony, the presentation was supposed to be at two," said Dr. Demos, who sat in the corner of the hut, mopping perspiration from his face. His shirt was completely soaked through. A small fire flickered in the hearth, where the woman heated more water for Tony's therapeutic bath. "It's almost four. We've been here for three hours."

"She said it takes time," Tony said. In fact, he could feel the healing power of the minerals seeping into his throbbing bones.

Outside, his bodyguards chased away the children with hisses and a few boots in the kidneys.

"This is my village, you know," said Tony.

The doctor nodded sleepily and fanned himself.

For some reason Tony had felt the need to return to his birthplace, and so he had accepted the invitation to speak at the dedication of a new postal station. As he had helicoptered over the rain forest, it had seemed that the entire jungle was aflame. Lent began the traditional time of burning and clearing, and plumes of smoke reached all the way to the clouds. Through the haze he could see the narrow, rotting Pan-American Highway turning to gravel and then to mud and finally expiring in the swamps and the overwhelming complexity of the jungle. From the top of Canada to the tip of South America, the only gap in the highway was here, in Darién Province. Modernity, what was left of it, stopped at his little home village of Yaviza, where the Chico and Chucunaque Rivers flowed into the broad and turbulent Río Tuira. Beyond Yaviza there were no roads and few houses other than the palm huts of the naked Chocos, who still hunted with arrows and spears. It was a paradise for monkeys, mosquitoes, and anthropologists.

"Whenever I feel lost, when I need to make a spiritual connection, I return here to my roots," said Tony. "I don't know, for some reason it relaxes me."

"You should take the Valium I offered you," said the doctor. "You're tense, your blood pressure is high. These folk remedies can only do so much, Tony."

Out of the murk, an old man stepped forward with his hat in his hand. His face was a wrinkled work of nature, like a jagged piece of driftwood on a beach, where the elements have had leisure to work their influence. "General, we are very honored," the old man began.

"What do you want, Uncle?"

"The children of the village have no schoolbooks. Many times we have asked the government for assistance—"

"Take a note, Doctor," Tony said to Demos. " 'Schoolbooks for Yaviza.' There, it's done. All Panamanian children should be educated. This is Tony Noriega's dream. So, what else do you want, Uncle?"

"That is all," said the relieved old man, who was already bowing and backing out of the hut.

"No offense, Uncle, but you ask for too little. You don't realize that you are already very rich. Everyone in this village is wealthy beyond their dreams."

The old man looked dumbfounded.

"Water!" Tony explained, splashing the rotten liquid. "Healing water! You can *sell* this, Uncle! Have you never heard of Lourdes? People will come here to be cured. You will build motels, restaurants, casinos. You know about Club Med?"

The old man shook his head no.

"Club Med! Club Med! Right here, Club Med Panama! Why not? Why not *Disneyland*? In the jungle. Here!"

The old man bowed again and backed out of the hut. He looked at the dirt roads and the chickens pecking at the ground and the Indians sitting on their haunches in the shade. They looked questioningly at the old man.

"He says Walt Disney is coming," the dazed old man said.

Tony's camera crew was waiting to record this visit for his weekly television show, *Everything for My Country,* which he cohosted with Felicidad. When the General finally appeared, rinsed and dressed, a bit sapped from the bath, the crew began shooting video of him walking among the Indians toward the tiny town square, which was opposite a falling-down Catholic church. "This is still the frontier," said Tony into the camera. "It's a trading town. Over here"—he pointed to the mud-colored river—"the Indians arrive in their wooden canoes, carrying yams and plantains. Cargo ships travel upriver from the Gulf of San Miguel. Now that we have completed the Pan-American Highway to this point, you see lorries arriving with goods from the city. Yaviza is entering the modern world. One day soon we will complete the highway across the swamp, and then the Americas will finally be joined."

"Is it okay to show their tits on TV, General?" the soundman asked.

About twenty Choco maidens were waiting under a tent for the ceremony to begin. They wore colorful wraparound skirts, but they were naked above the waist. They had painted their bodies with the black juice of the jagua plant. The patterns were mostly geometric—rows of equilateral triangles across their torsos, complicated bands of interlocking Vs twining around their arms, and bull's-eye circles around their nipples.

"Because they are Indians, yes, it's okay," Tony said, making up the rule for the occasion.

Tony sat in one of the aluminum lawn chairs that had been set up for the dignitaries. Next to him was the village cacique, Pericles García, dressed in a red loincloth and army boots. Tony had known him when they were boys here and used to swim together in the Río Tuira. They ate a feast of catfish soup and fried iguanas with rice, washed down with chicha, the Indian moonshine, which gave Tony an instant headache.

In addition to the Indians, Yaviza was populated by black shopkeepers who were descendants of escaped slaves, a few white missionaries, the odd American scholar or drug agent or rain-forest environmentalist, and an abundance of end-of-the-road riffraff. It was the kind of place where people went to get lost. Colombian guerrillas routinely sneaked across the border to hide out. There were still a few prospectors looking for gold, and some rubber tappers, and a delegation of government agriculture inspectors who were slaughtering all the pigs in the province because of hoof-and-mouth disease.

The new postal station was little more than a cinder-block depository where the mailman would come once a week to collect letters. Pericles made a brief speech, then the girls danced. As they swayed back and forth, a shaman chanted and waved carved batons containing the spirits of the forest, which he beseeched to protect the mail. At the end, a delegation of schoolchildren came forward with letters to send. Tony patted them on their heads and dumped the letters in the mail slot.

"Great stuff, General," the producer said. She was a brittle woman who never took off her sunglasses. "The whole country will feel good about this."

"Tony, have you got a few minutes?" the cacique said when the ceremony was over. The two old friends walked down to the wharf where they used to swim, followed discreetly by Tony's bodyguards. Beside the river were the vine-covered ruins of a sixteenth-century fortress built by the conquistadors.

"Remember when we used to climb those walls?" Tony said. He rarely felt nostalgic about old times, but many years had passed since he had returned to his village, and he wondered at the passage of time and at the distance he had traveled. He was also feeling a little woozy from the chicha.

"Many ghosts live here," Pericles said. "They come here to rest. Some say Balboa visits this place. One day, maybe your spirit will be here, too."

Talk like this sobered Tony up. Yes, he could imagine his immortal shade returning to his home village, looking for something—succor, meaning, love—whatever it was that life had not provided. But would he find it here?

A green lizard crawled across the encrusted stones and stared at him lazily.

"And how are things among your people?" Tony asked.

"Unfortunate, as usual. Iguana hunting is poor and the jungle is full of narcos. The people are restless because we have not been given cable."

"I've also had some difficulties lately," said Tony.

"Perhaps the curse of our people has been passed along through your mother's blood."

"What curse is this?"

"You mean you do not know our story, about how we came to be cursed by God?"

Tony thought back to the nighttime tales of his childhood, but he didn't remember any such legend.

"The elders tell us that in the ancient times God lived among his people," Pericles recounted. "One night he gets drunk from too much guarapo and falls asleep on the porch. The women come along and are laughing because God's balls are hanging out. Then the white man comes and says, 'Why are you laughing? You should cover up God's balls.' And then he covers God. When God wakes up, he's angry with us. He says, 'You don't even take care to cover my balls—the white man does it for you. From now on, you will always be poor and the white man will be rich.' And that is why the world is as it is."

"Do you really believe that, my friend?"

Pericles shrugged. "Why not? Is one belief more valuable than another?"

"I don't like to think that God is so stern that our people must be punished forever."

"Nobody likes to be laughed at, Tony. Especially God. We have learned this lesson at a great price."

Tony looked out at the broad brown river. Something caught his eye. Bubbles roiled the surface of the water. Below that, there was some huge, half-submerged object tied to the wharf.

"What is it?" Tony asked.

"A whale," said Pericles. "The captain of a cargo ship found the animal in the mouth of the river. He tried to tow it out to sea, but it kept returning. So for some reason he brought it here."

"Can't you let it go?"

"We try to, but it doesn't matter, the whale just sits there. His spirit has gone. We keep him here and talk to him to try to help him find it. But he will not be in this world much longer."

Tony walked to the end of the sodden pier and stared down at the immense gray animal. It was a humpback, the most romantic creature in the ocean, which roams the length and breadth of the cold Pacific singing his love songs and searching for a mate. The animal rolled slightly to one side and presented a giant eye, the saddest eye Tony had ever seen. The underside of his immense pelicanlike jaw was scratched and raw. For some reason, Tony felt that the entire universe was out of alignment. He was touched by a great sense of sadness, even of despair.

"Do you feed it?"

"It chooses not to eat," the cacique said. "Everyone feels very bad about this. We don't know what it means."

Just then, the doleful whale made a noise and sank itself out of sight. Despite the heat, Tony suddenly shivered. "It doesn't mean anything," he said, more to himself than to his friend. "This happens sometimes, whales beach themselves. Perhaps it's a chemical imbalance. You should not be so superstitious, my friend. It's the whale's bad luck, not yours." These brave words sounded hollow, even to himself.

When they came back to the town square, the camera crew had packed up and were ready to get back to the helicopter. "We're just waiting on you, General," the producer said impatiently.

"There's something else I must do," said Tony.

"You want to get it on film?" the producer asked, casting a glance at her watch.

"No, this I must do alone."

Yaviza was small but so disorganized that it took him a few minutes to find the road to the cemetery. He ordered his bodyguards to stand back as he walked among the elevated tombs. He had never come here before, and he knew he would never come again. It started to drizzle and within five minutes it began raining in earnest. Tony had neglected to bring an umbrella, but he didn't mind because it all felt so familiar—walking in the rain in the jungle, just as he had done so many years ago.

Finally he found the grave of his mother.

He rarely thought about her. She had been a poor Indian domestic who had worked for an alcoholic government accountant. Tony used to see his father, Ricaurte Noriega, on the streets of Yaviza. Although the father never acknowledged his son, their resemblance was unmistakable—Ricaurte had the pitted complexion that young Tony would also inherit. As for Tony's sickly mother, she had abandoned him so that she could spend her last year dying in peace. He didn't begrudge her that. Tuberculosis took a lot of Indians, even now.

María Felix Moreno. He could barely read her painted name on the worn and algae-covered stone. Half a century had passed already since her death. He had no real memory of her. If she hadn't done him the favor of dying, he might have remained in Yaviza. God had given Tony a way out, but in return he had taken his mother.

And now Tony stood alone in the rain and wondered why God had chosen him. He might just as well be bare assed and wearing a handkerchief over his penis like his friend, the village cacique. Divine fate had singled him out. But for what?

CHAPTER 12

THE SOUND OF HELICOPTERS roused Father Jorge just after dawn. He was sleeping on the balcony of Roberto's guest bedroom. Six Hueys rising out of the basin of the city converged on the mansion. Intrigued, he sat up in his sleeping bag and watched the helicopters position themselves. A convoy of armored personnel carriers broke through the fences and rolled up the lawn. It was all strange and wonderful. Soldiers spilled out of the carriers and surrounded the house. They wore helmets and gas masks and carried shields bearing the emblem of a snarling black dog, like some futuristic Gestapo. Next door, a neighbor holding a croquet mallet watched the invasion. He noticed Father Jorge and waved.

Someone opened fire.

Father Jorge fell against the concrete balcony floor. It was Roberto, he was sure; the sound of a single automatic weapon—*budderrrrrrrup budderrrrrrrup budderrrrrrrrup*—erupted from inside the house. In the yard soldiers pointed toward a second-story window and took cover behind the lawn furniture. Overhead the helicopters canted ever so ominously toward the house.

Suddenly the glass of the sliding door behind Father Jorge exploded as the helicopter in front of him raked the bedroom with deafening, flaming guns. Father Jorge somehow came unstuck from the balcony floor. He rolled across the shattered glass onto the bedroom carpet. All the windows were blown out and the king-size water bed was spewing like a sprinkler. People ran through the halls screaming. More gunshots and the unmistakable sound of boots as the soldiers burst through the doorways. Father Jorge inched through the shards of glass and crawled behind the raining bed.

Then the nature of the sounds changed. The gunshots ceased. Doors were kicked open; there were frightened shouts of surrender, followed by cries and groans and the ghastly crunching sound of people being clubbed and beaten. Father Jorge could actually hear the bones snapping. A sob of fear jumped out of the priest before he could stop it. He quickly bit his thumb to keep himself silent. He began praying furiously, praying that he would not be found. He was terrified but also deeply ashamed of his fear, and he made himself pray for the others who had already been captured.

He could see the boots in the doorway as the soldiers entered the room. He tried to stop his breath. One of the soldiers walked slowly toward the balcony.

"Blood," said the soldier.

Father Jorge realized that they must be talking about him.

"Maybe I will fire into the bed to see if anyone is hiding behind it," said the other soldier.

"No, wait!" said Father Jorge. He stuck his hands into the air. "I am coming out!"

The soldiers ordered him to stand, but when he tried to get up he discovered that his bare feet were full of glass splinters. He cried out as the soldiers pulled him to his feet. They were just two boys in uniform; their faces were young and excited.

"I am a priest," Father Jorge said, humbled by his need to be spared.

One of the soldiers pointed to the door. Father Jorge started to hobble toward it, but the glass in his feet was unbearably painful. He cried out and unthinkingly reached out to one of the soldiers for support.

He did not even feel the butt of the rifle as it broke the jaw below his right ear. He did feel himself being knocked off his feet—actually lifted off the ground—but the sensation was removed and dreamlike. He could see the soldiers standing over him like young giants, and he heard his own voice crying out as they kicked him again and again. And then he felt nothing.

THE NUNCIO WAS beside himself with anxiety. In the four days since the assault on Roberto's mansion, he had had no word from Father Jorge. Reports in the news said that Roberto had been beaten into a coma and placed on display in the Comandancia as a warning to other officers. But then a statement appeared over Roberto's signature saying that General Noriega was innocent of Hugo's murder. As for the others who were captured, there was no news at all. The rumor mill said that several people had been shot in the face and secretly buried. The Nuncio could not let himself think about this. If the worst had happened, he would never forgive himself. Why hadn't he been more insistent? He had let his affection for Father Jorge stand in the way of his judgment. He had always known that the price for resistance was high; now it seemed unbearable.

To keep his mind from dwelling on the terrible rumors, he began to quietly visit various government officials, seeking information about the missing protesters. He had lunch with Dr. Demos, a man he deeply distrusted, not only because of his association with Noriega, as his pollster and political adviser, but also because he was a Freudian and was inclined to talk analytical nonsense. They sat under the awning of an open-air café on Via Argentina while it rained heavily. A chubasco had blown in from the Pacific, drenching the city with a week of unseasonable rain. Demos was half Greek. He wore sunglasses despite the downpour and fiddled with a rosary.

"It's an interesting case, I only wish I could talk more about it," Dr. Demos said, referring to the General. "There are certain aspects of his personality that would make an intriguing monograph. Perhaps a classic."

"I'm certain," the Nuncio said politely.

"Of course, I've encountered similar kinds of religious mania in less celebrated subjects."

"What do you mean by 'religious mania'?"

"No offense, Monseñor. But if we can speak—let us say—off the record . . . ?"

The Nuncio shrugged in Gallic assent.

Dr. Demos paused dramatically. He was obviously thrilled by the opportunity to discourse upon his favorite subject. "Technically, I am referring to an affect-loaded fixation. If you had studied psychology, Monseñor, you would be familiar with the similarity between religion and neurotic behavior. I include in the term 'religion' the entire spectrum of spiritual practices, including magic and sorcery."

"I am very well acquainted with religious neurotics," the Nuncio said, bristling at Dr. Demos's condescension. "In fact, you might say I am a specialist in this area. But I don't accept that religion and magic are the same."

"No offense, Monseñor, but both the magician and the priest believe that inner thoughts can control outer events, through incantations or spells or prayer. From the perspective of the man of science, there is little difference between these actions. Similarly, the neurotic believes that his private ceremonies—compulsive toilet flushing, let us say—govern circumstances outside his actual range of influence. It is all magical thinking, and magic becomes religion once it becomes ritualized."

"So you are saying that General Noriega is neurotic? That seems a rather tame diagnosis."

"No, no, no! Not neurotic! Not in the sense that we commonly understand the term. He suffers from certain narcissistic disorders that I cannot in good faith describe." Dr. Demos hesitated. "Of course, everyone is aware of his bisexuality and the allegations of sexual perversion. My point is that neurosis is an affliction of modern man, and the subject in question is not modern. He's a savage who has read Nietzsche, and that's what makes him so dangerous and also so valuable from a clinical perspective."

Unfortunately, Dr. Demos was no help in the Nuncio's quest to rescue his secretary. "In matters of state, the General really consults no one," the psychiatrist said. "The best we can hope for is that he will be merciful in the face of public outrage. I've shown him my latest polls, which are devastating, as you can imagine. Unfortunately, the General usually reacts unfavorably to pressure. If anything, he is likely to strike back. I do not advise taking a public stand on this. Be patient and let events take their course."

The Nuncio returned to the nunciature in a dark frame of mind. He could not fend off the dreadful image of Hugo's headless corpse and the thought that Father Jorge might meet a similar end. As soon as he entered the rear door, he saw Sister Sarita waiting for him, looking deeply concerned, and his heart jumped. He immediately felt light-headed in anticipation of horrible news.

"Monseñor, you have a visitor," she said.

"Is it important? You know I'm not receiving until after four."

"This visitor I think you should see."

When he entered his library, the Nuncio found President Delvalle sitting at his desk with a shoe box in his lap. Ordinarily, Delvalle had the look of a dark-eyed 1950s Latin movie star, with slicked-back hair and flared nostrils, but now his large, fleshy face was pale with anxiety and his eyes were red and puffy—from either sleeplessness or crying, the Nuncio thought, perhaps both.

171

"Mr. President," he said politely. "May we offer you some refreshment?"

"Vodka tonic," said the morose president. The Nuncio placed the order with Sister Sarita.

"Everything is coming apart," Delvalle said.

"I completely agree. But is there something more that I don't know?" the Nuncio asked.

"Of course you know about the secret American plan?"

Everyone knew about the secret American plan. The Reagan administration was desperately trying to lure the General out of power with offers of luxurious exile. The results were so far quite predictable.

"Tony is only playing along with them," said Delvalle. "First he said he might resign, but now he says he won't. And this is after he has sent his own negotiators to Washington to make an agreement. They actually came to terms. And Tony turns down his own deal! It's becoming unbearable, I tell you. I suppose he has not responded to your request."

Twice the Nuncio had called Noriega's office on the president's behalf, seeking to arrange an appointment. "I'm sorry," said the Nuncio. "Apparently he chooses not to meet you, for whatever reason."

Delvalle sighed deeply. "You can't know what my life has been like these past several months. The humiliation, the insults. I never thought that public life could be so vulgar. I myself am losing money with this new sugar quota that the Americans have imposed. It's been a disaster, personally and professionally." The president took a long sip of his drink and then pressed the cold glass to his forehead. "I'm at the end. Really, the very end."

"What do you propose to do?"

"I shall simply fire him. I am the president, after all."

Of all the lunacy that had transpired in the last several months, the Nuncio thought that this must be the craziest notion yet advanced. He sat quietly—stunned, really—unable to respond.

"Everything will be constitutional," Delvalle continued. "One must do what is right."

"A commendable policy," the Nuncio said hopelessly.

"I've already been given assurance that the Americans will back me up."

"I would not be so certain of that if I were you."

"But they have indicted him in Florida! This has to be the end. Now we must do what we can to save Panama."

"I've observed that America is like the mythical Hydra," said the Nuncio. "It speaks from many mouths. You must be careful to hear what each of them says."

Delvalle slumped deeper into the Nuncio's chair. "I understand the point you are making, Monseñor, but I can't endure this state of humiliation any longer. It can only end in the complete loss of everything—my dignity, my family, my money, perhaps even my life. So what is there to lose? Do you mind if I have another vodka?"

When he had fortified himself, the president set the shoe box on the Nuncio's desk and announced that he had a considerable favor to ask. "I must make a speech to the nation, telling the people of my decision and asking for their support. If you don't mind, Monseñor, I'd like to tape the speech here, in your library."

"But—don't you own the television station?"

"In fact, yes, but if I tape it there, word will certainly get to the General. As you know, television personalities cannot be trusted; they will be stumbling over themselves to get to the phone to inform on me. If I go on live, it would be suicide, quite obviously. But, alternatively, if I make the tape here, it goes on the air later and I am . . . somewhere else."

"But, my dear Mr. President, what reaction do you expect?"

"My hope is that the people will take to the streets and support me. I realize very well that many of them do not regard me highly, but I am their leader, after all. I'm only trying to do honor to my country and my high office."

Seeing that there was little hope of dissuading the president from this course of action, the Nuncio agreed to let him use the library. "Would you like to stay in the nunciature once the speech has aired?" he asked gently.

"I'm afraid you are already housing too many government critics to make me feel welcome as a houseguest. In fact, I have a retreat of my own. I can wait there for the people to make their feelings known. Once they have declared themselves, I will emerge and together we will restore democracy to our shattered republic." The president then opened the shoe box and removed the tricolor presidential sash, which he draped across his chest. "There happens to be a cameraman waiting at your back door," he said as he patted down his hair. "If you would be so good as to admit him."

P AMPERED, STUCK-UP, white-assed bitch!"

"Pimple-faced toad!"

Carmen's pillow slammed against the right side of Tony's head just as he was taking a strategic step backward on her giant four-postered bed. He tumbled onto the mound of sheets that had been torn from the mattress in an earlier bout. Carmen fell on him and pinned his hands over his head. "Surrender," she demanded.

Tony stared helplessly at her shining breasts looming over him. Her neck was red and the freckles on her sternum throbbed with excitement.

"Okay, I give up. You can have anything you want. Just name it."

Carmen's eyes stared wildly at him through the cave of her unstrung yellow hair. "I want to watch the news," she said.

Tony groaned. Carmen was developing a depressingly active interest in current events. When they first got together she never asked about politics, but in the last several months she had been going at him with the zeal of an undergraduate, always full of questions and opinions. He suspected that there must be some law of female behavior that linked sex and complexity. Witness his relationship with Felicidad, which had become brutally simple.

Carmen switched on a news show that was a recitation of the week's events, starting with Delvalle's misguided attempt to exercise power. Only eight hours after announcing that he was firing Tony, Delvalle himself was dismissed by the more prudent National Assembly. The former president went into hiding. "Under article one eighty-four of the Panamanian Constitution," the announcer was saying, "Manuel Solís Palma becomes the minister in charge of the presidency, pending new elections."

"Why do you do this, Tony?" Carmen demanded. "Why do you keep making other men president? *You* should be president."

Tony laughed bitterly.

Carmen turned her inquisitive face toward him. She was propped up in bed wearing a pair of studious-looking wire-rimmed glasses. "Is that so funny?" she asked.

"It is not my destiny."

"'Not my destiny,'" Carmen echoed. "I hate it when you make these pronouncements. You're not making a speech. Why don't you just say what you mean?"

"What I mean is that the people who own this country would never let that happen," Tony said irritably. "To be behind the scenes, okay. To pull the strings. But when they look on the stage they want to see one of their own."

"But, Tony, you're just as rich as they are."

"I am the richest man in Panama," he said, although remembering his Colombian guests, Escobar and the others, he added, "at least, I am the richest *Panamanian* in Panama."

"Then what's your problem? That you're not in the Union Club? Is that what you want? To be a part of the elite? Look, they're not the people you think they are. I know, Tony. I've been around them all my life. Sometimes I think you have a complex, you know. You think you're inferior and it makes you crazy."

Tony could see that further lovemaking was out of the question. He put on his red underwear and began tying the ribbons around his ankles to ward off the Colombian hex.

"So suddenly you get in a bad mood," said Carmen. "I was trying to support you, and you start to sulk."

"Of course I'm inferior—in their eyes!" Tony snapped. "I'm not white. This is not something I'm imagining! It's not a 'complex.' The plain fact is that it would be easier for you to be president than me. Look at your skin—it's a passport for anything you desire. Me—I can't imagine what it would be like, even though I think about it all the time—Tony Noriega, with a clear white complexion! Do you think that people would make me into their demon then? No, it's because I'm a mestizo with this fucking pox on my face!"

Carmen sat for a moment and then wordlessly put her beautiful white hand on his. He stared at it, feeling drained by his outburst and overwhelmed by an emotion that he fought against, the one emotion that he should never allow himself to feel. He was in love, helplessly, hopelessly in love. And that made him so furious. He knew very well how vulnerable love made him, and how foolish. For him, love was a no-win proposition. It went only in one direction.

"You know, even when I was a boy, I understood where my life was going to lead me," he said, examining Carmen's lovely fingers. "I saw the white asses in their fancy cars and gigantic homes, but I knew in my heart that little Tony in the streets was smarter, he had bigger balls! And all my life I planned how I would become more powerful than they. It was like a mission from God. So I don't care that they don't love Tony! Nobody loves Tony! Even you don't love me. I know this. But respect. And fear. This is my language. Without power, I don't exist. Even for you."

Carmen pulled her hand away. "Honestly, Tony, sometimes I think you're only fucking me out of revenge."

CHAPTER 13

For MORE THAN A fortnight Father Jorge had lain in a crowded cell in the basement of La Modelo in a state of semiconsciousness. In his more lucid moments he listened to the conversation of the other prisoners, some of whom had been in this same dark, shit-stained cage since the Torrijos years. They were killers, by and large, except for a dozen political prisoners who lived in constant fear of the criminals. They huddled together for protection. Father Jorge was vaguely aware that they included him in their circle in order to guard him against the others, but he also knew that safety was out of the question.

The priest could not talk except through his clenched teeth. The slightest movement caused his broken jaw to work itself loose, with agonizing pain. He spent most of his time lying on his hammock because his feet were swollen and infected. He tried to avoid pondering the damage that had been done to him, but there was little else to think about. His thought processes were vague and fragmentary. His legs throbbed, but his feet had no feeling at all. He could see the infection and wondered if it was gangrenous, and if so, whether he would lose his legs. He might also lose his life, but that prospect was to some extent less awful than the thought of being maimed.

Even in his dizzy state, Father Jorge sensed the tension in the cage, the angry, unspoken currents of power that stirred beneath the interactions of the men. He had begun to understand that the central source of the conflict was him. Fear and resentment and other emotions that were not as clear to him swirled around the dim cell. One of the criminals, a bald and muscular man named Lucho, gave him a portion of his soup every day. They received only soup, beans, and bread. If soup wasn't served, Father Jorge couldn't eat at all, since he couldn't chew. More important, Lucho also gave him a straw to eat with. At first the priest simply accepted it without thinking, but he noticed the hostile expressions of the other criminals and he gradually realized that their anger was connected to his use of the straw. Later, he saw them snorting cocaine with the same straw.

The cage opposite theirs was filled with madmen. When they found out that the wounded man was a priest, they begged him to hear their confessions, but he was unable to respond because of his jaw. Now they spent hours every day screaming at him, and cursing God, and making bizarre boasts of their sins. Sometimes they pelted the cage with turds. The men in Father Jorge's cage crowded together away from the bars, trying to keep out of range. There was nothing to do with madmen, but they looked sullenly at Father Jorge, whose presence had unsettled the fragile balance of power.

"Don't mind them, Father, they are animals," Lucho said one afternoon as he gave him the straw and helped himself to the priest's bowl of beans. Lucho wore a copper bracelet on his wrist. Since all jewelry had been confiscated from the other prisoners, this bracelet became an object of fascination and envy. Lucho was the caretaker of the straw and apparently the supplier of the cocaine as well.

When Father Jorge sat up to eat, he felt light-headed and confused.

"Your feet look better today," said Lucho. "The swelling is going down. Soon your jaw will heal. In a week, perhaps. I am a patient man. I don't want to hurt you, Father. I will be gentle with you."

Father Jorge realized that he was being tended like a farm animal. And it wasn't just Lucho who watched his progress. Sometimes he would awaken to see men kneeling beside him, just staring at him or touching his hair. Sex was as common as drugs in the cage; there was little attempt among his cellmates to be discreet in their couplings.

He wondered why he had not been interrogated. When he heard sounds of torture he expected that soon someone would come for him. His head was full of dangerous knowledge, names of people in the resistance, places of meeting, plans for the future. With every ounce of will he would resist betraying the others—but how long would he be able to hold out? He prayed for the strength to die rather than talk.

The political prisoners were led by a wiry intellectual named Tristan Solarte. He had a vitality that made him seem like a living person among a horde of ghosts. Lucho largely left him alone, which was, in its way, a grudging homage to Tristan's quiet dignity and his political courage—he had been one of Noriega's most relentless critics. Tristan had "disappeared" from his house five months before, and Father Jorge was relieved to discover that he was still alive.

Tristan began sleeping next to Father Jorge and spent much of each day at his side, chatting in a friendly fashion despite the priest's limited ability to respond. Gradually Father Jorge realized that Tristan was guarding him against the sexual advances of Lucho and the other men. "You know what they charged me with?" Tristan told him one night. "Nothing! There's a new calumny law that allows them to lock up a person for five years in preventive detention just for being accused of slander. Isn't that absurd? Maybe that's what they've done with you, Father. All those masses you said for Hugo—they're getting even with you for that."

"Not even a hearing?" the priest asked through his clenched teeth. His only hope of getting word to the Nuncio was that he would be charged with a crime and allowed to enter a plea. That much would be on the public record. It had never occurred to him that he could remain here for years with no hope of being heard. He looked at some of the long-timers and imagined himself with a scraggly gray beard down to his navel.

One day he lay on his hammock with his feet raised against the wall. He had tried to keep his feet elevated after awakening to find a rat gnawing at his wounds. The rats and the prisoners lived in a surly coexistence. There was so much marijuana in the prison that the rats wandered around in a half-stoned state, boldly slaking their thirst from the bowl of the toilet. The rodents had a distinct family hierarchy. For a week or so there were only three regular rat visitors to the cell, but then the fourth one reappeared. The priest noticed that her teats were enlarged; she must have a nest of babies somewhere. Soon there would be an entire new litter to contend with. He watched the mother rat sniffing about under the hammocks, looking for shoes. They ate anything leather—for the salt, he supposed.

"Goddamn vermin!" Lucho screamed. He suddenly snatched the mother rat up by the tail and held it in front of his face. "You think you can get away with that?" The rat was squirming and snapping the air, but then stopped to look at Lucho as he yelled at it. They were probably both stoned, the priest thought; otherwise, the rat would not have let itself get caught. There was also something weird in the moment that passed between Lucho and the rat, as if there were a remote chance of communication, before Lucho swung the animal by its tail and brained it against the bars.

"Fuck, Lucho, you made a mess!" one of the criminals cried, wiping rat blood off his face.

The madmen across the hall came back to life, screaming at Lucho. They apparently regarded the rats as pets. They cursed and cried. Lucho taunted them by holding the carcass outside the cage, then he flipped it toward them. But the rat struck the bars of the other cage and then lay in the hallway, still seeping blood.

"Great, Lucho, now it's going to stink up the place!"

Lucho turned and hit the man who complained, then pressed his hands against the man's throat. "You want me to do the same to you?" The muscles swelled in Lucho's massive arms and his copper bracelet glinted in the faint yellow light. When he let go, the man dropped to his knees and coughed up blood.

For a while the men in the cage were quiet. They were all wary of what was going to happen next. Eventually the food cart arrived and Lucho came to the priest with his bowl of soup.

"You need to eat more, Father, you're getting too thin," he said. "The others will give you their soup as well."

"This is enough," the priest murmured.

Lucho touched Father Jorge's thigh. "You are like a broomstick. It's not attractive. You will eat what I say."

"He's doing what he can, Lucho," Tristan said evenly. "You cannot force a man to eat more than he can keep down."

Lucho darkened and looked as if he were going to strike the older man, but instead he turned to Father Jorge and kissed him fully on the lips. "Remember, I'm the one who is taking care of you. If you want protection, you have no choice." Then he glared at Tristan and walked away. Tristan looked helplessly at the priest. There was nothing to say.

Father Jorge slept fitfully. He could still feel Lucho's lips on his, no matter how often he wiped his mouth. The kiss posed questions about himself that he did not want to face. He was frightened of Lucho but more frightened of the longing that the kiss had awakened.

"Get up, Father," the pudgy guard said. He was holding a set of leg chains.

"What are you doing?" Lucho asked furiously.

"They want him," the guard said simply.

"He's mine!" Lucho said. "We have an agreement!"

The guard shrugged. He was a pig-faced man with eyes that were too indifferent to be thought of as cruel. "I have no control over this," he said. "They want the priest."

Father Jorge still had not moved.

"Get up," the guard said again as he opened the cage.

Lucho took a few menacing steps toward the open gate, but then he suddenly stopped and slumped onto his cot and began to cry.

Father Jorge tentatively put his bare feet on the floor. He had not walked more than a few paces in a long time, and just standing made him feel faint. When he put weight on his feet, pain shot all the way through his body and into his shoulders. The madmen were strangely quiet. The guard fastened the irons around his legs. The chains were absurdly unnecessary; he was far more hobbled by his feet.

The stairwell was full of blinding sunlight, but instead of going up into the courtyard, the guard led him down the steps, into a lower basement. The hallway was almost black, but there was a room with a bare yellow bulb, and the guard pushed him toward the crack of light coming from the half-opened door.

The floor of the room was covered with stained sawdust, stinking of the blood that had already been shed there. A large man with a club in his belt gave him an appraising look, then smiled dismissively. "Sit," he said.

Father Jorge sat in an armless wooden chair in the center of the room under the light.

The large man suddenly started coughing. He took an inhaler from his pocket and gave himself two quick bursts, and when he spoke his voice sounded high and wavery, as if he had been breathing laughing gas. "We have some questions for you, which you will answer. Don't think about the alternative. I realize that you are a priest, but that doesn't mean anything to me. I will gladly treat you just as we have treated the others—even worse if it suits me. Answer our questions and you can go. If you have any ideas about resisting us, put them out of your mind.

You can make it easy or we can make you regret you were ever born."

There were no instruments of torture that the priest could see. The pudgy guard and the other man both had clubs. He supposed that was all they needed. A few feet away a woman with a steno pad took a sharpened pencil from her purse and gave him an expectant look. In his cell, Father Jorge had rehearsed how he would respond to this moment. He had decided to face death with as much courage as he could summon.

"What do you want to know?" the priest asked. He was shocked at himself. The words seemed to come out of his mouth unbidden, as if they had their own right to exist. Within twenty minutes he had given them all the names that he could remember. He was surprised he had so little to say. His shame was great, but his longing for life was greater. Later he would believe that the splash of sunlight in the stairwell had undone him. After another hour the man with the inhaler opened the door and the pig-faced guard led him outside. His eyes filled with tears in the sunlight. He was free, but he was no longer the same man. No, he would never be the same man.

THE NUNCIATURE WAS subdued despite the many refugees who usually liked to congregate in the hallway or drink coffee and play bridge with the Nuncio in the dining room. For the past week the guests had been scrupulously silent, tiptoeing and whispering to keep from disturbing Father Jorge. Sister Sarita had been a nurse in her youth, and she had skillfully lanced the infection in his feet and extracted the remaining shards of glass. The bones of his jaw had begun to knit back together, but the priest was still in constant pain. One of the refugees, the owner of a Jaguar dealership, made a telephone call and soon a small package arrived at the nunciature. Sister Sarita took it into the kitchen, where the Nuncio found her mixing white powder into a saucepan.

"What is it?" he asked her.

"Heroin," she said nonchalantly.

"Sister! Holy Mother of God! You can't have such things in this place! Of all things!"

"It's a narcotic, like any other he would have if you would let him go to a real hospital," she said defiantly. "And if you think I'm going to let that beautiful young man suffer any more without painkillers, you are very much mistaken."

The Nuncio bit his tongue. He didn't want to let Father Jorge out of his sight, and he depended on Sister Sarita to take care of him.

Soon Father Jorge was resting better, although an intermittent fever still raged. Except for the penicillin and heroin injections, the Nuncio took on most of the nursing tasks himself. Some redness and signs of infection still remained, but after a few days the swelling subsided. Father Jorge slept and slept. It was as if he didn't want to be awake. Whenever he came to, they stuffed him with bouillon and Jell-O.

The Civic Crusade met Tuesday evenings in the library of the nunciature. These gatherings had become increasingly crowded, in part because of the refugees, who were always present, but also because the resistance movement had been revitalized by the American attempts to remove General Noriega from power. Spontaneous strikes and protests broke out nearly every day despite the brutality of the PDF. Noriega's spies planted rumors at a Lions Club luncheon that any demonstrator who was sent to La Modelo a second time would be raped by prisoners with AIDS. Most people thought it was a characteristic bit of psychological warfare on the General's part, but there were enough infected prisoners to make the threat sound credible. In any case, no one who had been there wanted to return.

One day, with no prior notice, the trial of Roberto Díaz Herrera came on television, interrupting a game show. A nun came running to the Nuncio and told him to turn on his set. Until then no one had known what had happened to Roberto since the attack on his mansion. Most people thought he had been killed, so the trial caught everyone by surprise. It was a weird piece of political stagecraft. The prosecutor was a harried young woman in an advanced state of pregnancy who waddled around the courtroom with her hands pressed to the small of her back. She charged Roberto with "an attack against the internal personality of the state," a crime no one had ever heard of. Finally the camera turned to the defendant. Roberto looked dazed but unmarked. The Nuncio suspected that he had been drugged. "Yes, I declare myself guilty," Roberto said in a slurred voice. The whole affair was over in minutes. Roberto was transported to a military prison on Coiba, which was famous for the number of prisoners who had "hanged themselves" in their cells.

So the mood in the library was both grim and pragmatic. Most of the members of the Civic Crusade were unwilling revolutionaries, more comfortable in their boardrooms or drinking cocktails in the lobby of the Marriott. They were frightened by the dark road ahead and the prospect of violence, exile, and personal ruin. They were also chastened by the revolutions of Nicaragua and El Salvador and the damage that had been done to those tragic republics. Until recently, no one had believed that Panama would ever sink into that circle of hell, but they had been to enough funerals now to realize that anything could happen. They were not even certain that they were secure in the nunciature; if Noriega was willing to stoop to assassination, why should he hesitate to violate the sanctuary of a foreign embassy? A truckload of soldiers waited on the corner of Avenida Balboa, making this scenario seem very likely.

The last thing the civic leaders wanted was for the Left to seize control of the opposition; indeed, the great paradox was that Hugo Spadafora, the martyred symbol of the resistance, was the creature they feared most—a romantic leftist revolutionary. If Hugo had still been alive, nearly everyone in the library would have secretly sided with Noriega. They wanted something unthinkable in Central America, a bourgeois coup. It troubled the

Nuncio that the entire revolution seemed to be a revolt on the part of the white upper class against the mestizo lower class that Noriega represented.

Some of the most prominent businesspeople and political figures in the country were present, including some who had been bloodied in the streets or in Roberto's mansion: Guillermo Endara, a corpulent attorney whose black glasses were perpetually sliding down his nose; Aurelio Barría, president of the Chamber of Commerce, who had succeeded the murdered Serafín Mitrotti as head of the opposition; and Ricardo Arias Calderón, the stern and slender philosophy professor they called "the Monk" because of his ascetic habits. Arias Calderón had been waging a fearless and nearly solitary struggle against the military dictatorship most of his life. Even Naomi Amaya, the country's most famous madam, was present. The Nuncio secretly admired her as a formidable source of information.

Jack Tarpley, the American ambassador, also slipped in the now-famous back door of the nunciature, along with a political attaché and a security officer who scanned the library for listening devices before the meeting began. The Nuncio was astonished that nothing was found.

The ambassador began by describing American efforts to persuade General Noriega to leave Panama peacefully. They were two-pronged. One plan being developed with certain Panamanian exiles (whose names were not mentioned but were known to everyone) provided that Noriega and his top officers would step down and new elections would be held. The negotiations were currently snagged on the question of the General's indictment on drug charges in Florida. Noriega wanted the indictment quashed; the Reagan administration was reluctant to interfere in an independent legal proceeding, even though it seemed unlikely that the General would ever face trial. Some monetary inducements surfaced to sweeten the deal. While that line was being pursued, the administration had also frozen all Panamanian assets in the United States. The strategy, as the ambassador explained it, was to paralyze the Panamanian economy and make it impossible for General Noriega to operate.

"You are talking about destroying the very people in this room—the people who are leading the opposition," said the head of the Coca-Cola bottling plant. "We'll be the hardest hit—and Tony will just laugh at us. Meanwhile, our employees will suffer. God knows how long we'll be able to pay them."

"Even General Noriega has to make a payroll," Ambassador Tarpley pointed out. "We think the best way of causing dissension in the ranks of the PDF is to make it clear that nobody gets paid until the boss steps aside."

"You're encouraging a military coup, in other words," Endara said.

"We'd certainly welcome a change in leadership, however it comes about."

"So we have a coup; what keeps us from getting another Noriega?" Arias Calderón asked. "As long as the military runs the country, does it really matter who runs the military? It's the system that needs to be changed, and the way to change the system is to eliminate the PDF altogether."

"Of course it matters who runs the military," said Marta Ungo, the wizened society columnist for Radio Impacto. She was eighty years old and had dyed her hair bright red. She was also the only Panamanian in the room who carried a U.S. visa in her passport, a matter of extraordinary prestige and gravity in this country. "We need a strong man to lead us. You know that Panamanians can never govern themselves."

This statement led to outbursts from all sides of the room. Ungo was not alone in her sentiments. There were still many Torrijistas who longed for the relatively benign paternalism of those days. They remembered that it was Torrijos who had negotiated the canal treaties, but nostalgia had allowed them to forget that it was Torrijos who created Noriega and used him to turn the country into a criminal police state.

"There is a much better solution than this policy of economic starvation," said a small man in a pink polo shirt whom the Nuncio didn't know. "It's obvious—the gringos should just open the gates of Fort Clayton and drive their tanks to the Comandancia. Who could really resist them? Seriously, do you think the PDF would engage them? Not at all. It would be over in minutes. And then you could take Pineapple Face to Miami and put him in jail, where he belongs. We would all be happy about this, wouldn't we? So I think the Americans should just do this favor for everyone, and tomorrow we can start building our country again."

From the way others were nodding assent, the Nuncio realized the man in the pink shirt was voicing the unspoken wishes of the majority of the people in this room. They dreaded seeing their businesses ruined, their employees out of work. The threat of La Modelo weighed constantly on their minds. Also, many of them frankly held the United States responsible for creating Noriega in the first place and supporting him as he helped the narcos extend their filthy empire. Why shouldn't the Americans take care of the problem they helped to create? Perhaps it was as easy as the man suggested.

As the Nuncio thought about it, however, he saw how easily such a plan could go wrong. Suppose the PDF resisted valiantly—how many casualties was the United States prepared to sacrifice? Even though Noriega was not an elected head of state, everyone recognized him as the Panamanian leader, and the precedent of knocking down a barracks to kidnap the commander in chief was a diplomatic taboo. One could only imagine the fuss this nouveau gunboat imperialism would stir up in other Latin countries. The Japanese and the Europeans would seize the opportunity to negotiate preferential trade treaties at the expense of the Americans. Moreover, Noriega was the prince of chaos. If he could hold off the Americans for a few weeks, he would gain the upper hand. He could use the opportunity to incite people against the Yanqui aggressor, making himself into a nationalist hero rather than a dictatorial drug lord. His Dignity Battalion would own the streets and wage class warfare in the name of national pride. And looming over the entire fiasco was the fate of the strategically critical but so vulnerable and easily sabotaged Panama Canal—the jugular vein of the Americas. It dawned on the Nuncio that the man in the pink shirt was probably an agent provocateur. Of course, Noriega would have his spies here. It would be naive to think otherwise.

And yet, what could be done about it? Without evidence, the Nuncio couldn't throw the man out, and even if he did, there were likely others in the room who were providing information. In the Nuncio's experience, the best way of dealing with a traitor was to feed him information one would want him to have, whether accurate or not.

"The United States has no interest in intervening militarily," the ambassador said quickly. "We have to work as best we can within the structure of legitimate authority. And so we must start by acknowledging that the United States continues to recognize Eric Arturo Delvalle as the legally constituted president of Panama—even though your parliament has nominally removed him."

The ambassador's voice was overridden by loud objections from the fifty-odd Panamanians present. "With all due respect, Jack, we can never support that clown," said Arias Calderón. "He doesn't even have the nerve to appear in public. He's still hiding in his vacation house at the racetrack."

"And how can you call him the legal president anyway?" Barría shouted passionately. "This man conspired to overthrow Nicky Barletta. This is a crime—even though Barletta was fraudulently elected in the first place."

"We need a clean slate," Naomi Amaya said as the others noisily agreed.

Ambassador Tarpley waved his hands to quell the uproar. "I know that Delvalle is tarnished goods, but whatever action is taken, it must have the appearance of advancing democracy. Believe me, we are looking for a Panamanian solution to this crisis, but until then we have to have someone—anyone—that we can deal with on a legitimate basis. And it must be someone that everyone in this room agrees upon. Otherwise, the opposition will be divided, and then—forget it. The revolution is over. Noriega will stay in control. So unless you have a sudden change in the power structure—call it a coup or whatever you will—our position is that Delvalle is the lesser evil."

"He may be less evil, but Delvalle is still worse than Noriega," said Ungo, pricking the air with her silver cigarette holder. "Delvalle is weak and stupid. We cannot have such a man in control. Who knows how he might be used? Besides, he's unforgivably boring."

The Nuncio looked around the room. On this point Ungo was victorious.

"Perhaps there is another alternative," the Nuncio said. "I advance this suggestion merely as an observation, since it is not my place to appear partisan. But were the Civic Crusade to create its own political party, with its own slate of candidates, then you would have the opportunity to endorse the restoration of Mr. Delvalle to the office of president while at the same time indicating your opposition by campaigning against him."

The ambassador looked at the Nuncio with undisguised admiration. "I think it's a stroke of genius," he said.

As the meeting was ending, the Nuncio put a hand on the shoulder of the man in the pink shirt. He felt him startle. "I appreciate your comment," the Nuncio said casually. "But the truth is the gringos will never overthrow Tony. They will buy him out— it's the best solution for everyone. He can't stay in power forever. This way, he gets paid for his trouble, and life goes on. What do you think?"

"Why—I suppose you're right, Monseñor," the little man said nervously.

"Yes, if we all behave sensibly, no one needs to be harmed," the Nuncio said, "on either side. Because one day Tony Noriega will be gone, and those who supported him will face the consequences. Better for everyone to find a peaceful solution."

The Nuncio could tell by the expression in the man's eyes

that the point had been made. He could only hope that the message would be delivered.

O F COURSE, NOTHING remains secret in Panama for more than a day," the Nuncio wrote in his weekly intelligence report to Cardinal Falthauser. These dispatches were collected just before lunch in order to make the afternoon Alitalia flight to Rome. "GENERAL NORIEGA has a source in the U.S. State Department who told him about the freezing of Panamanian assets the very afternoon the decision was made. He managed to get $10 million out of American banks before the door slammed shut. Meanwhile, the Americans have evacuated every liquid asset they can find. Overnight, money has disappeared from Panama. Most of the ready deposits were smuggled out of American-controlled banks disguised as trash. A garbage truck passed through the alleyways and picked up more than $100 million and transported it to Fort Clayton, where it was flown out of the country on cargo planes. Milk and bread have disappeared from the shelves. One sees fires burning in the streets, and gunshots break out with no explanation. Since no one pays taxes now, the government has been reduced to living off the revenue of parking meters and lottery tickets. We are living on canned meat and reading by candlelight.

"The Americans are clearly signaling their support for a coup, and yet, only a few days ago, several of Noriega's most trusted officers, including MAJOR FERNANDO QUEZADA, MAJOR JAIME BENITEZ, and the head of the Panamanian police, COLONEL LEONIDAS MACIAS, attempted to overtake the Comandancia. It seems clear that General Noriega knew about the attempt all along. When the plotters arrived at the headquarters, they walked into a fatal trap. They were easily captured by Noriega loyalists. The loyalists were led by MAJOR MOISES GIROLDI, who single-handedly defeated the coup even though he was held at gunpoint by the insurgents. One can only regret that he spent his courage on behalf of such an unworthy result.

"Thus the General has spun a web that entrapped his best officers, the very ones the Americans and the majority of Panamanians had hoped would put an end to this wicked regime.

"What concerns me is the possibility—one might say the likelihood—of Noriega's using the office of the papal nuncio as a target for political attack. I know very well of the Vatican's extreme reluctance to be drawn into local disputes. I am mindful, too, that part of my mission as an ambassador is to avoid controversy and to advance the standing of the Church as a political body. I am also bound by my obligation as a priest, however, and the daily increase in cruelty and danger that one sees everywhere in Panama tests the restraint of even the most jaded diplomat. As I am reminded again and again by younger charges in our midst, the Church must stand for certain moral principles. I know you find this paradoxical coming from me, Hans, as I have always been the most pragmatic of priests. But should we consider taking a stand? Should the Church issue a statement condemning General Noriega's actions and calling upon him to step down from power before more damage is done to this enchanted jungledom?

"I await your urgent reply . . ."

CHAPTER **14**

D O YOU THINK men would be different if they were not raised by women?" Tony asked. It was getting dark outside and twilight shadows crept across the bedroom.

"Have you had another fight with Felicidad?" César asked as he returned carrying a tray of cheeses and a bottle of Fonset-Lacour.

"Worse."

"Carmen? Really? Well, honestly, I'm not surprised." César set the snack tray on the bedside table.

"They can program us because they are our mothers and they have all the control over our lives. Something they do, you know; it's like hypnosis. We're under their spell. This is despite the fact that they behave irrationally and often have strange odors."

"Men aren't so perfect, either."

"She complains that I won't marry her, then she threatens to leave me."

"I think she has a right to expect commitment on your part, one way or the other. She's been very loyal, and look what you've put her through."

Tony took a slice of cheese from the tray and chewed it contemplatively. "In an ideal world, of course, I would marry her. She is the only woman I love. But I have made a commitment already—I'm a married man."

"How do I fit into that?" César asked as he poured them each a glass of wine.

"This is not exactly infidelity," said Tony. "It's a completely different relationship."

César laughed. "You have the morals of a rubber ball. Why do you even bother to justify yourself? You do what you want anyway. You used to tell me that we should rid ourselves of all morality."

"I still believe it is the responsibility of the man in power to act in his self-interest and not out of some idealistic notion of right and wrong. The ruler can never know what is absolutely right. He can only know what he wants. History is filled with examples of the harmfulness of moral actions."

"I'm not talking about matters of state, Tony. I'm talking about getting a divorce and making an honest woman out of Carmen."

"The people would not stand for it. I suppose it is a sacrifice on my part, an act of penance, perhaps. The people expect their leader to behave loyally to his wife in public, no matter what. It's unreasonable, but there it is."

"Shit, Tony, if you're going to do penance, try giving something up for the Colombians. These guys live by a code, you know. You hurt them, they kill you. Maybe you can get rid of Escobar and the Ochoas, but they have cousins waiting in line. You'll never get another peaceful night's sleep. I'm telling you as a friend. You can't double-cross people like that, Tony. You go too far."

Tony thought about that for a moment. "You know, all my life people have been saying this to me, that I go too far. But I keep going and going. And I never get to this place, 'too far.' Tell me, where is it? Can we see it from here?" He laughed and gulped down another cheese cracker.

"Okay, do what you want," said César. "But listen to me, Tony. God might forgive you. But I don't think you can ask that of the Colombians."

Father Jorge set his crutches outside the confessional and eased himself onto the unforgiving bench. A line of schoolgirls in white cotton blouses and green skirts awaited him with the most ingenious sins to confess, some of which seemed to have been invented for the sole purpose of confessing to the now notorious priest. His spell in La Modelo had made him into a hero of the resistance. People were beginning to point to him and look at him with a deference that was altogether unfamiliar. The irony was unbearable.

The last of the schoolgirls confessed to eating an entire chocolate flan by herself, believing she had committed the sin of gluttony. She was a slender thing, and Father Jorge tried to reassure her, but she would not be satisfied until he had dosed her with a Hail Mary and urged moderation in the future. When she had gone, Father Jorge remained in the box, reading *La Prensa*. The paper said that because some of the military officers in the failed coup had been to school in the United States, General Noriega was holding the Americans responsible—this despite the fact that the Americans had so conspicuously failed to aid the rebels.

"May we talk, Father?"

The raspy voice on the other side of the screen belonged to the intelligence officer who had been here before. "Do you want to make a confession?" the priest asked.

"Yes, but I'm not certain of my sin," the soldier said. "I've done something very disturbing. I thought I was saving lives. Now I don't know what I've done, or why."

"What is it that you've done?"

"I'm the one who stopped the coup attempt."

Father Jorge realized that he was talking to Major Giroldi, Noriega's savior.

"I know what you're thinking, Father, but I was not a part of any grand scheme to entrap the plotters, like people say. If there was a trap, I didn't know about it." The soldier said that he had been awakened by an AK-47 in his ear. He thought he was going to be killed, and he was filled with shame for the life he had led and with fear, knowing that he was going to have to face God. "Major Benitez told me to surrender my men. I insisted on seeing them face-to-face. I swear, until I walked to the parade ground and stood in front of the troops, I wasn't certain what I might do." His loyal men stood before him, and Benitez held his gun on him, prepared to shoot. The officer was torn between wanting not to disappoint his troops and fearing that he would be killed.

"The odd thing is that if Benitez had only awakened me that morning and asked me to join him, rather than threatening to kill me, I would gladly have gone over to the rebels. They were good men—Quezada especially. But I never thought he would lead a rebellion. We've known each other forever. I only wish he had come to me himself and asked for my help. But he put his trust in other men, and some of them betrayed him."

The garrison had been understaffed that morning, Giroldi remembered—scarcely two hundred men, all under his command. "I've gone over this in my mind a million times now. Tony is popular with the crooks at the top, but among the men he is an embarrassment. Most of the other divisions would have supported a quick, decisive action. I could see in the eyes of my troops that they were only waiting for me to declare myself, and I was sure they would support me, whatever I said."

Father Jorge sat silently. He had not known how close the coup had come to succeeding. He felt the loss even more.

"The words came out of my mouth, 'Seize him!' " Giroldi continued. "I surprised even myself. In a single moment Benitez was overcome and surrendered his weapon. I don't know why he didn't kill me. He said, 'You fool!' and I knew he was right, instantly I knew this. And yet the alternative might have been very bloody if General Noriega had been able to rally any of the other divisions. The situation was unpredictable. I thought that, this way, I would be the only one to die."

"What did you do then?"

"There is a machine gun on the wall of the Comandancia. I ran up and fired a burst into the air. These were the only shots of the coup, and they were mine. I only did it to awaken the remaining troops. They all came running to the parade ground, and we gathered the conspirators and locked them in the barbershop."

"Where was the General?"

"I don't know where he was during the attempt. He arrived about an hour later, after everything was secure. He took me into his office and embraced me. Then we went out on the balcony and watched the troops assemble. The General asked for the conspirators to be brought out. They had already been stripped and beaten, and now they were naked and wrapped in American flags. It was pathetic, really. They were such good men.

"The General saluted me in front of everyone and called me a hero. I heard the men cheering, but I saw Quezada looking at me as I stood next to the General. It was as if he was saying that General Noriega is my responsibility now. I had stolen the opportunity for change. Now anything that happens is on my head. I cannot escape this thought.

"And then the troops began to beat the conspirators with their rifle butts until the blood ran in the gutters. You could see nothing but blood everywhere. I thought I was going to vomit in disgust. And I knew it was my responsibility. Panama will be destroyed because I surrendered to the vanity of heroism. When the General put his arm around me and kissed me, it was like being anointed by the devil. And he said, 'I want you always at my side.'"

Father Jorge was silent for a moment, trying to digest the officer's story. Finally he asked, "What do you want of me? Are you asking for forgiveness?"

"I honestly don't know, Father. What I did was a terrible mistake, but is it a sin?"

"No, I cannot find sinfulness in your actions. Whatever you did was done from good motives, no matter what the outcome. For whatever reason, God has chosen to spare you. Perhaps he has a higher use for you."

O F COURSE, this is purely speculative at this point, General, but I believe we can find you sanctuary in Madrid, with a satisfactory stipend that should take care of your material needs." Mark Ortega, the Panamanian lobbyist from Nocera, Lemann & Fallows, produced a handsome brochure that detailed the payout plan, along with real-estate prices and the menus of some of the finest restaurants in the Spanish capital city. He held it upside down so Tony could read it. Tony was hanging from a bar by his Gravity Boots, a pair of shoes with hooks attached. With his arms crossed, he looked like a roosting bat.

"Madrid?" The disappointment in Tony's voice was evident.

"Madrid!" said Mark. "Latin country! Very chic! Famous nightlife! Just look—" He began flipping through the brochure, searching for evidence of Spanish good times.

"Madrid nightlife," Tony said dismally.

Mark tossed the brochure into the trash. "Okay, you don't like Madrid. Where do you want to go? You gotta give me some guidance. Nightlife—how about Monte Carlo?"

Tony shook his head. "The Shah, he tried to get into Monte Carlo. He had to come here."

"Yeah, I heard."

"I did the U.S. a big favor by taking him, believe me. The whole world turned its back on this man, but we welcomed him. We gave him first-class medical treatment. We put him up in a mansion on Contadora Island. All this we did for our American friends."

"And the boys at State appreciate it. They realize it's payback time. But you gotta help us, General," Mark said, cocking his head as he tried to get a fix on the General's inverted features. "Give us some guidelines. We can work with State. But you have to let us know where in the world you want to go."

Tony stared at the office furniture above his head. It was good, occasionally, to view the world from a fresh perspective. "I sure wanted to fuck his wife," he said after a moment.

"Excuse me?"

"The Shah. His wife. I've never been to Scotland."

"You want asylum in Scotland?"

"She used to water-ski topless. Really, for a woman of her age, she was magnificent. I've still got some pictures."

"Scotland," said Mark. "You'll have to remind me what the attraction is."

"People go fishing in suits there."

"And that sounds like fun to you?" Mark asked helplessly.

"Then tea and crumpets in the drawing room."

"I'll certainly check into it, General, although I gotta say, Scottish nightlife . . ."

Tony smiled, then burst into song. *"I love Paris in the springtime. I love Paris in the fall."* He had a surprisingly melodious tenor singing voice.

"Okay. Scotland and Paris." Mark assembled his remaining documents and stuffed them in his briefcase. "It's a start, at least."

THE NUNCIO RECEIVED his weekly diplomatic pouch from the courier and immediately retired to the library. He took the precaution of locking the door, although it was wholly unnecessary. Not one of the dozen refugees who were chattering in the hallway expressed any interest in Vatican politics, and he could tell by the heft of the pouch that there was no great bundle of cash inside to cover expenses. But prudence was built into his nature; prudence was the mirrored half of the scheming side of his personality. He instinctively protected himself against people like himself.

He broke the seal and pulled out the manila envelope inside. There were the usual receipts for the supplies he had ordered, a compendium of policy statements and bulletins, and the cherished *Rapporto di Informazione Riservata presso la Santa Sede,* a gossipy monthly newsletter that kept the diplomatic corps up-to-date on the fortunes of the Church hierarchy. It was by far the most secret document normally transmitted via diplomatic mail. This month featured a report handicapping the prospects for the successor to Joseph Cardinal Ratzinger—the Nuncio's nemesis—in the Congregation for the Doctrine of the Faith. He placed the report in his drawer for a quiet moment later in the afternoon, feeling a naughty anticipatory thrill.

The final item was a response from Cardinal Falthauser. It was under a separate seal. The Nuncio opened the letter and held it near the reading lamp, where he could read the narrowly spaced text.

Secretariat of State
Vatican City
March 28, 1988

My Dear Monsignor Morette:

As you know very well, one of your principal duties as Saint Paul's ambassador is to keep the Church officially uninvolved with local disputes. The Holy See is dismayed by the evident use of the nunciature as a plotting ground for rebellion. The laws of sanctuary are clear. We do not dispute the obligation to provide for the safety of citizens seeking political refuge. But we are amply persuaded that your role has leapt beyond what we can, in good conscience, endorse. We rather believe that you have encouraged the use of the Church's facilities to spread sedi-

200

tion, and in this you have very nearly approached our official rebuke.

It is not the nuncio's task to meddle in the affairs of the country to which he is posted. We urge that you keep this injunction in mind and conduct your behavior accordingly. This warning extends to your staff as well, whose actions reflect upon the Church as much as your own. We make special reference to Father Jorge Ugarte, your own personal secretary, whose active political involvement cannot have escaped your notice.

As for your ceaseless requests for financial succor, they are emphatically denied. While your situation is keenly appreciated, it is believed that any further assistance from the Holy See would only aggravate the situation that now attends the papal nunciature in Panama. Perhaps the natural limitation of resources will have the beneficial effect of encouraging your guests to seek refuge elsewhere.

In the meantime, we remind you that we are in the Lenten season, a time of penance and prayerful introspection . . .

The Nuncio couldn't read the final lines, his hands were shaking so. He set the letter on the leather tabletop and took a deep breath. His career appeared to be headed for a shocking conclusion. He had seen it happen before—priests who had lost favor got pushed to the margins, humiliated before their peers. At this rate he would end up with some squalid posting in Mauritania or Chad. Not that he was above serving in any capacity—that was his calling as a priest, to serve. But still!

There was another troubling nuance in Cardinal Falthauser's reprimand. Never in any of the Nuncio's official communiqués had he mentioned Father Jorge's political activities; indeed, he had carefully avoided any discussion of his secretary's imprisonment or the injuries he had sustained in the assault on Roberto's mansion. Now it was dismayingly clear to him that the Vatican had another source. He felt sick with surprise and embarrassment. Until now the Nuncio had persuaded himself that he was so far outside the Roman orbit that he was lost from view. The Vatican had given him little reason to believe otherwise. The larger world was full of startling and pressing developments. Communism was collapsing. Africa was starving. Asia was rising. Islam was advancing. God was forgotten in Europe. The Americans were liberalizing theology at the same time that they were Reaganizing politics. The Church had interests to defend everywhere. Its resources were stretched to the vanishing point. And yet, with all the hubbub of international turmoil, Cardinal Falthauser had found time to cultivate spies inside the Panamanian nunciature.

But who? Who was Falthauser's spy? The Nuncio had personally hired most of the staff, with the exception of the elderly driver, Manuelito, who had been here since Pope John XXIII, and Sister Sarita. She, of course, knew everything. Moreover, he doted on her. The very thought that she might be filing intelligence reports gave the Nuncio a chill.

As he was brooding about this, he became aware of the scurrying sounds of guests rushing up to their rooms. Doors closed, one after another. An instant later there was a knock on his door. Sister Sarita entered with what now seemed like an unusually complicated expression on her face.

"He's here," she said.

"Who?"

"Pineapple Face."

The Nuncio took a step back. Was there a plot against him? First he was rebuked for meddling in Panamanian affairs, and then the leader of the country comes calling, with who knew what agenda.

"Where's Father Jorge?"

"He's at the parish."

"Then I suppose you should send the General in, Sister."

She turned to go, but the Nuncio called after her. "You should bring us some port from the cellar—the special reserve. And if you have any of those little gâteaux in the kitchen, they would be welcome, I'm sure."

Sister Sarita sniffed and departed in an obvious huff. A moment later the General appeared at the library door. He looked pale and thinner than he had been at their last meeting. The bags under his eyes gave their own dismal report.

"General! What an honor," the Nuncio said, once again noting Noriega's curiously dead handshake. "Since we last talked, I admit, I've spent several hours rereading Augustine. I must say, I feel like I've been sent back to seminary."

Tony smiled tensely and looked around the impressive library. It was not grand, but it was very comfortable, the lair of a man who likes to spend time by himself but not too much time (as he could see by the stack of unanswered correspondence on the Nuncio's desk). Nor was it an especially religious room; aside from the garish color print of the pope on one wall and a portrait of Jesus and a simple crucifix on another, there were no sanctimonious artifacts. On the shelves were some authors Tony had in his own library—le Carré, Márquez, Gloria Vanderbilt on etiquette—in addition to the expected volumes of theology and diplomacy. Beside the Nuncio's desk was a chessboard with the pieces halted in mid-play. Tony sensed by the environment that he and the Nuncio shared certain fundamental qualities, such as a love of strategy and a need for control. From their first meeting, Tony had felt that they would become either friends or formidable adversaries. Of course, neither of them had much need for friends.

"Actually, there's another matter I've come to discuss with you, Monseñor. It concerns what I am to do with my future."

"I'm flattered that you would seek my counsel, General, but I can't imagine what would lead you to believe that I have any advice worth offering on such a serious subject."

"I need the views of someone with an international perspective," said Tony, ignoring the Nuncio's false modesty. "Besides, everyone else in this country comes to you for advice—why not me?"

Sister Sarita entered with a tray of port and sweets. She had on her most aggrieved expression—really, she looked like a galley slave—but Tony thanked her so meekly that she became flustered and avoided his glance.

"I understand the Americans have made you a generous offer," the Nuncio said as the nun left the room, making a furtive sign of the cross as she closed the door.

"I expect you can tell me every detail of the proposal. You have even better intelligence than I."

"In the Vatican, one learns to keep one's ears open."

"The Vatican—this is a culture I've always been curious about. The city where no one has sex. It's very peculiar."

The Nuncio laughed. "Yes, even I thought it was strange, although if one chooses celibacy, it's easier to be in the company of like-minded companions than in the sensual world. I spent many years there and I suppose I got used to its peculiar habits. Most of the time I labored in the Congregation for the Doctrine of the Faith."

"Isn't that what used to be called the Holy Inquisition?"

"These days we mainly investigate candidates for sainthood. I had the job of prosecuting the opposing point of view."

"So you were the devil's advocate."

"As it is popularly known, yes."

"All those years, you must have developed sympathy for the devil's perspective."

"You could say it enlarged my moral compass," the Nuncio replied blandly.

"And after holding such an important job, you must have done something very bad or very stupid to be sent off to a small tropical republic."

The Nuncio scowled impressively, his massive brows knitting together in stern reproof. "And now you find yourself in a similar position?"

"Well, I also have enemies," Tony conceded.

"But they seem very forgiving. I understand that the Americans have agreed to let you name your successor. You can even keep your money—this sounds too good to turn down!"

"All the same, I am conflicted." Tony tapped his breast pocket. "Here I have my resignation speech already prepared. It's my farewell address—a beautiful speech, I must say. I cried as I wrote it. Reason tells me resignation is the correct path."

"I hope you don't intend to deliver this speech in the nunciature."

Tony smiled thinly. "Poor Delvalle, he was such a coward. No, if I resign, I will speak to the people directly. I do not fear them."

"But you say 'if'—surely there is no alternative when the Americans have turned against you."

"The Americans do not control the universe, Monseñor."

"Just the civilized parts of it," the Nuncio said. "Perhaps there is a suitable compromise, one that can be rewarding for you and face-saving for the Americans. I don't mean to put a price on it, but can't you imagine a solution that would be acceptable? One that would satisfy your material desires and perhaps even give you a voice in the country's future?"

"That's an illusion," Tony said. "One holds the reins or one does not. Look at what happened to Somoza. He stepped down, and the bastards tracked him into Paraguay and blew him into microscopic fragments. They did not even find the hairs of his mustache. Torrijos used to say, 'The first duty of the man in power is to stay in power.'"

"Yes, and look what happened to him," said the Nuncio. "If only he had left when the time was right, perhaps his plane might not have crashed so—shall we say?—mysteriously."

"Your point is accurate, Monseñor. One rides the tiger. Tell me, do you read the Tao?"

"Eastern philosophy doesn't call to me."

"That's too bad. There is great wisdom there. Lao-tzu says that the master acts best by doing nothing." Tony leaned back and recalled the verse: *"He leads by emptying people's minds and filling their cores, by weakening their ambition and toughening their resolve. He helps people lose everything they know, everything they desire, and creates confusion in those who think they know. Practice not-doing, and everything will fall into place."*

"Are you saying, then, that you plan to do nothing?"

"It's a paradox, isn't it?" said Tony. "As long as this indictment hangs over me, there is nothing I *can* do. Money and power mean very little if I am sitting in prison. And frankly, Monseñor, there are people who will not want me to testify in an American courtroom. Some very dangerous people."

The Nuncio now understood the cause of General Noriega's sleeplessness. It was one thing to be named as a criminal defendant in a racketeering and narcotics smuggling case. It was another to be identified as a potential witness against the CIA and the Colombian mob.

"Have you spoken to the Americans about this?"

Tony scowled. "On this point, they refuse to negotiate. I think we need a go-between, someone who can speak to both sides. Someone like you."

The Nuncio leaned back in his chair and drew a deep breath. How should he respond? He wondered if his very words were being recorded and sent to the Vatican. It was a chilling thought.

"Of course, I will do what I can, General," the Nuncio said after a moment. "I only request that you keep my involvement a matter of strictest secrecy."

CHAPTER 15

THE AVIARY WAS Tony's special retreat. He spent many hours here feeding his birds and confiding secrets of state he could share with no one else. Recently, he had been able to offer several happy reports. His new policy of doing nothing had neutralized the Americans and kept the opposition completely off guard. His enemies were no longer talking about "post-Noriega Panama." They were talking about condo prices in Miami.

Romeo preened and clacked as Tony spritzed him. *"Darling darling love you darling,"* Romeo said as he nuzzled Tony's ear. Pepe, a neurotic sulfur-crested cockatoo, turned his back on the scene and began plucking feathers from his wings in a jealous fit.

Tony was so caught up in his birds that he failed to notice Felicidad storming across the lawn with a rolled-up copy of *La Prensa* in her hands, which she was waving like a machete.

"Monster!" she cried as she burst into the cage.

"Sweetness! Love!" Tony said as he retreated. "What have I done?"

Felicidad silenced him with a deafening whap across his left ear. But the newspaper was not enough. She tossed it aside and emptied a silver feeding bowl, then renewed her assault with single-minded fury. The terrified parrots banged into the mesh fence of their cage, crying and screaming curses.

"You think I don't know?" Felicidad shouted over the din. "You think all Panama does not know?"

The bowl made a resonant bong as it collided with Tony's head. "Please, please, Fela," Tony pleaded, "for the sake of our children . . ."

"How dare you invoke our precious daughters!" Felicidad redoubled her blows. "When it is you who has disgraced your children! Even in the newspaper they write about your 'Señorita Carmen.'"

"Forgive me, I'll have the newspaper closed at once."

"No more talk," Felicidad said ominously. "I'm going to discuss my options with my attorney. But in the meantime, if I ever see her in public, I'll scratch her eyes out! And yours, too!"

DR. DEMOS SEWED a final stitch in the cut over Tony's eye. "It's going to be pretty ugly for a couple of weeks, Tony. You should get yourself some very dark sunglasses to wear to the Carter reception."

Tony groaned. Having Jimmy Carter in town to supervise the presidential elections was another annoying development. Tony should have smothered the plan when it first arose, but who ever believed that the election would be genuinely contested? Now Endara, the human walrus, was making a race of it—as if it were a real election and not a ceremonial one, meant to confirm Solís Palma in his appointment to that office.

"Giroldi, what's the latest report?" Tony asked irritably.

"They say the vote is running three to one against our president," Major Giroldi said gravely.

"You are wrong, Major," Tony said. "The vote is actually in favor of the president."

"Sir?"

208

"In Panama, the civilians have a responsibility and the military has a responsibility," Tony explained. "The civilians must choose the right man to lead them. Apparently, they have failed. Now it is up to the military to correct this mistake."

"But Jimmy Carter is here . . ." Giroldi said anxiously.

"Carter! Carter! Fuck Jimmy Carter!" Tony exploded in fury. "If he knew how to run his own country, he would still be in office! Now we must act quickly in the Panamanian way to save the country from this terrible mistake. Get out there, Major, and bring me the election!"

STILL HOBBLING, Father Jorge marched with the crowd toward the Plaza de Santa Ana, where Endara and his vice presidential candidates, Billy Ford and Ricardo Arias Calderón, were scheduled to speak out against the stolen election. Polling places had been ransacked, ballot boxes confiscated and burned—and much of this outrage had been broadcast on CNN. Noriega's savagery was now obvious to the entire world. Conscious that they were in the spotlight of history and emboldened by the presence of television cameras and foreign correspondents, the citizens of Panama marched with a determination that Father Jorge had never seen. There was none of the festivity that had marked other demonstrations—instead, there was a formidable silence. The marchers wore white and waved white handkerchiefs in the air—white, white everywhere. Telephone poles all along the boulevard were studded with pineapples despite the new law that made it a crime to ridicule the physical features of government leaders. For the first time in his tenure in Panama, Father Jorge sensed a widespread resolve that change would have to come, and soon.

At the front of the parade, Guillermo Endara and his two vice presidential candidates rode in a flatbed truck, waving to their supporters as they led them toward the Presidencia. As usual, Endara's heavy black glasses looked as if they were about to slide completely off his nose. Obese, myopic, chronically short of breath, completely uncharismatic, Endara was an unlikely hero, but he had found the courage that the moment demanded. Few people knew the man's political views. Endara was for change, and change was ready to jump into his arms.

These thoughts came to Father Jorge through a sea of sadness and guilt. Although he walked among the leaders of the resistance, he knew that he was no longer one of them. He had informed on them. He had shared secrets with the enemy, and the shame of this fact was difficult to bear. He had not even been to confession since he left La Modelo. He knew that the Nuncio had desperately campaigned for his freedom, and he was grateful for that, but since his release he had allowed a silence to fall between them. This also weighed on him, since he could not bring himself to admit to the Nuncio that he was a traitor.

As the procession turned the corner into the plaza, the band suddenly stopped playing and the march stumbled to a ragged halt. The marchers in the back could not see what was happening in the front, so they continued to press forward until finally they had pushed themselves into the plaza. There they found the streets blocked by several dozen PDF troops in riot gear, carrying batons and shields.

Endara motioned to quiet the crowd, but the people were already silent, or only murmuring, and so the gesture seemed superfluous and strangely silly. He dismounted laboriously from the bed of the truck and approached the officer in charge, a pinch-faced colonel whom Father Jorge recognized as a member of the white middle class—the same people, by and large, that the officer was standing against. Perhaps for that reason the officer was unable to look into Endara's smiling, reasonable face. Once Father Jorge would have doubted that such a man could order his troops to attack his own social class, but he had learned how easily a man's allegiances could be perverted. He supposed the officer was the victim of some kind of sadistic loyalty test.

Once this man had declared himself in this fashion, he would always belong to Noriega. No one else would have him.

A stirring in the crowd caused Father Jorge to look into one of the side streets. He saw the Digbats massed there, wearing their colorful T-shirts and carrying chains and pipes. Some of them held boards with long nails protruding from them. They were just unemployed teenagers with handmade weapons, but their faces were hard and eager. Others in the crowd noticed them as well, and they began shouting like animals that have suddenly discovered that they've been trapped in the slaughter-house. With no avenue of escape, the people pressed even more into the center, into a compact, frightened horde. Father Jorge tried to push his way to the front, thinking that he might be able to persuade the officer to let the women leave, but he could scarcely move his arms in the crush.

And then the Digbats charged.

The plaza echoed with the shrieks of the mob and the wild cries of the Digbats. A woman next to Father Jorge dropped to the ground in a heap. He thought she might have been shot, but then he realized that she had fainted from fright. People around her were stepping on her in their panic. He lifted the woman's limp body and held her upright, but then he didn't know what to do with her. He simply stood there, stupidly hugging her to him and waiting for the Digbats to beat their way to them.

The Digbats advanced in a disorganized mob, swinging their bludgeons like crazed reapers moving through a field of wheat. Blood flew into the air as if it were raining upward. Father Jorge caught sight of Guillermo Endara just as a fist brushed past the candidate's face, knocking his glasses off. He looked confused and oddly denuded, the way people do who are never seen without their glasses. He dropped to his hands and knees, patting the ground and looking for his glasses, but then a pipe crashed across his skull and his face slammed into the pavement.

The woman Father Jorge was holding came back into consciousness. Her eyes were vague, but then they filled with terror.

For a moment she clung to him, but then she pushed away and began wobbling through the hysterical crowd like a sleepwalker. The entire scene was surreal—the cries, the violence, the movements that took place with hallucinatory slowness. Father Jorge struggled toward a car where he had noticed the vice presidential candidates were hiding. He wasn't certain what his own intentions were, but he felt the urgent need to act, perhaps to redeem himself. The Digbats had surrounded the car and were knocking out the windows with bats and pipes. There was a gunshot. Then Father Jorge recognized the lanky, white-haired figure of Billy Ford being pulled out of the car. His white shirt was covered with blood. Ford pushed one of the Digbats away, but just as he did another hit him squarely on the back of his head with a heavy steel pipe. Ford staggered. He began to paw the air as if he could claw his way through the mob, but they had him now. One blow after another landed. Ford's head snapped back and forth, but somehow he kept walking. It was as if he had some destination in mind and a superhuman determination to achieve it. He turned to the window of a video store where a bank of televisions was showing the stern face of Jimmy Carter lecturing the press. Ford waved at the pictures in confusion as a PDF soldier grabbed him and pushed him into a waiting armored van.

All of a sudden, as if responding to some unspoken command, the Digbats stopped their assault. Some of them tossed away their crude and bloody weapons. They looked tired and surprised by what they had done. The screaming died, and the moaning of the beaten protesters could be heard. In this moment of release, some terrible understanding passed between the Digbats and the protesters. It was the recognition that they were not separated by politics or class or generations but by their very natures; and that because of this, humanity would never be reconciled; peace would never be more than a pause in the eternal cycle of wars and revolution.

In this tragic moment Father Jorge noticed Teo Sánchez standing a few feet away with a pipe in his hands. Teo's clothes were splattered with blood and bits of gore. He was standing over the body of an unconscious woman whose face had been mangled. As soon as Father Jorge saw him, he realized that Teo had been staring at him for some time. Perhaps he was weighing whether to attack him. Father Jorge walked toward him, then fell to his knees beside the beaten woman and began to pray. Teo stood over him for a moment, then dropped his pipe and ran away. The pipe made a clanging noise in the street and then rolled over the cobblestones.

A few feet away from Father Jorge, the PDF colonel was vomiting beside his waiting jeep. Father Jorge held the hand of the woman whose face Teo had destroyed. Her nose was ruined and flat and bits of her teeth lay on the ground. He felt useless. He could tell that she was alive, but he didn't know what to do with her except to pray. He got back to his feet and walked through sticky puddles of blood to the presidential candidate. Endara was sitting up, holding a handkerchief on the wound to the back of his head. "I'm all right, Father," he said, "but check in the car—my bodyguard."

Father Jorge went to the car and looked in the shattered windows. The bodyguard had been shot in the face. Bits of his brain had scattered onto the upholstery. A fly crawled across the man's open eyes. For a moment Father Jorge thought he would be ill. He quickly blessed the bodyguard and made a cross on the man's gory forehead. Then he stared fixedly at the bright blood on his finger. Everywhere people are suffering and dying for freedom, he thought helplessly, and here I am, a traitor talking to a dead man.

CHAPTER 16

Tony stood in front of a three-way mirror examining the stylish reflections of himself. Señora Morales stood behind him and on either side. "There's nothing wrong with the jacket," she said. "It's your attitude."

"What do you think, Lollipop?" Tony asked.

Carmen sat sullenly in a stiff Danish chair. "I think you should listen to Mama," she said in a voice of weary experience.

Señora Morales tugged roughly at Tony's shoulders. "A jacket like this has a statement to make. You need to relax and let it speak for you."

Tony tried to relax, but Señora Morales was unconvinced. She took his wrist and shook it. "Loosen up!" she commanded. "This is not a uniform, General! If you want to look like Jack Kennedy, do like this—" And she slumped a bit, rolling her shoulders forward and sticking her hand where her jacket pocket would be.

"Like this?" asked Tony, trying to imitate her.

"No! Not like this." She replicated his stiff bend at the waist, a sort of Japanese bow that completely missed the point. "Like *this!"* She transformed the movement into an elegant, Eurotrash slouch. "Great men are confident! Great men carry themselves with grace and assurance! They do not poke out their chests like Tarzan. When you see them, you know what they are inside."

"You can't judge a book by its cover, Mama," Carmen said.

"Nonsense."

Tony struck another pose. Señora Morales stepped back and appraised him. "Better," she said grudgingly. "Remember, everybody loved Kennedy because he was so suave, so sophisticated. He dressed so well."

Tony stared at his reflections. He looked like a small, squat mobster in a stylishly shapeless jacket. In his opinion, the slouch made him appear a bit infirm.

"They will love you, too," Señora Morales said as she ran her hand across the rich Armani wool blend. "Now, when you speak, do this—" And she poked the air in a characteristic Kennedy gesture.

Aफ्TER CELEBRATING early Sunday mass, Father Jorge napped in the vestry. He fell deeply asleep almost immediately, and when he awakened it was with a jolt, as if he had stepped in a hole. He was disturbed without really knowing the reason why. He supposed he must have had a dream that he had now forgotten.

When he went outside the sun was so bright he felt almost blind. He squinted and limped toward a patch of shade under a banyan tree. As he was approaching, he recognized Major Giroldi sitting on a bench, waiting for him.

"May I walk with you, Father? There's something I'd like to discuss."

Father Jorge nodded.

"Let's go this way, away from the Comandancia," Giroldi suggested.

They turned down a narrow street filled with shuttered shops that had been closed since the economy died. They moved slowly because of Father Jorge's feet, which were almost healed but still tender.

"I trust I have your confidence," said Giroldi.

"Of course, although perhaps we should return to the confessional if there's something—"

Giroldi laughed grimly. "If it's a sin, I haven't committed it yet. Perhaps you could advise me."

"I will do as best as I can."

Giroldi cast an anxious glance down the street, then resumed walking and speaking in a low tone. "I am considering a desperate action. Can you imagine what this might mean? Pardon me for being so mysterious."

He wasn't being mysterious at all, in Father Jorge's opinion. The major reeked of conspiracy. "I can make a guess," the priest said.

They came to the remnants of the old walled city. Near the rubble of the wall there was a corrugated iron fence that was orange with rust and gaudily painted with graffiti. A vine had burst through the pavement and seemed to be tugging the fence into the ground, into the past, along with the vestiges of the ancient wall and the rotting apartments of Chorrillo.

"I am a Christian and a patriot, Father. Now I find these two sides of myself in a dangerous struggle. I wish to do something for my country that may place my soul in jeopardy."

"Sometimes men of faith take great chances," said the priest.

Giroldi stopped and looked directly at Father Jorge. The officer's eyes were haunted and filled with sleeplessness. "Do you ever think about the story of Abraham and Isaac? I have often wondered why God would place a man in such a position that he would have to sacrifice his son."

"He did not have to make the sacrifice, only to be willing," Father Jorge said. "God stayed his hand."

"But what if God had actually demanded the blood of Isaac? This is the question I ask myself. Can it ever be right to kill in cold blood?"

"I don't believe God would ask this."

Giroldi stared at him intently, then he began to walk again. "This is a great burden off me, Father."

"Whatever you do, you must take care to protect yourself and your family."

"Believe me, this is very much in my mind. And for that reason, I have a big favor to ask. I cannot think who else to turn to." Giroldi looked at him in embarrassment. "I want you to take a message to the CIA."

"The CIA? I don't know any such people!" Father Jorge said under his breath. "Besides, I am not sophisticated in these matters. I'm afraid I would place you in greater danger than you already are."

"Father, I need someone I can trust. At least I know where you stand. You are a hero. You have suffered for the cause. In you, Hugo's spirit lives. That is a rare thing in this country, where so many play both sides. Besides, no one would suspect you of being a conspirator with the army."

The sound of it made Father Jorge draw a quick breath. "No, no, it's too risky, too absurd."

"I can't do this myself," said Giroldi. "If I am seen, then it's over for me. There will never be an end to Noriega. But if my plan succeeds, with the help of the Americans, think how much good we can accomplish! You said yourself that men of faith must take chances. If we don't act for the good, then why should we expect goodness to follow?"

I THOUGHT WE WERE on an enemy-reduction plan," Gilbert Blancarte said as he surveyed the curses on Tony's voodoo altar. There was a photo of Ronald Reagan under an ashtray; a picture of Guillermo Endara stuck in a ball of cornmeal; and an article by Sy Hersh wrapped around a rotten tamale. Father Jorge's name was inscribed on a slip of paper and nailed to a cow tongue. Joining the pin-filled dolls of Pablo Escobar and Jesse Helms were George Bush, General Honeycutt, and a huge, menacing female figure that the witch doctor failed to recognize.

"Felicidad," Tony admitted guiltily. He was deep into a bottle of Old Parr.

"You are also having marital difficulties?"

"She's a very powerful woman. You've got to give me something for her."

Gilbert looked at the lingering yellow bruise under Tony's eye. "Do you want her dead or merely terribly punished?"

"No, no, not dead. Something like, I put it in her coffee and she becomes pleasant. And thin. Something like that."

Gilbert sniffed in his patronizing, too easily exasperated manner. "Honestly, Tony, where do you get these ideas? First, we must consult the orisha. I need a few minutes to prepare things. Why don't you get your offerings together?"

Gilbert wrapped a black turban around his head, then briskly set about clearing a space on a coarse wooden table upon which a concrete head of the god Elegguá reposed. The icon had a mouth, eyes, and nose made of cowrie shells and a knife blade sticking out of its forehead. Gilbert lit five black candles and set a coconut on the table. Then he pressed his hands together and looked around the room. Apparently everything appeared satisfactory. "Okay," he said, "what do you have to offer?"

Tony came forward and made the sign of the cross, then placed a rooster carcass on the altar, along with a bottle of rum and one of Fidel's favorite cigars. Gilbert examined them noncommittally. "*Omi tutu, ana tutu, loroye, tute ilé,*" he intoned, placing three drops of water on the god's head. "Now we will see if the orisha accepts our sacrifice." He took a hammer from his kit and with a single powerful blow split the coconut into several pieces. Milk and bits of shell flew into the air. He then tore off three pieces of rind and knelt on the floor.

"*Akueyé owó, akueyé omá, ariku babagwa.*"

"*Apkwaná,*" Tony responded.

Gilbert threw the coconut rinds on the floor. Two of them

were brown side up, one was white side up. Tony looked at the rinds and then at Gilbert.

"I don't know, Tony, it doesn't look good."

"Can't you throw it again?"

Gilbert shrugged. "I can do it, but the orisha may not like for us to be asking again without improving the offer. Haven't you got something else for him?"

Tony looked suspiciously at Elegguá. The cowrie-shell features had a kind of surprised idiot look. "What does he want?"

"That's the thing about gods, Tony. You don't know what they want until you give it to them. This Elegguá, he's the trickster. He usually likes food, he likes goats, he likes toys. But you take a chance when you're dealing with him. He's the justice giver, the score settler. If you cross the line with him, he'll punish you. You could put down a perfectly good sacrifice, but if he's turned against you, forget it. My experience is that he usually wants the thing you don't want to give."

Tony thought about this for a moment, glumly. "I don't have a goat on the premises," he said.

"Well, what do you have? It better be good."

Tony rummaged through his drawers and came up with several parrot feathers and an ornamental Japanese dildo. Gilbert placed them in front of the god and repeated the incantation. When he threw the coconut rinds, all three sides were brown side up.

The back of Tony's neck began to prickle.

"I told you we should have made a better sacrifice," Gilbert said. "You should have listened to me. I didn't want to throw the coconut again, but you insisted."

"What am I going to do now?"

Gilbert put up a silencing hand and then closed his eyes. Tony sat anxiously for several minutes as Gilbert's breath became shallow and his head lolled to the side. Finally his eyelids opened to reveal a mass of garish veins racing through the pupil-less eyeballs. Tony shivered and took another gulp of whiskey.

219

"Bad signs," said Gilbert in his helium voice. "Many enemies. Many problems. Oh, you have been bad, Tony. *Baaaaaad.*"

Baaaaaad? Hadn't he tried to get out of the narcotics business? Now the Colombians were trying to kill him. Hadn't he tried to placate the Americans? Now they were trying to remove him from power. Every step he took got him in deeper trouble. He was beginning to get a little impatient with moral reforms.

"Bad vibrations," Gilbert said. "The universe is so angry with you."

"What? What do you see?"

"Storm clouds coming. Chaos! War! Disaster!"

"Enough!" Tony cried, slamming down his whiskey glass.

But Gilbert was still lost in his trance, foretelling the awful future. "Bombs! Fire! Many people dying! Oh, Tony, it's all your fault, you really fucked up so bad . . ."

Tony poured a pail of chicken blood on Gilbert's head. The witch doctor snapped to in a violent spasm. "What's happened? Oh, my God! Blood!" he said in alarm. "Am I injured?"

"Go. Get out of here."

Gilbert looked bewildered. "You did this to me?"

"Get out of Panama," Tony said. "Leave immediately. No more of this superstitious prophecy."

Gilbert collected as much dignity as possible, given the chicken blood dripping from his nose. "I don't know what's wrong with you, Tony. You offend the gods, you got to expect punishment. That's the way it is. Me, I tried to help you. And look at what you've done. You've made a big mistake. You need all the friends you can get."

"I need you? I'm the ruler of the goddamn country! I've got an army! Millions of dollars! Everybody who does business in this country needs Tony Noriega! So don't try scaring me with your hocus-pocus. You and your *'bad vibrations'*—hah!"

"You're crazy, Tony."

"Don't forget your herbs." Tony poured a bowl of dried cieba leaves on Gilbert's head. They stuck like feathers to the chicken blood.

Gilbert rose to his feet. His face was as dark as a thundercloud. "Blasphemer! I tried to save you! But no! You can't stop yourself, can you? You have to go and do something so stupid you'll never redeem yourself. You've really fucked up now."

"Get out," said Tony. "You're lucky I'm letting you walk away."

"What you've done to me is nothing compared to what's about to happen to you, my friend. You've offended the gods, and they will destroy you! *Akwaté omú bilabao!*"

When Gilbert was gone, Tony looked around at the mess that was left behind—his ruined sacrifice, the blood on the table that was spilling onto the floor, shattered bits of coconut. He was flooded with remorse. Gilbert really was very powerful—no doubt he'd be joining the Colombians in the wanga war—and now Tony was alone, utterly alone. He looked fearfully at the impassive concrete god. Suddenly his legs went weak. He dropped to his knees and begged forgiveness. "I know I've screwed up. I don't know what got into me!" But the god radiated disfavor. "Please, please forgive me, Elegguá! I know I've made a fool of myself—it wasn't meant to show you disrespect! I was mad at Gilbert—that guy really annoys me. I know I've offended you with my sacrifice, but if you'll just grant me your blessing, I'll give you anything you desire—anything!"

When he looked up from his prayer, Tony gratefully spotted his half-empty bottle of Old Parr, but as he reached for it, he inadvertently knocked it off the table. Or had the bottle leaped away from his grasp? It seemed like another warning from the universe of the unbridled punishment in store for him.

"Okay, what do you want?" Tony cried.

Silence.

"Money? I can give you money. Goats? You can have a whole goddamn herd of them! Just tell me what you want!"

Tony was finally beginning to realize the full measure of the orisha's displeasure.

"Okay, okay, I know what you want," Tony said. "Okay, I will give it to you. But remember this sacrifice! It's enough! After this, we are even with each other!"

Tony staggered to his feet. He was woozy and disoriented, but he struggled to move the bulky pharmacist's cabinet where he stored his precious herbs. Once the cabinet was out of the way, Tony wedged himself into the dusty space behind it. There was a wall safe behind a false panel. Inside were several hundred thousand dollars in cash, a U.S. military code book, secret formulas for casting spells, and a large goldfish aquarium covered with a paisley drape. He lifted the aquarium and carried it carefully into the room where Elegguá was waiting.

"Here," said Tony as he removed the drape. "I hope you're satisfied!"

Inside the aquarium, floating in the viscous liquid, was the head of Hugo Spadafora.

Gods were never happy until they had tasted blood, Tony thought bitterly. Until now, Hugo had been his alone. But what good had it done him, really? One thing after another had gone wrong ever since Hugo passed into the other world.

Hugo's eyes were askew—one looking upward and one down at Tony's shoes. His skin was slightly green and coated with whiskers. An artery trailed out the severed neck like an unplugged electrical cord.

There was just enough Old Parr left in the spilled bottle for Tony to salvage a few last sips. He clinked the side of the aquarium in a farewell toast—a toast he had never shared with the living Hugo.

All the things Tony had wanted, Hugo had. He had wanted to be a doctor, like Hugo, but the most that a poor boy like him could expect or hope for was to become a pharmacist's assistant. Even when Tony turned to the military, he had been overshadowed by the protean Hugo. While Tony was issuing traffic citations and learning drill in the National Guard, Hugo was waging revolution in the jungles of Africa and Central America, writing best-sellers about his adventures. But what did it matter? Tony could not go back and create a happy childhood for himself, or a loving family. He would never be handsome; instead, he was pocked like a Peg-Board and given lizardlike eyes that frightened children and even caused grown men to draw away when they saw him. In his home village there was a she-devil named Tuli Vieja who had a face like a sieve. She sneaked along the stream-sides looking for children to steal. The people said if you looked at her directly, she would suck out your life through the holes in her face. For this reason, some of the Choco avoided looking at Tony to this very day despite the postal station and all the other favors he had given them. They thought he was the male incarnation of Tuli Vieja. Sometimes Tony wondered that himself.

There had been a moment when everything might have turned out differently—that was the first time Tony had ever seen Hugo, at a little outdoor cantina in Colón during Carnival. Hugo was at his peak then—glamorous, handsome, rich, famous, surrounded by fans and beautiful women, women that Tony could only dream about. There was a samba band, and Hugo had danced like a prince. Everything he did was so naturally cool and filled with grace and courage. Tony had sent a bottle of fine champagne to Hugo's table, a gesture he could scarcely afford. Hugo, however, did not invite Tony to join him and his beautiful friends. He did not even acknowledge the gift. He simply received it as tribute. He drank the champagne and left, trailing laughter and contempt.

"But, Hugo, the universe is so fickle," Tony said now as he contemplated the chain of events that had led inevitably from that moment to this one. "You can be up so high and I down so low. Now look at us. Somewhat reversed, right? I guess somebody up there is watching out for me, eh? What do you think, Doctor? It's funny, isn't it?"

Hugo's hair swayed like seaweed and his puzzled eyes looked high and low.

"I don't see you laughing," said Tony.

CHAPTER 17

ROLLINS HAD SUGGESTED meeting Father Jorge at what he said was a "dentist's office" in Punta Paitilla, and the priest was surprised to find that it really was a dentist's office and not a safe house or CIA front. "You sure you don't mind?" Rollins asked when they met. "I have to spend half my life sitting in this chair being tortured. My gums." He raised his upper lip to display a pulpy gum line and several missing teeth. "It's genetic," he explained.

"You do know why I contacted you?" Father Jorge asked under his breath.

"Oh, everybody in this country has a secret to sell," said Rollins. His skin was clammy and he smelled faintly of rum.

"I'm not selling anything!" Father Jorge said indignantly.

"Sorry. I didn't mean to offend you, Father. Most of our agents come to us because of financial distress. You don't see too many idealists in this business." Just then the dentist walked in carrying a hypodermic with a six-inch needle. Rollins shrank a bit. "Maybe you should give me last rites, Father," he said. "Hah hah hah."

"This may pinch a bit, but believe me, you'll be glad for it in a little while," said the dentist, plunging the needle into Rollins's tender upper gum. "Don't move around so."

Rollins made a cry like a little bird.

"This will take a few minutes," said the dentist. "I'll be back when you're numb."

"I wish they used gas here," said Rollins when the dentist had gone. "I'm such a coward about these things."

This was the CIA? Father Jorge worried about Major Giroldi placing his trust in an agency that was so shabbily represented. Nonetheless, he forged ahead. "I assume that a certain PDF officer has been in contact with you," he said.

"I talk to dozens of them," said Rollins. "What's his name?"

Father Jorge paused, then whispered Giroldi's name.

"Oh, right. So you're our contact?"

"I'm only delivering a message."

"Okay, then, what shall we call you?"

"Excuse me?"

"Tradecraft. Every agent gets a moniker. We don't want to have to use real names in our reports."

"I'm not an *agent*."

"Okay, whatever, but suppose Giroldi wants you to get in touch with me again. Maybe you don't want people to know who you are. You just use your trade name. Safer. More discreet."

This was absurd, Father Jorge thought, but on the other hand, he certainly didn't want anyone to know about his involvement. "What do you suggest?"

"I've got my own system," Rollins confided. "What's your favorite Disney character?"

"Mickey Mouse?"

"Taken," said Rollins. "Maybe something a little less obvious."

"Can't we just say something like 'José Rodríguez' that sounds like an ordinary name?' "

"It is an ordinary name, Father, too ordinary. Do you know

225

how many guys there are with that name? Suppose some guy who really is named José Rodríguez calls me up—it could get very confusing. Listen, trust me, you want a name that's memorable but not exactly real. Anyway, it works. All my guys do it."

"Oh, well, this is ridiculous. You can call me anything you want."

"It has to be something meaningful to *you*. Otherwise, you might forget it, and then where would we be?"

"In that case, maybe you can call me Pinocchio. I think that would be very appropriate."

"I like your thinking, Father. It's symbolic and memorable. Unfortunately it's also taken."

"Goofy, then."

"The really mainstream ones are pretty much picked over. Donald, Daffy, the nephews. I had one of the Seven Dwarves left till last week. I encourage you to think a little less conventionally. Like 'Thomas O'Malley.' "

"Thomas O'Malley?"

"You never saw *Aristocats*? He is the alley cat who rescues Duchess."

"No, but I like the name."

"Like I said, it has to be meaningful to you. I can suggest some ideas, but it should come from within."

"But I'm not that experienced with these movies. I can't really think of any."

"Oh, come on, Father—think back! You must have seen dozens of them when you were a kid. Everybody did."

"Apparently so."

"What was your favorite? *Sleeping Beauty*? *Fantasia*? *Cinderella*?"

"*Bambi*, I suppose."

"*Bambi* happens to be available. You're a luppy man, Fadder." The Xylocaine was taking hold.

"I really don't want to be called Bambi."

"How 'bout Thumper?"

"Okay, okay, can we just go ahead with this?"

"Sure, sure, but how would you like to be paid?"

"Paid?" Father Jorge snapped. "I'm a priest! I've taken a vow of poverty. I'm certainly not going to violate that to take a bribe from the CIA."

"It's not a bribe, Fadder. It's a gesture of appreciation. And if you don't want the money, we can give it to somebody else. Even to your church, if you want."

Father Jorge paused. "How much money are we talking about?" His parish really was very poor.

"Not millions but not hundreds, either. Depends on the relationship. How it debelops."

"It's not going to *develop*. I've just come here to deliver a message for a friend. A man who is placing his life in danger and needs your help."

Rollins rubbed his tongue across his deadened incisors. "Well, then, talk. Nobody's stobbing you."

Father Jorge took a deep breath. The import of what he was about to say was so serious that the fate of the entire country depended on it—but he seemed to be trapped in some bizarre farce. "My friend asked me to inform you that there will be a sudden change of leadership. But he will need your support."

Rollins eyes widened. "A coup? Wow, that's—"

Just then the dentist returned. Rollins shot a frustrated look at Father Jorge, then opened his mouth wide.

"How are we doing?" the dentist asked impatiently. He was a brisk and efficient type. He had a pair of magnifying lenses pushed up on his forehead. "We should get started. Can you feel this?" He stuck a metal probe in Rollins's gum.

"Ow!"

The dentist looked at him in surprise. "Again?" he said.

"It hurbs."

The dentist shook his head in amazement. "I've never seen anyone so resistant. I guess I'll have to double up on the anesthetic."

When the dentist had left the room, Rollins turned to Father Jorge. "Quick, I don't want another shot! When's this going to happen?"

"Wednesday at dawn."

"Doesn't give us much time."

"Secrets don't keep in Panama."

"What do you want us to do?"

"Block off the roads to the Comandancia. You don't have to do more than that—just make sure that reinforcements can't get through. Pretend you are doing one of your regular exercises."

"That's all?"

"This is a Panamanian solution, Mr. Rollins, just like your president has been calling for. All you have to do is to block traffic. And fly over the airport to keep the aircraft from taking off."

"The U.S. cannot be party to any plan that results in the death of a foreign leader."

"Believe me, Mr. Rollins, that's the last thing our friend has in mind. He only wants a change at the top."

"That's what we want, too, Fadder."

"One last thing: during the coup, his family will seek refuge at Howard Air Force Base. You must ensure their safety."

The dentist returned with another giant injection.

Rollins put his hands in front of his face. "No, no, it's dead! I don't peel a ting!"

But the needle slipped through his defenses, and as Father Jorge left the room he noticed Rollins's feet curling toward heaven.

I THINK WE should talk," said Tony.

"If you got something to say, okay, I can listen," Pablo Escobar replied. "But private and in the open. Neutral territory. Not on the phone."

"Why don't we go for a jog?" Tony suggested.

An hour later the two men met at Fort Amador and began

running along the causeway. Escobar was not in such bad shape for a heavy man, but he sweated through his Hard Rock Cafe T-shirt before they had gone half a mile. He mopped his face. His thick black mustache glistened.

"Here we can say what we want," Tony said. He was puffing a little himself, and he could smell the Old Parr sweetly working its way through his sweat glands. "I carry this along for insurance, in case they are listening." He turned on a transistor radio. The U.S. Armed Forces station was playing "Okie from Muskogee," a Merle Haggard tune.

"At least change the station," said Escobar.

Tony turned the dial. "Okay, but you should pay attention to such things. The words to their songs are a window to the gringo soul. They are such Protestants! Sex and infidelity, all the time!"

"Catholics are just as bad," said Escobar. "Fucking guilt, always on your mind."

"Right, I agree. The difference is the Protestants think the world is coming to an end at any moment, and in their heart they know it is their fault. Which, this is probably true. The world will go up in a big bang, just the way it was created, only this will not be God's intention. He makes the world, and then the Baptists destroy it."

"Every religion is full of cranks," said Escobar. "You can't put it all on one group. It's just as likely that the Jews and the Muslims will put an end to things as the Baptists. Hell, the Hindus."

"Yes, but the Baptists think the apocalypse is coming soon, and they will all get to heaven before everybody else. People like this should not be in charge of the American nuclear arsenal."

"It's scary," Escobar agreed. "Whenever you mix religion and politics, watch out."

"I think the real problem is sexual," said Tony.

Escobar nodded enthusiastically. "If everybody got more pussy, the world would be a lot safer place. That's the problem with religion—it gets in the way of natural appetites."

"But why? Why does religion stand in the way of sexual fulfillment? I think we adopt religious beliefs as a way of avoiding sex as much as possible."

"Tony, with all due respect, that makes no sense to me."

"Tell me, Pablo, what is religion after all?"

"Fairy tales," said Escobar. "A story we tell ourselves about life everlasting. Helps us go to sleep at night."

"I agree that religion has this quality. But all creatures die, and yet man is the only one that we know of that creates religions. Why is this? Because he is aware of his solitude." A beautiful girl in sunglasses ran past them in the opposite direction, with an exhausted white dog the size of a large rat. The dog's tongue hung limply to one side of his mouth and his toenails clicked on the sidewalk. Tony and Escobar both turned to look at the girl's ass as she passed. "Why do you want sex in the first place?" Tony continued. "Because you don't want to feel alone. You want to have union with another person. Say this girl—you'd like to fuck her, right?"

Escobar grunted.

"But afterwards, maybe it's not such a good feeling, right? You feel *more* alone. Then maybe you want another girl, this time a different one. But the outcome is the same. It is like drinking salt water—you finally die of dehydration. A cruel paradox, isn't it?"

"I still like fucking. I'd fuck the dog, as a matter of fact."

"Of course you would—because you love life and you're afraid of death like everybody else. It's perfectly natural. When you're fucking, you're saying yes to life, and yet death is the whole point of sexuality. You merge with another person in order to escape the loneliness of existence and the fear of death, but with every sexual act you are reminded of your mortality and the prison of identity."

"Jeez, Tony, you're a morbid son of a bitch."

"There's only one escape from this existential dilemma. Love. If you're really in love, you can never be entirely alone."

"Now I believe that," said Escobar. "I got a good woman. She puts up with a lot of shit, I can tell you that."

"You're a lucky man," Tony said enviously.

They had come to the base of the Bridge of the Americas, which spans the canal. Tony immediately started up the slope.

"I don't know," said the panting Escobar. "It's a long way across." He stopped and bent over to catch his breath.

"We don't have to go all the way, but the view is really something."

They jogged slowly up the pedestrian side of the immense bridge, which arched like a cat's back over the waterway. Escobar lagged behind, grumbling and perspiring. His pudgy legs were quivering. "Slow down," he complained.

The bridge traffic roared past them, emitting foul gusts of diesel.

"We're almost there."

A Liberian tanker slipped quietly past underneath them, its radar mast scooting just under Tony's Reeboks. Finally they reached the apogee of the bridge. "No one should visit Panama without seeing this," Tony said proudly. "Here, you can see practically the whole country—the mountains in the west and the jungles in the east."

Escobar held on to the rail, gasping.

The sky was very close today; the heavy black clouds were impaled by the flagpole on Ancón Hill. Immediately below, on one side of the canal, was an American naval base; on the other side were Quarry Heights and the busy port. In the distance another ship was slowly rising in the Miraflores Locks. Tony could just see the machinery turning, the tourists taking photographs, the vendors selling T-shirts and Panama hats. He felt a rush of national pride. "Ask me any question about the canal," he said. "I know everything."

"I'm really not interested in the goddamn thing."

"Ah."

"It's a ditch," said Escobar. "I don't see what's so impressive."

Tony couldn't help feeling wounded by Escobar's insensitivity. It was hard to reach out to someone who was so unmindful of another's national feelings. "It's a common misunderstanding that one ocean is higher than the other," Tony finally said.

"I thought that was the whole point of the locks."

"Not at all. The tides are somewhat different, but the levels are essentially the same. In point of fact, the locks raise the ships well above sea level. Much higher than you probably thought."

"How high?" Escobar asked grudgingly.

"One hundred seventy-seven meters."

"That's pretty high," Escobar conceded.

"You know, our two nations were one before the gringos came and built this thing."

"I know very well."

"We should not let them come between us again," said Tony. "That's why I wanted to talk. There's been a terrible misunderstanding."

"A misunderstanding," said Escobar. "They gave you a fucking award in Washington."

"I know, I know! But still, it was a huge mistake. Okay, yes, I did authorize the raid, but only because the gringos already knew about the plant. The whole thing was a tragedy that could not have been prevented. I only hope you can forgive this unfortunate episode so we can get back to business as usual."

"I thought our mutual friend in Havana told you the price of forgiveness."

"A billion dollars is unrealistic, Pablo. I'm not a king. But I have given you sanctuary. Another leader might have taken your money and put you in jail."

"Another leader might find his dick stuck through his ears."

"What I am saying is that we have much in common. We can still help each other. What's the alternative? War with each other? I don't want this—do you?"

"Tell me something," Escobar said gruffly. "How the fuck did the Americans find out about the plant? It was buried in the god-damned jungle. They couldn't pick it up on satellite. There was nothing around there for a hundred miles, no roads, no people.

Somebody had to tell them. Somebody with connections. Somebody on their payroll."

"I know what it sounds like, but I am not the only person in Panama who consults with the Americans. They have their sources, like everyone else."

"If it is not you," said Escobar, "then it is somebody in your operation. You see how that compromises everything? We cannot resume our business relationship without trust. You give me the son of a whore who betrayed us, then maybe we'll talk again."

CHAPTER 18

THE NUNCIO ENTERED the grotesque modern chapel in the Comandancia in the company of an elegant crowd of civilian guests, all of them dressed in their finest party clothes. The occasion was the christening of General Noriega's first granddaughter. Many of the guests were among the leaders of the Civic Crusade. Was there another country in the world, the Nuncio wondered affectionately, where a party could stop a revolution?

Although it placed him in an awkward position, the Nuncio had acceded to the General's request that he perform the ceremony. Such a gesture might be well received in the Vatican. In any case, the grandchild was an innocent and required the Church's blessing. Who could criticize a priest for performing such an office? But still, the Nuncio felt compromised.

There were three or four hundred people in the chapel, about half of them military officers. Among the civilians, the Nuncio spotted several of the famous Colombians, including Escobar. There must have been a reconciliation between Noriega and the cartel. This was alarming news. The Nuncio wondered what

Noriega had done to appease them. Whatever it was, the price must have been high: the General was already quite drunk. It was eight o'clock in the morning.

The Nuncio stood at the baptismal font and offered a prayer. Then he asked for the family to stand, along with the godparents. Wobbling and grinning like a madman, General Noriega came forward with his grandchild in his arms.

"Do you renounce Satan and all his works and pomps?" the Nuncio asked.

"I do renounce them," the General said on behalf of the infant girl in her lacy white gown. The smell of alcohol on his breath was slightly nauseating.

The Nuncio dipped his hand in the baptismal font and dribbled the water in a nice even flow over the baby's forehead. She looked surprised and began to wail. The General laughed and held her up over his head like a trophy.

The reception followed in the courtyard. Young soldiers wearing aprons walked among the partygoers, carrying canapés and drinks.

"Tony, you shouldn't drink any more, you're making a fool of yourself," Felicidad warned.

Tony started to take a defiant sip of his Bloody Mary, but the celery stalk in his drink got stuck in his nose.

"See what I mean!" she hissed.

"I need to check on security," he said sourly.

Tony walked up the steps to the fortifications that surrounded the Comandancia. From here there was a clear view of Quarry Heights, the Olympus where the Americans spied down on them. Why, Tony wondered, did his enemies have to be so powerful? Life would be so much easier if he had more manageable opponents. On the other hand, the size and number of a man's enemies say something about him. They are history's yardstick, a way of measuring a man in his time. Where would Nelson be without Napoleon? Lincoln without the Confederacy? No one achieves greatness without struggling against formidable opponents, so in that sense perhaps Tony really was blessed. He had stirred up the most impressive enemies of his era—the Church, the Colombian mob, and the Americans. He had a lot to be thankful for.

Major Giroldi was at his command post on the ramparts overlooking the party. He snapped to attention as Tony approached, then jumped to give him a hand when his commander tripped on a step.

"Are you all right, sir?"

Tony examined his new suit in dismay. It was a pinstriped Hugo Boss that Señora Morales had picked out for him, now stained with tomato juice. "Major, if you see any American helicopters flying over, shoot them down," Tony said, loudly enough that many of the guests in the courtyard could hear.

Giroldi laughed in a tolerant manner.

"You think I am joking?" Tony shouted.

"You're not joking?" Giroldi asked in alarm.

"That's an order, Major! No American aircraft flying over our party!"

All the guests in the courtyard were now staring at Tony, their mouths open in surprise and dumbfounded agitation. They suddenly looked like guppies in a pond. Tony imitated their bug-eyed expressions and then burst out laughing.

Many of the guests slipped away immediately, not wanting to take the chance that the Americans might inadvertently fly within range of PDF rockets. The effect of their departure on Felicidad was obvious despite her attempt at composure. She was red-faced with humiliation and near tears. Tony, however, was oblivious.

"Enrique, you filthy dog," he said to the chief justice of the Supreme Court, a bald man with a self-important air, whose standard of living depended on the brown envelopes he regularly received from the PDF. He was in the company of a buxom teenage girl in a scoop-necked dress who shyly looked at the ground. "She is young enough to be your daughter."

"She *is* my daughter, General," said the chief justice. "Lorena, this is the famous Tony Noriega."

Tony kissed the daughter's hand, then impulsively buried his head in her virginal bosom. "Mmm, life!" Tony said. "Enjoy it while you can, Lorena."

The remaining guests gasped. The chief justice went deathly pale. "Is he completely insane?" one of the guests muttered under her breath.

"It is possible," the Nuncio said. "A man in his position, subjected to the pressures he must face—yes, even insanity would be a refuge. Men do crazy things when they feel that they have used up their rational alternatives."

"Now he doesn't even have César to put the brakes on him," said another partygoer. "No one else had the nerve to tell him when he was out of control."

"César Rodríguez?" asked the Nuncio. "What happened to him?"

"You didn't hear, Monseñor? They found César's body in Colombia. He had been given the necktie."

"The necktie?"

"It's a filthy Colombian habit. They slit the throat of an informer and pull his tongue through."

"I didn't know this," said the Nuncio. "Well, perhaps General Noriega's behavior can be explained by the fact that his best friend has died and he is overwhelmed by grief."

"Or guilt," said the partygoer under his breath as the General walked toward them, carrying his granddaughter around as if she were a ventriloquist's dummy.

"Bless you, my children," Tony said in a high, girlish voice, making the sign of the cross with the baby's tiny hand.

The Nuncio smiled uneasily.

"Any response from the Americans?" the General muttered.

"It's going through channels," the Nuncio quietly replied.

The General cleared his throat in a manner that was meant to draw attention, and as the other guests turned to notice, he patted the Nuncio on the shoulder and handed him a manila envelope.

The Nuncio left in a furious mood. There was really nothing wrong with accepting a contribution for a pastoral service, he told himself on the ride back to the nunciature. It wasn't as if he were selling indulgences! And it was just like the General to make it appear that he had the Church in his pocket.

On the other hand, it was a very generous contribution.

"TONY, WE COULD HAVE eaten in my apartment," Carmen said under her breath.

"I am sure the food is better here." Tony looked around at the affronted faces of the other diners in Las Polvidas, the seaside spot that had become the most expensive restaurant in the entire country. Part of its ambience derived from the fact that it was a former dungeon. Condemned prisoners had been locked in the caves in the lower part of the structure, which flooded during high tides. One could imagine their screams as the waves lapped against the walls and their cells began to fill. Now the sounds of jazz filled the stone rooms and the smell from the kitchen was heavenly. All of that lent a romantic air to the place, which was the reason that Tony had chosen it for this special night.

"Everyone is staring at us," Carmen muttered.

Tony picked up the menu and smiled. "It's a good thing I'm so goddamned rich!" he said loudly. "But how do these other bastards afford this place? *They must not be paying their taxes.*"

Heads in the room abruptly turned to other conversations. Carmen's eyes rolled in embarrassment. "You don't understand these people. It's one thing to behave as we do in private. Okay, it is even expected. But they will never accept this—Tony and his mistress, in public!"

"Is that how they see it?"

"That's how it *is.*"

Tony reached into his jacket and pulled out a small gold box. "I see it differently," he said as he handed the box to Carmen. "I see Tony and his fiancée."

Carmen gasped. She stared at the box in shock.

"Aren't you going to open it?" Tony asked.

"Have you told Felicidad?"

"Not yet," Tony admitted. "I don't want to upset her until it's absolutely necessary."

"I'm glad," said Carmen. "I'm glad you haven't told her because I can't do this. It would be wrong for everyone."

"But this is what you wanted!"

"I know, I thought it was what I wanted. I guess it was. But I finally realized something, Tony. All my life I've belonged to someone else—my mother, you. I never did anything for myself. Now I'm going to do something I want to do, just for me."

"What?"

"I'm going to be a fashion designer in Miami."

Tony choked on the champagne.

"I know what you're thinking," Carmen said hurriedly. "It sounds vain and shallow. But Tony, I *am* vain and shallow. I'm not the kind of woman who can be the first lady of Panama. Felicidad has it in her nature. She loves power and fame. That doesn't mean anything to me, Tony. I'm not a queen. In my heart I know what I was born for."

Tony stared at her in disbelief. "You're leaving?"

"As soon as the semester starts."

"But, Carmen, if you like fashion, I'll give you a fashion business! I'll appoint you minister of fashion! Everyone in Panama will wear what you tell them to wear!"

"God, Tony, you really miss the point."

"What's the point?"

"It's not just fashion—I need another life!"

"But . . ." Tony's mouth opened but he didn't know what to say. Finally he sputtered, "Don't you know how much I want you?"

239

"Want? Want?" Carmen said furiously.

"Don't get excited. People are staring."

"Do you know what it's like to be *wanted* by Tony Noriega? It's like a prison! I feel like one of your caged birds. You don't know, Tony. You don't know what I've had to put up with. I have things I want, too! But nobody ever thinks about that! No! Nobody ever says, 'Carmen, what do *you* want?' It's always, 'The Americans are trying to screw me!' or, 'Fidel doesn't understand me!' Well, for once in my life, it's my turn!"

"Carmen, my dear little Carmen," Tony pleaded in a low voice, desperately trying to calm her down. "Carmen, please listen to me. Let's be reasonable. We can work this out. Look, you give me what I want, and I'll give you what you want. That's fair enough, isn't it? I've only been waiting for you to tell me what is your heart's desire. Think about it! What is it that I can't give you? Money? Love? Power?"

"Respectability," said Carmen. "I just don't want people hating me all the time. It takes a toll, Tony."

Tony was stopped. "You just can't do this," he finally said.

"Well, what are you going to do about it? Put me in prison? I mean, come on, Tony—I'm a free woman! You don't own me! What gives you the right to tell me what I can do?"

"I love you," Tony said simply.

At last Carmen subsided. She studied him for a moment. "Okay, if you love me, prove it."

"Anything you ask, tell me."

"Become a regular person."

"I don't even know what that means," said Tony.

"It means quit this crazy job. Then maybe I'll consider your offer."

"What kind of thinking is this? I'm the boss! I'm somebody! I can give you things! What good am I if I step down? Who will care about Tony Noriega then? You? I don't think you know yourself very well, Carmen. I am not an attractive man, it's no secret! You don't stay with me because of my personal qualities. No one does! And now you ask me to give up the very thing that makes me what I am. You want me to become nobody? You think you could love that? Are you loco?"

"Maybe," said Carmen. "Maybe I am."

LIEUTENANT CHEEVER followed General Honeycutt at a trot into the brilliant tropical dawn. It was always hard to keep up with the huge commander, who walked in mammoth strides across the manicured grass toward the officers' mess. On the long slope below them they could see the soldiers squaring up on the parade ground. Everything was orderly and in its place.

"God has done a good job today," the general observed with satisfaction.

"Yes, sir. But, sir, shouldn't we be scrambling some aircraft, General? The coup is supposed to happen in fifteen minutes."

"Giroldi," said the general. "How much can we trust this guy? Could be a trap."

"I don't know, General, but we've obligated ourselves to provide air cover and to block the main roads. We're supposed to enact what appear to be routine maneuvers."

The general looked pained. "I thought we were talking hypotheticals. Just spook talk, maybe this, maybe that."

"Well, evidently Major Giroldi has taken us at our word."

"Something in my gut tells me this would be a horseshit mistake."

"Ten-hut!"

The officers in the dining room jumped to attention as General Honeycutt entered. He paused for a moment to savor the cholesterolic odors of bacon, sausage, cheese grits, eggs, pancakes. "Smells like America," he said happily. "At ease, ladies and gentlemen."

"But, sir," Lieutenant Cheever said, trying to hold the general's attention as he passed through the lengthy buffet line, "we've spent months trying to get the Panamanians to do some-

241

thing, anything! We've practically been begging them to hang him from the courthouse clock."

"Throw in some more hash browns, Irene," the general said to the server. "I'm a starving man."

"Yes, sir, General. You want another plate?"

"No, just dump 'em on top of the pancakes."

Cheever took a half bagel from the pastry shelf. "I don't mean to pressure you, General, but we've made a commitment."

The general stopped and looked his aide sternly in the eye. "Look here, son, you're Manuel Noriega."

"Sir?"

"You're the dictator of this godforsaken mosquito factory. You're getting pressure from all sides to step down. People talking coup, people talking revolution. What do you do?"

"What, sir?"

"You appoint your most trusted man, this Giroldi fellow, to provoke the Americans into making some threatening maneuvers, then he can point to us and say we're playing gunboat diplomacy. It's a setup. You can smell it from here to Timbuktu."

"But what if it's not? They say Giroldi is a real righteous guy. This could be a golden opportunity if—"

"If! If!" the general shouted. "How do we know Giroldi isn't another Noriega? He's PDF! The whole institution is rotten! And suppose this really is just a show. Don't you think Noriega is smart enough to stage this whole thing? How many people do you think might get killed in this little drama? I say let's let it play out a bit and see what happens. Irene, I don't think I can live without a brace of sausage to go with that omelet."

CHAPTER 19

Tony awakened feeling woozy but strangely elated. He had never felt exactly this way before. There was something wrong with the mood and also with the circumstances, now that he noticed them. He was not in his own room, or any place he recognized. It was a plain white room with barred windows. The bubble-gum odor of industrial disinfectant made him a little nauseous. That, and a hangover that belonged in an alcoholics' museum.

His eerie serenity was a bit disturbed by the discovery that he was wearing a green hospital gown. Have I been in an accident? he wondered. An assassination attempt? He tried to recall the events that had led him to this unexpected place, but all he could remember was breaking up with Carmen, and that was too painful to think about.

The door was locked.

Tony sat on the bed for a moment and then began to scream.

"Tony?"

It was the voice of Dr. Demos on the other side of the door.

"Let me out of here!"

"Tony, calm down. We can discuss this, but you have to be in a receptive state."

"Let me out or I'll have you killed."

There was a long pause. Finally the door opened, and Dr. Demos cautiously stuck his head in. "How are you feeling today?" he said cheerily.

"Where are my clothes? I need to go to the office."

"Well, actually you arrived without any."

"How long have I been here?" Tony asked. "I don't even know what day it is."

"You had a little breakdown, Tony." Demos came in and sat in the white plastic chair. His sunglasses made his eyes unreadable. "They brought you here last night."

"Who? Who did this to me?"

"Your friends. That's all I'm going to say. I don't want you to start threatening people who only want to help you."

Tony slumped onto the bed. A breakdown!

"We got you on some medication that was supposed to calm you down a bit. You were really a handful, I can tell you. Convulsions, fits of rage."

"I can't remember anything."

"That's not unusual in cases of hysteria."

"Are you saying I'm crazy?"

"We don't use that term," said Demos. "I could offer you a diagnosis, but frankly it requires a bit more study. In the meantime, we have lots of ways to help you—drugs, therapy, analysis—but mainly what you need is rest."

"I think maybe you're the one who's crazy, Doctor. Who knows I'm here?"

"No one, really. We've got you registered under another name."

"Good. Get my uniform here immediately. If we hurry, maybe I can get to the office before anyone suspects."

"Honestly, Tony, as your doctor I can't really permit this. You're in a pretty fragile state of mind."

Tony ripped off the thin hospital gown and hurled it in the

face of Dr. Demos. "Look at this, Doctor!" he said, grabbing hold of his balls. "Do you have a pair like this? I didn't think so! Now get my uniform and my driver and let me out of here. I've got a country to run."

An hour later, dressed in his highly pressed khakis, Tony slipped out the back of the Paitilla Clinic. His bodyguard opened the door to the armored Mercedes and Tony collapsed into the backseat. The bodyguard was a sweet-tempered young man nicknamed Scar because of a traffic accident some years ago in Colón. The path of the injury tugged down one corner of his mouth in a perpetual frown, so that no matter what his mood, his expression always appeared to be full of menace and wrath. Now he also looked guilty and a bit scared.

"Chief, are you okay?" Scar asked tentatively.

"No, I'm a fucking lunatic," Tony snapped.

As they rode through the city, Tony looked out the window at the sky, which was being bled white in the punishing morning sunshine. Unwelcome fragments of the night before entered Tony's mind. Girls. Drinks. Empty hangers on Felicidad's side of the closet. He was alone. That wasn't a paranoid delusion. He was born to be abandoned by everyone he loved.

Half an hour later the Mercedes passed through the guard station and entered the parking lot of the Comandancia. The barracks were unusually quiet for midmorning. A single soldier leaned against a tank in the courtyard, his M-16 hanging from his shoulder. He snapped to attention as Tony stepped out of the Mercedes. Tony halfheartedly saluted and followed Scar toward the entrance. A few feet past the soldier, Tony heard the ominous sound of a round being loaded into a chamber. Scar suddenly wheeled around with his Uzi drawn, pointed at the wide-eyed young soldier.

"Something going on, Corporal?" Tony asked the soldier, whose face was a pale, tense mask. His nameplate said *Alvaro*. "N-n-no, sir, General, I wa-was just ch-checking the c-c-c-cartridge."

"Checking the cartridge?"

The stuttering soldier slowly lowered his weapon and opened the chamber for Tony to inspect.

Scar kept his Uzi pointed at the corporal. "General, let's go to Fort Amador," said Scar. "There's something going on here. It's not safe."

Tony looked into the pale and clammy face of Corporal Alvaro. He was mestizo, like Tony.

"Is Major Giroldi here, Corporal?"

"Yes, sir. He's in the b-b-b-barracks."

"Hmm. Very well. Let's go inside," Tony said to Scar. "Giroldi will know what's going on."

As soon as Tony entered the building, he heard a warning gunshot from the traitorous corporal outside. It was followed by the sounds of scattering footsteps and doors closing. Tony felt a chill of terror—and remorse. How could he have believed that the soldier would not betray him just because he was mestizo?

Scar pointed his weapon into the empty corridor. "This is not good, General. Let's get out of here."

Tony drew his pearl-handled pistol. His hands were shaking so violently he could hardly hold it. "I just want to get to my office," he said.

"Don't do what they're expecting, General."

"They will have locked the gates by now," said Tony. "We can't just stand here."

The two men crept down the hallway, Scar looking to the front and Tony to the rear. A machine gun broke the silence. Tony dived to the floor.

"Cease fire!" a familiar voice cried.

Scar fired a burst from his weapon and then knelt beside Tony. "Chief! Are you all right?"

"I'm okay. They just surprised me." Tony heard the clicking of automatic weapons locking into place at both ends of the corridor. "There's no way out. We'll have to make a run for the door."

They ran fifteen feet to the entrance to Tony's office. It was locked. "Have you got a key?" asked Scar.

Tony fumbled in his pockets.

"Quick!"

He found the keys, but he couldn't make his hands work well enough to get the proper key in the lock. Scar snatched it out of his grasp. He quickly opened the door and poked the muzzle of his weapon inside. There was no one there.

As soon as they got inside the office and bolted the door, the phone rang. "General, it's no use," said the voice that Tony now recognized as that of his trusted Major Giroldi. "Look out your window."

Tony peeked out through the slatted window toward the battlements that surrounded the Comandancia. Hundreds of soldiers lined the walls, their weapons pointed directly at Tony's office. As soon as Tony's face appeared between the tiny crack in the blinds, a dozen weapons fired, shattering the windows and sending the blinds flying. Tony hit the floor and rolled under his desk. The bullets ripped through ceiling tiles and exploded the fluorescent lights.

"No one should die for this, General," Giroldi was saying on the phone. "It's time for you to give up power. I am speaking to you now as a friend, not as a soldier. You see that we have taken care of everything. There is no escape. I can only ask you to respect your office and surrender peacefully. If you do, we will protect you. You will not have to fear for your safety. You have my word."

Scar whispered into his other ear, "Have you got any weapons here? Any extra ammunition?"

Tony shook his head.

"Give up, General," Giroldi said impatiently. "Throw your weapons into the hall. Otherwise, we will have to kill you."

"I need a few minutes to think."

"I'm sorry, General, there will be time for thinking later.

247

Throw the weapons into the hall now or we will fire. This is the truth."

Tony slumped in defeat. Scar cracked open the door and sent his machine gun into the hall. It went skittering across the waxed floor.

"Your pistol as well," Giroldi said.

A moment later the door opened, and Giroldi entered with a dozen other mutinous officers. Two of them pushed Scar against a file cabinet and frisked him. Tony recognized them all—some of his most trusted men, but none of them more so than Moisés Giroldi. His savior! The man he trusted most in the world! Tony had been best man at Giroldi's wedding. The betrayal was complete.

"You have done the wise and honorable thing, General," Giroldi said. He looked self-consciously triumphant, as if he were posing for a postage stamp. "Now I'll have to ask you to move over there against the wall."

He gestured to a spot covered with civic awards and photographs of Tony with world leaders.

"What are you going to do?" asked Tony.

"Please, just move over there," said Giroldi. "I am giving the orders now."

But Tony's feet wouldn't move. A wavy-haired lieutenant named Contreras shoved him hard. "Don't you understand orders, General?" Contreras said. He roughly led him to the window and jerked open the blinds, holding Tony forward like a trophy. "Look at him! Here's the monster, Tony Noriega!"

A great cheer arose from the men. "Kill the bastard!" some of them cried. Several of the officers in the room agreed. "Yes, let's kill him," they said. Their voices were thick and excited. "Let's get it over with now."

Tony's legs went to rubber and he sank to the floor. The rebels laughed at him. "Get up, General," Scar said encouragingly as the rebels jeered. Then, under his breath, he added, "Be a man."

Tony wanted to be a man, but he found himself weeping.

Giroldi looked at him with pity. "Don't be afraid. No one is going to die here."

"What do you want of me?"

"We have a few documents for you to sign. It's a very simple procedure. I think you'll find that we've been more than considerate about your well-being."

Tony accepted the papers, but when he tried to read them his eyes couldn't take in the words.

"I've got a pen, General."

"Just—just give me a few minutes, Moisés. I need to pray."

Giroldi hesitated.

"Don't trust him, Major," Contreras said urgently. The other officers quickly agreed.

Tony sat on the floor like an infant.

"He must be treated with respect," Giroldi said. "We will leave him alone to make peace with himself and with God. What can he do? You see for yourselves he is not dangerous anymore."

When they were gone, Tony quickly grabbed his private phone. It was unbelievable to him that they had not cut his line immediately.

Carmen answered, her voice thick with sleep. "Tony? How dare you call me!" The line went dead.

Tony dialed again. "Carmen, don't hang up! The son of a bitch Giroldi is throwing me out. They're going to shoot me, I'm sure of it."

"Tony, that's terrible."

"I agree."

"I wish you hadn't behaved so badly last night."

"Carmen, please! I need you to call my supporters! Find somebody! There must be somebody loyal! The Mountain Men division, the Dobermans, even the Digbats—"

There was an insistent knock on the door.

"You don't remember the things you said?"

"Carmen, I beg you! Forgive me! I was stupid, I was hurt! I said things I didn't mean."

"I hope that's true."

"Listen, if the Americans aren't in on the coup, there's still a chance. Get the chief of police! Tell him to round up the families of the headquarters staff—Contreras and the others."

"General?" said Giroldi's voice. "We're coming in."

"Carmen, this is your chance to be free of me. But if you don't save me, I'm a dead man. So think about what you really want."

THE WHOLE CITY is throbbing with rumors of a coup," Father Jorge said as he burst into the library. "Has there been anything on television yet?"

"Not yet," said the Nuncio, "but it's true—rebel officers have taken over the Comandancia and gunshots have been heard."

"Gunshots?" Father Jorge looked grim.

"Gunshots, then silence. I suppose that means he's dead now." The Nuncio was surprised at his own reaction as he said these words. Certainly Panama would be better off without the General, and the Nuncio had to admit that his own life would be made considerably easier without the press of refugees and the constant focus of international attention on Panama. He would happily return to the obscure existence that he had led before Noriega became the world's most despised villain and the Vatican turned its withering eye in his direction. Still, there was a sense of loss, as if something vital had been subtracted from the universe. "It's to be expected, I suppose. I'm sure we'll hear something official, but in the meantime—" The Nuncio suddenly noticed the expression on Father Jorge's face. "You had no part in this, I hope?" he said.

Father Jorge's complexion darkened. "A very small part," he conceded.

The Nuncio shook his head in exasperation. "You have no idea how perilous our situation is here! I realize where your sympathies lie, but really, Father! You are jeopardizing everything! We can only hope this coup succeeds. You may be lucky and the Vatican will forget about you. I'm not even speaking about General Noriega. If he survives this, then we are all in great danger. A wounded lion is much more dangerous than a sleeping one."

T ONY STARED AT the sheet of paper in front of him. "But this is a resignation," he said.

"Of course," said Giroldi.

"I can't sign this."

Giroldi smiled tolerantly. His face was full of compassion and goodwill. "I know it's hard to accept, General. But you realize that the terms are extremely generous. You get to stay in Panama and no charges will be filed."

Tony nodded without looking up.

"You only have to remove yourself from your present office and then you are free to go on with your life, with my personal guarantee for your safety."

Whatever that's worth, Tony thought as he watched Contreras out of the corner of his eye. "There are several items for discussion," Tony said. "In theory, I agree to your demands."

"What does that mean, 'in theory'?" Contreras said darkly.

"I just need a legal reading before I can make such a commitment."

Contreras snorted. "Why do you even talk to him?" he said to Giroldi. "There is no negotiation! We all agreed to this! These are the final terms."

"And we are very close," Tony said reasonably. "There are only a few items to clarify. For instance, there is nothing in here about my pension."

"*Pension!*" Contreras cried.

"It may seem a small thing to you, Lieutenant, but I must consider my family."

"You've stolen enough to keep your family rich for fifty generations! You've taken half the wealth of the country—never has there been such a robber, never in the history of the world!"

"You exaggerate," said Tony. "I may have taken a little here and there, but I have shared with my fellow officers. Giroldi can tell you, can't you, Moisés? We have all benefited. Even you, Contreras."

"We are here to change all that, General," Giroldi said stiffly. Every word he said seemed to be measured to fit into a history text. "We're going to pull the corruption out by the roots. Even from our own pockets."

"If this is so, then I congratulate you. Panama has long needed such principled leadership. Indeed, I will join you in your efforts."

"You can't join us," said Contreras. "We're revolting against *you*."

"Very well, if you feel that way." Tony shrugged indifferently. "But for your sake, I do feel compelled to ask if the Americans have examined this document."

"This is not an American action," said Giroldi. "It is purely a Panamanian action."

Tony looked grave. "So you are declaring independence from the gringos as well?"

"It is time for Panama to behave like a normal country and not a colony of the United States."

"This I also approve. But even a normal country wants to have good relations with the superpowers, especially when one of them has twelve thousand troops stationed here."

"Of course we will treat the Americans with respect."

"I assume you have already discussed the coup with them?"

"In general terms," Giroldi conceded.

"That was prudent," said Tony. "The next step is to fax this resignation letter over to them and get a reaction."

Tony started to hand the letter to Giroldi, but Contreras blocked him. The man's face was murderous. "It's a trick, Major," he said.

Tony ignored him. "Major, if you are going to be running Panama, you may as well know that the Americans want to have their
thumb in every pie. It will set a good precedent, believe me. You
will show them that you are independent but cooperative. Flexible. They will see you as a man they can do business with."

"This is a ruse!" Contreras cried. "Send it to the Americans
and we will be here in the next century waiting for a response
from the State Department."

Tony's eyes never left Giroldi. "Really, Major, it is only a gesture. A simple courtesy."

Giroldi was paralyzed.

"Major, he's stalling for time!" Contreras warned. "He's up to
something!"

"I don't see what possible harm it would do," said Giroldi.

Tony smiled. "Your first executive decision. I must admit, I'm
impressed."

What the hell am I supposed to do with this?" asked General Honeycutt as he waved his copy of the fax in the air. A special response team had assembled in his office in reaction to the
communiqué.

"It appears there really is a coup in progress, General," said a
young intelligence officer. "We've got visual contact on the Comandancia. The rebels clearly have control."

"Actually, General, we've got information that a countercoup
is also under way right now," said Rollins. The man was wearing
a stained guayabera and smoking a perfumed Latin cigarette.
"The Mountain Men division is being airlifted from Río Hato.
Two transports have already landed."

"Coup? Countercoup? How do we know what's real?" the
general cried helplessly.

"Maybe we should give Giroldi the backup he requested, sir,"
Lieutenant Cheever suggested. "We can easily block the Moun-

tain Men by rolling a few tanks out on Avenida Fourth of July. They'll get the message right away."

"I'm still not convinced that this isn't being staged for our benefit," the general replied. His stomach was also beginning to rebel. "What wisdom can the agency bring to this, Rollins?"

"From the agency's point of view, this is a disaster," Rollins said. "We'd be losing our most cherished intelligence asset. Tony Noriega has been pouring gravy on our biscuits since the Eisenhower administration."

"But our entire foreign-policy establishment has been negotiating for his removal," said Lieutenant Cheever.

The general looked distrustfully at Rollins. "I thought the agency was working with Giroldi," he said. "You brought him to us in the first place."

"We just gather information, General. The old shake-and-bake days are over. You ask my opinion, and I say hands off. If Giroldi takes control, he'll deal with us; if not, well, we haven't lost anything."

General Honeycutt stared out his window. He had a splendid view of the Miraflores Locks, that masterpiece of turn-of-the-century engineering. A tanker bearing oil from the North Slope of Alaska was edging through in one direction as a Norwegian cruise ship waited to go the opposite way, toward Tahiti. The general felt like a glorified transit commissar. "What are we doing in this Third World puzzle box in the first place?" he grumbled. "Guarding a goddamn ditch!"

AT FIRST, TONY mistook the sound of light artillery for thunder, since the sky was low and ready for an afternoon downpour. But then Corporal Alvaro rushed into the room and disclosed in a hushed, distressed voice that the Mountain Men had arrived and had engaged in combat with a rebel roadblock on the airport highway.

Carmen!

"But the Americans must have blocked the roads," Giroldi said.

"Do you see them?" asked Contreras, looking out the slatted windows. "Where are they? I don't see any American aircraft, either. You said they would be performing maneuvers."

"You didn't get their written guarantee, Major?" Tony asked. "I hope you didn't just accept their word."

Giroldi looked at Tony in annoyance.

Tony shook his head sympathetically. "Well, perhaps all is not lost. You could call the Americans and demand that they honor their commitment."

The rebel officers looked at each other uncertainly. "For once, I agree with him," said Contreras.

Giroldi fished in his pocket, looking for a telephone number.

"It's eight two zero seven nine four," said Tony. "That will get you straight to General Honeycutt's office."

"Thank you," Giroldi said reluctantly as he dialed the number.

"His aide is named Henry Cheever."

The line rang and rang.

"They must have gone to lunch," said Tony.

"Major, let's kill him now," said Contreras. "Everything is falling apart. If we kill him, we have still achieved our goal."

"No."

"Then what do you propose?" Contreras said urgently. "Do you want a battle with the Mountain Men? We're minutes away from it. They will bring heavy weapons—it is going to be a bloodbath."

Giroldi turned to Tony. "Do you absolutely refuse to sign this?"

"I can't sign it without further consultation. If you'd just let me get my lawyer on the phone . . ." In the background he could hear additional gunfire, closer this time.

"In that case we will have to deliver him to the Americans," said Giroldi. "They say they want to put him on trial—okay, they can have him!"

"It may already be too late for that," said Contreras. "You hear the sound of the M-60s? That is the Mountain Men. You know how small our guard is! They will be overwhelmed in no time!"

Corporal Alvaro rushed in. He couldn't be more than twenty, Tony thought. "M-m-many of our troops have sur-surrendered," he said in a voice that was cracking in panic. "They refuse to f-f-fight. They think we have f-f-failed."

Contreras chambered a round, but Giroldi pushed his weapon away. "Let's be calm," he said. "We need to think about how our actions will be perceived in the future. We haven't failed! After all, we still have the General. What can they do? Don't you see that we are the ones who are in control? The only thing we have to worry about is losing our heads."

The phone rang. Tony and Giroldi both reached for it.

"Hello," said Tony. He listened a moment, then a smile came over his face. "It's for you," he said, handing the phone to Contreras.

"Me?" Contreras looked confused. "Who knows I am here? I told no one." He took the phone from Tony's hand. "Lucia?" he said in disbelief. "Where are you?"

As Contreras listened, the blood drained from his face. "The police have my family," he said when he had hung up. "Even my mother."

"My God," said Giroldi.

Carmen!

"There are other family members being held as well," said Contreras to the other officers in the room.

Tony waited until all the eyes in the room had turned toward him. "What happens to me, happens to them," he said simply.

Just as he spoke, an explosion shook the room. The rebels instinctively ducked, but Tony sat calmly at his desk. "How much time do you have, Major? You know the situation better than I. How many troops can you count on? What are their capabilities? Can you rely on the other divisions?"

Giroldi couldn't speak. All the power had been sucked out of him.

Tony turned to Contreras. "If you value your family, put your weapon on my desk."

Contreras hesitated only a second, then did as he was told. Tony did not even bother to pick it up. Most of the other officers in the room did the same. Corporal Alvaro hurled his weapon on the desk and stared at Tony with pure contempt.

The sound of the battle intensified. Tony could hear small-arms fire now and the cries of the frightened soldiers on the battlements. "It's over for you, Giroldi," he said.

Giroldi began dialing the number of the American general again.

Tony shook his head. "This is your moment of decision, Major. Kill me or kill yourself."

The phone rang and rang. Giroldi hung up and stared vacantly into space. Tony stood up and began walking toward him. "Kill me or kill yourself, Major! Your choice!"

"Don't make me do it, General!" Giroldi said, pointing his weapon at Tony but taking a step backward.

"Personally, I propose that you kill yourself," said Tony. "It is the only honorable exit from this farce."

"It's against my religion."

"All right, I respect that. In that case, give me your weapon and place your fate in God's hands." The two men began to circle each other, separated only by Giroldi's M-16, which rested on Tony's chest. Gunfire now echoed in the corridor. Time slowed deliciously. The other rebel officers began to weep and pray, but Tony's senses unfolded like blossoms. He could smell the fear in the room. Then the gunfire ceased, and Tony could hear the Mountain Men running through the corridor to his rescue. It was almost as if he were out of his body, running along with them, participating in their excitement. Every movement, every sound was subdivided into a thousand comprehensible shards of revelation. Tony radiated power and happiness, knowing that for

257

this moment he was experiencing what it would be like to be God.

But Giroldi still stood in the middle of the room with his M-16 pointed at Tony's chest. Tony danced around him like an angel of death. "Of course, you could still kill me, but you can't do that either, can you, Major?"

Giroldi's finger quivered on the trigger.

"General?" cried a voice in the hallway. "We're coming in!"

Tony seemed oblivious to the gunfire that blew out the lock on his door. He continued to dance with Giroldi. "You don't have the balls for it, do you, Major? What are you going to do? Kill me? Act! Act now!"

The door burst open and a dozen Mountain Men rushed into the room. Like a man breaking out of a trance, Giroldi dropped his weapon and raised his hands.

"Are you all right, General?" asked a captain who had led the assault.

Tony nodded without looking at him. "You should have taken my advice, Moisés," he said gently.

Giroldi's eyes fell away from Tony's stare.

"Is the compound secure?" Tony asked the captain.

"Yes, sir."

"I'm tired of all this shit!" Tony suddenly cried. He picked up Giroldi's weapon and fired it into the face of Corporal Alvaro. The top of the young man's head disappeared.

Tony threw the weapon back on the desk. He looked into Giroldi's weeping eyes. "Can you believe this?" Tony asked him. "Is this luck? I should be dead! I should be lying there with my head blown off like that poor whore's son!"

There were five other rebels in the room besides Giroldi. Now they shrank back against the wall, ashen with fear and shaking like trees in a storm. Giroldi dropped to the floor and began pounding his head against the linoleum tiles.

"It's a miracle!" said Tony, "a fucking miracle! Do you believe in miracles, Giroldi?"

Giroldi sobbed and continued to beat his head against the floor.

"You're a religious man, I assume you do." Tony reached for a ceremonial machete above the couch. It had been given to him by the president of Venezuela, who told him that it had once belonged to Simón Bolívar. It was one of Tony's most cherished trinkets. He felt the edge of the blade.

"Kneel down," he said to Contreras.

Contreras dropped to his knees.

"Love is a miracle," Tony continued. "Until now, I never felt its force. But I have been saved by the love of a woman and by the grace of God. It's amazing, isn't it? What did I do to deserve it? I can't think of anything, can you?"

Giroldi appeared to be going completely mad.

"I don't know where I get this power," said Tony. "Somebody up there is taking care of me." He looked again at Contreras. "Stretch your hands out on the desk."

Contreras looked up at him, his eyes pleading, but Tony stared back with a gay implacability. Then the wavy-haired lieutenant placed his trembling hands on Tony's desk. Everyone in the room was silent and agog.

"You pushed me, remember?" asked Tony. "That was rude." He looked out the window where the Mountain Men were now commanding the walls. He waved his arms over his head and grinned as they cheered. Then, with a movement so rapid and powerful it was difficult to see, Tony brought the machete down across Contreras's wrists, slashing cleanly through the bones. Contreras withdrew the stumps of his arms and stared wordlessly at the arterial blood gushing out of them like firehoses. On the desk, his severed hands twitched eerily.

Several of the Mountain Men began to retch.

"I want a little more respect around here!" Tony shouted.

"Oh, God, please stop this!" Giroldi prayed. "Kill me! Kill me! Somebody kill me now!"

"Oh, Major, that would be so disappointing. Stand up," he

said. Giroldi struggled to his feet and looked in Tony's eyes. Tony brushed the bloody machete against Giroldi's cheek, then rested it on his neck. It was so tempting. But then Tony turned to the captain of the Mountain Men. "Major Giroldi says he wants to die, but I don't think he wants it enough. Besides, we have a few questions to ask him. Then we'll consider his request."

Tony took a handkerchief out of his pocket and meticulously wiped the blood from Giroldi's face. "Moisés, you were my friend," he said. Then he kissed Giroldi on the lips—a long, furious kiss. He could feel Giroldi's soul disappearing.

"Just don't kill him," Tony told the captain. "Everything else."

CHAPTER 20

To-ny! to-ny! to-ny!"

Tony stood before the cheering crowd and waved the bloody machete over his head. In his other hand he held a carved icon of Christ. The worshipful crowd in the little provincial town of Santiago de Veraguas swelled the square and choked up the streets and alleyways. They reached out their hands to Tony, their eyes filled with tears, their mouths filled with the sound of his name. Somehow he had found the key to their love. They knew now that he was blessed.

"Thank you, my friends!" Tony cried. He waved the machete, then he waved Christ, and then he basked in the roar of their response.

"What do you think about Tony Noriega now?" he said.

The deafening cry of their love embraced him. Even Torrijos never had a moment like this, he thought. He was everything to them.

He waved for silence now. Reluctantly, the crowd subsided. "First, a prayer of praise and thanksgiving to the just and merciful God of the universe, whom we may call Jehovah, or we may call Allah, or Yahweh, or Buddha, or the Universal Conscience of the cathedral of our souls. To him, to this God of the rich and poor, of whites and blacks: We beseech you to bring your presence here today. We ask that all Panamanians overcome their differences and aid us in the mighty struggle ahead. Amen."

"AMEN!"

"Now it is time to be serious," Tony continued. "I will tell you what transpired on this amazing day. The traitors conspired with the gringos! They asked me to resign, to hand over my country. I said *never*—never will I leave my beloved country!"

"*Never! Never!*" the frenzied crowd responded.

"You will have to kill me before I give away my country! It will never happen!"

"*Never! Never!*"

"Do you know what occurred? They were such cowards they couldn't kill me! Even the mighty United States was too frightened of Tony Noriega!"

The cheers drowned him out. Tony danced around the stage for a moment, then motioned again for silence. "In my heart, I pity the traitors. They trusted the monster of the north, and they themselves were betrayed. Just like the Bay of Pigs, they were left to die. So we learn a lesson. We learn that we cannot trust those who do not love us, who only want to use us. We must put our faith in ourselves. We must learn to be vigilant. Yes, we are surrounded. The enemy is everywhere! He is even inside us, like the worm of death. It's time for the patriots to stand up. You know who the traitors are. You know who celebrated when they thought Tony Noriega was dead. I want their names! I want their names!"

"*Names! Names! Names!*"

Tony waved them into silence again. They were like a sea of children—his children. "We will cleanse our country of traitors. We will run the American imperialists out of our sacred Canal Zone! We will purge the spies that infest our military institution! We will throw out the seditious foreign priests who are stirring up the malcontents! We will make Panama our country again!"

They loved it. They were crazy for him.

"Good men died today," Tony said, "soldiers in the coura-geous Mountain Men division, strong and patriotic warriors. But their blood will not be lost! They have spilled it on their country's soil, and we will grow strong from it. We will become hard and resolute from the blood of the patriots! From now on, our policy will be a bullet for our enemies, a club for the undecided, and money for our friends!"

The friends in the audience cheered.

"We can no longer play the game of democracy while we are dealing with this enemy from within. I stand here today to de-clare myself your maximum leader for national liberation."

More cheers as he eliminated the façade of democratic rule.

"You know me! I'm Tony Noriega! A man of peace! A man of patience! But my patience is at an end. Once again the United States has threatened the peace and tranquillity of our country. Once again we have been equal to the task. But I say enough! Enough! Enough! From this moment on, a state of war—"

The cheering stumbled to a confused halt.

"A state of war exists between the peace-loving republic of Panama and the monster of the north! We will stand on the banks of the canal and watch the bodies of our enemies float by! *War! War!*" he cried jubilantly into the abrupt stunned silence.

I N THE FOLLOWING DAYS, the Nuncio received reports of Ameri-can troops arriving in Panama to reinforce the already massive garrisons. Every night the air swarmed with American heli-copters, and during the day jets traced cloudy lines in the sky. It would seem suicidal for General Noriega to attempt any attack on the American bases or personnel, and yet soon after the infa-mous war speech a campaign of harassment against Americans stationed in Panama began in earnest.

Lieutenant Cheever awakened General Honeycutt with the news that a U.S. Army private had been beaten and locked in the trunk of his car while PDF officers raped his wife. "Not only that, sir, but three American officers have been locked up on trumped-up charges. We've already filed a protest, for whatever good that might do." For the next several nights American military personnel were roughed up by Panamanian police, who appeared to be under orders to provoke an incident. Meanwhile, a small-scale guerrilla war targeted U.S. bases in the zone. In his top-secret report to the Pentagon, General Honeycutt disclosed that American marines had engaged a squadron of commandos attempting to blow up the fuel tanks at Howard Air Force Base. Several of the commandos were killed, some others wounded, but the Americans covered up the incident when they learned that the guerrillas were Cubans. The provocation could easily have escalated into war with Castro, but for whatever reason, the Americans declined the opportunity. The atmosphere was electric and ready to ignite, but still the affronts continued. All this was taking place during the Christmas season, when the city was lining itself with lights and the streets were filled with posadas instead of demonstrators. Five thousand children had been brought from the interior to view the parades.

There was nothing like a declaration of war to awaken the interest of the press. They quickly filled the rooms of the Marriott, and one could see them at the better restaurants in town, interviewing members of the Civic Crusade and buying drinks for government spokesmen, or filming outside the downtown shop-window where Guillermo Endara lay in a hospital bed in the third week of his hunger strike. The press had cash, and they were greedily welcomed everywhere.

It was all very exciting and dramatic, much like the atmosphere the Nuncio remembered when the Olympics had come to Rome in 1960. There was that same sense of theater, of being at the center of the world's stage. But so much attention demanded a resolution. Once the curtain rises, the actors tend to play out their roles.

The Panamanian government reacted to the unwanted press

invasion by staging a raid on the reporters' hotel. A heavily armed PDF squad burst into the lobby of the Marriott and beat up members of the Civic Crusade who had been having drinks with reporters at the bar. When several reporters attempted to intervene, they were beaten as well. All of this, by the way, was captured on videotape and aired on the U.S. evening news. The world press reacted by sending vast reinforcements. One couldn't venture out in the evening anymore without fifty requests for interviews.

The Americans made sure that the PDF was aware of their immensely superior force. Nearly every day there were tank exercises outside the zone and overflights by warplanes. Hundreds of body bags were shipped to Gorgas Hospital. At the diplomatic level, the Americans organized an international boycott of Panamanian products. The country was coming to a complete halt commercially.

Despite the hostilities between the two countries, negotiations continued between Noriega and the American State Department, with the Nuncio acting as a go-between. He tried to keep the Americans flexible, but after the rape of the soldier's wife and the attack on American bases, it was all the Nuncio could do to keep the ambassador on the phone. "This time he's gone too far," the ambassador kept saying, and yet every day there was some new outrage to add to the media bonfire. The latest American position papers showed an increasing reluctance to negotiate—another sign that the military option was gaining favor.

The Nuncio thought that there was still a chance that General Noriega would listen to reason. Clearly, the advantages of staying in power were quickly disappearing. Moreover, the Nuncio had finally achieved a breakthrough: the Americans agreed to drop the indictments. The U.S. Justice Department was howling, but the key to the settlement was on the table at last, the Nuncio believed. He tried to contain his euphoria, but he had to admit that it was a diplomatic triumph. Perhaps even the Vatican would recognize it as such, should the secret dealings ever come to light. (They always come to light.)

He persuaded Sister Sarita to prepare the sugared biscuits that General Noriega had so enjoyed on a previous visit to the nunciature. At four in the afternoon, the nun showed the General into the library, where the Nuncio was waiting with a bottle of rather extraordinary sherry that he had been saving for a special occasion.

"Don't you find her attractive?" Tony asked when the nun had left them alone.

"Sister Sarita?" the Nuncio said in disbelief. "She's nearly as old as I am, if that could be possible."

"Still, there's something sexy about her."

"Indeed?"

"And I rarely find nuns that appealing."

"Nor do I, thank goodness."

Tony giggled. "This must be evidence of my disturbed mental state. Everyone is saying that Tony is crazy." In fact, his laugh did sound a little hysterical.

"I assume you are not so crazy that you actually want to go to war with the Americans."

"Want it? No. But I am ready."

"But really, General, the Americans could destroy this charming little country in the space of a few minutes. The prospect of seeing those awful machines turned on Panama fills me with horror. I mean, you're a military man—can there be any question about the inevitable conclusion to such a contest?"

"They thought the same about Vietnam."

"Somehow I don't see you as another Ho Chi Minh."

Tony's eyes narrowed. He liked the Nuncio, but he knew that behind those silken vestments there was a skilled manipulator whose cleverly chosen words could prod a man along a path he might not have chosen. "I'm a creature of the jungle, Monseñor. We'll see who is more suited to combat in the tropics."

"I sincerely hope it doesn't come to that!"

"You know what Machiavelli said about the Prince? War should be his only profession."

"Ah, Machiavelli," the Nuncio said in disgust. "I used to read him in seminary. Under the bedsheets. The pornographer of power."

Tony laughed. "Yes—'the pornographer of power.' I like that! It's very good. Of course, you and I may disagree on the merits of pornography, but on the subject of power, I believe we have a common understanding. And so I am surprised that you condemn Machiavelli."

"I don't see what you get from him."

"Mainly, that the secret of success is to imitate the great ones of the past."

"That's useful, yes," said the Nuncio. "And who, General, do you model your own life after?"

"Omar Torrijos and Jesus of Nazareth."

The Nuncio arched his brow. "Once again, I see we have something in common."

"You priests simply don't understand that Jesus wasn't just a religious figure. He was profoundly political."

"The-brown-skinned-Third-Worlder-standing-against-the-imperial-power sort of thing?"

"Exactly."

The Nuncio sniffed. "The Marxists held a similar view."

"And you don't approve of it."

"I'm reluctant to see Jesus depicted as a political leader. He told us himself that his kingdom was not of this world."

"Revisionism," said Tony. "Look at his actual life—it was an unrelenting struggle against Roman occupation. The Romans were not satisfied until he was crucified."

"In your case, I don't think it needs to go that far," said the Nuncio as he handed the General the latest American proposal. He tried to keep a neutral tone in his voice, but it was difficult,

267

given the significance of the breakthrough. As the General read the document, the Nuncio uncorked the sherry and poured them each a handsome dollop.

The first few pages were reworkings of previous agreements, with new language designed to make the General's abdication appear to be more like a routine retirement package, permitting nominal health benefits and pension contributions. Tony paused over this section, then turned to the key clause, in which the Americans agreed to drop all charges in exchange for his immediate departure from Panama. He read it through quickly and set it aside.

"The principle remains unacceptable," said Tony. "They want me to leave power. This is the one point I cannot concede."

"But what else are we negotiating?" the Nuncio asked, unable to keep the exasperation out of his voice. "I tell you in all seriousness, this offer is the last one that the Americans will put on the table. If you do not accept it, you are inviting a devastating response. We are talking not just about pension contributions but about your very existence."

Tony sipped the sherry and weighed the Nuncio's words. "Tell me, Monseñor," he said after a moment, "would there have been a Christian church if Jesus had not been martyred?"

The Nuncio stared at him, dumbfounded. "Well, other great religions have been established by leaders who lived long lives and died natural deaths," he said cautiously. "Muhammad and Gautama Buddha did not have to be sacrificed in order for their doctrines to be spread. The difference is that Christ's death is meaningful. He suffered for the sins of all mankind. Through his sacrifice, we are redeemed. That's the basic Christian message, and it is sealed in his blood."

"I would like to believe that. But to me, the crucifixion is a favor God gave to Jesus because he loved him above all others. Without becoming a martyr, Jesus would have been just another Old Testament prophet, like Hosea or Joshua. But because God loved him more, he allowed Jesus to be sacrificed. By this action a whole new religion arose that worships the death of a single man." Tony selected one of the biscuits from the tray. "Death is a high price to pay, but I would say that Jesus got a good bargain, wouldn't you?"

"Is that your object—to be worshiped?"

"Of course, this is the fundamental appeal of politics, Monseñor. I don't deny it. One wants to be loved." Tony looked past the Nuncio to a dreamy portrait of Jesus on the library wall. Jesus was wearing a gleaming blue robe and was placing his hand on the head of a leper. There was a halo above his golden hair. "Do you really think Jesus was so pretty? I see all these calendars and stained-glass paintings, and he looks gorgeous. But is it historically accurate?"

"Well, we really don't know what Jesus looked like," the Nuncio replied. "Isaiah, of course, prophesied that the Christ would be despised by all men, he would be without comeliness, his complexion marred—"

"I knew it!"

"Of course, we can only speculate," the Nuncio quickly added. This whole conversation left him deeply unsettled.

CHAPTER 21

L OYALTY DAY MARKED the anniversary of Torrijos's return to Panama in 1969 following a failed coup attempt. In fact, it was a tribute to Noriega more than Torrijos, since it was Tony who had thwarted the overthrow. He had arranged to smuggle Torrijos back into the country by a private plane, which landed in a jungle airstrip in Chiriquí that was lit by the headlights of jeeps and trucks. By this daring action, Tony had made himself the only man that Omar Torrijos really trusted.

Just like Moisés Giroldi.

That was the danger in letting people get too close, Tony thought as he finished tying his necktie and adjusting his ski-slope hat. He could not allow himself to make that mistake again. He was in a country now without maps, one in which his friends were more dangerous than his enemies.

The troops were awaiting his inspection in the courtyard. Tony stuck his pearl-handled pistol into his holster and took a final look in the mirror. He snapped off a salute to himself, then marched out to see his men.

There they were, a thousand men frozen at attention. It was

like being in a museum by himself, walking among statues. He looked closely into their faces, but they did not blink or return his stare. They looked fixedly into space, frozen by duty and terror. Since the coup attempt, Tony had ordered the executions of more than seventy officers.

As closely as he looked, however, he could not see into their souls. He could not see if loyalty was really there.

He put a finger on the cheek of a handsome corporal. The man's skin flinched.

"You need a shave, Corporal," said Tony.

"Sir, yes, sir!"

Tony smiled. He might have some fun with this one. But some other time. He turned to the garrison commander, a small, wiry officer with a narrow face and a rodent's mustache. "Colonel Macías, assemble the five ranking officers. We are going across the street to visit an old friend."

FATHER JORGE WALKED in a daze through Chorrillo, led by forces he did not want to acknowledge but could no longer resist. How could he have been so naive?" He asked himself furiously. The more he considered his behavior in the last year, the more he concluded that he was a failure as a priest—a dangerous one at that. When Father Jorge was in this black mood, there was no end to his self-loathing. He placed himself in the witness seat and prosecuted his actions remorselessly. He had fooled himself into believing that he could help the people of Panama through political action, but so far the protests against Noriega had led only to repression, murder, and economic collapse. People were poorer and more desperate than ever before—thanks, in part, to Father Jorge! He had joined the movement and then betrayed it—completely! Naming every name! And yet in the morally reversed world he was living in, he had become a hero because of his "resistance"! He was far too great a coward to admit his betrayal. Even worse, he had fooled himself into believing that he understood God's will. He had persuaded Giroldi that God would not demand violence. But what did he know of God's intentions?

His despair filled him with defiance and a longing for annihilation. And every step took him closer to the object of his buried obsession. The landmarks that he passed—the Marlboro Man, the graffiti fence, the New and Slightly Used Tires store, were warning signs that he was drawing nearer to his own moral destruction. In his shame he could think only of the promise of consolation offered in the apartment of Gloria Sánchez.

Her face registered surprise and pleasure. "I'm just getting Renata fitted for her Communion dress," she said as she invited the priest in. Renata was standing on a stool looking angelic as a Chinese seamstress hemmed her white organdy dress.

"Oh, Father, it's you!" Renata said delightedly.

"Be still, child," the seamstress fussed as she expertly looped the thread around the bottom of the dress.

In one corner of the room there was a small Christmas tree decorated with colorful paper cutouts and garlands of aluminum foil. An Advent calendar filled with candies hung on the wall, marking five days till the blessed event. The small room smelled of freshly made bread pudding. Father Jorge patted Renata on the head. She had a red Christmas bow in her hair, and she looked at him so adoringly that he felt deeply abashed. Strangely, everyone accepted his presence as being completely natural, as if this moment of heightened religious feeling had somehow summoned him up, rather than his own loneliness and sexual longing.

"Do you know your catechism, Renata?" he asked dutifully.

She laughed charmingly. "You know I do, Father."

"It's true, you are a clever young lady."

She hugged him. How ironic that she called him "Father," when he would never know the true meaning of that word! A wave of recognition washed over him, presenting him with a vision of himself surrounded by the sounds and smells of children—his children—and the comforts of physical love. Ordinary happiness could have been mine, he realized—not for the first time, but never so intensely as now. The Church often called itself a family, but it was really more like a multinational company, with colleagues and bosses rather than siblings and parents. The clergy were tied together not by blood and familial love but by an idea. All of a sudden he knew with absolute heartbreaking clarity the joy that would have been his if he had not made such a radical choice of profession. He wondered if he had ever really acknowledged, until now, the depth of his sacrifice. And for what? To serve a God he didn't understand!

Within minutes, the Chinese seamstress had finished her task and taken the new dress away to be pressed. Gloria sent Renata to the convent school to help package groceries for the poor. Despite her protests that she wanted to stay, Renata skipped away singing a carol.

"Do you want some pudding, Father? It's still hot."

She came and sat beside him on the futon. One bite of the rum-soaked pudding and his eyes filled with tears.

Gloria took his hand. "If there's something wrong, you can tell me." Then she laughed and said, "I've never actually received a confession from a priest."

Father Jorge smiled ruefully. "I'm afraid that I am not much of a priest."

"You've been very good to us, Father."

He looked at her and then looked away. "I wish, for once, that you wouldn't call me 'Father.' "

Gloria was silent, but she seemed to be reading his thoughts. He felt the uncertainty in her hand. Although he was ashamed, he was also desperate for her to simply understand. He wished that words did not have to be exchanged. His longing was so great and so unlimited that to explain it would be like trying to capture the air in buckets.

"I guess everybody has times they want to be someone else," Gloria finally said. "It's okay, but it is a little hard for me to think of you as an ordinary man."

"Just because I'm a priest doesn't mean I am not weak and filled with natural human desires. In fact, I am even weaker than other men, but until recently I have been able to hide this knowledge from myself. To be ordinary—this is what I want more than anything in the world! That would be a promotion from the life I now live. It is such a farce! People think of me as some kind of hero or a saint, but I'm a coward and the worst kind of sinner—the kind who does not even allow himself the pleasure of enjoying his sin."

"But there's nothing wrong with desire, Father." Gloria stopped herself and said, "Jorge." Then she giggled.

"Is my name so funny?"

"No, I'm a little nervous," she admitted.

"Tell me something. What do you desire?"

"I want my children to be safe."

"That's not the same thing as desire," said the priest. "God also wants this. When I talk about desire, I mean selfish things, things that you want for yourself that maybe are not right or not deserved."

Gloria's face emptied and she looked away. "I don't have desires any longer, not the way I used to. Of course, I understand what men want of me, but I don't have the same feelings for them. Physically, I mean. Sometimes I long for a man, but what I really want from him is that he talk to me, that he take me seriously as a person. This thought excites me more than sex. I know that I am not worthy of respect. Men will never want to just talk to me. Let's be truthful, it is not what you came for."

"I just want to be with you, an ordinary man with an ordinary woman."

Gloria pushed a lock of hair away from the priest's eyes and studied him for a moment, then she kissed him cautiously on the lips. "I don't want you to break your vows," she said before he could kiss her back. "It makes me feel like a criminal or something."

"I broke my vows from the moment I started wanting you."

"Well, there's a difference between thinking and doing, I don't care what the Church says." She began unbuttoning her blouse. Father Jorge's face felt as if it were on fire. He was filled with desire and confusion about her intentions. "You're nice to me," she was saying. "You were always nice, even from the beginning. I just want you to talk to me. It doesn't matter what you say. Just don't lie to me."

When she opened her blouse, Father Jorge found himself staring at her brassiere. He put his index finger on the stiff white material and slowly traced the border along the soft brown skin of her breasts. Gloria watched him do this as if he were drawing a sketch in the sand. It was not as if it were her own body that was being touched. Physically she was somewhere else. He did not know how to reach her or if he should even try.

Nor did he know how to get past the brassiere. Certainly there was some simple and probably obvious means of removal, but it presented an inscrutable barrier to the priest.

"In the back," Gloria said, leaning forward helpfully so that he could reach around her. He felt the clasp in the middle of her back. He pulled at it, but desire and guilt had made him fumbling and incompetent.

Gloria gently pushed him away and easily unfastened her bra.

The priest stifled a sob. It had been years since he had actually seen a woman's breasts. Now that they were being offered to him, he felt awed, as if he were in the presence of something mysterious and holy. Was this blasphemy? he wondered. How could something so commonplace and profane as a prostitute's body fill him with a sense of worship?

But these thoughts fluttered past and he lost himself again in sensation. The shape and feel and smell of her were dizzying. He was attached to her breast like a baby.

Gloria suddenly pushed him away. "You're not keeping your end of the bargain," she said. "You have to talk to me."

"What do you want to hear?"

"Whatever is in your mind. You don't have to worry, Father.

Men tell me things—things they would never even say in confession. You won't shock me."

"I was thinking about my mother," the priest said. "I don't know why she came into my mind. She never wanted me to be a priest. She was not especially religious. I think she wanted grandchildren too much."

"I approve of this mother," Gloria said, smiling.

"I think she would have liked you, too," Father Jorge said. "I was young when she died, but I remember that she judged people by her own standards. It didn't matter to her who you were, but how you treated other people."

"I think you have the same nature."

The priest looked again at Gloria's breast, cradled in his hand. "I keep wondering if my life has completely changed," he said. "I've never felt what I'm feeling now, and I don't know if I ever will again. There's so much I don't understand. I think I'm committing some terrible sin, but at the same time I feel like getting down on my knees and thanking God that I can be here with you."

"I think I hear Renata coming," Gloria said, as she quickly redressed. "Now you should eat your pudding, Father, and put these thoughts away. Renata loves you too much. You will have to be a priest again now."

THE CURSE OF Panama, the criminal class," Tony said as he led the small delegation across the street to La Modelo, where curious faces stared out at them from every barred window.

None of the officers said anything. Some of the faces in the windows belonged to the hundreds of men who had been their friends and colleagues only a few weeks before. Many others were buried in La Modelo.

The director of the prison hobbled forward to greet them, a large, crooked man named Pujols. "Welcome, General, we've made the preparations you've suggested," he said. He led them through the courtyard to a wooden door that was reinforced with iron bands. "This is where we keep our special cases," he explained.

"You once lived here yourself, didn't you?" said Tony.

Pujols made an eerie noise that may have been a laugh, then he stuck an inhaler in his mouth and took a deep breath.

Inside the door a spiral staircase led down to a foul-smelling basement. The stairs were lit by bare yellow bulbs, which gave a sickening luminescence to the perspiring concrete walls. The sound of screaming became very clear.

"You hear that?" said Tony. "That's the sound of the Traitor Bird."

The officers looked at each other. Pujols tapped on the door of the room at the bottom of the stairs. A pudgy guard opened it and the officers followed Tony inside.

"Is he dead?" asked Tony.

At first, in the dim light, it was difficult to see the naked body lying motionless in the straw.

The guard kicked the body savagely in the kidneys. There was a small moan.

"Trust," said Tony. "Who do you trust these days, you know what I mean?"

The officers nodded uncomprehendingly.

"I trust you, but I trusted him once, too." Tony ground his boot into the prisoner's crumpled hand. The finger bones cracked. But the man no longer registered pain. "My old friend. How are they treating you?" He turned to the others. "You all remember Major Giroldi?"

"Yes, sir!"

"That's right. You all knew him, didn't you? And what I know is that the major could never have done what he did without cooperation. Without his friends knowing. This being Loyalty Day, I'm going to offer you the opportunity to show some loyalty."

The officers exchanged desperate and uncertain looks.

"Remember, trust!" said Tony. "It is the highest quality of friendship."

Colonel Macías unholstered his pistol and waited for the others to do likewise. Then, at his nod, they each began firing. Giroldi's body jumped at the first volley and then lay motionless.

CHAPTER 22

THE NUNCIO WAITED in the antechamber of the cardinal's office. It had been three years since he had been in Vatican City, and he walked through the black-and-gold gate of Porta di Sant' Anna with a mixture of nostalgia and humility, nodding to the familiar faces among the mass of unfamiliar ones in the Sacred College and wondering what their thoughts might be. Everyone seemed to know something about him that he didn't. Probably this was a feature of his own paranoia, he decided, but to be summoned back to the Holy See with no explanation left him feeling vulnerable and on edge.

After fifteen hours of travel, the forty-five-minute wait he had already endured in the cardinal's antechamber was more insult than was strictly required. Struggling to stay awake, he leafed through a foreign-policy journal, but the words kept melting and sliding off the page.

The cardinal's door opened and a page exited, carrying an envelope. The boy had entered fifteen minutes before, and now he walked directly past the Nuncio without a sideways glance. Every action seemed unbearably charged and ominous.

Time passed and the Nuncio's ruminations became disjointed and fanciful. He was engaged in a pleasant reverie about having a meal with the *Wheel of Fortune* lady when he suddenly became aware of Cardinal Falthauser's massive roseate face in front of him.

"Henri? Are you awake now?"

"I must have nodded off," the Nuncio said.

"You were snoring like a locomotive," the cardinal observed uncharitably.

Hans Cardinal Falthauser's office was self-conscious in the manner of a genuinely powerful man who still needs to impress others with his power. A bank of muted television sets covered one wall, with satellite reports coming in from a dozen countries. Three computers sat on a console, apparently doing something on their own as numbers and tables scrolled across the screens, making unfathomable reports. There were some intermittent electrical noises that the Nuncio recognized as modern computer sounds, but he could not grasp their function. He felt suitably diminished and antiquated, a sad old relic snatched out of the provinces and brought to the home office to give an accounting.

"Sherry?" asked the cardinal.

"I think espresso would be more appropriate for my condition."

The cardinal ordered the coffee and then sat on the divan, smoothing out the wrinkles in his immaculate cassock. At least he had the grace not to receive me behind his spacious, clutterless desk, the Nuncio thought. In front of the window, on a highly polished ebony credenza, was a photograph of the pope looking like an awed student as the cardinal lectured him on some important point.

"So, Henri, you find yourself in a bubbling pot. Perhaps you could be so kind as to give us a quick assessment of the political situation in Panama."

Was this really the point of his sudden recall to Rome? In his best professional voice, which he hoped was not too buoyant with relief, the Nuncio described the essential failure of the popular revolution, the ongoing international boycott, and the disastrous coup attempts, which had only served to reinforce the General's power. Reason said that Noriega would have left long ago, but he persisted despite logic, despite threats, despite the will of his people and the massing of immensely superior American forces. He was a stain that would not be washed away.

"He must be a very resourceful man."

"I would say his abilities are chronically underestimated. He reminds me at times of Mussolini, a genial monster, although lately he's become more brutal. He's crushed any remaining rebellious elements in the military. The lack of formidable internal opposition coupled with uncertain signals from the U.S. have allowed him to remain in control. Chaos seems to favor him. That said, however, General Noriega simply cannot continue to behave as recklessly as he has toward the United States without expecting consequences." The Nuncio then related an incident that had occurred just before his departure, in which an American soldier was shot and killed in Panama City as he tried to run a PDF roadblock.

"So you predict a response?"

"I believe that the U.S. has been waiting for just such an incident. They have been building up their arsenals for weeks."

The cardinal gravely shook his large head. "This is what our intelligence tells us as well. I understand that you have been involved in the negotiations to persuade the General to resign."

"Ah, yes," the Nuncio admitted. "He came to us for his own obscure reasons. I have tried to be a neutral mediator. Certainly I have not attempted to interject myself or the Church into these discussions."

Cardinal Falthauser turned slightly and stared thoughtfully out the window at the thousands of tourists who were filling Saint Peter's Square for the Christmas season. "You realize, of course, my dear Henri, that the Holy See does not intend to become party to the political quarrels of other nations. This is a recurring problem with our Latin American bishops. Haven't we repeatedly instructed you to remove yourself from this process, not to meddle, not to mediate? And yet you continue to receive members of the opposition for clandestine meetings, and you encourage your secretary in his seditious political goals. This partisanship is directly contrary to the instructions you have been given again and again concerning your mission in Panama."

The Nuncio flushed and sat quietly. Cardinal Falthauser's spy in the nunciature obviously knew everything—and reported on it most unfavorably.

"I cannot hide my disappointment," the cardinal continued. "Again and again I have represented your position to the Curia, along with your constant requests for money. I must say that you've been a source of annoyance to the other members for quite some time now."

The Nuncio bowed his head. "Apparently I was not meant to serve in this capacity," he said humbly. "I can only hope that the Church has some other task more suitable for my inadequate abilities."

"I did not say that you were inadequate, Henri, only that you were disrespectful and annoying. However, you have other qualities. No one doubts your political skills, least of all me. Moreover, I'm reluctant to replace you immediately. The situation is too volatile to throw in someone new."

The Nuncio gratefully seized on the grudging reprieve that the cardinal was offering. "Certainly, the situation is perilous. One can't know what will happen next."

"But you must do all in your power to keep the Church out of the negotiations," the cardinal said sternly. "If the General uses you as a political counselor, then people will hold the Church responsible for whatever develops. That could be disastrous, depending on the outcome."

"I see your point. And yet, between us, I must confide that General Noriega does not really come to me for political advice.

We do talk about the various proposals concerning his resignation, but he doesn't really appear to be at all interested in stepping down. He seems to have another goal in mind. A religious one, if you can believe it."

Cardinal Falthauser looked at him questioningly. "Is Noriega a religious man?"

"A confused one, to be sure, but he is deeply interested. I've even wondered whether this entire saga of his rise to power and his assault on convention is some odd kind of religious theater. He seems to be testing God."

"So in this case you have been acting more as a priest than as a political adviser."

"I believe so."

"Then I must ask you, Monseñor, what is the current state of your own religious belief?"

The Nuncio looked into his superior's unforgiving eyes and then glanced away. "I'm afraid that my faith is as tattered and insubstantial as it was when I left," he admitted. "I pray, I read my office, but no one could say that I am devout. Whatever force it was that drew me into the service of God has apparently deserted me."

"In that case, you are even less qualified as a spiritual adviser than as a political one," the cardinal observed. "I will agree to let you return to Panama for the time being, until the immediate situation resolves itself. But I caution you one last time to remain out of the fray. Become invisible. Do not counsel, do not presume to insert yourself in matters of state or of spirit. You are to hold the fort, no more. And when the turmoil has subsided, we will reevaluate your future."

Tony, you keep fucking up. Now you're really in trouble."

Fidel's unwelcome voice was on the other end of the line. Tony listened impatiently. He was on his way out the door—a date with Carmen!

"A wing of American F-16s has just crossed our airspace," Fidel continued. "Shit, we thought they were invading *us*. But they kept going. Which means they are headed your way."

"Don't worry, they're not going to attack," Tony said. "I've got Bush by the balls."

"Okay, Manuel Antonio. But he doesn't seem to think so."

Fidel's warning did little to dampen Tony's mood. He skipped out of his office and told his driver to step on it. He had told Carmen eight o'clock, and Fidel had made him late.

Carmen answered the door wearing blue jeans. "Oh, Tony, I forgot we were going out," she said distractedly. Her hair was in a frayed bun. "Do you mind if we just order in? I've got to finish wrapping my shoes."

Tony entered the bare apartment. To his astonishment, Carmen's lush environment had been erased. It was now an empty shell, like a theater after the set has been struck. The furniture was gone. There were shiny rectangles on the walls where pictures once hung. Even the drapes had been pulled down. Several dozen cardboard boxes were scattered across the room, taped and marked with an address in Florida. Tony felt like he was falling out of the sky.

"Where's your furniture?"

"It's all been sent to storage in Miami. For the first several weeks I'm going to be staying with my cousin." Carmen went into her closet and emerged with an armful of shoes, which she began wrapping fastidiously in tissue paper. "She has an apartment in a really nice part of Miami Beach. Then when I get enrolled and everything, I'll find my own place."

"Enrolled?"

"Tony, we talked about this, remember?"

"Well, I thought you had changed your mind."

"I'm sorry you thought that, but it is not the case." She stopped packing and looked at him with a serious expression that he could not quite read. She was wearing her glasses again, which made her look less sexy but somehow more deeply appealing. The Carmen he knew was disappearing into those studious brown eyes.

"I'm really taking charge of my life now, Tony. This means everything to me."

Tony slumped onto one of the boxes in confusion. The rules of love were so cruel and paradoxical. He laughed hopelessly.

"Is this funny?" Carmen asked.

"Funny? I guess it's funny that leaving me means everything to you and having you means everything to me. If you were going to break my heart, why did you save my life?"

Carmen knelt on the floor beside him and put her head on his knee. She was quiet a moment. "Maybe I need to find out what you really mean to me. I can't do that here, Tony. You don't give me any room to breathe. It has to be a choice for me. Here I feel like I've got a leash around my neck. I know you want me, but that's not enough. I have to want you to want me."

"And you think that might happen in Miami?"

"I'm not making any promises."

Tony felt as empty inside as Carmen's apartment. There was practically nothing left of him. This was exactly what he had feared the most about love.

"You're not going to stop me?" Carmen asked quietly.

Tony shrugged. "I'm really not so powerful, you know. I can tell you to go, but I can't make you want to stay."

NOW ALL HE COULD think about was drowning himself in depravity.

Tony picked up Ari Nachman and Dr. Demos, his favorite whoring companions, and they went to Naomi's, drinking whiskey along the way. "I'm going to fuck every woman in the place," said Tony.

"I'll vote for that," said Nachman.

When they arrived, however, the waiting room was empty of

girls. There was an American hippie watching television. He had long, stringy blond hair and a red-blond beard, and he wore a New York Yankees hat. He looked at Tony with open-mouthed delight.

"Hey, hombre, I have desire to shaking your hand!" the American said in barely understandable Spanish. He started toward Tony, but Scar rudely stepped between them and shoved the American against the wall. "*Por favor,* simply to say *mucho gusto,*" the American complained.

"No weapons," Scar reported after frisking him.

"Where are the girls?" asked Tony.

"They to disappear," said the American. "Here are only one, she is."

"What's going on?" Nachman asked in English.

"All the GIs have been called back to their bases," said the American. "In fact, I'm one of the few gringos around. The embassy told me that all nonmilitary personnel were supposed to leave the country. But I don't give a shit about politics, man. I'm on a spiritual journey—drivin' from Fairbanks, Alaska, headed for Tierra del Fuego. I mean, how'm I gonna avoid Panama? War or not."

Tony smiled thinly and wondered whether to have the American killed. That might pick up his mood.

Presently Naomi appeared. When she recognized Tony her nostrils pinched together involuntarily. "I thought you were supposed to be retiring to Monaco," she said.

"I would go, but my friends all beg me to stay."

"Really?" Naomi said flatly. "*These* friends?"

Nachman and Dr. Demos shrank in their chairs.

Six months ago she would not have felt so free to mock me, Tony thought. Now it was all she could do to keep from sneering.

"We came for some relaxation, not for politics," said Tony wearily.

"You picked a bad night. We've only got one girl tonight and she's with a client."

"What about you?" said Tony. Naomi was middle-aged and a little formidable, but still. . . .

She looked at him as if he were a fly that had just landed in her food. "I'm retired, like you ought to be. You can go over to Aquarius, but it's the same everywhere. No soldiers, no girls."

Were they all part of some female conspiracy? Tony was getting desperate.

"Hey, man, you can take my place in line," said the helpful American. "It'd be a fuckin' privilege."

Tony acknowledged this gesture with a cold stare. As if he was going to wait in line!

"One girl? Doesn't give much for us to do," said Dr. Demos. But he didn't say it very loud. Tony's frame of mind was a little frightening, even to his psychiatrist.

Naomi went back into her office, leaving the men to watch a soap opera on TV. Ten minutes later, an obese college student sauntered down the hallway, rubbing his glasses on his filthy shirt. When he put them back on his face, he recognized Tony and his mouth fell open. Then he bolted for the door.

The idea of following such a cretin was so disgusting that Tony nearly got up to leave. But then the girl appeared, and he kept his seat.

She was his type, thin but with nice full breasts like welcome baskets. She obviously knew who he was, but her face registered no reaction. She fluffed her hair and looked around the room and yawned.

"What's your name?" Tony demanded. He could take only so much insouciance in one evening.

"Gloria."

"Gloria, it's time for you to do something for your country."

She shrugged and led Tony down the hall.

Because of his pitted complexion, his narrow shoulders, his short stature, and his inclined-to-be-rotund figure, Tony had always felt an extreme sense of physical inadequacy; and yet, with all his shortcomings on display, nothing made him happier than stripping naked. It was liberating and decisive. Somehow, when he took off his clothes with a woman, especially a woman he didn't know, he also took off his self. Being with a whore was even better in some ways than being with Carmen. With a whore, there was no history and nothing to explain. Whores were so forgiving, so accepting of who he really was. If only God could be so merciful! With Carmen, he longed to dissolve in her arms and merge into a single egoless being; but he could never quite reach her. There was some final membrane between them that he could not penetrate. (If he did, he'd be in heaven!) But with a good whore he always felt he was on the edge of something—an explosion!—blowing himself to kingdom come!

Gloria gave a pitying little smile when Tony was undressed, which he accepted as the inevitable toll on the road to pleasure.

"What do you want?" Gloria asked.

"I wouldn't mind if you hurt me a little bit," Tony admitted.

"You want to be punished?" She stood up and her breasts moved in a slow rhythm, as if they were constructed of some heavy element. Her waist was tiny, but when she slipped off her pants her ass swelled up admirably. Tony loved it with all his heart. Her ass was a place of mystery and his hope for glory, the very reason he had been born. God was in there, he knew it.

Gloria took a pair of handcuffs from a drawer. Tony compliantly placed his wrists around a bar on the brass bed. The cold metal click signified his surrender. He was helpless now, hers to do with as she wished.

Gloria studied him, like a doctor doing an examination, and with the same aura of authority. She ran a sharp green fingernail down Tony's torso. He quivered in pleasure, verging on pain. "You've been bad," she said.

"I've been very bad," he agreed.

"Someone needs a spanking."

Tony crossed his handcuffed arms and rolled over onto his belly, presenting himself for punishment. He could hear Gloria rummaging in the drawer again, and then he felt the touch of a leather strap being drawn across his buttocks.

"Whap!"

Oh, my God! It really hurt!

"That's too much!" he cried.

"Don't complain, you little weasel!" She lashed him again, much harder. His whole body levitated. His internal organs huddled together in a defensive knot. "Somebody ought to pay you back for all the harm you've done."

Tony groaned. "I didn't mean it!"

The lash did its work. Again and again. Then she stopped.

"Don't look," she said.

She was back in the drawer. In a moment Gloria ordered him to spread his legs. As soon as he did, he felt a lubricated dildo being shoved up his ass, only it was way too long for a dildo! Tony screamed, but she kept pushing, and there was nothing he could do to resist, she was going to shove it all the way through him! This was the end! Impaled in a whorehouse! Explosions rang in his ears. Then the entire room bounced as if the house were going to leap into the sky. What was happening? A mirror blew off the wall and shattered in the air. Gloria screamed. Everything was exquisitely strange and painful.

And then suddenly the door opened and Nachman stood there, looking at Tony handcuffed to the bed with a broomstick up his ass. Nachman was dazed and covered with a dusting of ceiling plaster. "Shit, Tony—it's the Americans! They've invaded!"

CHAPTER 23

"WHERE ARE THE goddamn keys?" Nachman said after he had removed the broomstick. Gloria had vanished with the first explosion.

"There's a drawer," said Tony. "Look in there."

"I can't see a damn thing." The power was blown. Aircraft were roaring five feet overhead. Bombs going off right and left. "Fucking whore was probably in on the whole thing," said Nachman. "Wait, this may be the ticket."

As soon as he unlocked the handcuffs, Tony curled into a fetal ball.

"Get up, Tony. We've got to make a run for it. What's your plan?"

"My plan?"

Another explosion rattled the room. "Yes, your plan! You've got a contingency plan, don't you? The goddamn gringos are blowing the shit out of this country. Where are you supposed to be? Where's your remote command headquarters? Who's the contact with the civil defense squad?"

"There is no plan," Tony admitted.

"No plan? Tony, you got the fucking United States knocking

290

down your door, and there's only one thing they want. You."

But Nachman's words were drowned out by the screeching of jets overhead and the awesome sound of a 105-millimeter howitzer blowing holes in the planet.

Tony started to put on his uniform. He was having a little trouble making his legs work.

"Wait!" said Nachman. "You can't wear that! Everyone will know who you are. You need a disguise."

Just then Scar came into the room, pushing the longhaired American ahead of him. "He was trying to run off," said Scar. "I thought maybe he knew something."

"*No sabe nada!* I'm a fuckin' hippie, man!"

"You're an American," said Nachman. "Your goddamn army is blowing the shit out of this country."

"Like, I'm highly aware of that, dude. I was just tryin' to get the fuck out of Dodge."

"First, give the General your clothes."

The flash of a nearby explosion illuminated Tony in his red silk underwear.

"Okay," said the American reluctantly as he stripped off his Bermuda shorts, "but what am I gonna wear?"

"Put on the General's uniform."

"I don't know, man. That could be unwise."

"I can't find my ribbons," said Tony.

"We don't have time for that," said Nachman. "You got to get dressed and out of here—now!"

The men rushed outside, cursing Dr. Demos, who had taken the Mercedes, along with a suitcase of cash that Tony kept in case of emergency. The only car left in the lot was a tiny white Hyundai covered with bumper stickers. *Save the Whales. Visualize World Peace. Onward Through the Fog.*

"See if the keys are in your pocket," said Nachman.

Tony found the keys in the Bermuda shorts just as the American came racing out of the whorehouse, wearing Tony's uniform. "Hey, don't steal the car, dude!"

"It's not stealing," said Tony. "It's war."

"But it's still *my car!*"

"And it stinks," said Nachman as he got into the driver's seat, which was draped with a seat cover of wooden beads. "Tony, roll down the window."

"What about me, Chief?" asked Scar.

"We'll meet at La Playita," said Nachman.

"No, they'll know about that," said Tony. "Our friends will help us. Check with Señora Morales—she'll know where we are."

Nachman spun the Hyundai onto the highway. "I should have guessed that they would wait for the full moon," he said. The city was in a yellow twilight of fires and tracer bullets. The air churned with half-seen aircraft. Noise fell on them like an avalanche.

"My God—look!" cried Nachman. All around them, paratroopers were landing and pulling in their billowing parachutes, and above them the sky was filled with thousands more. The undersides of the silken chutes glowed from the reflected explosions.

Nachman swerved and jammed the car into reverse. "Tony, pull your hat down!" The paratroopers were close enough for Tony to see the camouflage on their faces. He crammed the Yankees hat down over his eyes.

Nachman drove through the luminous night without his headlights. When they arrived on the airport highway leading out of town, they saw people scattering everywhere, racing for home or looking for cover. Nachman navigated through the disoriented mob. Cars passed indiscriminately on both sides of the highway. Tony had never seen such madness.

"Look—they're fighting back!" Tony cried excitedly. An anti-aircraft battery fired into the sky from the barracks at Tinajitas, on a hilltop above the Río Curundú. "The men are still with me!"

Nachman shook his head in soldierly admiration. Tracers flew out of the fort like a fireworks display.

"Do you want to go up there and give the men some courage?" asked Nachman. "They need leadership."

"As an officer, I agree," said Tony. "On the other hand, I am also the leader of the country. I think my first duty is to protect myself."

Above them, the immense black shadow of an aircraft Tony had never seen before suddenly darted into view and then roared low overhead like a passing Death Star. In its wake, the mountain flew into the air in a blinding red-orange flash. Everything was gone—like that! The armory ignited in a secondary explosion. The guts of his defense! Gone!

"Jesus," Tony muttered.

Nachman drove quietly through the chaos.

Ahead of them was a queer sight—the baseball stadium was filled with people in the stands and on the field. They were staring into the sky, watching the war. Whenever a new explosion shook the fundament, they cheered.

"They think they're at a rock concert," said Nachman. "It's crazy, completely fucking crazy."

"They're cheering for the Americans," Tony said glumly.

"Maybe you better lie down in the backseat."

F ATHER JORGE WAS awakened by what sounded like surf crashing against the walls of Our Lady of Fatima. He sat upright in a panic. A tidal wave? he wondered. But then he heard the sound of the helicopter hovering directly overhead. He threw open the window and looked outside. The backwash from the helicopter blades blew the curtains off his wall.

It was midnight, and the rest of Chorrillo had never gone to bed. The apartments across the street were brightly lit. Father Jorge could see the silhouettes of his neighbors standing on their balconies. They were looking into the sky and waving and shouting, but their words were drowned out by the powerful mechanical drone. Then came an even louder sound, the accented voice of an American soldier broadcasting in Spanish from an immense amplifier on Ancón Hill. "Soldiers in the Comandancia! You must surrender! We have you surrounded."

There was no answer until the defiant sound of a machine gun erupted from the Comandancia. The helicopter abruptly swerved out of the line of fire. Instantly three aircraft converged on the Comandancia from different angles, firing rockets into the center of the structure. Father Jorge had never seen anything so sudden and frightening—and exciting. Then the lights of the city abruptly went out.

Father Jorge groped in the dark for his clothes and sandals. By the time he was dressed he could see that dozens of refugees were already headed toward the parish, many of them carrying children. He rushed downstairs to let them in.

Nuns entered the sanctuary in bathrobes and immediately set to work attending to shrieking babies. The orphans from the parish house wandered around in their pajamas, wearing dizzy expressions of amazement. When Father Jorge opened the patio door another river of people flowed inside.

"Why are you coming here?" he asked.

"The gringo soldiers told us to come," a woman in a flowered housecoat said.

Father Jorge muttered a quick prayer and then stumbled into the kitchen. Two harried nuns were making coffee and tamarind tea by candlelight. "Sisters, have we enough food for these people?" he asked.

"We don't even have enough water, Father," one of them replied. "The utilities are dead. We have no milk for the children. And we were supposed to go to the market this morning, so the pantry is virtually empty."

An explosion rattled the walls and sent spices flying off the shelves. Father Jorge heard screaming coming from everywhere in the parish complex—from the orphanage, the dining room, the sanctuary, the basketball court, the home for the elderly— hundreds of voices from every room and corner. He pushed his way through the frantic hordes. All around, mothers were crying out, seeking their lost children. Elderly people vomited in panic. Fear was transforming itself into illness and passing through the crowd in a sudden contagion.

"Father, come here!" a voice cried. "There are wounded people here!"

The priest pressed his way toward the jammed patio between the orphanage and the sanctuary. Overhead the voice in the helicopter was again calling for surrender. Father Jorge could make out the shapes of hundreds—perhaps thousands—more people massed outside in the street, pushing to get in. The confusion was multiplied many times by the darkness. Near his left ear a match was struck. Terrified faces stared at him, looking for him to tell them what to do. At his feet there was the body of an old man whom Father Jorge knew as a beggar he often encountered outside the Economic Café. The front of his shirt was soaked in blood, which appeared black and full of bubbles.

"The gringos have killed him," someone said.

"But I'm not dead!" the beggar protested.

"No, no, it was the Digbats who killed him," another person said. "They're in the streets, everywhere, firing into our apartments. It's crazy! No one is safe out there."

"I'm not dead!"

"Take him into the dining room," Father Jorge said. "It will serve as our hospital."

He started to follow them, but he noticed a little girl with a red bow in her hair.

"Renata, where's your mother?" he asked. Even in the dimness he could see that she was pale and frightened. She looked at him but couldn't respond. "Have you seen her?" he asked.

She shook her head no.

"Do you think she may be looking for you?"

Renata burst into tears and clung to Father Jorge's side.

"Don't worry, little one, I'll find her for you," he said.

He knew it was wrong to leave the parish when so many depended on him, but he couldn't do otherwise. He was drawn by a force he couldn't resist and hesitated to name. The streets were filled with a strange yellow light. The sound of small arms and machine-gun fire erupted nearby. He heard glass breaking and footsteps skittering over the cobblestones. A huge flash suddenly turned the world into a yellow afternoon, and then it went dark again—even darker, it seemed. Father Jorge blindly pushed his way through the tide of refugees who were coming to the parish from all directions. Some of them looked at him as if he were mad. "They're killing people, Father! Where are you going?" But he scarcely heard them. He ran through the shadows calling Gloria's name.

He could smell the fire in Mariners Street even before he saw it. There was a bright glow coming from one of the apartments. The fire had gotten onto the balcony and was creeping along the sagging timbers. For a moment, it seemed to rest there, faltering, but suddenly another flame appeared in the upper story of the apartment building next door. There was nothing to stop it now. Chorrillo was made of matchsticks. Glimmering cinders flew into the air—tiny emissaries of destruction.

Voices inside the apartments cried out for help, but Father Jorge could not stop for them. People were dragging their belongings into the street. Two men were absurdly trying to shove a piano through a doorway. The people trapped behind them were screaming in terror and rage. The strangeness was so powerful that he was not even sure which entrance led to Gloria's apartment, but when he stumbled into a doorway, he recognized the broken bicycle in the ruined foyer. He tripped on the missing steps and vaguely registered that he had cut himself somehow. But he could think of nothing else but her.

Her door was open. Glass from the windows lay scattered all over the floor and the wall was pocked with bullet holes. The Christmas tree had been knocked to the floor, its ornaments strewn around the room. He looked in the closet. She was nowhere. He ran back into the smoke-filled hallway and stumbled downstairs into the blazing street.

She must be looking for Renata at the convent school, down by the bay on Avenida de los Poetas. Father Jorge ran through the dark street where the fire had not yet arrived. There were television sets and odd appliances lying around that people had tried to carry with them but then had jettisoned in the confusion.

Ahead of him the shadows moved. A figure stepped forth, and then a dozen more. The priest could see the darker outlines of their weapons.

"Who are you?" The voice was very young.

Father Jorge wanted to rush on past them, but there was something predatory and taunting in the way they held themselves, like a pack of wolves. He identified himself and slowed down but decided that stopping altogether was dangerous.

They demanded his money. He was surprised to find that he had a few dollars in his pocket, which he tossed onto the street.

"Are you really a priest?" one of them asked. The tone of his voice was insistent, not curious. "Stop, I want to talk to you."

Father Jorge kept walking.

"Are you a priest?" the boy repeated.

"I said I was."

"Am I going to hell, Father?"

Father Jorge stopped. He looked at the boy. In the light of the fires and the moon it was difficult to tell how old he was, but he looked no more than fifteen. No facial hair. Still some baby fat in his features. His youth served only to make him more menacing. Father Jorge asked the boy his name.

"You don't need to know my name, Father. Just answer my question."

"The answer is yes."

Father Jorge heard them all giggling like children as he hurried away.

The convent school was closed. The windows had been broken and the school vandalized. Father Jorge thought he heard some noise or movement inside. He pushed the broken casement of a shot-out window and the entire structure collapsed into one of the schoolrooms. He stepped into the room and again called Gloria's name.

Every room appeared to be empty, yet the chapel was still lit with candles. Father Jorge took one of the candelabra and walked through the wrecked hallway. Then he heard something quite distinct and he went into the small gymnasium.

It wasn't easy to see beyond the glow of candlelight, but he made out two figures on the bleachers.

"Gloria?"

"Is that you, Father?" It was Teo's voice.

He was sitting on a bleacher. Gloria was lying against him. She seemed to be staring at him, but when he could see her more clearly he realized that her eyes were fixed and no longer full of questions. Teo was holding her bloody head in his lap, like some perverse *Pietà*. Father Jorge knelt beside her and took her hand, which was already cold as marble.

Teo was stroking her hair and staring into the candlelight in a trance. The Boba Fett doll hung around his neck.

"Who did this?" Father Jorge demanded.

Teo turned his dull eyes toward him, then looked back into the candles. "Does it matter?"

The priest fought an impulse to slap the boy. "How did it happen?" he asked.

"It was just a mistake," said Teo. Some kind of automatic weapon lay at his side.

"Tell me," the priest insisted.

"We were doing our business, and she got in the way."

"You killed her?"

"No, one of the boys. She was running toward us, shouting something. He just shot her. It was a mistake. It was all a big fucking mistake."

For a moment, Father Jorge hated him. He hated the stupidity, the anger, the craziness of the mob. He hated Teo for being a part of it. Then he realized he was angry at God, not at Teo. It was God who had tempted him with the prospect of an ordinary happy life. Now God had taken that possibility away. He wanted to scream and cry. Instead, he put his hand on Teo's, which were sticky with his mother's blood, and the boy fell sobbing into Father Jorge's embrace.

GENERAL HONEYCUTT entered the command center of the Tunnel to the sound of a great ovation. His officers were cheering and slapping high-fives, along with a contingent of civilians that the general had never seen before.

A huge relief map of Central America dominated the room, with the individual units of American and PDF forces indicated by flags. No one was paying attention to that, however. The real interest was directed to the bank of television monitors on the wall that broadcast the war from low-orbit satellites and high-flying observation aircraft in infrared and with special thermo-sensitive devices. The atmosphere in the room was like that of a sporting event. On one of the monitors there was real-time footage of the wounded soldiers stumbling about in the dark ruins of the Comandancia. The thermal images of the dying men were gradually fading from the screen.

"Resistance is very spotty, General," said Lieutenant Cheever. "Mainly at the airport. A squad of SEALS got hit when they tried to take out Noriega's jet. No casualty report yet. Other than that, about a dozen broken legs in the Eighty-second."

"What about Panamanian casualties?"

"Too early to tell. Some Digbats are shooting up the place."

"When this settles down, there'll be hell to pay to get those characters to disarm," said the general.

"That's when the new modifications we made to the Sheridans will really show their stuff, General," said one of the civilians, who wore a beautifully tailored khaki shirt with epaulets and a watch that cost as much as a cruise missile.

"The invasion really does appear to have been a complete surprise," said Cheever.

"A slam dunk," said another civilian, who was wearing some kind of safari outfit from L. L. Bean.

"Who are all these people?" the general asked under his breath.

"Industry people," Cheever replied. "Pentagon sent 'em down. Lockheed, TRW, Northrup, General Dynamics—this is a huge tryout of new products, after all."

"But these guys aren't engineers."

"No, sir."

The general realized with a start that he was in a roomful of lobbyists.

"We're particularly proud of our new F-117A stealth fighter," said a man who therefore would have to be from Northrup. "Absolutely no radar picture at all. Slipped into local airspace like a cat burglar. They never knew what hit 'em."

"Unfortunately, that aircraft bombed the wrong facility," said Cheever. "It appears to have struck a school a thousand feet from the air base we targeted."

"Oh, my God—a school?" the general said.

"We're trying to get casualty figures now."

"Pilot error," the Northrup man said. "Even the best piece of equipment can't overcome human frailty. But we keep trying!"

"How 'bout them AC-130 SPECTREs?" said the Lockheed representative. "They turned the Comandancia into Swiss cheese in seventeen seconds. I timed it."

"Terrific success, General," said the safari suit. "A really great war."

"Operation Just Cause is not a war," the general snarled. "It's not even a proper invasion. It's a goddamn abduction, and so far it's been a catastrophic failure. Unless one of you geniuses has a gizmo that will kidnap a foreign leader and extradite him to Miami, then I'll ask you to keep out of my way."

General Honeycutt turned and stormed out of the Tunnel, muttering to himself. Thirty years had passed since he'd been in combat, and now, as he came out on the hillside, the actual war lay at his feet, unfolding in front of him in earsplitting splendor. Irregular spats of gunfire erupted in pockets all across the city. Madness was afoot as always in war, and yet the fighting was scheduled to end in forty-five minutes. After that, it was a matter of mopping up, keeping the looters under control, and finding the man who had brought this all down on himself.

"I'll find you, you moonfaced son of a bitch," the general vowed. Then he said a quick prayer, asking for forgiveness. He had forgotten how much he loved war.

IN THE MIDDLE of the night, the American ambassador's car picked its way through the potholes and debris on Avenida Fourth of July. The fires of Chorrillo were still burning, illuminating the entire city in an orange glow and brightly outlining the looming shapes of the office buildings. Christmas decorations— bells and angels and stars—festooned the unlit streetlights.

As he watched Chorrillo burn through the darkened windows of the ambassador's Lincoln, the Nuncio worried about Father Jorge and silently prayed for him—and all the desperate citizens of that accursed neighborhood. He also wondered what fresh catastrophe would be awaiting him at the nunciature. He steeled himself for the worst.

"It looks bad now, but it's all cosmetic," Ambassador Tarpley was saying. "Insurance will cover most of the damage. No doubt my government will provide emergency loans and reparations as well. In a few months, this place'll look better than ever."

Tarpley had been a real-estate developer in San Diego, and the Nuncio supposed his assessment was correct. On the other hand, he remembered the dozens of body bags that were laid out in a field outside the gates of Albrook Field when he arrived an hour ago. Death was not a recoverable asset, even for the mighty United States.

Downtown there was a blaring traffic jam. Except for the headlights of the cars and the floodlights that the Americans had established around their positions and the spooky beams of helicopters roaming between the skyscrapers, there were no lights. Despite the fact that it was three o'clock in the morning, people were swarming all over the streets, plodding along under tottering loads of merchandise. Some were wearing five or six layers of clothing, with the tags still attached. The Nuncio watched as looters brazenly sledgehammered shopwindows and loaded grocery carts with cameras, furs, and electronic equipment. Burglar alarms screeched and clanged. A cabdriver waited patiently as a young woman filled his trunk with dresses still on hangers. At a Texaco station, a team of men methodically removed the gasoline pumps. A dozen young boys emerged from a sporting-goods store riding brand-new bicycles and carrying scuba tanks and water skis. Not one of the boys could be older than ten. They must think that the Americans have come to turn them into Americans, the Nuncio decided ungraciously, considering the courtesy the ambassador had extended him and the delirium with which Panama welcomed the invasion. Several times, as the Lincoln stopped in traffic, people had come up to the ambassador's car and pressed their joyous faces against the tinted glass. Another gang of looters rushed out of a bank and ran right through a nativity scene, knocking over a statue of Joseph in their haste to break into another store. Across the street a shopkeeper with a pistol in his hand nervously watched the thieves, who were also armed. Then the shopkeeper and the looters both noticed the American flag on the Lincoln and they spontaneously burst into applause. The Nuncio thought it was the strangest encounter he had ever seen.

On the corner several soldiers stacked sandbags around a machine gun. Two American military policemen, their faces painted in camouflage, sat in a Humvee at an intersection, listening to the radio and chatting with a pair of schoolgirls as looters paraded by, modeling their new outfits. "It's a damn disgrace," said Tarpley, "but my people tell me it's the best way of defusing resistance. Half the looters are PDF or Digbats, and we'd rather have them out stealing stereos than fighting us. In the meantime, our troops will consolidate control. On balance, it's less costly in human terms."

The Nuncio breathed easier when the ambassador's car turned into the drive of the still-standing nunciature. The residence was completely dark except for candlelight coming from some of the rooms.

"I'll see you to your door," said Tarpley.

Sister Sarita answered the knock carrying a kerosene lamp. "Oh, Señor Ambassador! Welcome!" she said in a stage whisper. "And Monseñor—I can see you are so tired from your trip. Let me get Manuelito to help you with your bag."

"I wish I had a bag, Sister. Unfortunately, it was lost," the Nuncio said testily.

"We had to put the Nuncio on an air force transport from Miami to get him here," Tarpley explained. "Somehow, in all the confusion . . ."

"Invading small countries is such a lot of trouble, it's no wonder that luggage gets lost," the Nuncio said. "Here, I won't require your bullet-proof vest any longer." As he removed the cumbersome object, the Nuncio felt embarrassed and somewhat cowardly for wanting to keep it.

"Remember, Padre, if you hear any news about that rascal's whereabouts, you must give me a call."

"I'm flattered to think that the United States of America, with its listening devices and satellite reconnaissance and its army of paid spies, would have any need for the intelligence of a simple man of God."

"Well, if you actually were a simple man of God, I wouldn't bother asking," said the ambassador.

As the ambassador left, the Nuncio followed Sister Sarita into the reception hall. The lamp in the nun's hand cast spectral shadows onto the walls.

"Is everyone safe?" the Nuncio asked. "Where is Father Jorge? I've been—"

"Shhh! Lower your voice, Monseñor."

Only then did he notice the shapes of bodies splayed out on the floor of the hall and lying on the couches and chairs. "Lord above! What have we here?"

"Narcotraffickers, police torturers, members of Noriega's death squad, a Basque terrorist group, even the minister of immigration," said the nun in a hushed tone. "The nunciature is overflowing with them."

"Señor Ortega?"

"Apparently the gringos found a cocaine laboratory in his office. Also President Solís Palma and the head of the secret police. He climbed over the garden wall about an hour ago."

"How many are they?"

"Around three hundred," the nun replied, "and they continue to come. Every hour there is another knock on the door."

The Nuncio sighed in resignation. Cardinal Falthauser would never believe this.

Fortunately his library remained sacrosanct. Sister Sarita set the lantern on the Nuncio's desk, beside a pile of mail and newspapers. Despite the circumstances, he was relieved to be back in this comfortable room. He realized how much he was going to miss it when the reckoning came.

He spent an hour sorting through urgent messages from other diplomatic missions, reporting their own distressed situations, and from desperate Panamanians looking for missing family members. Although he was exhausted from travel and confusion, there was no time to rest. Food and bedding for the refugees had to be secured, new quarters found for most of them, medical aid rendered, and then the inevitable report to Cardinal Falthauser written. The Nuncio wished that he had been able to sleep on the bumpy air force transit; it was hard to know when he would be able, in good conscience, to lay his head down again.

At dawn there was a tap on his door, and the Nuncio looked up to see the haggard face of Father Jorge. The two men embraced and then stared at each other wordlessly for a moment. The Nuncio immediately detected that there was something deeply changed in the young man's expression. For the first time since he had known him, his secretary appeared no longer young. But there was no time to explore this now. "I can't tell you how worried I was about your safety," the Nuncio said. "Is everything in the parish destroyed?"

"The entire neighborhood has burnt to the ground," Father Jorge said mournfully. "And yet somehow the church and the parish buildings escaped damage. There was a small breeze that kept the fire moving west. Had it gone in the other direction, we would have lost it all, but God chose to spare us, apparently. Despite that, the gringos shut the church down and ordered us to stay out of the neighborhood."

"What happened to the refugees?"

"The Americans set up centers for them at the high school in Balboa. There are thousands of them camped on the football field."

The Nuncio sat heavily in his library chair. "We've got a refugee camp of our own, evidently. I suppose we can put some of them in the convent school, at least until the new government gets a chance to establish itself."

"But they are seeking sanctuary. I doubt they will want to leave the nunciature."

"In fact, the nunciature is wherever I say it is. If I wish to extend its province to the convent school, that is within my power. And certainly we cannot support three hundred refugees. We will have to find other embassies willing to accept them. This must be made clear to everyone in the morning."

"I've already spoken to the Cubans and the Nicaraguans," said Father Jorge. "They're overwhelmed as well."

"Then we must turn to the Europeans. Believe me, the Vatican is not going to supplement our meager allotment, no matter how great the catastrophe. At this rate the nuns will be reduced to pilfering the grocery stores like everyone else. We cannot have it."

"I'll make some calls right away," said Father Jorge.

"What about Noriega? Do we have any idea where he is?"

"People say he is in the jungles calling for armed resistance."

The Nuncio laughed. "More likely he's in a Colombian whorehouse calling for a whiskey soda."

"In either case, the borders are sealed, his army is collapsing, even his closest aides are making deals with the prosecutors. He has no one to turn to. I hear the Americans have placed a million-dollar bounty on his head. He's a cornered rat."

"And do we have any idea where this cornered rat will turn?"

"His wife and daughters have taken sanctuary in the Cuban embassy."

"Too obvious. The Americans will be waiting—with their rat traps." The Nuncio stroked his unshaven chin. "There is, unhappily, a more likely alternative," said the Nuncio. "He will come here."

"And what if he does?"

"It's a diplomatic disaster! We could be stuck with him forever! Remember Joseph Cardinal Mindszenty? He took refuge in the American embassy in Budapest in nineteen forty-eight, and the communists wouldn't let him out for twenty-three years!"

"But how can we deny Noriega sanctuary if he asks for it?"

"We can't let it get to that point. We must tell the Americans to put a cordon around the nunciature. Under no circumstances is Noriega to believe this sanctuary is available to him. I can see by your expression that you disapprove of this," said the Nuncio, acknowledging Father Jorge's pursed lips. "I know that international standards of diplomacy require us to protect political refugees. But the fact is that the Church does not wish to be involved in political matters, not at all! Unfortunately, everyone in Panama now sees us as an asylum for fugitives. When it was just an occasional political dissident who needed to be out of circulation for a few months—well, that was a different matter. Now we're housing crooks and terrorists and even assassins. I can guarantee you that the Vatican will be furious! And despite the fact that Noriega is the de facto head of state, he is also a wanted man."

Father Jorge got up to make his calls. "By the way, Monseñor, what I feel is not disapproval but relief. I've never hated a man so completely. I am ashamed to admit it. If he were here, I don't know how I might behave."

"Be careful, Father," the Nuncio said gently. "In my experience, it's exactly the questions we don't wish to face about ourselves that God likes to pose."

Citizens of Panama! Join me in resisting the Yanqui invader! Rise up and kill the enemy! A vast army of resistance is forming. Join with your neighbors and the patriots of Panama!" Tony's dim, scratchy voice played across the airwaves of a pirate radio station on the other end of the phone line. "Together we will drive the gringos back into the canal and reclaim our country. Follow me! In the names of Bolívar, Guevara, Sandino, Villa, Martí—resist the imperialist! I salute you! This is your maximum leader, Manuel Antonio Noriega, signing off on Radio Free Panama!"

"Tony, would you like another California roll?" asked Mrs. Escobar. She was standing beside the pool with a platter of sushi when Tony hung up the phone. In the background Elvis Presley was singing "Blue Christmas" on the stereo.

Tony helped himself.

"You don't think they can track the call, do you?" asked Mrs. Escobar.

"They need at least three minutes," Tony told her authoritatively, pleased to be able to display his technical expertise.

"They don't know who they're dealing with, do they?" she said admiringly.

Tony was a bit alarmed by the fact that Mrs. Escobar was so young and beautiful and yet he was unmoved by her. The tension must be getting to him. Here he was in hiding, with a million-dollar bounty on his head and thousands of American soldiers hunting for him, and all he could think of was Carmen. Carmen Carmen Carmen. In all likelihood he would never see her again. She was probably lying in the sun in Miami Beach with her nose in a book, not giving him another thought. He had come so close to real love—or at least he thought he had. Carmen had saved his life, but she had done it more out of pity than love. Or out of obligation. Or whimsy. Who knew why women did what they did? Now he would never know. But at the time Tony had thought it was love. It felt like love might feel. And having experienced that feeling, even if it was a one-sided illusion, he could think of nothing else.

Scar had been listening to Tony's broadcast with an excited look in his eye. As soon as Mrs. Escobar returned to her chaise longue and began coating her long brown legs with cocoa butter, Scar leaned over and whispered eagerly, "Is that what we're gonna do, Chief? Go to the jungles and fight the gringos?" He clapped his hand over his heart. "All my life, this has been my dream! You only have to say the word and I am at your side!"

Tony looked at him wearily and took another sip of his drink. Mrs. Escobar made a clever little concoction of rum and crème de mocha in a coconut shell. Pablo called it a Poison Pussy. Pablo was currently floating in the pool like a small island.

At first the sound of diesel engines did not cause alarm in the poolside coterie, but suddenly the clatter of boots caused Tony to leap out of his deck chair. "How do I get out of here?" he cried.

Mrs. Escobar motioned him toward the cabaña. Tony and Scar ran inside and hid behind the bar, but of course it was the most obvious place imaginable.

There was a deafening pounding, which Tony recognized as the sound of the front door being battered down. Then a Blackhawk helicopter leapt above the house out of nowhere; it seemed to have sprung out of the grass like a jaguar.

"What are we going to do?" Tony asked frantically.

"Go over the fence?" said Scar.

"They'll shoot me as soon as I show myself. Besides, it's too high."

"We can fight it out."

"Your Uzi versus the American army?"

Tony heard the door give way. The soldiers were racing through the house now. Scar made a motion and then dashed toward a pair of garbage cans in an alcove behind an acacia tree. Tony paused for a millisecond, then raced to the other can, clambering into it and placing the aluminum top on his head like a Chinese hat. He scrunched himself into as small a space as possible. The can was already partially filled with kitty litter and shrimp shells, and the top would not quite close. He could just see out a crack as the soldiers broke open the French doors and spilled onto the patio—about twenty of them, wearing armored suits and futuristic headgear and carrying weapons that Tony had never seen before. They looked like visitors from the twenty-second century.

He noticed that Mrs. Escobar had taken off her bikini top and was painting her toenails on the chaise longue. You had to admire that woman.

The soldiers stumbled to a breathless halt. "We are American soldiers," the platoon leader said in halting Spanish.

Mrs. Escobar looked up blankly. "Yes, you are."

The soldiers stared at her for a moment, taking in her terrific breasts. She went back to painting her nails.

"We are looking for General Noriega."

"Yes, I know," said Mrs. Escobar.

"Is he here?"

"Do you see him? Then he's not here."

"Who's that?"

"That's my husband."

Pablo waved lazily.

The platoon leader motioned for his men to fan out and search the area. Tony stopped breathing. The soldiers followed the barrels of their weapons in different directions, poking into the cabaña and the garden and the back side of the house. One of them fired into the dense foliage of an overhanging guayacan tree, spewing branches and the remnants of a squirrel nest into the sky and prompting a furious burst of curses from Mrs. Escobar. Tony suddenly got smaller. The lid of the trash can closed. He shut his eyes and crossed his fingers and began to pray.

"Nothing?" said the platoon leader's voice.

"Zip. Nada."

"Okay," said the platoon leader. "But we'll be watching. First sign of him, we may drop a bomb on this place. Comprende?"

"I'm sending you a bill for my door," said Mrs. Escobar.

Tony sat in the garbage and a pool of his own urine for another six hours, waiting for dark. There was a nearly constant whapping of helicopters passing overhead. Finally the lid was lifted and Tony looked up at Pablo Escobar. "This is it, Tony," said Escobar. "You got lucky. Now you got to get gone. Jesus, what a smell."

"Are you sure they've left?" Tony crawled out of the garbage, casting an envious look at Scar, whose can had nothing but paper trash in it.

"The street is blocked at both ends," said Escobar. "Look, don't ask me to do anything else. You already brought too much trouble on my house."

"But the Yanquis are everywhere!"

"I've thought about this before," said Escobar. "There's a manhole in the street. I don't know where it goes, but it may be your only chance."

"Be careful, Tony," Mrs. Escobar whispered.

Tony and Scar crept through the house and the shattered doorway, which the servants had already begun to repair. Out-

side, they hid in the shrubbery while a helicopter passed overhead, shining its theatrical searchlight through the treetops. Beyond the gate was an old cobblestone street bathed in shadows.
Barricades blocked either end of the street. Less than fifty feet
away soldiers were talking to one another. One of them stood in
front of the rearview mirror of a Humvee, applying a fresh coat
of camouflage to his face.

"There it is," Scar whispered.

Tony could just make out the darker circle in the shadows,
like a puddle of oil in the street.

"Wait for me to open it," said Scar. He crawled into the street,
struggled with the manhole cover, then suddenly rolled back into
the shrubbery as a Humvee at one end of the block started up
and filled the street with its headlights. The soldiers were coming directly at them. Tony and Scar squeezed against each other.
Scar clicked off the safety on his Uzi.

Clink, clink! The Humvee rolled over the half-opened manhole. But the soldiers in it did not seem to notice. They were listening to a report over their radio. "Roger, confirm the capture of
General Noriega at twenty-two hundred hours," the radio said.

"But that's not possible," said Scar as the vehicle passed.

"Of course not."

The men stood there for a moment. "It must be that American in the whorehouse," said Tony. "They've captured one of
their own people!" He began laughing out loud.

"Shh, Chief. I don't think they'll be fooled for very long."

Scar wrestled the cover off the manhole, then insisted that
Tony enter first so he could close the lid behind them. Tony
balked. It was utter blackness down there. A light, funky breeze
from the sewer blew into his face. Tony already smelled so bad
himself that this new degradation seemed foreordained. He—
who had once been so mighty! so charmed!—was being dragged
back into the gutters whence he came. He placed a foot on the
rusted ladder and began his descent. Every step echoed in the
darkness. He sensed water somewhere below, but it was impossi-

ble to gauge dimensions. He looked up and saw stars glimmering in the sky, as bright as they might be if he were looking through a telescope. He was leaving the surface of the planet for some new chthonic existence in the netherworld. When Scar pulled the cover of the manhole back in place, even that little circle of light was snapped out. Now there was nothing. Foul oblivion.

And sewage. Tony felt the liquid rushing into his tennis shoes. He drew his foot back and clung to the rungs of the ladder. Mixed into the sewage smells was some ammoniacal odor that cut through his sinuses like a switchblade. He wanted to cry out in despair, but he was so numbed by fear and disgust and the shock of the smell that he couldn't speak. He was also gripped by a sudden chill. Plus he was becoming aware of a high-pitched squeaking noise that he desperately wanted not to identify.

"Chief, keep going. I don't want to step on you."

Tony drew a short breath, then stuck his foot back into the sewage. He did not feel the bottom.

"We can't just stay here," said Scar several minutes later.

Oh, to hell with it. Tony let go. The sewage was not as deep as he had feared—up to his crotch, no more. He waded a few cautious steps, waving his hands in front of his face as he groped for a wall. Every breath felt like acid down his throat. Moreover, the squeaking was hard to ignore. Tony sensed motion all around him. He heard Scar drop into the water behind him.

"Chief?"

"I'm here," said Tony. "Have you got a match?"

A few seconds later, Scar struck a match. A thousand beady bat eyes caught the reflection.

Scar screamed. The match died in the gutter breeze.

"Stop that," Tony commanded.

Scar choked and coughed.

"Apparently we're at an intersection," said Tony. "There are four directions. How many more matches do you have?"

Pause. "Three."

Strangely enough, Tony was beginning to feel resourceful.

"We want to head toward Río Abajo. Nachman will meet us there."

"Gee, Chief, that's miles away, and I don't even know what direction we're facing."

"This way is west," said Tony. "At least we're safe here. All we have to do is keep walking."

He turned into the flurry of wings and began to slog through the turbid liquid.

CHAPTER 24

WHERE WAS HE? For three days the twenty thousand invading soldiers, plus the twelve thousand Americans already stationed in Panama, plus a substantial portion of the Panamanian population, in the interest of rewards or vengeance, had combed the country looking for a single individual. There were alleged sightings of him everywhere, some of them supernatural—for instance, his face was manifested in a tapioca pudding served at the Pavo Real restaurant, exciting a group of legislators in Noriega's party to make daily pilgrimages to the restaurant's kitchen, hoping to adduce further evidence of the General's divinity. Straw-filled effigies with pineapple heads hung from telephone poles all over town. But the real Noriega seemed to have been transported to some other dimension.

During that time, looters had systematically appropriated every material object in every unguarded store in the country. An expanded economy of black-market entrepreneurs sprang up on the streets, openly hawking goods in front of the stores from which they were stolen. At Bon Bini and Felix B. Maduro, upper-class housewives with discerning eyes scoured the shelves, removing bolts of Japanese textiles and place settings of Wedg-

wood china. Strange disparities occurred. Because of the short-
age of refrigerated meat, two pounds of hamburger could be
traded for a television set—televisions suddenly being in surplus.
The downtown turned into a kind of street fair, with shoppers
pushing heavily laden carts stolen from the supermarkets as last-
minute looters stood in the desolate stores stripping window
treatments, and television news crews filmed the naked man-
nequins and the festive mob while delivering moral judgments to
the rest of the world. It was the best Christmas anyone had ever
heard of.

The Basque terrorists spent the entire day decorating the
nunciature and serenading the kitchen staff with traditional
songs of the holiday season. The Nuncio could almost forgive
them for being responsible for General Noriega's getting the
Légion d'honneur. Even the nuns were in a cheerful mood despite the tireless effort they were making to feed the refugees,
many of whom were quarrelsome and dangerous characters. Fortunately the Nuncio had been able to establish a separate colony
of asylum seekers across the street, and Father Jorge had managed to place several dozen of them at various other legations.
Most of the drug dealers and PDF officers had been farmed out
to the Europeans, or to the Japanese, who had a bottomless interest in Panamanian affairs and had proved to be unusually ac-
commodating. No doubt Japanese intelligence was feasting on
their stories at this very minute. Sister Sarita had put the remaining refugees to work baking cookies and cutting out chains
of paper angels.

Father Jorge joined the Nuncio for a small lunch in the garden. So much had happened in the past few weeks that the two
of them had not had time for their usual intimate chats. Father
Jorge longed for the innocent pleasure of a time that now seemed
beyond claiming, a time when he knew his calling and felt secure
in God's service. Now he even doubted the goodness of God's intentions. Evil flourished, and wherever he saw the work of God
there seemed also to be the trace of mischief.

They began with a tureen of chilled soup. Both men were so exhausted they could scarcely eat. "The snoring," said the Nuncio. "Last night sounded like Roman traffic in the middle of the day."

"The Hungarians took five more," Father Jorge reported.

The Nuncio stared stupidly at a blue butterfly that had settled on a hibiscus blossom.

"You'd think there'd be more outrage," Father Jorge said after a while.

"Mmm?"

"It's been a continual party ever since the Americans landed. I've never heard of a people who were so happy to be occupied by a foreign army. And yet I still wonder at the need for the invasion. If the goal was to kidnap—or kill—Noriega, did they really need such a massive display of force? All those soldiers, and so far they've failed."

"It suggests that there is a larger design behind their stated goal," said the Nuncio.

"The canal?"

"It's obvious, isn't it? The U.S. wants to continue to control it despite the treaty that makes them surrender it a decade from now."

"You think they will abrogate the treaty?"

"Control can be achieved by other means. The Americans had the opportunity to encourage a moderate successor from within the ranks of the PDF. For whatever reason, they failed to do this. Perhaps it was incompetence or uncertainty about the nature of the successor. Perhaps it was a debt to Noriega because of his long service to the CIA. But I think the real reason is more profound. The Americans have decided that the way to control the canal is to eliminate the PDF. That way the Panamanians will permanently depend on the Americans to defend the canal. This entire kidnapping scheme is a pretense for the destruction of the Panamanian military."

"But is that bad?" asked Father Jorge. "The whole institution is completely corrupt. Perhaps now the Panamanians have a chance to reform their country."

"I suppose," said the Nuncio doubtfully. He forced himself to take another helping of the soup. "Soon this entire adventure will be over," he mused aloud. "Given the present climate of opinion in the Vatican, I've begun to consider retirement. But the truth is, I don't think I'm well suited for it. Compared to other alternatives, it may not be the worst destiny to befall a man my age. But I simply cannot picture myself sitting beside a cozy fire in some provincial cottage, much less rocking in a file of drooling priests on the porch of a geriatric monastery."

Father Jorge said, "I've been considering retirement as well."

The Nuncio was rarely caught so completely off guard. "You? But you are a fine priest with a golden future! I can't imagine what would make you think otherwise. I've seen how your congregation has grown, how they value your spiritual leadership. I realize that you are politically at odds with the Holy See, but the Church is not so rich in talent that it can afford to ignore a priest with a following."

"It's not the politics that concerns me," said Father Jorge hesitantly. "In the past few months, I've made some unhappy discoveries about myself. I'm a weak man, weak in spirit and in flesh. Until recently, I thought I had a certain moral authority. I believed I knew how the world worked and what was right and what was wrong. Now I realize that the world is more mysterious than I thought. I don't know anymore what is right or wrong. I used to think I was a force for good, but now I'm worried that I'm actually doing harm. I'm not a moral authority, I'm just a poor naive priest with a good education and a very limited experience in the world."

"We're all limited by our experience," said the Nuncio. "Perhaps you have made some mistakes—I know you hold yourself responsible for poor Giroldi—but you acted in good conscience.

317

He would have done what he did with or without your guidance. The consequences would have been the same."

"My mistakes are more than just errors of judgment, I'm afraid," he said. "I've violated my vows."

The Nuncio looked at his secretary with great concern. He knew that there was more that the younger man wanted to say, but he was desperate to keep him from saying it. "Whatever is on your mind, I urge you to wait until this chaos subsides. We're all depleted by the press of events. Things that are said in the confusion of the moment cannot always be taken back."

Just then Sister Sarita come running into the garden. "It's him," she said.

"Who?"

"On the phone. The Little General. Pineapple Face."

The Nuncio and Father Jorge exchanged a meaningful look. "It's just as I predicted," said the Nuncio. When he picked up the phone, he heard the familiar grating tenor of the fugitive dictator.

"Merry Christmas," said Tony.

"How kind of you to call," said the Nuncio. "Merry Christmas to you as well."

"I understand you've taken in many of our friends. We wanted to thank you for that."

"Indeed, we're deluged, as you know," the Nuncio replied. "Crammed with refugees. We're sleeping in shifts and nearly starving. Everything is rationed, down to the razor blades and toilet paper."

"Still, you do the right thing," said Tony.

"The bare minimum. Only what international law requires, no more."

"And yet everyone in Panama appreciates your hospitality."

"Not *everyone*, I hope, although we've served far more than our share."

"If another refugee sought sanctuary, would he be safe?"

"Some refugees are more conspicuous than others," the Nuncio said, silently praying that the Americans were monitoring his phone. "Moreover, there is the matter of protocol. In certain cases I would have to submit a request to the Vatican."

"How long would that take?"

"Perhaps three days, if it is expedited."

"I don't think you have such high requirements for your other guests. However, I understand the need for consultation. So I propose to allow you ten minutes to make the call. We can do the paperwork afterward."

"Ten minutes! One cannot even get a Roman operator in that time!"

"I find myself at a crossroads, Monseñor. There are two directions open to me. One is to seek the sanctuary of a friendly legation. The other is to go into the jungles with my ragged army and wage years of guerrilla warfare against the imperialist puppet regime. Who knows how many will die in the struggle? It would be a tragedy if you felt personally responsible for the death of so many brave soldiers."

"Indeed," the Nuncio said reluctantly.

"So I leave it in your hands, Monseñor. Merry Christmas."

The Nuncio hung up the phone and without a pause he picked it up again and began to dial a number.

"What are you doing?" asked Father Jorge.

"I'm calling the Americans. I warned them he would be coming here, but apparently they didn't believe me." He listened incredulously as the phone rang and rang. "Have they no one in the entire embassy?" Finally he hung up and turned to Father Jorge. "What's the name of your contact at the CIA?"

Father Jorge was too shocked to answer.

"Quickly, there's no time for temporizing," said the Nuncio.

"Rollins," said the priest.

"Call him immediately and tell him the situation."

Father Jorge dialed the number and asked for Rollins.

"Who shall I say is calling?" said the secretary.

"Thumper," the priest said under his breath, but not so quietly that the Nuncio failed to hear.

"Not a good time to talk, Thumper," said Rollins, when he got on the line. "Everything's gone to hell around here."

"I just wanted to let you know that General Noriega is seeking refuge in the nunciature."

"By all means, give it to him," said Rollins.

"What?" Father Jorge said stupidly.

"I'll even cut you another check for your church."

"But aren't you trying to arrest him?"

"Not us. As far as the agency is concerned, he's one of our own. I hope we'd do the same for you, Thumper."

Father Jorge hung up and started to say something to the Nuncio, but the expression on the priest's face said enough. "Well, in that case, we'll have to think of something else," said the Nuncio. "Our obligation is to keep the pope from inheriting this . . . time bomb! Believe me, the Vatican will want nothing to do with this. Whatever justification we use will be lost on Cardinal Falthauser. Moreover, we will have to hand him over to the Americans in the end, so we will wind up looking like cowards. They have a warrant that appears to be perfectly legal."

Father Jorge sank into the wing-back chair. "I suppose we could hand him over to the Panamanians."

"Excellent idea," said the Nuncio. "Either they put his head on a stick or they let him run the country again. Which of these outcomes do you prefer?"

The phone rang again.

"Hello, General," the Nuncio said unhappily. "I don't believe it has been ten minutes."

"And yet I think you have had time to make your decision," said Tony.

The Nuncio sighed.

"You will need to pick me up in the embassy car," Tony continued. "I don't trust the Americans to let me in if I just show up. It's too dangerous."

When the Nuncio hung up, he sat at his desk and glowered. Father Jorge had never seen such an expression on his mentor's face.

"So you agreed?"

"He's waiting at the Dairy Queen," the Nuncio said.

"Shall I have your car brought round?"

"Yes," said the Nuncio, "but I'm not going. You are."

"I distinctly heard you say that *you* were meeting him."

"It's far more important that I reach the ambassador and get the Americans to intercept him. You put on my vestments. No one will guess you're not me."

"Noriega will! He knows us both. He'll suspect a trick, and frankly I don't like to think what he might do."

"Don't worry, he has no choice. When the flood comes, even the goats climb the trees. Here—" The Nuncio took off his skullcap and placed it on Father Jorge's head. "I promote you. Go get my robe and take the papal Toyota. I'll call the Americans. Don't worry. They'll ride to your rescue like the cavalry."

THE STREETS OF Panama City looked like the aftermath of a hurricane—nearly deserted except for the American soldiers, who were at long last arresting looters. As the Toyota cruised slowly out of town, Father Jorge passed several hog-tied young men lying on their bellies on roughly torn strips of corrugated cardboard. There seemed to be no urgency about collecting them; they were just deposited there, like trash. The priest was growing accustomed to extraordinary sights. He no longer exclaimed at the weirdness all around him. Even his imposture of the Nuncio seemed somehow natural and understandable. He was attired in the full splendid regalia—the collar, the cassock, the velvet cincture, and even the same cordovan moccasins that the pope favored. Father Jorge couldn't keep from surreptitiously stroking the satiny cassock. There was promise in it.

But these thoughts were interrupted by a *bing! bing! bing!* coming from the dashboard.

"What's the problem?" he asked Manuelito, the white-haired driver whose head did not quite reach over the perimeter of the steering wheel.

Manuelito said something, but Father Jorge couldn't understand. Manuelito slowly pulled over to the curb, then reached into the glove compartment and took out a set of false teeth. "It's about to run out of petrol," he said when his teeth were in.

"Isn't there a station nearby?"

"Many."

"What? Are they all closed?"

"It's Christmas Eve, Father."

"Ah." Father Jorge thought for a moment. The Dairy Queen was still some distance away, on the outskirts of the city. "Do you think you can make it to the Benedictine abbey? The monks may have a car. Or some petrol at least."

Manuelito maneuvered the Toyota along the bay toward Old Panama, where the Benedictines maintained their small monastery. The tide was out and predatory terns congregated on the glistening rocks of the shoreline. At the edge of the rain forest stood the ruins of Old Panama. The graceful spire of a gutted cathedral rose above the loamy jungle soil. There was something spookily alive and emergent about the ghostly city that the pirate Morgan had put to the torch three hundred years ago. Father Jorge reflected on the fact that there was nothing more charming than seeing the wreck of a former civilization—but then he remembered the charred remains of Chorrillo and the heartbreak of his parishioners. Soon, no doubt, the entire neighborhood would be razed and planted over with far superior apartments, financed by American reparations, but it still seemed a loss that nature wasn't allowed to reclaim some part of modern civilization—to dignify it by letting it go to ruin.

These guilty thoughts were interrupted by a coughing from the engine. The Toyota lurched forward violently, sputtered, and lurched again before slowing to a halt and expiring in a last frustrated burp. Father Jorge got out and walked the last half mile.

He turned down a cobblestone path. Here the walking became precarious, especially since the Nuncio's shoes were rather too small for him. They were little more than carpet slippers anyway—thin, Italian made, so that every pebble made an impression underfoot. A boy passed by pushing a bicycle cart and nearly fell off as he observed the spectacle of Father Jorge in the Nuncio's grand costume; then the boy laughed and began honking his rubber horn.

At the end of the street there was a rotten wooden gate, with the seal of the Benedictine Order hanging from a single rusty nail. The abbey itself was quite old, a colonial remnant, with the charm of great age but the liability of being situated in a swampy backwater. Fewer than a dozen monks remained, most of them contemplatives with little connection to the world. Father Jorge strained to remember the name of the abbot, who had invited him to a barbecue once, not long after he arrived in Panama—a thoroughly dismal social occasion.

"Brother Martín!" The name came to his lips the moment the door creaked open and the owlish, gray-bearded monk squinted out of the gloom.

"Your Reverence," the monk said uncertainly, taking in the impressive vestments.

"It's Father Jorge," the priest reminded him.

"I hadn't heard the news of your promotion."

"It's only temporary," said Father Jorge. "As it happens, I'm in somewhat of a rush. Do you by any chance have a car that I can borrow? The papal Toyota has run out of petrol."

"Ah." The monk stood in the gateway, rocking back and forth on his sandals as if he were waiting for instruction. "I never trusted the other fellow anyway," he said.

"Well, yes, however, the matter of the moment has to do with petrol and automobiles. I have a very pressing appointment and most urgently require your help. This goes to the highest level," Father Jorge said, and then emphasized, "the very highest level."

The monk's eyes grew wider with the implication. "But there's none of us here that drives, you see, Your Holiness. Now there is a housekeeper that buys the groceries, but she isn't here at present."

"If you had some petrol, that would suffice," Father Jorge said impatiently.

"We might have."

"Might?"

"Petrol is quite dear, as you know."

"Is it?"

"To a poor order such as ours. We cherish the little that we have."

"I assure you that you will be repaid," said Father Jorge, who then felt the need to add, "with interest."

That seemed to be exactly the incentive Brother Martín was waiting for. He opened the gate and permitted Father Jorge to enter.

"It's only that we have some sizable expenses. Just look at the broken glass," the monk said as he led Father Jorge through the dim mission. "We have more than a score of windows to repair. It's been one window after another with all these strange explosions. I don't know where we'll get the money for all the repairs."

"The whole city is in a shambles," said Father Jorge.

"I'm not surprised. It's been *boom, boom, boom.*"

"Well, there was a war."

"Really? There's a war?"

"*Was* a war. It's over now."

"You hear so little news here," Brother Martín said regretfully.

Twenty minutes later Father Jorge drained the contents of a five-gallon can into the Toyota's tank. He kicked the side of the car to wake up Manuelito and said his farewells to the insufferable Brother Martín, who held the empty petrol can and cast a gloating look at them. "Remember the windows, Your Reverence!" he called. "We are dependent on the charity of our fellows!"

"Merry Christmas," Father Jorge said sullenly. Charity, indeed! Father Jorge now had a list of requisitions that ran on to a second page. He sighed and stuffed the list into the pocket of the Nuncio's cassock.

Manuelito peeked through the spokes of the steering wheel and pointed them toward Via España.

The Dairy Queen was well attended for Christmas Eve. Seven or eight cars waited at the speaker stations, which were entwined with plastic poinsettias, while roller-skating waitresses whizzed among them like bees going from blossom to blossom. One of them stuck her head partially in the window and stared ironically at Father Jorge. "What would you like?" she asked.

"Uh, Coke, please."

"That's all? What about you, Grandpa?"

"I'll have a Beltbuster and a large fries and a medium Dr Pepper," said Manuelito.

As they waited for their order, Father Jorge called the Nuncio on a pay phone and told him of their delay. "I may have missed him altogether," he said.

"It's just as well, since I haven't been able to rouse the Americans anyway. Apparently there has been some sabotage of their phone lines. You may as well return."

But first Manuelito had to eat. He put his teeth back in and began to nibble.

Thirty minutes later, Father Jorge noticed that a Land Cruiser with tinted windows was passing by for the second time. It slowed, then pulled into the slot next to them just as Manuelito was finishing his last french fry. The driver's window lowered and a man with a ferocious facial scar peered out. Suddenly both doors opened and two men abruptly got out and jumped into the

Toyota, the scarred man in the front seat with Manuelito and the other man in back with Father Jorge.

Tony recognized Father Jorge immediately. "Is this some kind of priestly trick?" he demanded.

"Yes."

"Where is the Nuncio?"

"He was indisposed. He sent me instead."

"Even the Church betrays me," Tony said furiously.

"If you want to go to the nunciature, you can come with me. Otherwise, we'd be happy to drop you elsewhere," Father Jorge said. "The Libyans, the Iraqis?"

Tony clenched his teeth. The men rode in silence for a while. This was actually the first time Father Jorge had seen the General up close. He seemed remarkably harmless despite the weapon that was visible under his T-shirt.

"What are you looking at?" Tony said sharply.

"I didn't realize you were so small."

Tony turned away in disgust. "I had a file on you. You were the pig who was always preaching against me. I could have gotten rid of you like that." He snapped his fingers.

"Why didn't you?"

"Because my heart is soft."

Father Jorge smiled slightly. "I can't imagine that my humble sermons caused you such distress. I was only saying masses for Hugo. My reputation for being outspoken is more than I deserve."

"You look a bit like him, you know," Tony observed. "Pretty."

"Thank you," said Father Jorge.

"Handsomeness is a serious fault in some men. They think that because of their looks they are morally superior, that God has cast them in the leading role. That was Hugo's problem. He had the face of a movie star but the mind of a chorus girl. I don't really think he was destined for greatness in life."

"Perhaps he would not have been so important if you had not had him killed."

Tony pulled his cap down over his eyes and said not another word.

I'M AFRAID OUR QUARTERS are quite spartan," said the Nuncio as he led Tony upstairs. "We've made a little dormitory in the parlor. Your bodyguard can sleep there. Meanwhile, we've made the best room available for you. Father Jorge and I are at either end of the hall. Yours is right here. *Voilà!*"

He opened the door to a cubicle containing a cot, a crucifix, a window air conditioner, and a black-and-white Philco television set with a taped-together antenna. "It's small but it's clean. I'm afraid the appliances don't work very well, the air conditioner not at all, the television set only occasionally. In any case, dinner is at seven and there is a Christmas mass at midnight."

"Thank you," Tony said numbly. The room already looked like prison to him.

The Nuncio went down to the kitchen, where the staff was assembled. There were four nuns, including Sister Sarita, who acted as their mother superior; the driver, Manuelito; and a young Chinese gardener from Uruguay. The Nuncio looked them over carefully. Any one of them could be the Vatican's spy.

"Under no circumstances is the General to use the phone or receive outside messages," the Nuncio told them. "We don't want him setting up office here. We also need to maintain control over the information he receives. In the end, this is a Panamanian matter and we must treat it that way. We will offer General Noriega respect and try at all times to ensure his safety, but remember that our ultimate goal is to spare the Holy Father any further embarrassment. Sister Sarita, will you hide the fax machine?"

That evening the Basque terrorists prepared a large turkey with sausage stuffing and candied yams for Christmas dinner. The dining room was festooned with plastic ivy and garlands of immortelles. The remaining refugees made a touching effort to dress for the occasion, given that most of them had arrived with nothing more than the clothes on their back.

"Isn't the General going to join us?" the Nuncio asked Scar, who was enthusiastically helping himself to a second portion of turkey.

"Oh, he would never eat this," said Scar.

"I didn't realize the General had dietary restrictions."

"He's a vegetarian," said Scar. "Two things you never do around General Noriega: eat meat and smoke. He's a fanatic on these subjects."

The Nuncio absorbed this information without comment.

The radio was playing Christmas songs and the guests were chatting so volubly that the Nuncio did not hear the commotion outside. Suddenly he noticed that the silverware was chattering and the candelabra began to shimmy as if there were a small earthquake. Conversation died and the guests looked at each other in confusion.

"Monseñor! The building is surrounded by gringos!" Sister Sarita reported.

"Now they come!" the Nuncio exclaimed.

As he came out of the front door, the Nuncio shielded his eyes against the glare of the headlights from a dozen tanks. The rumble was deafening. Past the glare he could see the dark forms of the war machines and the toadstool helmets of thousands of American soldiers. The muzzle of a tank cannon pushed against the gate of the nunciature, which was straining and about to burst open.

"Monseñor, I understand that you are harboring an international criminal," the American general shouted through the bars.

"Apparently we have been chosen for this purpose."

"I want you to get your people out of there. Either you hand him over to us or we're coming in."

"Do as you wish," said the Nuncio. "I'm delighted that you're taking this problem off my hands. But this is not the way to go about it."

"We've got thirty thousand troops who've been hunting night and day for this turkey. I don't see how you're going to stop us."

"Obviously, I can't. If you choose to enter against my will, I cannot prevent it."

"I'm glad you see my point."

"However, you should consider the fact that once you pass through this gate, you will be standing on the soil of the Vatican. As far as international law is concerned, that would be equivalent to invading Saint Peter's Square. Certainly it would be a brilliant moment in your career, General. Thirty thousand American troops assaulting the Catholic Church—this could be the most memorable public-relations disaster since the Huns entered Rome."

General Honeycutt rocked thoughtfully on his heels while his mighty machines gurgled and thrummed like hungry animals.

"In the meantime, I hope you'll excuse me," the Nuncio said. "We're at dinner."

FROM HIS WINDOW Tony had been watching the massing of troops—more soldiers than he had ever seen anywhere, more than his entire army. Helicopters hovered like a swarm of mutant mosquitoes. He had seen the Nuncio go out and talk to the American general and he wondered what arrangement they had come to. For a few cherished hours, Tony had actually felt safe in this room; now he expected that he would be hurled into the arms of the waiting Americans at any moment, or else that some specially trained squad of men in black would suddenly burst through his window and snatch him. Or murder him. They were capable of anything.

He missed his beautiful daughters. He missed his birds. He missed Carmen.

He was sitting in his bed, cradling his pillow, when he heard the knock on his door.

A potbellied man stood there in his undershorts. It took a

fraction of a second for Tony to realize that he was looking at himself.

"I thought you might need a mirror," said the Nuncio. "Our own rooms don't have them, but we realize that our guests have different considerations."

"Thank you," Tony said, mustering up as much dignity as possible.

The Nuncio propped the mirror against a wall. "I'll have one of the nuns hang it for you in the morning."

"You spoke to the Americans."

"Yes, they seemed to require a lesson in international diplomacy. But I think now they at least understand the concept of sanctuary."

"They are still here, however."

"Of course it would be too much to hope that they would simply leave us alone. I'm afraid we're in for a long siege."

"How long?"

"That will depend entirely on you. You can stay here as long as you wish," the Nuncio said reassuringly as he produced a large meerschaum pipe, which he had saved from his college days, and filled it with a particularly sweet tobacco called Three Nuns. It amused him to think of it as Catholic tobacco. He hadn't smoked in nearly thirty years. "I would never consider forcing you to leave. But perhaps we should discuss your future plans."

"I prefer to go to Mexico or Spain," said Tony as clouds of tobacco smoke began to form in the room.

"Unfortunately Mexico has refused to respond to our query and Spain has withdrawn its previous offer."

"Did they say why?"

The Nuncio shrugged and puffed.

"Cuba, then," said Tony.

"Yes, but the U.S. will never allow that, and I doubt the Panamanians will, either. Frankly, we haven't had a good response to our requests for asylum. As I see it, there are three alternatives. Stay here"—puff—"turn yourself over to the Panamanian authorities"—puff—"or trust yourself to the American legal system. Who knows what a good lawyer might do for you?" Puff puff puff.

Tony coughed. "I think I'd rather stay here," he managed to say.

"And you are welcome. Certainly, we will enjoy your company. But do you want to know my real concern? I am afraid the Americans will let the mob break through."

Tony stole a look at the river of people dammed behind the loops of razor wire. There seemed to be no end of them. Many were holding candles or flashlights. The line stretched all the way down Avenida Balboa until it disappeared behind the skyscrapers. He could hear the people banging pans and honking horns. They were crying out for the Nuncio to push him out the door.

"After all, why should they stop them?" said the Nuncio. "The Americans certainly don't intend to stay here forever. One day they'll leave, but the people will still be there. I would hate to see you wind up like Mussolini, hanging by your heels like a butchered hog. It's so undignified."

THE NUNCIO FOUND Sister Gertrude, the youngest of the nuns, puzzling over the copying machine in his library. Occasionally members of the staff came in to make copies without his permission, but it was rare, and she looked startled when he entered. "There's some problem with this machine," she said. "The green light won't come on and I don't know how to fix it." Her face was purple with embarrassment.

The Nuncio saw immediately that there was a paper jam. He was no expert on such things himself, but he knew enough to open the back of the machine and pull out the offending sheet— in this case, a partially copied private letter from President Endara, discussing the new government's position on Noriega's extradition. "Is this yours?" he asked the nun.

She shook her head nervously.

"May I see what you're copying?"

The nun lifted the lid and showed the Nuncio a handwritten recipe for pâté. "We were using the turkey liver," she said. "I asked one of the Basques for a recipe. I should have written it out. I'm sorry if I've—"

"No, not at all, Sister. Go ahead, I think the machine will accept it now."

When the nun had finished, the Nuncio unlocked his desk and found President Endara's original letter still there. Obviously someone else had a key.

At midnight, the refugees crammed into the nunciature's tiny chapel for Christmas mass. Sister Magdalena and Sister Hortensia played carols on handbells, rather inexpertly, unfortunately.

"All the loyalties fall away," the Nuncio preached that evening. "Only God is loyal until the last minute." When the Nuncio had finished the first part of the liturgy, Father Jorge filled the silver chalice, and they offered Communion. This was one of the ceremonies that the Nuncio had always loved, even as a child, when the mystery and the ritual of the Church had overwhelmed his senses. Whatever tatters remained of his faith, he was still devoted to tradition and to the majesty of certain ceremonies.

When Sister Sarita received the wine, she crossed herself and left the rail. She was replaced by General Noriega.

"What are we going to do?" Father Jorge muttered as they moved down the line of communicants. "He can't possibly receive Communion!"

"Why not?" the Nuncio whispered back.

"His soul is not pure!"

"How do you know it's not?" the Nuncio said. But he also felt conflicted—after all, it was a mortal sin for a sinner to receive Communion without confession, and the General hadn't practiced Catholicism for some years. But here he was, in his T-shirt and Bermuda shorts, kneeling at the Communion rail with his mouth open and his tongue outstretched, waiting to receive the host.

The Nuncio gave it to him.

The Communion wafer reposed on Tony's tongue like a frog on a lily pad. Tony looked up expectantly as Father Jorge stood in front of him with the chalice.

"No," said Father Jorge. "I refuse."

A few minutes later, as they changed clothes in the vestry, the Nuncio chastised Father Jorge.

"But he must make a confession!" said Father Jorge. "It can't be right to let a man commit such a sin if a priest can prevent it."

"It's his sin, not yours," said the Nuncio. "We are not the judges. We are only the servants of God's will."

"Really, Monseñor! Do you truly believe that God loves this man?"

The Nuncio looked at his protégé in amazement. "Isn't it obvious?"

CHAPTER 25

"Good morning, Panama!"

The disc jockey's voice broke through the Nuncio's slumbering consciousness like a sledgehammer. He bolted upright and then clutched his chest. The sun was not yet up. He fell back on his pillow, feeling light-headed and delusional.

"Hey, in there! Rise and shine! Doot do doodle doodle do! Doot do doodle doodle do!"

The Nuncio had never heard anything so loud. The sound transcended mere wave patterns and became a physical event, like a sandstorm or a hurricane.

"Sounds of the great lawbreakers of the past! You're gonna love it! This goes out to Tony from Uncle Sam!"

The Nuncio could not believe that the music could actually be louder than the announcer's voice. All of Panama must be on its feet. He opened the door to the corridor and saw Father Jorge stumbling into the hallway at exactly the same moment, his eyes goggled and his hair electrified. The priest's mouth moved but all the Nuncio heard was a blast of Linda Ronstadt singing, "You're no good, you're no good, baby you're no good."

Downstairs the refugees were running around like rats in a

334

cage. The nuns huddled in their bathrobes, holding their ears. The Nuncio walked past them. Everyone was trying to tell him something but he could only shake his head.

Outside, the sky was just beginning to lighten. The American general was still standing at the gate, only now he was grinning and wearing enormous earmuffs possibly designed for nuclear explosions.

"Please, General! You're only torturing a bunch of poor nuns and priests!"

The general grinned wider and pointed at his earmuffs. The Nuncio made a pleading gesture to turn down the volume, but the general affected not to know what he meant.

So this is war, the Nuncio thought as he returned to the nunciature. He was angry, but it did occur to him that he and the American general had the same object in mind: to get Noriega out of the embassy as quickly as possible. Their method might be crude, but he had to admit it might be effective. Certainly it was working on him.

Already a certain degree of order had asserted itself inside. The refugees had crammed toilet tissue in their ears. The nuns had the coffee ready and were beginning to roll out pastry dough for croissants.

> *These boots are made for walkin',*
> *And that's just what they'll do.*

The Nuncio wrote on a piece of paper, *"I'm going mad."*

Father Jorge nodded and responded with his own note: *"Nancy Sinatra = psych. warfare."*

"& Gen. Noriega???"

Father Jorge put his hands together under his chin and closed his eyes, imitating sound sleep. The Nuncio looked at him in disbelief.

"Narcotics?"

Father Jorge shrugged.

* * *

IN FACT, TONY had awakened several moments before, surprisingly rested despite several vivid sexual dreams. Strangely enough, his libido had returned here in this monkish room, surrounded by the American troops and a Panamanian lynch mob. Who could account for the promptings of desire?

Also, he had never minded American popular music.

Tony discerned another beat that didn't quite accompany the music. He opened the door to find the old nun holding his clothes. They must have done his laundry in the middle of the night. Oddly enough, she was smoking a cigarette and seemed to make a point of blowing smoke in his face before he quickly closed the door.

On television there was a report from Romania. The dictator, Ceauşescu, had been murdered. A mob paraded his bullet-ridden body before a CNN camera crew. It struck an ominous note.

Tony raised the mirror to the window and studied his situation. In the reflection he could see troops everywhere, in the streets and on the rooftops. APCs and reinforced gun emplacements barricaded the streets. A thoroughly professional encirclement. Tony canted the mirror toward the front gate, where he saw the Nuncio engaged in another conversation with the American general. Both men were nodding as they conversed—another worrisome sign.

Several degrees to the east, however, Tony spotted dozens of television cameras on the balconies of the Holiday Inn across the street and a thousand reporters with binoculars trained on his window. Some of them were waving at his reflection. The whole world peered back at him on the other side of those cameras. To be so universally watched, so widely hated, so intensely sought, was perversely sublime. It was almost like salvation, Tony thought.

Then the music died.

*   *   *

THROUGH THEIR restaurant contacts, the Basques had managed to smuggle a whole young pig into the nunciature, which they spent the morning preparing. At noon the pig went into the oven, slathered with oil and garnished with thyme, basil, sage, and juniper berries. All afternoon the smell of roasting pork wafted through the embassy. It was a dish designed to drive a vegetarian to delirium.

When the Nuncio had finished his letter to Cardinal Falthauser, he placed it in the diplomatic pouch and summoned Manuelito. The old man came into his office without his teeth. He seemed to get smaller every time the Nuncio saw him.

"Manuelito, take the pouch to the airport straightaway. If the Americans try to stop you, remind them that this is traveling under diplomatic cover and they have no legal right to restrain you. Do you understand me?"

Manuelito said something incomprehensible and took the locked bag. The Nuncio waited a few moments, then walked out the back door of the nunciature where the elderly driver was warming up the Toyota.

"I left something out," the Nuncio explained.

Manuelito gave him an alarmed look. The Nuncio unlocked the bag and looked inside. He was not surprised to find a separate envelope there, addressed to Cardinal Falthauser, and containing, among other things, a copy of President Endara's letter.

"Hand me your keys, Manuelito."

Manuelito actually seemed proud of himself and rather happy to be exposed. He handed the Nuncio a set of keys that duplicated every one of his own—including the desk, the safe, and the diplomatic bag.

"You are discharged as of this very moment," the Nuncio said sternly. "Take your teeth and get out of here."

* * *

FATHER JORGE LAY on the couch, staring at the water marks on the ceiling as if he were trying to divine some message therein. "You don't really think God loved Hitler, do you?" he finally asked.

"Of course he did, although Hitler failed to express God's love in his own life. It was his failure, not God's."

"God could have stopped him."

"But he didn't—because even Hitler was an instrument of his will. History is, after all, the expression of God's unfolding story. At least, that is our doctrine. And if we adhere to it, we must believe that God has anticipated all things, and welcomes them, just as he expected the suffering and sacrifice of his son."

"That's different from loving Hitler, or Stalin, or Noriega."

"You place the General in a rather exalted pantheon of villains."

"He may differ in scope but not in kind," said Father Jorge. "It is as if all these big European monsters fruited and left behind the seeds that produced Marcos, Somoza, Sukarno, Idi Amin— the monstrous second-generation Third World progeny that includes Tony Noriega. Maybe they didn't get to operate on the same scale as Hitler, but we are still talking about enormous evil—murder, drug trafficking, criminal enterprises on a grand scale, not to mention the corruption of a nation and innumerable lesser sins of the flesh. Surely God shuns such wickedness. How can he love the man who commits such crimes?"

"General!" said the Nuncio. "I didn't hear you knock!"

Father Jorge abruptly sat up. Tony Noriega was standing in the doorway. The General gave him a look that was hard to read.

"There was something disturbing on television," said Tony.

"Ah, you got it working," said the Nuncio.

"Cigar?" said Father Jorge, offering Tony a box of green-leafed Havanas. Tony drew back in revulsion. Father Jorge shrugged and lit one for himself.

"They said you made an agreement with the Americans," Tony said accusingly.

"Yes, I did," said the Nuncio.

"You signed a paper allowing them to invade the nunciature."

"In the unlikely event that you decide to hold us hostage."

"Do you really think that of me?"

"Certainly not. But it permitted the Americans to say that they have made progress in their negotiations. And frankly, if we had not come to some arrangement about the music, I would have handed you over myself."

Tony drew a chair well away from Father Jorge's cigar. "But if you say I am not cooperating, then the Americans will say that you are my hostages. They only want an excuse, and now you have provided it."

The Nuncio tapped ashes from his pipe and refilled it from the tin of tobacco. "Let's be honest with each other, General. This is a political matter with me, not a religious one. I don't want to die for politics."

"For me, it's the opposite," said Tony. "My political life is over. I've entered a new stage. I have a request, Monseñor. I want you to hear my confession."

The Nuncio held the lit match in his hand for a second, then blew it out. "Well, yes, of course, this is a very important matter, and I am glad to hear you make such a request. But in fact I am in a bit of a bind. My role is to mediate the interests of all the parties involved and bring this affair to a peaceful and satisfactory conclusion. I don't know that I would be able to serve those ends if I was also your priest."

"I thought a priest was obligated to hear all confessions."

"Absolutely," said the Nuncio. "And I will if you wish me to. But I must caution you that such an action might compromise my status as a neutral third party."

Tony scowled and cast an accusing glance at the pope's portrait.

"Father Jorge, on the other hand, suffers from no such conflict," the Nuncio said.

Both Tony and Father Jorge looked at the Nuncio in undisguised alarm.

AT FOUR THAT AFTERNOON, Tony entered the confessional box. Father Jorge waited unwillingly on the other side of the screen.

"Bless me, Father, for I have sinned."

"What are your sins?"

"I have not loved God sufficiently."

"What other sins have you committed?"

"Really, that's the main one."

There was a lengthy pause from the priest. "Certainly, you can think of others," he finally said.

Tony thought. "No."

"If we reflect on them, they will surely come to mind."

"You are probably thinking of adultery," said Tony. "I will confess it if you like, but God doesn't really mind that."

"God expressly forbids it in the seventh commandment. And it is well known that you have been with many women other than your wife."

"The same was true of every one of God's special kings. Look at David and Solomon. God gave them many wives and hundreds of concubines. Was that adultery? No! God spells it out in Leviticus. You can't sleep with your mother, your sister, your daughter, your granddaughter, your aunt, your in-laws, your neighbor's wife, or a woman in her period. I never do these things. Therefore it is not adultery."

"There are nine other commandments that may not be so easy to rationalize. I urge you to consider your behavior and seek God's forgiveness. Confession is not a game, it's a holy act. This is not a time to dissemble or bargain. God knows what is in your soul! There's no use in trying to make a defense. You must lay your soul bare and beg for God's forgiveness."

"That's exactly why I'm here!" said Tony. "People have accused me of many crimes, but I don't see them as sins. The money I've accumulated—well, it was largely in the form of gifts. I didn't *steal* it. I merely *accepted* it. I don't bear false witness, I don't curse God, I never work on Sunday—in all these ways, I obey the commandments."

"But you've killed."

"Yes, but even there God has published exemptions, and I fall within the guidelines."

This was sacrilege! Father Jorge was furious. "Major Giroldi didn't deserve to die," he said. "He protected your life, and look what you did to him in return."

"Yes, the poor deluded bastard. If he had killed me quickly, he would have gotten away with it—people would have called him a hero. But he thought he was carrying out God's directives. Fortunately he lived long enough for justice to be served. Those who rose up against me were properly punished, according to biblical standards. So many people make mistakes by reading the scriptures superficially."

"Hugo Spadafora?"

"It's true I wanted him dead. I never ordered it. I never even asked that he be arrested. But I did pray for it, and apparently God answered my prayer. For some reason, Hugo's death fit into God's plan."

"We cannot know what God intends," said the priest heatedly, "and I think it's blasphemous to attribute Dr. Spadafora's savage assassination to divine will. It was your own soldiers who murdered him, not the angels of the Lord."

"Maybe we can't read the mind of God, but I do believe that he has picked me out for a special destiny."

"Many people believe that. Most of them are in mental hospitals," the priest said before he could stop himself.

"I am not a schizophrenic," Tony replied defensively. "I've never claimed to hear the voice of God. But the evidence of my own life tells me he is at work behind the scenes, arranging events for my benefit. I came into this world with nothing. I was despised and abandoned. And yet God exalted me. He paved the way for me. How else can you explain my life?"

"You seem to think that God has his hand on your shoulder, pardoning your misdeeds and leading you to wealth and power, when it was your own ruthless ambition that encouraged you to cheat and steal and slaughter your opponents. God certainly did not ordain these actions, no matter how cleverly you rationalize them."

"This, I don't accept," said Tony. "You think a bastard mestizo orphan could rise so high without the help of God? I cannot believe a priest would think this. God has chosen me, Father. Why, I cannot say. You tell me—you know so much. Why would God allow me to stay in power all these years if I really were so wicked as you believe? You must have prayed for my downfall, but he listened to my prayers, not to yours."

"Until now!" the priest burst out. "Even if God did have a special place for you, as you like to believe, your situation has certainly changed!"

"I thought the same thing. But I realize that every time I have tried to understand God, I have failed. When my most trusted men turned against me, God saved me! There is no other way to explain it! I am a sinner, but he loves me anyway. All those righteous men—Hugo, Giroldi, and the others—they died very badly, you know. I would not want to have ended up like them! And so God must have a plan for me. Maybe he intends my sacrifice to be a lesson to mankind. Haven't you seen the cameras outside? The whole world is waiting for little Tony to surrender! God has not rejected me, he has only found a new way to extend my influence. Incidentally, Jesus came to the same conclusion."

"Do you really think your situation is comparable?" the priest said in disbelief.

"What bothers me is that you don't even know what my sins

really are," Tony continued. "You think you understand me better than I do myself—better than God. You don't sound like a priest anymore. You sound like a prosecutor. That's not what I'm here for, Father."

Father Jorge felt somewhat chastened. "I apologize for letting my personal feelings invade this sacred relationship. It's true I hold you responsible for many crimes, but it is up to God to say whether or not they are also sins. Your conscience has to prompt you in these matters."

Tony stared at the shadowy figure behind the screen. "For this, I forgive you, Father. See, we are all sinners, after all."

"I don't know what you want of me," Father Jorge said in exasperation. "I thought you wanted to confess. Instead, you seem to be waging some kind of theological assault on human decency."

"But I did confess!" Tony protested. "I confessed that I didn't love God sufficiently."

"It's not a sin if you don't love God."

"Really?" Tony was stunned. "How can that be so? Isn't loving God the reason for life? Maybe you're mistaken, Father. Maybe what you mean is that it is something bigger than sin if you don't love God. It's so big we don't have a name for it. And I am guilty of this big thing! I confess this to you! Please, Father, give me your blessing."

Father Jorge bit his lip. For the first time, the General made sense to him. Once, he also had thought he understood what God wanted in the world and where he stood in God's plan. Now he had lost faith in that understanding. He had been just as deluded as Tony Noriega—and perhaps for the same reason: he had failed to love God. The priest wondered whether it was a mistake ever to try to understand the ways of the Lord. It was too easy to fall into confusion and despair. Still, he wished he could be as certain of God's love as was General Noriega.

In any case, there was little he could do to change the General's conscience. His sole duty as a priest was to make certain that the confession was sincere and contrite. In these matters, there was no doubt. In all other things, doubt abounded.

"You understand what your penance must be?" he asked.

"Trusting God, I am ready to accept it," said Tony.

"In that case, *ego te absolvo.*"

As soon as he came out of the confessional, there was stunning evidence of God's forgiveness. Sitting on the divan in the foyer, smacking gum and jiggling her foot, was Carmen. She looked at him with an expression of wonder, almost of awe.

"Tony, you're in so much trouble!"

He was so shaken he could barely speak.

"What? What?" said Carmen. "Aren't you glad to see me? Is there something wrong?"

"No, nothing wrong," said Tony. "The very opposite!" He took her long, freckled fingers in his. "I was sure you were already gone."

"I was going, but we got caught in the invasion. And then I didn't know what I wanted. I guess I just wanted to make sure you were safe."

"It means that much to you?"

"They showed a picture of you on television. Where'd you get these clothes?"

Tony flushed. "It's not dignified, is it? As a fugitive, it was necessary to assume a disguise. Now I regret it."

"That's why I brought your uniform."

Tony's delighted eyes fell on the laundry bag draped over a chair. "But what about shoes? I can't wear the uniform with these sandals."

"Here," said Carmen, handing him a shopping bag, "I stole these for you."

Tony's eyes misted over in gratitude.

"Damn you, Tony, why didn't you quit a week ago when there was still time to negotiate? We could have lived together in Paris."

"But you left me! You were going to be a fashion designer in Miami."

"We both know that's not the point. The point is that you still wanted to be the leader of the country and I didn't know what I wanted." Carmen took the gum out of her mouth and wrapped it in a tissue. "What I really wanted was you, Tony, not Mister Ruler of All I Survey. You were too big for me. I couldn't reach you. But now you're kind of a nobody. You don't have anybody except me. It's the first time in my life I've really been needed." Then she put her arms around him and kissed him hard.

Tony's heart was beating so fast he thought he might have a seizure. "You really love me?" he asked breathlessly.

"Yeah, but it's going to be a little hard to be with you. The Americans say they're going to put you in prison for a hundred years."

Tony held her to him, and her body felt familiar but also somehow new. It was the body of his beloved. "We don't have much time," he said, "but for this moment, I swear that I am completely yours."

I KNOW IT ISN'T SANCTIONED by the Church, Monseñor, but true love, isn't it divine, no matter what people say?"

The Nuncio looked at Tony with unexpected affection. The two men were saying good-bye in the library. Outside, the black American helicopter that would ferry Tony off to justice awaited, its blades idling impatiently. Television lights ringed the nunciature, waiting to record the departure. Tony appeared to be completely transformed—and not just by the freshly pressed uniform and the last-minute haircut that Sister Sarita had given him. His face glowed. And when the Nuncio had offered him—and Carmen—Communion that evening, it had been one of the most moving experiences he had ever witnessed. They had knelt before him, holding hands. Their love for each other was so obvious that the air in the chapel was charged with it.

"Love is always precious," the Nuncio said.

"Now God has given me everything," said Tony.

"I find myself in the odd position of envying you," said the Nuncio, surprising himself with this admission. Of course, he had long since renounced any notions of romantic love in his own life, but he had never given up on the love of God. Clearly Tony was deluded about God's particular interest in him, but there was power in the delusion, and consolation. Perhaps it was a form of madness—a similar madness shared by monsters and saints, who all feel divinely entitled to their freedom.

Tony stood up and the two men embraced.

"Go with God," said the Nuncio.

Downstairs, the staff and the refugees were waiting. Tony said farewell to each of them, particularly to Scar, who was also wanted by the Americans, but not so much that they would pursue him after Tony was gone. Father Jorge stood beside the sturdy oak door. He handed Tony a Bible. "Something to read on your journey," he said.

Tony accepted it gratefully. "When I read it, I'll think of you, Father. I'll remember your blessing."

Father Jorge bowed and looked askance. He felt oddly proud of that moment as well.

Tony opened the door. The lights blazed into the room, and then he vanished, as if he had been swallowed by the light.

The Nuncio was drawn after him. Once he got outside, he could feel the draft of the helicopter's eager blades. He saw Tony opening the front gate. The Nuncio walked quicker, trying to catch up to him, but two huge Americans clapped handcuffs on Tony and picked him up under his arms. They hurried toward the helicopter as if all the ghosts in Panama were chasing them.

The helicopter door opened, and Tony turned around. He saw the Nuncio and smiled, and then said something that the Nuncio couldn't hear.

"What?" the Nuncio cried, and put his hand to his ear to indicate that he hadn't understood. But now Tony was pulled into the helicopter. As soon as his shoes left the ground the door closed on him, and the helicopter leaned forward, then leapt into the air, spewing wind like a wave. The Nuncio's skullcap blew off his head and went tumbling into the street.

From the window of the helicopter, Tony caught a last glimpse of the Nuncio, with one hand on his bare bald head and the other waving frantically. In another second he saw the lights of Panama City spilled along the coastline like pearls carelessly thrown in the sand. The sea, the jungle, the mountains were all below him now, and only the sky and his future awaited him. Next to Tony, an American drug agent was trying to explain his legal rights, but Tony could not pay attention to him. The moment was too powerful. "Why me?" he asked himself again. "Why does God love Tony Noriega?"

There was no answer. But then, Tony really didn't expect to hear one. He wouldn't have answered, either, if he were God, and God were Tony Noriega.

This novel does not pretend to be a journalistic account of General Manuel Antonio Noriega and his seven-year reign in Panama. Some of the people chronicled here are part composite, part invention. This was done to allow myself the freedom necessary to imagine the thoughts, feelings, and actions of literary characters. In the case of the Nuncio and his secretary, for example, I have imposed my own characters in place of their real-life counterparts. The book largely follows the true events that occurred between September 13, 1985, when Dr. Hugo Spadafora was assassinated, and the U.S. invasion of Panama on December 20, 1989.

My character, Tony Noriega, is a creature of my imagination. Although his actions are structured upon the facts of General Noriega's life as I understand them, my goal in this book is to create a personality who lives plausibly within these pages. It may help the reader to know that, in addition to General Noriega's conviction for racketeering and conspiring to manufacture and import cocaine into the United States, for which he is currently serving a thirty-year sentence in federal prison in Miami, he has also been convicted in absentia in Panama for his involvement in the murders of Hugo Spadafora and Major Moisés Giroldi. The scenes of his direct participation in those murders are my own creations. Hugo Spadafora's head has never actually been found.

Thanks are due to many helpful people who contributed their knowledge and insight in the preparation of this book. At the top of the list is my friend and invaluable guide Berta Ramona Thayer, a lawyer and journalist whose universal access to people in all ranks of Panamanian society made my visits there both productive and delightful. I would also like to offer special thanks to Mario Rognoni, General Noriega's former spokesman and one of Central America's great raconteurs; Roberto Eisenmann, founder of *La Prensa*; Guillermo Sánchez Borbón, whose outspoken and wonderfully mischievous columns for that paper helped bring Noriega down; José Blandón, who was Noriega's chief political adviser; Roberto Díaz Herrera; former president Ernesto Pérez Balladares; former vice president Ricardo Arias Calderón; and Mayín Correa, a brave journalist who became mayor of Panama City. In addition, I am happy to acknowledge the debt I owe to Aquilino Boyd, Pablo Thalassinos, Carlos Duque, Daniel Delgado, Escolastico Calvo, Ricardo Bermudez, Dr. Gioconda Gaudiano, Pedro Rognoni, Fernando Quesada, Lucho Delgado, and Manuel Solís Palma, each of whom afforded me generous amounts of time and precious observations about their country and the complicated man who held it in his grasp.

Several books were also extremely helpful to my understanding of Noriega and Panama; in particular I point to Kevin Buckley's *Panama,* Frederick Kempe's *Divorcing the Dictator,* John Dinges's *Our Man in Panama,* Roberto Díaz Herrera's *Panama: Política y magia;* R. M. Koster and Guillermo Sánchez's *In the Time of the Tyrants,* José de Jesús Martínez's *La Invasión de Panamá,* Steve Albert's *The Case Against the General,* Mayín Correa's *Sin concesiones,* and Luis Murillo's encyclopedic *The Noriega Mess.* General Noriega wrote an autobiography with Peter Eisner titled *America's Prisoner,* which presents his version of events. Stephanie C. Kane's delightful book on the Choco, *The Phantom Gringo Boat,* helped me understand that culture.

In this country I was assisted by David Adams, Ricardo Ainslie, John Burnett, and Mac Chapin. Several friends read the manuscript at various stages and offered their guidance, including Lee Aitken, Matthew Fox, Nancy Hardin, Jan McInroy, James Magnuson, and Wendy Weil. I am also grateful to David Rosenthal and Geoffrey Kloske at Simon & Schuster for their valuable editorial guidance. Stephen Harrigan's counsel has always been wise and generous, and his friendship has lit the lonely path of the writer's life for nearly twenty years. Finally I must acknowledge my wife, Roberta, whose love and good humor have sustained me through many uncertain times. For all the help I've been given by these friends and colleagues, I say thanks and thanks again.

ABOUT THE AUTHOR

Lawrence Wright was born in Oklahoma City in 1947 and reared in Dallas, Texas. He is a graduate of Tulane University and the American University in Cairo. He is a staff writer for *The New Yorker* and the author of five previous books of nonfiction: *City Children, Country Summer* (1979), *In the New World: Growing Up with America, 1960–1984* (1988), *Saints & Sinners* (1993), *Remembering Satan* (1994), and *Twins: And What They Tell Us About Who We Are* (1998). This is his first novel. He has won the National Magazine Award for Reporting as well as the John Bartlow Martin Award for Public Interest Magazine Journalism. In 1992 he received a grant from the National Endowment for the Arts. For the past twenty years he has made his home in Austin, Texas.

Panamá City

Miraflores
Locks

CANAL

RAILROAD

VIA SIMÓN BOLÍVAR

VIA ESPAÑA

Military
Bases

Port
of Balboa

Ancón
Hill

U.S.
Embassy

BALBOA

GOLF
HEIGHTS

CALLE 50

Union
Club

CAUSEWAY

TERREPLÉN

AVENIDA CENTRAL

AVENIDA BALBOA

Nunciature

Bridge of the
Americas

CHORRILLO

AVENIDA DE LOS
POETAS

Presidential
Palace

Kms.

Fort
Amador

Comandancia

0   1/2   1

Miles

© A. Karl / J. Kemp. 1999

Caribbean

Sea

COSTA RICA

BOCAS DEL TORO

COLÓN

COCLÉ

CHIRIQUÍ

David

VERAGUAS

PAN-AMERICAN HIGHWAY

HERRERA

LOS
SANTOS

Coiba
Island

Pacific Ocean